I0631815

Luna City Compendium #4

The Comic Diversion

By
Celia Hayes
& Jeanne Hayden

Geron GA *& Associates*

San Antonio, 2025

Dedications and Acknowledgments

Thank you to the readers who love the series, and demanded a further chronicle of events, lives, and loves in Luna City. To my family, friends, my dear little son James Alexander-Page, and to the friendship and memory of those Marines whom I served with, and to those who came before, and after. *Semper Fidelis!*
Jeanne Hayden

The Luna City series is dedicated with affection to those residents of Texas small towns who have not only welcomed us over the past decades of doing book events and markets, but who have also served as an inspiration by telling stories which are woven into these chronicles: Fredericksburg, Boerne, Bulverde, Beeville, Goliad, Gonzalez, Comfort, Richmond, Junction, San Saba and Harper, Giddings, Llano and Lockhart, Richmond, New Braunfels, and Kerrville. All my thanks and gratitude to those reader fans who love Luna City and waited impatiently for yet another story, and to the late Professor John Igo, of San Antonio, who read an early version of the first chronicle and encouraged us to continue with the tale.

Celia Hayes,
San Antonio, 2025

Contents

Luna City & Environs

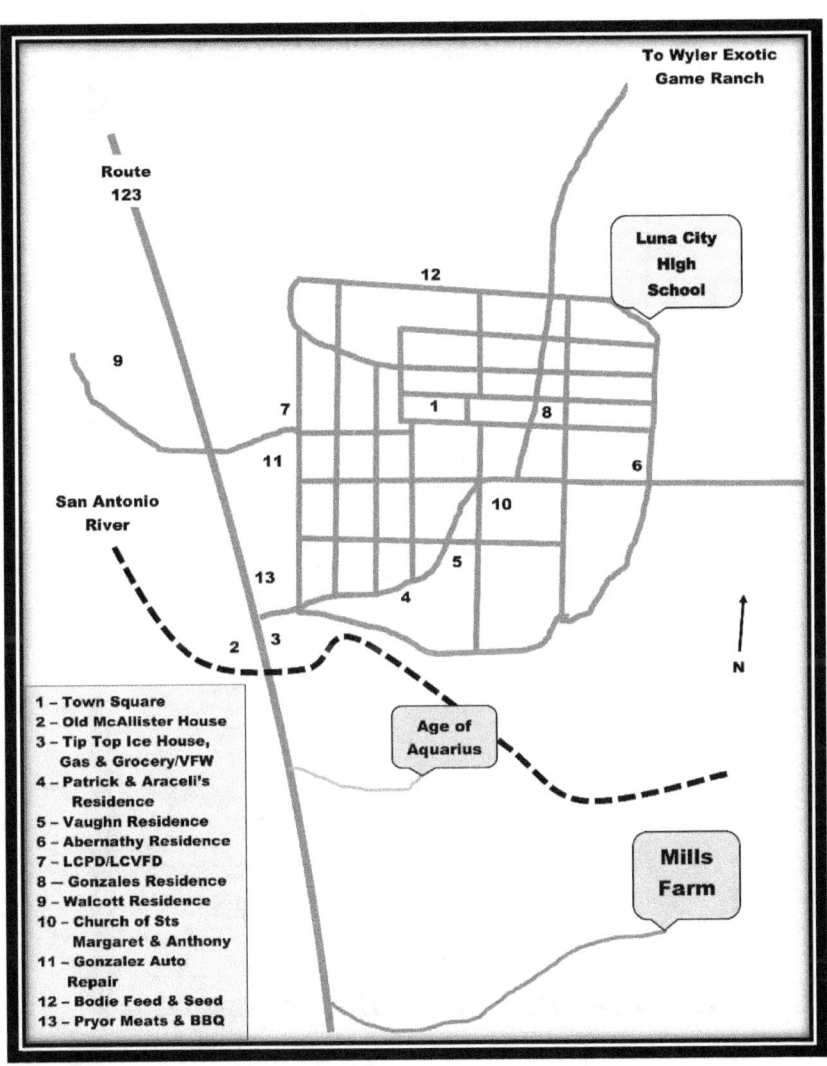

1 – Town Square
2 – Old McAllister House
3 – Tip Top Ice House,
    Gas & Grocery/VFW
4 – Patrick & Araceli's
    Residence
5 – Vaughn Residence
6 – Abernathy Residence
7 – LCPD/LCVFD
8 — Gonzales Residence
9 – Walcott Residence
10 – Church of Sts
     Margaret & Anthony
11 – Gonzalez Auto
     Repair
12 – Bodie Feed & Seed
13 – Pryor Meats & BBQ

Luna City Town Square

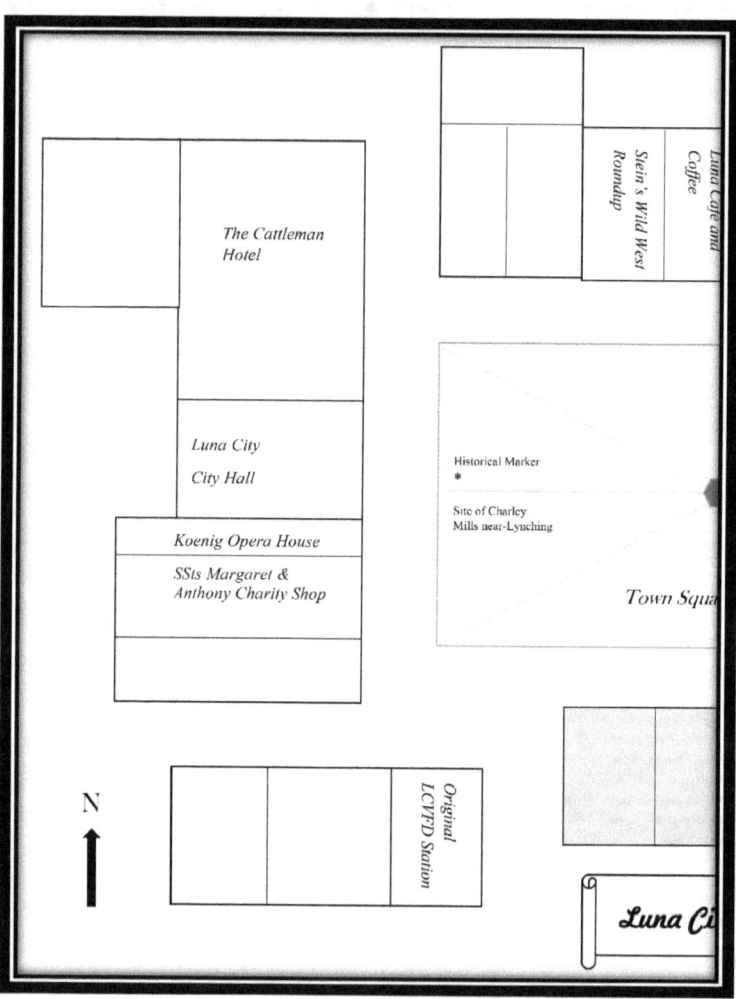

The Cattleman
Hotel

Stein's Wild West
Roundup

Luna Cafe and
Coffee

Luna City

City Hall

Historical Marker
*

Site of Charley
Mills near-Lynching

Koenig Opera House

SSts Margaret &
Anthony Charity Shop

Town Squa

N

Original
LCVFD Station

Luna Ci

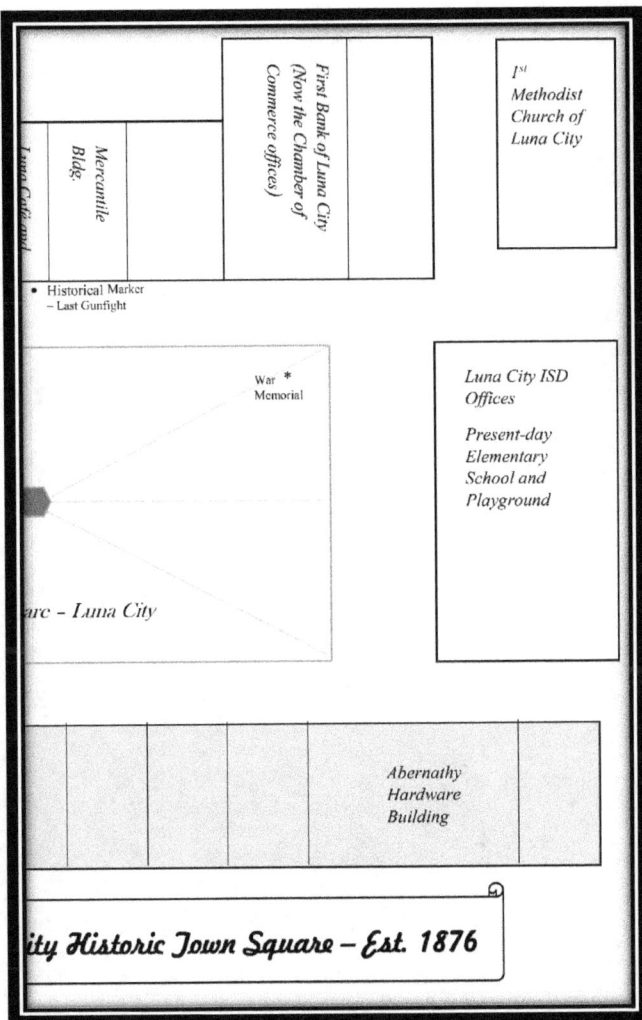

First Bank of Luna City
(Now the Chamber of
Commerce offices)

Mercantile
Bldg.

Luna Cafe and

1st
Methodist
Church of
Luna City

• Historical Marker
– Last Gunfight

War *
Memorial

Luna City ISD
Offices

Present-day
Elementary
School and
Playground

arc – Luna City

Abernathy
Hardware
Building

ity Historic Town Square – Est. 1876

Cast of Characters

(An asterisk marks those who are deceased)

Richard Astor-Hall *(Ricardo to his friends in Luna City, Rich Hall in his previous life)*	A former celebrity chef, who through a chain of circumstances, manages the Luna City Café and the occasional catering event.
Martin Abernathy	Widower, father of Jess, mayor of Luna City, hereditary owner of Abernathy Hardware.
Jessica "Jess" Abernathy Vaughn	Daughter of Martin, qualified CPA, Air Force Reservist, champion barrel-racer, married to Joe Vaughn.
Benny Cordova	The devious and ninja-skilled general manager of Mills Farm.
Samantha "Sammi" Colquhoun	Sometime actress, media personality, and ex-girlfriend of Richard, now married to Collin Wyler
Lucien "Lew" Dubois	Director of Marketing for the corporation which owns Mills Farm.
James Wyler "J.W." Ellis*	Grandson of Doc Stephen Wyler, once boyfriend to Jess Abernathy, best friend of Chris Mayall.
Dwight David "Music Man" Garrett	Coach of the Mighty Fighting Moths and band music master.

Alberto "Berto" Gonzales	Student and part-time limo driver, younger brother of Araceli Gonzalez, friend of Richard, and grandson of *Abuelita* Adeliza Gonzalez.
Sylvester Gonzales	Gaming geek, computer nerd, USMC veteran.
Roman Gonzales	Construction contractor.
Roman "Romeo" Gonzales	Cousin of Berto and Araceli, former oilfield worker, currently top male model, married to Susannah Wyatt, no longer an unwitting focus for strange and unearthly energies.
Adeliza "Abuelita" Gonzalez	The revered and feared matriarch of the Gonzales/Gonzalez clan, dedicated Food Channel watcher, and Richard's biggest fan.
Araceli Gonzales-Gonzalez	Older sister of Berto, married to Patrico, mother of Angelika and Mateo, manager, assistant cook, head waitress at the Luna Café & Coffee.
Patrico "Pat" Gonzalez	Husband to Araceli, drives a tanker truck for an oil company in the Eagle Ford Shale Oil Field.
Hernando "Nando" Gonzalez*	Korean War fighter ace, local hero, for whom the high school gymnasium is named.

Judith "Judy" Stillwell Grant	With her husband Sefton, the owner of the Age of Aquarius Campground and Goat Farm, the last two holdouts of a 1960s commune.
Sefton Grant	Husband of Judy, landlord of Richard.
Brianna "Bree" Grant	Youngest grandchild of Judy and Sefton, willful and intelligent, former apprentice at the Café.
Katherine "Kate" Heisel	Gonzales cousin, reporter for the *Karnesville Weekly Beacon*, significant other to Richard.
Lucas "Luc" Massie	Junior chef at the Café, drummer in a local band known as OPM.
Christopher "Chris" Mayall	Manager, Tip-Top Icehouse, Gas & Grocery, bartender at the VFW, Navy veteran, amputee participant in marathons, medic - Luna City VFD, best friend of J.W. Ellis, and friend of Richard.
Allen Lee Mayne	Former pro football player, Food Network star, host of roving restaurant show *A La Carte With Quartermayne*.
Leticia "Miss Letty" McAllister	Oldest person in Luna City, WWII Red Cross service, kindergarten teacher, friend to Chris Mayall.
Douglas McAllister, Phd *	Miss Letty's older brother, professor of history, and author of *The History of Luna City*.

Ozymandias-King-of-Kings "Ozzie"	Richard's one-eyed cat, mascot for his cooking-for-kids blog "Captain Kitten's Kitchen."
Xavier Gunnison-Penn	Unsuccessful international treasure-hunter, about to marry Dr. Miranda "Mindy" Rodriguez-Gonzalez.
Andrew Pryor	Oilfield geologist, headquartered in Karnesville, owner of small BBQ restaurant.
Patricia Wyler Pryor	Granddaughter of Dr. Stephen Wyler and Miss Alice, wife of Andrew Pryor, HS girlfriend of Joe Vaughn.
Dr. Miranda "Mindy" Rodriguez-Gonzalez	Granddaughter of Don Jaimie, owner of the ranch which was the original Gonzales landholding, about to marry Xavier Gunnison-Penn.
Georg Stein	Native of Germany, a retired corporate lawyer, passionate reenactor, owner of Stein's Wild West Round-up, married to Annise.
Annise Stein	Co-owner of Stein's Wild West Round-up.
Joseph "Joe" Vaughn	Army veteran, local football hero, chief of the Luna City Police Department, married to Jess Abernathy.

Joseph James Vaughn, Jr.	Infant son of Joe Vaughn and Jess Abernathy-Vaughn.
Harry Vaughn	Great-uncle of Joe Vaughn, retired federal marshal, and former police chief in a small town in Alaska.
Clovis Walcott, (Colonel, USAR/Ret.)	Retired US Army Reservist, currently consulting engineer, keen reenactor.
Sook "Isabel" Walcott	Korean-born wife of Clovis, socially ambitious, and the tiger-mother from Hell.
Jeremy "Jerry" Walcott	Oldest child of Clovis and Sook, a student nurse and family care-giver.
Robbie Walcott	Younger son of Clovis and Sook, bright and wildly curious, part-time cook at the Café.
Belle Walcott	Daughter of Clovis and Sook, student at the Julliard School of Music.
Susannah Wyatt-Gonzales	Former regional manager, at VPI, sexually stalked Richard, got over it and married Romeo Gonzales.

Luna City

Collin Wyler

Son of Doc Wyler and Miz Alice, father of Patricia, international financier, serial husband, and treasure-hunting enthusiast.

Dr. Stephen Wyler

Owner of the Wyler Exotic Game Ranch, a qualified veterinarian, part-owner of the Café and second-oldest resident. Father of Collin, grandfather of Patricia Pryor and J.W. Ellis.

Luna City X

The New Plan

"I brought down the mail for you, Ricardo," Sefton Grant tapped politely on the metal door of the small airstream trailer that Richard called home, late on a chilly January day. "Saw the lights on, knew you were home."

"I have mail?" Richard replied, wooden spoon in one hand. "'Strewth, I do almost everything on-line with my phone, these days. I almost forgot that there was such a thing as a stamped envelope with paper printed documents contained within. Who's it from?"

"None of my business," Sefton replied, with stalwart dignity, considering that he was clad in his usual costume for a mild late winter day — cowboy boots and a hand-loomed loincloth which barely covered the naughty bits. The seventyish co-proprietor of the Age of Aquarius Campground and Goat Farm was a stringy and well-tanned character who mostly resembled a fitter and less-run-to-seed Willie Nelson. He added, "Official mail on one — something to do with your immigration status, I would guess. Look, if you need it, Judy and I can declare this place a sanctuary for the undocumented. Our old Communards will go to the wall for you, as a person fleeing political persecution for your beliefs … you do have beliefs, Ricardo?"

"In good food, well-prepared and expertly served," Richard replied with a sigh. "Hardly the stuff of which international political martyrs are made. But I do appreciate the sentiment, Sefton."

"The other is hand-written," Sefton Grant handed over the two envelopes. "You know someone in France?"

"My parents," Richard answered, after a gander at the second envelope. "They live in France now … don't know for how much longer, with all this Brexit faffing about. But they have the extensive property there since I bought it for them out of my take from my first season as a TV chef. I understand that my dear old Dad is making a go of the vineyard attached to the property. Lord only knows how he does it — he was an investment broker when he retired with a hefty pension and a boodle of earnings on personal investments. I can't think how he ever managed to learn about making wine, although I suppose that anything is possible."

"A filthy capitalist, then?" Sefton queried.

Richard replied, "No, Dad has always been scrupulous about bathing. And he has excellent instincts about investments, and how they can work for you. Honestly, Sefton – I've always been a piker about that kind of thing. You earn money, you have money, you spend it ... compound interest and all that is a closed book to me. Might as well be a species of voodoo magic, as far as I am concerned. Look, Sefton. I've decided to make some life changes. And you're the first to know."

"Oh?" Sefton shifted uneasily, on the doorstep to the tiny vintage aluminum caravan, in which Richard had made a home for ... how many years was it? Richard had lost track. "You're not going to come out of the closet are you, Ricardo? Me and Judy, we're open-minded as sh*t, so that's OK with us, regardless..."

"No!" Richard regarded his host and landlord with mild exasperation. "No, not out of that closet. I'm as straight as straight can be. Totally hetero – I like the girls and they like me. In bed and otherwise. No, I've come to some life-decisions. I'm going to come out as American and ask Kate to marry me."

"Is that all?" Sefton looked ... well, not as jolted as Richard thought he might have been, on the occasion of that momentous announcement. "Well, congratulations all the way around. Don't know how all that legal BS will go, being natural-born Americans, Judy and I. It was all sorted for us, on account of where we were born. A bit different, I think – making the active choice. Lotta hurdles to go over, or so they say. I prolly ain't the one to best advise you on that – mebbe Jess is the right person to go to. Even Doc Wyler – he's got the power juice an' all. 'Specially as you work for him, at the Café, an' all." Yes," Sefton definitely looked in a brighter mood. "See what 'ol Doc W. can do for you, Ricardo. But if all else fails, Ju and I can declare this place a sanctuary space for the undocumented immigrant."

"I believe that you and your good lady won't have to go to that extreme," Richard replied, somewhat heartened by Sefton Grant's gesture of support, and the implicit support of all the Old Communards, original members of a commune founded at the Age of Aquarius in the 1968 Summer of Love. Most of them were now ensconced with tenure in the upper rungs of higher education, so possibly they possessed at least as much communal social justice juice as the aged and irascible owner of the Wyler Ranch, for whom the concept of social justice was merely a nasty and disruptive rumor. 'But nonetheless – it is appreciated. Your support and all. I will go through with it all, you see. This is a place that ..."

"Gets a hold on you, Ricardo," Sefton agreed. "Kinda grows on ya.'"

"Like moss and mold," Richard agreed, and Sefton laughed. It was a friendly and companionable laugh.

"Hey look – wet your head, in a metaphorical way of speaking – now that you're about to become one of us. Let me bring you a jug of the newest ..."

"Your vintage white?" Richard was immediately all ears. "Or your best red. It matters not, Sefton. I'll drink a health to my future as an American, a married man, to Kate and ... well, really – anyone and anything you propose a toast to. Bring it on, man. Bring it on."

"Sure," Sefton shuffled the toe of his cowboy boot in the small dust which had blown across the space of concrete pavers which formed the brief sheltered patio below the vintage Airstream caravan which had been Richard's *(and latterly Ozzie the Chef Kitten's)* home since arriving in Luna City. Sefton looked as if he was the bearer of unfortunate intelligence. "Say, Ricardo ... have you really thought about where you will live, once you and Katie are a thing? This place is really small, an' I know you love it,   but once you and she are a family sort of thing ... a dinky trailer like this just won't cut it. Katie has all her own stuff, ya know. Books and all that. Ju and I built the yurt for the family. We needed the space, you see. A space big enough to swing a cat in..."

"I have no intention of swinging Ozzie," Richard replied with some indignation. "I am certain that he would object most strenuously to that exercise. I suppose that I would have to consult with Kate. I suppose that we would have to establish a somewhat roomier joint domicile. Honestly, Sefton, I would keep the caravan as a *pied-à-terre* ... a sort of holiday or weekend retreat. It's a small space of my own ... and dammit, I do appreciate the solitude and peace of your little refuge. I'd go on paying the rent, of course, even if ... when Kate and I establish a residence elsewhere…" Left unvoiced was a certain kind of sinking-in-the-heart realization that he and Kate would <u>have</u> to live someplace together – a larger place, with room for Richard's kitchen things, Ozzie's litterbox and all that Kate would bring to a union of their two households. Which wouldn't fit into the Airstream, not even with the aid of a dozen shoehorns.

"That's fine, Ricardo," Sefton shuffled the toe of his cowboy boot into the dust again. "A man does need a refuge, 'o course. So, where d'you think you and Kate will settle?"

"I don't know," Richard answered. "That will be up to Kate's preference and my own hopefully well-fattened checkbook. I am perfectly agreeable to my ladylove making that momentous decision. It all depends on how well-fatted that checkbook might be, in the long run. I … well, I was a fool about money, and left a good quantity of financial debris behind in London. Debts and all; we might have to settle in here, after all."

"A country boy can survive," Sefton grinned crookedly, but with complete understanding.

"No matter what country, eh?" Richard answered. "You've been a pal, Sefton. I should thank you again for being so… although quite a lot of people who claimed to know me well have insisted that I'm a selfish, inconsiderate git. I don't really deserve the consideration that I have received from you all…"

"Never mind, Ricardo," Sefton flashed those amazingly good straight teeth again in a smile. "We all have our weaknesses, ya know? I'll bring that jug of mustang red for ya … if you don't answer the door, I'll leave it by the step. I suppose you wanna do some thinking about your letters?"

"I do, Sefton – and thanks for the consideration," Richard replied.

The official letter he cared little for – but the letter from France had his complete attention, after reading the salutation and the opening paragraph.

His parents were going to visit Texas, late in spring, or early summer. And that presented yet a third complication to a life which was already sufficiently challenging for Richard.

Spring 2019 Newsletter

Spring 2019 Newsletter

Luna City Chamber of Commerce

5 North Town Square, Suite 4

Check out our Facebook Page

The Karnes Company Living History Association marks Texas independence with their annual three-day encampment under the oaks of Town Square. Opening of the encampment begins with a military drill and ceremonial flag-raising at 9 AM Friday, April 12. Bring the kids for demonstrations of 19th century technology, from starting a fire with flint and steel, to making felt, casting lead bullets, making lace by hand, and cooking over a campfire with authentic 19th century pots, pans and implements. See displays of military gear and drills, products produced in Texas in the early days, and ride the hayride, around Town Square. Make Texas history live again!

An Addition to Luna City History

Sefton Grant and other local volunteers have finished clearing scrub cedar trees and other brush which for decades obscured an antique folly, which once adorned the elaborate gardens surrounding the long-gone Sheffield Mansion. The 'folly' was a stone circle of native limestone on top of a low rise at the western end of the garden, duplicating a prehistoric Irish stone circle. Morgan P. Sheffield was an enthusiastic researcher and amateur folklorist, who came to Luna City for his health, and hoped to establish a resort and spa on property now occupied by the Age of Aquarius Campground and Goat Farm.

Upcoming Events

February 16

The Luna City VFD holds their yearly pancake breakfast at the 1st Methodist Church Parish Hall, from 7 – 10 AM

April 6

Yearly Spaghetti Feed, Sts Margaret and Anthony Parish Hall, from 5-8 PM. Kitchen prep work to be done April 4th, from 12 noon on, in the Parish Hall.

April 12

Spring Rally Encampment on Town Square for the Karnes Company Living History Association. Live demonstrations of 19th century life, drill, and displays, all weekend long.

Book Club Readings

The Luna City Book Club meets on the first Tuesday of each month at 7 PM in the Parish Hall of the First Luna City Methodist Church. January's selection is Trish Creighton Doyle's *Those Boleyn Daughters*.

Luna City ISD News

Summer School Classes

Summer school begins on Monday, June 3. Besides make-up classes for students who receiving failing grades during the regular school year, a number of elective and shop courses are offered. Contact the school administrative offices for a list of courses offered.

Life Guard Certification Course

In cooperation with the ARC and the Karnesville City Department of Recreation, the Luna City ISD offers a life-guard certification course for those aged 16 and older who wish to work during the summer at public or private pools and waterparks in that capacity. Students must pass a swim-qualification test to qualify for acceptance to the course. The course will be held from 9-3 every Saturday in April and May. A school bus will depart from the parking area by the Nando Gonzales Memorial Gymnasium at 8:15. Students taking this course should bring a packed lunch, a swimsuit, towel and change of clothes.

Mighty Fighting Moth Audition & Band Practice

8th Grade musicians who wish to audition for a place in Mighty Fighting Moth Marching band for the 2019-2020 school year are asked to schedule an audition during the first two weeks in May. Contact Mr. Garrett through the school office to arrange a time mutually convenient.

Marching Band practice will begin July 23rd, every Tuesday, Thursday and Saturday at 8:30 on Moth Field. In the case of rain, practice will be held in the school gymnasium.

Community Marketplace

Valentine's Day Special

Judy Grant is offering bespoke baskets for Valentines' Day; the perfect gift for your loved one! Baskets will vary in price according to contents, which may include any or all of the following: essential oils, bees wax candles, lotions, and specialty goat-milk soaps in various romantic and erotic shapes. Order by February 9 for best selection and delivery.

From Chief Vaughn, Luna City PD

The young, reckless and bored are reminded that informal drag racing on Rte 123, or various deserted backroads adjacent to the Wyler Ranch is strictly forbidden by local, county and state laws. The movie series "Fast and Furious" is not a documentary.

Luna Café Spring Blue Plate Lunch Specials

Tuesday – Chicken Pot Pie with Flaky Crust
Wednesday – Salisbury Steak with Mushroom Gravy
Thursday – Baked Ham with Sweet Potatoes
Friday – Tuna Salad Sandwich with Pomme Frit
Saturday – Pot Roast with vegetables
Sunday – Baked Lasagna

All selections served with a green salad dressed with Chef Richard's special dressing and include dessert of the day.

Going For Broke

* ring * ring * ring *
"Hi, Mum," Richard said, as soon as his mother's voice came over the line. Well, strictly speaking, not a line. He supposed that he and his parents were speaking through invisible waves bounced off satellites and radio towers. He was taking a break, out in back of the Café, now that the breakfast rush was over. He had finally gotten the knack of calling his parents in France in mid-morning, catching them in early evening instead of the wee hours of the night. "I got your letter about visiting Texas this summer..."

"Oh, darling, won't it be such an adventure?" His mother replied. "Your father is so looking forward to touring the new wineries, seeing how things are done in Texas. And to see you again, now that you are doing so very well."

"You and Father are doing very well too, or so I understand," Richard surveyed the three raised beds of herbs which took up a large portion of that otherwise uninspired space back of the Café formerly dominated by the refuse bins. The herbs looked slightly wilted. While he was out there, he had better sprinkle water on them. Much of his success with the Café over the last few years had been due to his expert use of fresh herbs in the Café's signature dishes. "You know, when I bought you that place in Provence for a retirement bolt-hole, I didn't think that Father would take it on in such a professional degree ... I just thought you would renovate the house and lease the vineyards to a local to manage."

"Oh, yes!" his mother replied. "But you know your father – never anything done by halves. Besides, total retirement is quite terribly boring – he says that really what it means is that you can do the work one wants to do, rather than what one has to do. We thought of it just as having an enjoyable and rather strenuous hobby, early on. But your father just got ... rather interested in the whole process, and how it could be improved in small ways, here and there. And having our label honored by those awards ... all our old friends in Bickley were just awfully chuffed at getting cases of our most recent prize-winning vintage as Christmas presents from us."

"Where is Father now," Richard asked, knowing that it would only be mid-evening in Provence, and rather puzzled that his mother had not passed her cellphone to him. "I have some rather good news for you both."

"He's gone to meet some vintner friends at their favorite estimanet in Saint-Didier," His mother replied. "You would be amazed at how fluent he is in French, now, darling! But your Aunt Moira is here! Go ahead and tell us your good news, and I'll share it with your father when he gets home."

Richard's heart sank, slightly, when he heard Aunt Moira's voice, in the background. His scarily competent and well-traveled Aunt Moira, who without any visible means of economic support other than a passport which unconvincingly described her profession as "journalist" nonetheless had a four-decade long history of having been in the vicinity of countless international developments in the weeks and months before such international developments unaccountably turned up as screaming headlines and lead stories in the print and broadcast media. It had been Richard's private conviction since he was a schoolboy that Aunt Moira was a high-level operative for an obscure department designated M-something; a distaff 007, as it were. Her grasp of martial arts, her demonstrated skill at knife-throwing and marksmanship with small arms were undeniable, as well as her forty-year-long record of turning up, fresh from what she artlessly described as *just a routine assignment, darling!* after a trip to locality which frequently devolved into civil unrest, a change in government or an open war in which the international media were forced to take an interest.

"Hullo, darling – how is that little restaurant of yours doing?" Aunt Moira asked, her voice rich and so very upper-class.

"Fine, Aunt Moira," Richard replied, although thinking that probably Aunt Moira already knew. She had ways, means, and reliable informants. "Look, Mum. I'm going to ask a woman to marry me."

"That's very ... sudden, dear," he heard through his phone, and he was brought to protest.

"No, Mum – it's not. We've known each other for ... practically all the time that I've been here, although we only started seeing each other seriously a couple of years ago."

In the background, Aunt Moira remarked, "A couple of years? Darling, you're losing your touch. You used to rush the girls as if the publican were about to call 'time, gentlemen, time.'"

"She's ... special," Richard argued. "And her name is Katherine – everyone calls her Kate. Kate Heisel. She works for the local newspaper, and produces my cooking podcasts – they're hugely popular, locally. I've met her family... we had Christmas dinner with her parents. Her family approves ... well, her grandfather doesn't. But he has a long-time grudge about the English, not improved in the least when I nearly dropped the flaming pudding in his lap. But it turned out that everyone loved the pudding, and they stopped the grandfather from going after me with an electric carving knife. We have a lot in common, including a pet. She loves my cooking and I love to cook for her."

"It sounds terribly eventful," his mother ventured in dubious tones. "But as long as you can work out these little disagreements between you and your Kate. You're a grown man, darling – I am certain that you know what you are doing."

Richard didn't think that he ought to unload the other bit of startling news on them – that he was going through the process of becoming an American citizen. *No, not at this time. Save it for when the 'rents had gotten past the initial shock.*

"I'm going to propose, the next time that we have a supper together. We meet once a week, although we do message and talk all the time."

"Oh, that," Aunt Moira interjected. "All very well, I suppose. Doesn't substitute for a good rousing boink now and again, just to cement the relationship."

Richard heroically and successfully restrained the impulse to inquire that if a good rousing boink did anything to cement a relationship, then why was Aunt Moira conspicuously unattached in a strictly relationship sense?

"We respect each other," he replied, instead. "I fully intend to present her with a ring at soonest opportunity. And not to ... err – suggest a good rousing boink until then."

"Excellent," Aunt Moira replied, and Richard could hear her very clearly. His mother was doubtless holding out her cellphone so that they both could be heard. "I have a family ring. It was your great-grandfathers'. Heirloom thing and custom-made from Garrards' when they were top-drawer. Ugly central stone – harlequin brown jasper, and as vulgar as you can imagine, but the rest of it is in diamonds and pearls, and the rest is hallmarked 20 carat gold. I'll put it in the post, special delivery for you. Use it if you wish – and if you want to have it remade, don't worry. Your great-grandfather had the most appalling taste..."

"Thanks, Auntie M.," Richard said, gratefully – and he was, for he had not made any particular provision for a ring, and that – he had been given to understand, was one of those obligatory things. How awful could his great-grandfather's taste be, anyway? "Look, Mum ... tell Father about me proposing to make an even more honest woman of Kate when he gets home from tomcatting around the bistros in town with his wine-making pals. Ok, bye-eee. Love you, Mum and Auntie M. Talk to you in a couple of days, all right?"

click

Karnes County Legends: The Stone Circle

From the Karnes County Beacon Website –
by Katherine Heisel, Staff Writer

At the crest of a low hill covered with a scrub wood of small live oaks, hackberries and native laurel which have grown up in the century since the old Sheffield mansion burned down, there is a circle of shaped limestone blocks. This stone circle is part of the landscaping around a long-vanished mansion. The property which now houses the Age of Aquarius Campground and Goat Farm was once was the home of Morgan P. Sheffield, who had discovered upon having a well drilled to provide household water, a natural hot mineral spring on his homestead property. Morgan Sheffield hoped, after this happy discovery, to build a small spa hotel and curative refuge, in the event that the San Antonio – Aransas Pass Railway would make Luna City a regular stop. Alas, that was not a dream which came to pass. Before the failure to make Luna City the queen city of Karnes County, Morgan Sheffield had built a palatial and stately mansion with an extensively landscaped garden, a garden which included a series of formal rose beds, a large summer house and a series of ornamental follies. All these but one succumbed to the depredations of time, including the mansion, which fell into ruin and were burned following a lightning strike during a summer thunderstorm. The single element of mansion and garden remaining after decades was the circle of stones intended to replicate the Irish Drombeg prehistoric stone circle. Morgan

Sheffield was an amateur folklorist of a certain dedicated breed common to the late 19th century. There is absolutely no historical evidence that any kind of orgies or human sacrifice ever occurred, local legends to the contrary. Morgan Sheffield merely liked the look of the stone folly, and as his five acres contained a nice selection of limestone slabs and boulders, he directed his landscape and garden architect to make full use of them. In time, as the estate and gardens decayed, the stone folly was overgrown and forgotten.

When the derelict acres became the property of Morgan Sheffield's great-grandniece, Judith "Judy" Stillwell Grant in the early 1960s, Judy with her husband Sefton Grant and a circle of friends from the University of Texas at Austin established a communal settlement in the summer of 1968. The commune members, in clearing away brush for their tents, yurts, teepees and free-range shacks, discovered the stone circle, and made it a centerpiece for various nighttime revels and celebrations. Judy Grant and her circle of friends still observe the Celtic solstice and equinox rites every three months at the stone circle, which is located approximately a quarter of a mile south of the main compound of the Age of Aquarius Campground and Goat Farm. Permission should be asked there for those interested in visiting or taking photographs of the stone circle, as it is on private property.

Starting the Wheels Churning

On a Tuesday morning, the start of a brand-new week, Richard rode his bicycle to work – to the Café on Town Square, a place of business which had been the cynosure of his life, ever since stumbling into Luna City by the grace of a Deity in which he barely believed, and on the wings of a black-out drunk some five years before. He liked to think that he had been accepted – nay, embraced by the locals, most of whom were fairly normal humans, moderately studded with those of varied eccentricity, much like preserved fruit and currents scattered through the sweet yeast dough of a traditional hot cross bun.

This was his place, and he would die under torture rather than confess that he had come to love it, fiercely and without reservation. Just as he had come to love Ozzie, the one-eyed brindle cat, riding behind Richard in the plastic crate strapped to the back of the trail bike, and Kate ... his media-savvy and creative soon-to-be fiancée, the star reporter for the local weekly newspaper, the *Karnesville Weekly Beacon (Your Beacon on The News in Karnes County!)*. Now, he had determined to take the final plunge, into pure citizenship and marriage alike. Well, he could tell the staff at the Café of his plans for one but the other must remain a private decision, at least until he had consulted with Kate and appraised her of his plans.

"I've decided to apply for naturalization," Richard announced to his best gal-pal, the head waitress and manager of the Café, in a lull during the breakfast rush, to Araceli Gonzales-Gonzalez. And coincidentally, second cousin to his intended. Richard was certain that this intelligence would pass through the Gonzales/Gonzalez kin gossip network with the speed of light. "And be a full-blooded American. Any thoughts from you all how that might be accomplished, but don't share with anyone − I want it to be a surprise. I'm in a bit of a hurry over the whole thing, too."

"No notion, Chef," Araceli replied, in mid-flight, a full coffee carafe in one hand, and the pitcher of cream in the other. Richard had firmly established a routine for the Café's coffee − only fresh-brewed, every morning, and full cream to accompany, although backsliders could make do with half-and-half. Chalk-based artificial creamer was an abomination and not allowed to pass through the doors – back or front – of the Café. "I'll bet Jess would know … and definitely the Steins would know, too; they voted in the last election for the first time, and Annise was just thrilled to bits."

"I'm meeting with her after the breakfast rush," Richard noted with pleased relief. "It shouldn't be that hard … should it?"

"It took the Steins almost ten years of filling out forms and doing interviews – and he was a lawyer, too," Araceli pointed out, as further comment being halted by the silvery jingle of the bell attached to a spring on the Café's front door.

Oh, dear, thought Richard. *Perhaps this wouldn't quite so be a doddle, a walk in the park...*

Jess Abernathy-Vaughn, the CPA who acted for the elderly owners of the Café came walking heavily through the shady green forest of massive ancient oaks at the appointed hour, pushing the stroller containing her lively toddler son, Joe Junior. Jess supervised her family's hereditary business, Abernathy Hardware, on the far side of the square which denoted the beating downtown heart of Luna City. Abernathy Hardware was housed in a tall four-story brick Beaux Arts-style late Victorian structure which currently housed the hardware store, Jess's business office, and the apartments over the store; the homes of Jess's widowed father *(and former mayor, now on an extended round-the-world cruise)* and her grandfather and grandmother. Jess herself lived with her husband, Luna City Chief of Police Joe

Vaughn, in a quaint Craftsman-era cottage on Oak Street, in what passed for a suburb in Luna City. Richard hurried out of the Café when he saw Jess carefully picking her away across the road and pulled out a chair at one of the sidewalk tables for her.

"Oof!" Jess exclaimed as she sank gratefully onto it. "Thanks, Ricardo. I think I may have overdone it. Give me a moment to catch my breath."

Richard eyed her covertly as he took the chair opposite. Jess was hugely pregnant. Although he claimed no further knowledge of these matters than paparazzi snaps of pregnant celeb baby bumps on the front page of the *Daily Mail*, it seemed to his inexpert eye that she was much bigger than expected.

He forbore to make any other comment than, "I'd have come over and met you in your office – you didn't have to overdo it in your condition."

"No problem," Jess insisted. "As Pooh says – bother my condition. I needed to get out of the office for a bit of fresh air and Little Joe kept asking for a 'tcookie' and wouldn't be content with a Nilla Wafer, which is all that Gram had in her pantry. I think he wants one of those lovely, frosted sugar cookies that you make for the Café..."

"Your wish is my command, young Master Vaughn," Richard sketched a hasty salute toward the Vaughn sprog, who favored him with a scowl which made the family resemblance to his father even more marked. "And do you want coffee? Can we interest you in a bit of lunch, perhaps?"

"No coffee," Jess replied. "My OB recommends against it, now that I have only another month to go."

"Then we will offer you a glass of fresh orange juice and a small dish of sliced fruit drizzled with our special honey-ginger-yoghurt dressing then," Richard replied. He was guardedly fond of Jess, who really did not look to be in the best of spirits. "It's no trouble," he added. "Salad special for today. After we go through the financials for this week, I have a special question on which I need advice. A personal one ... given that I am considering changing my legal status here."

"We're friends," Jess assured him, already looking somewhat less flushed. "No charge for an initial consult. It's not to do with the Café, then?"

"Only peripherally," Richard answered, and went to ask Bianca the junior waitress to bring Jess's light fruit-cup luncheon, a frosted cookie for Little Joe and a coffee for himself to the table outside. When he returned, Jess had her laptop out and opened, and Little Joe was chomping on his infant fist, regarding Richard with a baleful stare.

"Now then," Richard reported, opening up the folder in which he secreted the various weekly bills for comestibles for the Café, along with reports of the wages paid, and a print-out of customer receipts for the previous week. Jess reviewed them with a gimlet eye, only slightly distracted by the arrival of Bianca with the fruit cup and cookie for Little Joe, upon which that infant patron of the Café fell upon with savage joy, gumming the crumby sugar-cookie frosted delight into submission.

"You're looking at the best quarterback hope for the 2032 Moths Varsity," Jess observed. "Joe is already tossing around the Nerf football with him on the front lawn when he comes home after work. These figures look very well, Ricardo. Doc Wyler and Miss Letty will be quite pleased. Now, you said that you had a personal question."

"Yes," Richard answered, determined to lay all of his cards out on the table. "I've decided to be an American citizen."

Jess grinned. "You can always go to Mexico, sneak over the border and pray for the next amnesty to come soon. That seems to work for most, these days."

"Legally," Richard clarified. "All 'I's dotted and all 't's crossed, correctly and legally, ship-shape and Bristol-fashion. I've been here on a legal green card for ... five years, going on six. What else do I need do?"

"Let me call up the government website," Jess took a long swig of her orange juice and opened her laptop. "Hmm ... well, you have the five-years residence all squared away, it looks like. You have been here for a solid five years – I can testify to that, so far so good. You aren't serving in the US military or married to an American citizen ..." She looked at Richard interrogatively, and Richard confessed with some reluctance.

"I am going to propose to Kate, but that's going to be an entirely separate matter from pursuing citizenship. One job at a time, for me, you see."

"That's the easy short-cut you know," Jess replied, "But it's a shortcut that's been too easily abused. Let's go on; neither of your parents was a citizen? That would shorten the time required, I guess from what I read – oh, no luck on that last, even if your mom or dad was an American citizen, since you're over the age of 18. There's a form to fill out. It asks for a metric butt-load of personal information, past addresses, employment history, criminal record – everything but a sample of your belly button lint. Looks pretty daunting, Ricardo, as it's 21 pages long, although I can probably help you with it all, since I speak fluent bureaucratese. One of my gifts." Jess scrolled down a little bit further. Richard waited, with rising impatience. *She wasn't eating her fruit cup! An affront against the Café and their patent ginger-honey-yogurt dressing!*

"There's a test," Jess continued, after another moment. "For facility in English. I don't think you will have any problem with that, seriously – or for knowledge of American civics and history. I can download the recommended study guides and print them up for you at the office this afternoon. There are some fees involved ..." She sent Richard a searching look, and Richard answered,

"I'm certain that I can pay them – I've been earning good money from the Café, and catering ..."

"Those fees have a way of multiplying," Jess prophesied darkly. "And then there's a lengthy interview, based on what you answered in the form. I would suggest that you answer all questions by the interviewer and the firm with absolute 100% honesty."

"Lies being harder to remember," Richard agreed.

"Mmmm," Jess took a bite of her fruit cup, and continued scrolling through the laptop page, while Little Joe gummed his cookie. "Two passport sized photos of yourself, copied scans of the front and back of your green card ... hmm. Do you have any previous marriages on the record? They'll want documentation, if so – and if annulled or divorced, then copies of the testimonial paperwork. Criminal record ... Do you owe back taxes? I know that you don't from here, since I have done all your W2s and returns since Doc and Miss Letty hired you. What about before."

"I ... I might still owe creditors for the failed restaurant dodge," Richard admitted, slowly, thinking of his decade or so of employment and lavish travels as a celebrity chef. Well, he supposed that consulting the stamps in his passport would provide a full accounting of his globe-trotting. "I'm not entirely certain, you see. It was a total disaster. A spectacular disaster, and they were left holding the bag. I was not in very good shape; I just could not cope. And well ... honestly, I've always been afraid to go back and see what was left after the debacle. I had bank accounts, and the freehold of certain valuable City properties. I suppose those were drained by the baying mob of creditors, but I've just never cared to ... umm, poke the sleeping bear, and see if there was anything left over, or if I still owe. I just didn't care to know," he added, aware that Jess was regarding him over the fruit cup like a severe teacher forced to deal with a catastrophically slow pupil.

"Did you have a financial manager?" Jess sounded crisp and professional. "Someone legally empowered to deal with your money matters?"

"I don't know, actually," Richard confessed. "Seriously, Jess, a lot of all that, the last year or two or three from before – I can't recall. It all happened to someone else with my name, but just another 'me'. A doppelganger, with stupid, impulsive bad habits and no sense of responsibility. I never wanted to deal with it all, once I came here, once I left that life behind."

"You have to deal now, Ricardo," Jess forked up another bite of her fruit cup. "Welcome to adulting; it comes with the territory. The debts attached to that former life of yours; you will probably have to resolve them, as part of becoming an American citizen with a clean background."

"I know," Richard sighed. "I probably should ask my father about all that. I might have asked him to deal with certain aspects of my financials, although I can't remember for certain. Most of the last year before opening Carême is a decided blur to me. He and Mum are going to visit this year – some kind of tour of Texas wineries this summer. They want to come and visit. I suppose I can have a heart-to-heart with him then. He's a retired investment broker, but he has had a go for the last ten years over the French property that I bought for them when I first hit it big. I can't wait to see his face when I introduce him to Sefton Grant and show him Sefton's little wine-producing operation."

"You know," Jess cleared her throat, delicately. "Doc Wyler and Miss Letty think the world of how you've brought the Café up to scratch. But they just can't afford to pay you more, even if it would clear your old debts. You've maxed out your value to management, at this point. Well, Doc <u>could</u> pay off your old debts, theoretically, but…"

"I wouldn't ask," Richard returned, rather stiffly. "Not the done thing between gentlemen."

"Doc would agree," Jess nodded. "He's a businessman, not a charitable function. But you have done well out of the independent catering." She ate another bite of fruit cup and licked the ginger-honey-yogurt dressing from the spoon with appreciative appetite, which Richard observed with guarded satisfaction. "You've got a good team in the Café, you know. Araceli. Your freaky drummer, Robbie Walcott, the girls. Honestly, I think the café is as big as it's ever going to be. Speaking strictly as a friend, Ricardo, if you wanted to ease back from the day-to-day operations here and consider what Lew Dubois offered you as the senior chef at the Cattleman, that might offer you more scope, and certainly a higher income. Not quite the high-flying international chef gig, but I can read the signs. You've built a good thing; don't let yourself get stale, when the place practically runs itself. Boredom is as much of a career-killer as …"

"Instant celebrity? I take your point," Richard acknowledged, although he did feel a twinge of discomfort at how accurately Jess had pegged his own small spasms of boredom with routine at the Café. *Was he that transparent to every intelligent woman in Luna City? Apparently so.* Meanwhile, Jess continued.

"If you like, I'll help you with the application form, and the study materiels, and you can start collecting up all the documentation. I'll have to be taking a break from work for at least a couple of weeks after the baby... Meanwhile, if you are serious about doing more catering – Roman told me last week that Lew and Mrs. Lew will be in town next week, overseeing a new project, before the summer season begins. You can touch bases with him and see if his offers still hold."

"They will? My god, I'd love to see Lew and his good missus again," Richard found himself oddly pleased at this ripping good news, fresh off the Luna City bush telegraph. "What brings them to town again? I thought he was in near-blissful retirement."

"Lew?" Jess giggled. "Oh, never. Maybe when they fasten the coffin lid down and start throwing clods of dirt upon it – and I bet that at that point, he will pop up and gently chide the mourners for their failure to maintain good clod-pitching skills. He and Anne are overseeing a new project; expansion of the stable program and a new building project – an exclusive little executive-only enclave, in that little grove of trees near where the old Sheffield place used to be; part of what Judy and Sefton sold to Mills Farm for the extension. From what Roman says – a little compound of luxury guest cottages and landscaped gardens for the use of high-level executive staff residences, visiting C-level executives and majority board members. Can't be expected to rub elbows with the ordinary run of customers, you see."

Richard whistled, low under his breath. "Very nice. I suppose that I will see Lew again, when he appears. And I would welcome your help in filling out the interminable form. I am entirely serious about this, Jess. Fraught as everything seems to be at this moment ... I can't help feeling that this place is where I mean to be, this is the place where I must belong. And I mean to propose to Katie. Miss Heisel, you see. I ... must provide a future for us both."

"You are doing good, Ricardo," Jess replied. "And you'll be an amazing American. Even better, since you're already a good Texan. One more thing, though," and Jess frowned. "You might want to be tactful, if you are serious about proposing to Kate, and applying for citizenship; her big brother had a bad brush with a girl he met overseas when he was in the Army."

"Matt – now with the Karnesville FD," Richard nodded. "I met him and his wife when Kate and I went to Christmas dinner with her family. Solid bloke, and happily married – wife is a pip, as well."

"This was before," Jess explained, "When Matt was on his first tour overseas, young and dumb and full of ... the stuff that horny young guys are full of. He began dating a local buy-me-drinkie girl, who spun him a song and a dance about love, marriage, and baby carriages ... oh, and he would take her to the States. I was away myself, at the time, only heard about it much later from 'Celi, but poor Matt was really broken up when it turned out that Drinkie Girl was just leading him on for a green card and a one-way ticket to the land of the Big BX."

"That's not anything like Katie and I," Richard protested. "I don't see how there could be any comparison!"

"Probably not," Jess agreed. "But still — a word of warning — make sure that one has nothing to do with the other."

"I won't even mention it." Richard gathered up his collection of papers. "Best not to even bring it up."

Possibilities

"Chef," said Beatriz the waitress, as she fetched the dessert order for a foursome having lunch on one of the outside tables, "They have a question – they all adored the salad dressing, and they want to buy a bottle of it, to take home – can we do that? They said it was the absolute best in the world."

It was a mild weekend, just after Richard's consult with Jess over his citizenship application. The afternoon after that consultation, Jess had provided a thick folder full of questions and answers which might be on the citizenship exam. The weather as mild as a summer day in Bickley, and new green leaves had begun coyly peeping out on the bare branches of the venerable oaks in Town Square.

"It's our special house dressing," Robbie Walcott elaborated. "Blood-orange reduction and orange-infused olive oil, and Chef's twenty secret spices."

"Not twenty secret spices," Richard replied, slightly miffed. "Only the basic half-dozen. No point in overegging the pudding."

"It's not pudding, it's salad dressing," Beatriz looked desperately puzzled, and Richard sighed a little.

"Merely an expression, Beatriz, merely an expression. Certainly, they might have a bottle of it. I made up a batch yesterday, it's in the large square vat in the cooler. It's emulsified, so the proportions should be correct."

"You can use one of those Dublin Bottling works soda bottles in the recycle bin," Araceli suggested, "But sterilize it good, first. There's a box of corks in the back room. I was saving them from the wine bottles for Matty to make a boat with. Charge them – how much, do you think, Chef?"

"Eight dollars, plus tax," Richard made a swift calculation, and thought no more about the matter, as absorbed almost completely in studying for the exam in his few off-hours. But the next weekend, one of the couples returned for Saturday brunch, and brought three more friends, and both parties asked for another bottle of the Café blood-orange salad dressing.

"You know, Chef," Araceli suggested, "if this salad dressing thing is going to go on being popular, why don't we have bottles made up already."

"Yeah!" Robbie Walcott piped up. "Expand the Café brand by offering our exclusive small-batch chef-prepared dressings ... and sauces, too!" Robbie, having graduated the previous May from Luna City High School, had begun taking courses in restaurant management from an institution of higher learning in San Antonio. Richard could have advised the teenager that the motto over the gate of that place should have read *"Abandon hope all ye who enter here."* Still, Robbie appeared to be taking the whole enterprise with serious purpose and a simply exhausting degree of enthusiasm. Richard had no notion of what Clovis Walcott, or his wife, Sook, the most demanding tiger mother in Karnes County thought of their son deciding against an illustrious professional career following upon acceptance at and graduation from a prestigious university. Perhaps, like his own parents, they hoped that a career in food service was something their son would grow out of, if they didn't make much fuss about it.

That would be a hope stillborn, if Richard had any grasp of judgement in human matters. Robbie Walcott and his best gal-pal Brianna Grant had been trained by him several summers past in the strict French kitchen-brigade old-style tradition, and they were both irritatingly still keen as mustard. Robbie was at duty as a sous-chef without fail every weekend, and Brianna every day that her own upper-division studies could spare her, buoyed up by their out-of-the-blue-sky win of a local chili cooking contest at Mills Farm, a win that had made the Luna City Café and Coffee a destination restaurant for aficionados of small-town charms and chili-heads everywhere.

"Do what you want with this," Richard allowed, certain that the prospect had a better than even chance of flopping entirely. "I leave it on you to clear it with Jess ... Miss Abernathy. Mrs. Vaughn. There will an extra expense for the proper bottles for a retail product. Do investigate requirements for food processing for direct sales in this kitchen. I think that we can legally do it, but you might want to make certain. Just ... put my name on the label if Mrs. Vaughn gives it the go-ahead. It's my recipe, after all."

That was the last that Richard expected to hear about selling his signature spiced blood-orange ready-made salad dressing commercially. The notion would briefly bloom, wane, and die, once the enthusiasm of his junior staff withered on the vine, and he had other metaphorical fish to fry, now that his studies had moved on to necessary citizenship knowledge. But it didn't – the following Tuesday, he noticed a new display rack by the cash desk at the front of the house: a rustic set of slanted shelves made of cedar, filled with several rows of bottles, all neatly and attractively labeled, in a style which combined country chic with a touch of charmingly down-home quaintness. *"Chef Ricardo's Special Café Salad Dressing"* in a typeface which looked like cross-stitch, with the Café's coffee-cup logo at the bottom and the whole surrounded with a wreath of cross-stitched oranges and leaves.

"Got a friend at school whose boyfriend is a graphic artist," Robbie explained with becoming pride. "He did the label design. Great, isn't it?"

"It is all that, indeed," Richard replied. "Where did the shelf come from?"

"Mr. Grant wanged it out for us, in his workshop," Robbie answered proudly. "He says it can be adjusted for other items, and if we need it, he can do another to match. He's got plenty of cedar planks!"

"Well, tell him not to hold his breath," Richard advised, mordantly, but within days, the serried ranks of bottles showed gaps — and the shelves were all but empty by Sunday afternoon.

"I guess we better make a double batch, and bottle half for sales," Robbie's enthusiasm was unbounded, and Richard had so many other things on his mind that he assented without protest.

The shelf emptied even faster, the following week, which rendered the junior staff even more obnoxiously bright-eyed and bushy-tailed than before.

"The bottled salad dressing is a hit!" Robbie exclaimed, flushed with triumph, as they discussed this after the breakfast rush on Tuesday morning, as they worked in the kitchen to prep for lunch. "A triple batch, this week, Chef!"

"We might consider expanding the product line," Bree enthused, from her corner, where she was assembling fillings for sandwiches. "I know — Miss Letty's mother's recipe for apple butter! That was a hit for sure, Chef!"

"It was, indeed," Richard replied from the corner where he was whisking the ingredients for the Reuben sauce, which made certain toasted sandwiches a hit with clients. Miss Letty's sainted mother's personal recipe for apple butter had been used as a filling for Café-made Danish pastries with enormous success. "I approve, contingent on Mrs. Vaughn's approval for the additional cost of apples, and other ingredients, and a range of suitable jam jars, as well as the overtime in wages that it will no doubt involve. Do please figure out the cost ratio. This is a business, as Mrs. Vaughn keeps assuring me, and one which must be kept operating at a clear profit. Are there any other Café-made singular products which you are now considering unleashing on an unsuspecting public?"

"Well, there are, actually," Bree explained in touching earnest. "Your traditional English wedding cake – the raisin fruitcake that we made for the big Wyler wedding event. Only not as a wedding cake," she added hastily. "But just the cake itself, in small loaf pans. We have a ton of those mini-loaf pans for doing individual shortcakes in the back room. We could use those, and package them in the same cellophane wraps that we use for those cinnamon rolls that we send to the Tip-Top every day. That might go, very well, especially for Christmas. Everyone likes fruitcake at Christmas. And that special spicy cranberry confit that we did for the turkey supper special, the week – maybe a special for the holiday season."

"Guarded approval," Richard conceded, slightly abashed that he had not kept track of what his juniors were getting up to.

"For seasonal sales. Although I am convinced that there is only a limited quantity of fruitcakes, passed around through unsuspecting victims for years. Anything else?"

"That extra-spicy mustard," vouchsafed Luc Massie, the tatted and pierced junior chef and ambitious drummer for a local band practically guaranteed to go nowhere, especially as they had never finally decided on a name for themselves. "The stuff you mix to put on sandwiches, Chef. The bomb. Everyone loves it. I took some to a gig last week, and the guys did everything but put it up their nose."

"Well … err…" Richard was slightly taken back that Luc, whose personal peculiarities included a decidedly erratic relationship with his fellow human beings, had actually spoken up on a relevant matter. "Yes; the spicy mustard would be a good addition to the Café line of products. Only in small jars, as a little…"

"Goes a long way," Luc replied, and then appeared to go mentally wandering off into his own space, as he scraped and prepped the grill for the luncheon rush. This would be Luc's single venture of relevant commentary with regard to the orbit of his fellow human beings. It might be days before another communication of similar relevance.

"Ginger syrup!" Araceli exclaimed from the doorway. "Everyone loves it – on the pancake breakfast, and on ice cream, and in the fruit cup with yoghurt. You could sell twenty bottles this week alone!"

"The secret spicy mustard," Bree added, with a look towards' Robbie. "And the apple butter. The ginger syrup, in the same kind of bottle as the salad dressing. Got it. The tiny condiment jars, then. If it's OK, Chef – I'll put in the order for a couple of flats of tiny and medium bottling jars. Rob, ask your friend's friend to do specialty labels. I suppose we'll have to pay him eventually. The fruitcake and cranberry confit can wait until later in summer, nearer to Christmas, then."

"As you wish," Richard replied. He had other things on his mind; the study questions, and working out his proposal to Kate.

He did notice, in a vague kind of way, that the shelves for bottled products – for Robbie and Bree did have to ask Sefton Grant to construct another rustic cedar shelf unit, twice the size of the first – did seem to require constant restocking. The need to brew up yet another vat of ginger syrup, salad dressing, mustard, and apple butter as well as canning and bottling them in an endless series of sterilized jars and bottles seemed to be a constant. The last time that he met for a regular Tuesday sit-down with Jess Abernathy-Vaughn to review the financials for the Café, Jess made note of that category of sales.

"You know, this sideline of prepared sauces, syrups and fixings looks very good. The profit margin for those products are amazing. Was it your notion to go into providing them for sale at the counter?"

"No, it was Robbie Walcott and Bree Grant, mostly — backed up by the rest of the junior staff. It was their notion, and blessedly, they are willing to do most of the heavy lifting on it."

"That's the way to get things done," Jess agreed. "Let the ones with the bright ideas put in the time and labor that it takes to pull it off. They'll either have second thoughts about the whole thing or make a good go of it."

"Young Robbie says it's all a part of expanding the Café's brand," Richard replied with a weary sigh and a shudder. "Something that he picked up at that desperately down-market public uni of his. I sometimes wonder why he just doesn't settle for drinking heavily, going to protest marches, and doing the old rumpy-pumpy with willing undergraduate girls, like a normal university-aged chap. That boy is just too earnest and old-school for words."

"Robbie Walcott is too much of a Boy Scout to even consider that kind of extra-curricular," Jess giggled. "Honestly, I think he only has eyes for Bree anyway. They make a darling couple. Does your Boy Scout and his team have any other plans for Café-style packaged goods?"

Richard fetched up another deep sigh, although he was not altogether disapproving. If it came to it that imminent marriage with Kate meant moving on to employment with Venue Properties as their local restaurant chef and catering overlord, he would at least be leaving the Café in capable hands, and with a reputation and practice well-established. "Luc and Bree are working together on a dry spice combination that will be mixed by the customer with the usual ingredients to reproduce something like the prize-winning chili – still experimenting with that but expect to have it available next month. Otherwise, the team is planning to do small fruitcakes, using the recipe that I used for the Wyler wedding cake – a kind of raisin fruitcake, for sale during the holiday season. And that cranberry confit, lightly spiced with chili peppers for an amusing bite – that's for the holiday season again."

"Sounds logical," Jess nodded. "A limited release, guaranteed to tempt the customer in a rush. *Oh, buy it now, before it goes off the market!* Very shrewd of your kids, Ricardo. I have always suspected that the Girl Scouts operated on the same principle."

"You've lost me there," Richard confessed, in some puzzlement, and Jess replied, indulgently.

"Thin Mints, Ricardo. Thin Mints. Cookie sales. Once a year; limited time availability. Dad is a Thin Mint junkie. He used to buy a case or two from each and every Girl Scout troop in Karnes County and stash them in the garage deep-freeze. Heck, we only had room for regular stuff because we had another deep-freeze for deer season and runs to the Costco in Karnesville." Jess sighed nostalgically in return. "Yeah, all the troop leaders around here love Dad. He's good for their sales figures. Just like the work of your people in producing tasty stuff that people want to take home and enjoy something of, long after they have eaten a meal at the Café. A bit and a bite of what you love does you good. Mom used to say that ..." and Jess momentarily had a melancholy expression on her face, until Little Joe began to grizzle, in his stroller. "Oh, the Soup-Monster is getting pissy because no one is paying attention to him. Look, I had one more thought. You might think about coordinating with Chris and having some of these items for sale at the Tip-Top."

"On the same basis as the cinnamon rolls?" Richard agreed, a little shamed that he had not thought of that before – only that he has so much else on his mind. "Right you are. There's many a traveler on the road who stops at the Tip-Top for a spot of petrol and to use the loo, who never come into Luna City proper. I'll mention it to Chris next Friday at the VFW, if I don't run into him earlier. See you next week," he added, as Jess gathered up the contents of her folders, filed them neatly into her briefcase/purse, and stowed it into the carrier underneath the stroller seat.

"Got to take a raincheck for next week," Jess demurred. "I have an appointment with my OB – make it the week after."

"We'll manage until then," Richard assured her, and Jess grinned, wearily.

As it turned out, that was the last Tuesday confab with Jess for many weeks. Although the chili-spice packet was finally done, and on the shelves by the end of the month, where it was a consistent best-seller, to the enormous satisfaction of both Bree and Luc.

Impediments to Bliss

It was with pure relief, several days after consulting with Jess that Richard spotted Lew Dubois; craggy, genial, charming as only a man from French Louisiana could be, the hard-working at the ground-level director of – whatever it was that Lew Dubois was director of, in the august corporate precincts of Venue Properties International, the hospitality and resort corporation which owned Mills Farm. It was purely due to the herculean efforts of Lew Dubois that Mills Farm had not been transformed into some ghastly down-market water-park resort but continued in a discreet boutique fashion as a purveyor of near-to-luxury class spa, retreat, and upscale experience in a well-curated down-home Texas experience. The new and expanded Mills Farm offered pony trekking, hunting, kayaking on the San Antonio River, and stays in the tastefully renovated and gloriously historic Cattleman Hotel which dominated the western boundary of Town Square. Lew had repeatedly tendered offers of employment as the executive head chef – as had his predecessor at Mills Farm; offers seasoned with aggressively sexual overtures. Richard had served a resounding no to the first such offers and had prevaricated with regard to Lew's comparatively gentlemanly proposals, which came without a generous side-serving of sexual predation, unlike the offer from Susannah Wyatt, known far and wide across Mills Farm as the Witch in Pink Boots. *(Who was now happily and bountifully married to the most handsome Gonzales in three generations. Richard tallied up his good luck over this, every time he spotted Romeo Gonzales on the cover of GQ, or of Romeo and his wife Susannah Wyatt-Gonzales and their three handsome little sons on the cover of some glitzy lifestyle magazine.)*

But now Richard also was going to be a married man, a responsible and upright American citizen. He would have to settle previous debts, slap himself on his manly thorax and dig himself down into the Heisel family trench, all to gain the everlasting devotion of Kate, not to mention gaining the secret and historical family BBQ recipe as a lagniappe. Never mind the glowering presence of Kate's paternal grandfather, who had in the course of WWII service been arrested once and nearly shot as a German spy twice. There were, Ricard devoutly hoped, some familial grudges which would die.

Lew and his good lady wife Anne, accompanied by another lady of certain age who looked to Richard to be vaguely familiar, appeared unexpectedly at the outside table of the Café on one glorious spring morning, when it was not too hot to sit outside. The lawn in the Square was green and lush. Outside town limits, the meadows and pastures were thickly strewn with blooming wildflowers, all shades of blue, yellow, and pink. Miss Letty's hydrangeas, around the historic McAllister cottage bloomed in magnificent balloon-like bouquets in pink and pale blue. Richard spotted the trio and took out a plate of the Café's signature cinnamon rolls to them with his very own hands.

"Mr. Dubois – Lew!" he exclaimed, as he came out through the Café's silver-bell strung door. "And Anne! So happy to see you returned to Luna City. I knew that you had promised to do so, since this expansion of Mills Farm is so very dear to your heart..."

"It is, *cher* Richard," Lew beamed over his coffee and scrambled eggs, sided with two rashers of the Pryor enterprise's finest cured bacon. "'Ave you come to reconsider my latest offer, at last?"

"I have," Richard acknowledged with a deep interior sigh. Lew had offered him several times the position of executive chef at the renewed and revived Cattleman Hotel. It was a bit of a wrench, succumbing to the fate which he knew awaited him. He only wished that he might be able to resist the other temptations, those which might be lying in wait for him. "I wish to accept it, at long last. I want to get married; you see. And I have some old debts to clear, which I cannot possibly, on my present salary."

"Excellent!" Lew beamed approval, as did Anne. Their friend only looked down at her tablet with an absorbed expression, seeming to let the conversation wash over her, like a flood tide. "A wise decision, *mon cher* Richard – a doubly-wise decision! For marriage and for your employment with us. Neither will be a decision that you regret. Upon that, I would stake my own life. All the rest; management of the Café, your timetable of employment ... a mere bagatelle, minor details. We are willing to wait upon the date of your availability, of course. Perhaps the beginning of summer, then, when families are taking their school holidays."

"I am agreeable to that. And there's one more thing," Richard took a deep breath and plunged into the last lap of his personal odyssey and grand confession. "I'm going to apply for American citizenship. It's time, I think, for a new kind of beginning. May as well begin as I mean to go on."

If at all possible, Lew and Anne looked even more radiantly-approving, at this announcement.

"Richard, *mon cher*, I approve most heartily! It is said that there are those who are born American and have the misfortune to be raised elsewhere, yet the luck and foresight to be aware, and to come home at the earliest opportunity. You are one of those, dear Richard! Congratulations!"

"Err ... thanks, all," Richard mumbled, embarrassed to have such effusive notice taken of what was, after all, a simple decision to regularize his position. "I have to tell Kate, of course. Make it clear..."

"Pardon me," Lew and Anne's companion looked up from her tablet. She was a woman somewhat in her fifth decade, not bad looking for all the milage and expert maquillage, with a somewhat dreamy expression on her face, and a taste in dress – flowing and filmy – which brought to Richard's mind somehow the robes of Judy Grant and her friends when they went all druid-gothy in their various Celtic-seminal celebrations. "Do you know the Grants? Owners of the property which once was the Sheffield gardens? I would like to visit their stone circle, you see. For my latest work-in-progress. All part of my research. I do a lot of research, you see," she added, with a confiding air, as she took a notepad and a pencil from out of her purse. "Exacting research – I take photographs of the settings."

Richard looked from the Dubois' amiable countenances to their friend. "Yes, of course, I know them," he replied. "I know them very well, indeed. I live at their property, and I am certain that a visit to the stone circle wouldn't be any problem at all. Look – this is Judy Grant's cellphone number. But don't call her at this moment. She's likely doing her meditation time..."

That Judy Grant was most likely doing that meditation time in a yoga pose and completely unclothed, Richard forbore mentioning. Anne Dubois stepped gracefully into the conversation.

"Trish, forgive me – we did not introduce Richard at once. Trish, this is Richard Hall, who runs this Café, and does the most splendid catered suppers. Lew has been trying to hire him away for a management position at the Cattleman for simply months. Richard – Trish Creighton Doyle. She writes novels," Anne added confidingly. "We've known her for years – she came to stay at the Chateau Venasque, back when we first opened it, and she was researching her novel about the French Revolution. We got to be such good friends. Trish writes historical novels. She makes all kinds of best-seller lists and now she's staying at the Cattlemen for months to research her next book."

Those books must sell very well, if Trish the writer could afford the freight at the Cattleman these days, Richard thought. The name meant very little to him. His favorite recreational read was *Larousse Gastronomique* in the unabridged version, alternating with those vintage Hardy Boys mysteries procured at irregular intervals by Georg and Annise Stein, who dealt in Texiana, western and rare books from the premises next door to the Café. The Steins were regular customers, and Georg was a standout star at camp reenactments organized by the Karnes County Rangers, although a man who looked less like a 19th century Comanche warrior in loincloth and red blanket could hardly be imagined.

"Do they?" Richard made an effort to sound as interested as good manners required. "I can't say that I have ever read any of them, but how bloody fantastic for you. Congratulations are in order. I only had one of my books – my only book – crack the

NYT list, and it was an international travel guide with some recipes attached. Most of it was written by a ghost-writer hired by my publicist back in the day. The lavish pictures of scrumptious eats were taken by someone else, although I did pick the recipes, so I have that. What's the new book about, if you can talk about it?" he added hastily.

This was apparently reassuring to Trish the writer of historical fictions, for she beamed at Richard, and replied, "Oh, it's all finished in first draft. It's about a woman who has a strange experience at a stone circle ... goes back in time and falls deeply in love with a gallant yet sensitive Comanche warrior chief. I'm just filling in the research gaps at present." Trish the romance writer made a vague gesture with her hand, and Richard barely kept his expression neutral. The front door to the Café opened and closed; the Steins had finished their breakfast at the *stammtisch*, the regular's table in the Café. They waved to Richard, across the scattering of other diners at the outside tables.

"Gallant and sensitive wouldn't be the description which would leap immediately to my mind with regard to the Comanche, generally," Richard found his voice after a moment. "From all that I have heard, in just a casual way. But I'm not a historical expert. Georg Stein is. He and Colonel Walcott of the Karnes Company Rangers Living History Association. Speak of ... George and his missus just left. They keep the gallery next door. Give them a minute to get settled and open the place, and then go and speak to them. And any other members of the

Colonel Walcott's organization. They can put you in touch with some other local historical experts. Very knowledgeable experts, they are, all of them. Put you into a coma with the intricate details, they can, given half a chance."

"I believe that I shall," Trish Creighton Doyle replied, with great enthusiasm. "Thank you for the referral, and for the phone number for the Grants. I will want to visit the circle and take some pictures. For verisimilitude, and to get the feel for the setting of an important scene exactly right."

"And I must get back to my kitchen," Richard murmured. "Lew, you have my cellphone number. I can come up to your office to talk about the management project."

"Any time, *cher* Richard," Lew replied, and Richard took himself back to his work. More than ever, the kitchen was a refuge, but he had begun feeling cramped in it of late. There was so much more that he wanted to achieve, but which the Café itself lacked the scope … yet he did owe so much to Miss Letty and Doc Wyler …

Araceli was filling up the coffee carafe from one of the two large urns which served the breakfast crowd.

"Have you ever heard of a writer named Trish Creighton Doyle?" He asked, in passing. "She's famous and best-selling – and here in Luna City doing historical research for her next novel. She's out on the terrace with Lew and Anne Dubois."

"Sure, I have," Araceli replied. "Yeah, I saw her this morning – thought she looked familiar. I guess that I should be impressed … and she's here doing research? Well, that's a laugh."

"Not your cuppa, then?" Richard ventured. Araceli giggled.

"Nah, I'm strictly a sweet Regency fan. Georgette Heyer is my literary idol. Trish Creighton Doyle, on the other hand, is the complete opposite."

"Oh?" Richard raised an eyebrow, inviting further literary discussion. Araceli was a woman of decided opinions on many subjects, but this was the first he was aware of this particular aspect. "That bad, eh?"

"No, not bad, in the strictly descriptive sense," Araceli conceded. "Just not the teensiest shred of a ghost of an imagination in plots. The book club read one of hers early this year, a Tudor romance about Anne Boleyn's sister and I kept thinking all the way through that I had read it all somewhere before – which I had, when it was written by Philippa Gregory. Different words, but more or less the same plot and the same characters. Then there was the multi-generational family saga about the noble English family with a humongous stately home and three daughters with their hectic and very graphic romances ... that one, I think she took from a TV series. And there was the one about a doomed and unsuitable romance on the Titanic."

"That came from a movie, I'm sure," Richard ventured, and Araceli nodded.

"OK writer, not the least an original plotter. You'd recognize her books on sight, though. The cover of every single one has a bare-chested handsome stud embracing a woman with long flowing hair and a long flowing diaphanous gown on the front. Only the exact period details differ from one to the next –

that and the color of the heroine's hair. What's this next one supposed to be about, or did she say?"

"A woman who goes through a stone circle and falls in love with a gallant and sensitive Comanche warrior chief, or so she said." Richard answered, to be surprised when Araceli blanched and set down the coffee carafe.

"Oh, my god!" Araceli exclaimed. "Really? I swear, I can hear Georg Stein and all the rest of the Karnes County Rangers face-palm from here. Don't tell me; Chief Rama-Lama Ding-Dong of the Quixotic Comanche..."

"At the very least," Richard attempted to console her. "It will not be the fantastical crap-fest that Pip Noel-Barrett's movie turned out to be."

"Some comfort," Araceli replied. "I only hope that it doesn't get picked as a selection by our Luna City book club. That could get embarrassing."

(The book did eventually turn out to be richly embarrassing; not for the book club, or the Karnes Company Rangers Living History Association, but for someone else entirely.)

* * *

Monday loomed in Richard's mind like a mountain, that ghastly haunted mountain in *Fantasia* that turned into Chernobog after dark, a movie which had scared him into wetting his pants when he first saw it as a three-year old, back in the distant past. He was determined yet again, to ask Katie if she wanted to marry ... no, he wanted to marry her; no again, were they both agreeable to marrying. Chernobog flapped his leathery wings in Richard's imagination.

Oh God, there was something he had nearly forgotten! A ring! A ring was obligatory on such a momentous occasion as this, or so he had always been led to understand by movies, television shows and sentimental novels without number – and he didn't have one readily to hand! The ring promised by Aunt Moira – although from her description it sounded as if it were desperately unsuitable anyway. This was a disaster! How could he have overlooked such an important element for weeks! There was certainly no place in Luna City itself to purchase such a thing, unless it was in the old-fashioned coin-op dispensers in the entryway of Abernathy Hardware, which for the price of a quarter, would produce a plastic ring, a gargoyle figure, or a fake tattoo, all tastefully contained in a plastic sphere the size of a golf ball. It was too late to cadge a ride to Karnesville with any of his friends, since Kate would arrive at any moment...

Mercifully, his cellphone rang at that moment.

"Hey, you," he said into it, as it was Kate's number and name on the screen. "I've got ... something special – Chicken Fricassee – and I've a very important question for you..."

"Oh, lover – save it for next week!" Kate croaked into the phone at her end. "I'm as sick as a dog. Can I get a raincheck for next Monday? I love you for your food, and I wish that I had Ozzie to keep by feet warm, but I'm so miserable and ill, I don't even want to think about getting out of bed." She sounded like she was about to cry with regret and misery, but unaccountably, Richard's spirits lurched upwards.

"It's all right, My Kate of Kate Hall," he replied, almost limp with relief, torn between that and worry for her. "Where are you? I'll ask one of the guys for a ride and bring you some chicken soup or something ..."

"Not to worry," Kate replied. "I'm at home, Mom and Dad are fussing over me. Mom would have me bathing in a tub of chicken soup, if that would help. I think I have the flu or something. But look; next week for certain, OK, lover? Give Ozzie a good skritch and let him know it's from me."

"Sure thing," Richard felt a tide of unworthy relief rising in him; unworthy because he honestly relished those Monday evening suppers with his Kate, and because feeding her something remarkable and classically French in accordance with his training, concocted over the tiny hob or in the miniscule stove in the Airstream ... well, that was the apex of his week, a few hours with the woman whom he loved, and who apparently and against all sensible inclination, loved him and his eccentric one-eyed cat. But relieved, because that left him another week to secure a suitable ring, and to consider how best to suggest marrying their lack of fortunes together. He thought that he might consult with Araceli and Jess on the next day.

* * *

He waited at mid-morning for Jess to appear for the usual business consultation during the slow time between the end of the breakfast rush and preparations for luncheon service.

The minutes crawled slowly by, and finally he said to Araceli, "I don't know what's taking Jess so long. She's always been insanely prompt, and I needed to ask her advice on a personal matter."

"Didn't anyone tell you?" Araceli finished breaking open a roll of coins and emptying them into the cash drawer with an almost musical clattering.

"Tell me what!" Richard answered, annoyed. "No one tells me anything. It's as if you all believe that I am psychic or something."

Araceli sighed, a deep and theatrical sigh. "She's been admitted to the hospital in Karnesville for observation. She had an episode last night and Joe was worried. He called the hospital and they said to bring her in right away, so he drove her into Karnesville rather than wait for the ambulance."

"I thought at our meet last week that she was really close to delivering the baby," Richard acknowledged with some relief, and Araceli grinned.

"Babies, Rich – <u>babies</u>. She and Joe are having twin girls but keep it under your hat for now. They didn't want people to be making a fuss about it all."

"Good night, nurse!" Richard exclaimed. No wonder that Jess had seemed so stressed-out, at last weeks' confab. "Well, nothing like twice the results with only a single effort. Are ... is the gyno just going to wait for the calves to drop, as it were, or are they going to rush things along?"

"No idea," Araceli replied crisply. "Little Joe is staying with the Abernathy great-grands for now. Joe is driving to Karnesville every night after his shift to be with her, so I imagine that the babies are close to being delivered. What did you need to ask her about, then?"

"The best place to shop for an engagement ring," Richard confessed. "I mean to ask Kate if she would do me the honor. Nothing vulgar or flashy, even if I could afford a big chunk of diamond — just something attractive and meaningful to both of us. I have a family heirloom ring coming to me, but from what my aunt says of it, it's the most ghastly and vulgar thing ever created. I am convinced on that score that Kate will take one look at it and take a vow of chastity and enduring spinsterhood."

"Hmmm," Araceli looked thoughtful. "Give me some time to think it over. There must be some nice places in Karnesville for a better and nicer ring. Maybe even an estate jewelry place. Katie would like something unique, one of a kind, you know."

"But don't tell her," Richard pleaded. "I want it to be a surprise."

"Sure thing, Chef," Araceli promised, indulgently. "The only one I will tell is Abuelita. You know that she is awfully fond of you, and Katie, too. Maybe Abuelita can give you both good advice..." Araceli looked quite thoughtful at that, and Richard replied, with a deep sigh,

"Mostly because I look like your late grandfather, I suspect. But she is an old dear, she has done so much to uphold me from day one. Honestly, if I didn't already have a perfectly formidable old gran of my own, I would ask to be adopted by yours."

"She likes you for your cooking and recipes, too," Araceli added, seeming to be mollified. "So when do you plan to ask our Katie for her hand and the rest of her in marriage?"

"On our next day off," Richard answered. "Monday. This time, for certain. She had an emergency with her grandfather two Mondays ago and had the flu last Monday. Third time is the charm, I hope."

Now that he had confessed his intention to Araceli, and by extension, the formidable absolute female ruler of the combined Gonzalez-Gonzales clan, he absolutely had to go through with it. Because otherwise …

Getting This Baby Off the Ground

"Have I ever told you," Jess Abernathy-Vaugh said, through gritted teeth, "How f**king much I hate hospitals?"

"For shame, Mrs. Vaughn." Her husband replied equably. "When it was f**king which got us here in the first place. Now, are you going to eat that supper, or just look at it? You know, you can't have a single bite to eat or drink after eight tonight."

"I know," Jess replied, balefully. "And the third option; I can throw it at you, and you can eat it."

Joe belched, purposefully, deliberately. "Sorry, Babe, I already ate. You know, the food in the hospital cafeteria isn't that bad at all. I'll try and get admitted here when they have to do another round of surgery on my knees."

"Bastard," Jess remarked, feelingly, and picked up the fork, lying next to the dinner plate. "Salisbury steak … bet it's not a patch on your mom's."

"Probably not," Joe agreed. He was looking at her with guarded concern. Yes, he did know that she hated hospitals, dreaded those infrequent occasions when she herself was confined in them. Hospitals were a haunted place for Jess since she was eleven years old. A hospital was the place where her mother Beth had died, wasted inexorably away by an inoperable, undetected-until-too-late swift-moving cancer. The last time that Jess saw her mother, Beth was reduced to a shriveled remnant of her vibrant, lovely, loving self – with tubes in her arms, up her nose, down her throat and in other places. Jess, bewildered and grieving, had a horror ever since of hospitals; the mechanical beds with metal bars on either side, the ever-present medical apparatus, the sterile smell, the intermittent beeping of monitors dispensing intravenous medications and fluids, the noisy traffic in the corridors, constantly being awakened for yet another round of checks by doctors or nurses. Although the Karnesville Med-Center did make an effort to cut down on the noise. The nurses all wore soft-soled athletic shoes, and mostly, the trollies and beds moved silently in the corridor outside of room to which she had been confined to for … how many days and nights, now? Jess had rather lost track of how many days and nights she had spent in the antenatal suite; well sort of a suite, in that it had a little sitting area, with a fold-out sofa, a small table, a pair of chairs, and a rather nice set of daylight blocking drapes over the window. It might have been a hotel suite, if it weren't for the hospital bed and the bank of hook-ups for medical impedimenta, which mercifully were sited on the wall at the head of the bed. In the long run, it didn't matter to Jess. The only thing that did matter was survival and successful delivery of the girls. The twins; Elizabeth Myra and Alice Leticia. Their survival hung by a thread, the thread of the umbilical cord which fed them nutrients and oxygen, which had recently been observed to be intermittently constricted. It had also been impressed on Jess that her own obedience to the advice of her OB also mattered, hugely. That was, to remain in bed under medical observation if she wanted to deliver live children.

For the girls, Jess would endure anything, even a hospital. She already loved them dearly. She and Joe had 3-D sonogram pictures of them both, of their small faces outlined in black and white, slumbering within her burgeoning belly; their eyes closed, hands and feet fluttering in the sealed pool of amniotic fluid. Elizabeth was the more placid twin. That was already plain. Alice was a ball of frenetic prenatal energy; squirming and fussing, hiccupping incessantly. Jess was absolutely certain that Alice's tiny sharp elbows and knees were responsible for most of the activity behind her navel.

You haven't really lived, she observed to Joe, when she was carrying Little Joe, *until you have been kicked in the navel ... from the inside.*

"I do so wonder what they will look like?" Jess pondered, as she ate without relish or appetite, merely nourishment to relay to the girls. She longed to be home. Home – the little cottage in Luna City, the comfortable daily routine now seemed so far away. A simple supper with Joe, watching a movie after Little Joe was tucked safely away. "They're identical. Blue eyes, of course. Mine are hazel, yours are blue, so that works out. I think that they will have medium-brown hair. On the last sonogram, the girls already have hair, so that's a given..."

"Not long enough to braid," Joe replied, and Jess giggled.

"Long enough to tell what color it will be," she replied.

Joe said, "We'll know for certain tomorrow. Now, eat your supper, and we'll watch a movie together – Maybe Jerry can take five and watch it with us."

"Not if he's on duty," Jess replied. For the last week, Jerry Walcott, oldest son of Clovis and brother of Belle and Jerry, had been the night duty nurse on the antenatal ward; soft-spoken, responsible Jerry, the quiet and comforting caregiver. Watching Jerry insouciantly balance a small baby along his forearm with that small round head held secure in his hand was a rebuke to anyone who ever assumed that men had no skill at handling small children.

Jess had known Jerry since he was in high school. She was obscurely glad that he would not be the one to prep her for surgery first thing the next morning, although he had chuckled and said, *"Don't worry about me and a razor blade. I do it to my own self every morning,"* and then with another chuckle, had

74

added that certain areas needed to be shaved as a laser scalpel used to make a lower abdominal incision had been known to set inconvenient pubic hair on fire. Joe, hearing that, had laughed, and made a coarse comment, and Jess had wished to throw something heavy at her husband, saved that she knew that Joe was likewise deeply worried. For her, and for the girls. Crude and very, very dark humor was a safe refuge for him. Now she said,

"You brought your things? After I take a shower, you take yours, and we can both cuddle up and watch ... I dunno. Something safe and simple and predictable. We haven't watched *Funny Farm*, in a while, and it's on the hospital movie system. Let's watch that tonight. Chevy Chase always makes me giggle."

"Sure, Babe. Then I sack out on that fold-out sofa," Joe replied. "I'll need my beauty sleep. Tomorrow's going to be a long day."

"For me, especially," Jess replied, reconsidering something to throw at her husband, who laughed again.

"You'll have the good drugs," he replied, "But I'll have to go through it all cold turkey."

* * *

At about nine-thirty, Jerry tapped on the door of the suite, and put his head around the half-opened door.

"All decent?" he asked, and Joe answered,

"Are you kidding? If I wanted to be indecent, I'd pick a better place than a hospital."

The movie was almost over – nearly to the part where the pair of ducks ran into the house. Jess felt like she would have to prop up her eyelids with toothpicks at this point. This pregnancy drained her, as if some malign entity tapped her for several quarts of blood at a time.

"Time for bed-check, is it, Jerry?"

"Big day for you tomorrow, Mrs. Vaughn," Jerry answered, and Joe chuckled, as he rolled off the bed, where he had squeezed next to Jess. There was just barely room for the two, if Jess scooched all the way to the railings, and Joe lay on one side, with his arm around Jess, and the enormous mound of the twins. Jerry went through all the regular checks; blood pressure, listened to the twins and Jess's heartbeat, while Joe hovered anxiously.

"You washed with the antiseptic gel?" Jerry asked, and when Jess nodded, Jerry continued. "Then shower again with the rest of it tomorrow, by eight at the very latest. I'll leave you with a cup for a urine sample – do that, first thing as well. Silvia will be along at about 8:15 to prep you for surgery. She'll bring along a set of overalls and stuff for you, Joe. Then she will take you to the delivery room for final prep. Dr. Agostino will be there, to administer the epidural. When it's taken effect and they're ready to go, Silvia will come and get you, Joe. It won't take long. By a bit past nine, you'll have your girls in your arms."

"Promises, promises." Joe remarked, cynically, and squeezed Jess's hand – that hand which he had not let go of, all during the evening.

"We promise, you deliver," Jerry replied, with a comforting smile. "It all looks good, Mrs. V, Joe. Have a good night; seriously, try and sleep. We'll be extra-quiet at this end of the ward. But call me, if you have to. I want to see if your girls are as beautiful as their pictures on the sonogram promise."

"They will be, guaranteed," Joe assured him, and grinned at Jess. "They'll be the spitting image of Jess."

"Flattery will get you nowhere," Jess replied, obscurely comforted by the assurance, while knowing very well that she was about a six or seven on the one-to-ten scale of physical beauty. She was beautiful to Joe and that was all that mattered.

The girls will be perfect. On that note, she went to sleep very soon after the door whisked closed, hearing Joe's breathing across the room. It was strangely reassuring, that sound. He was standing on the wall, looking out at the threatening darkness, undismayed, unafraid. Joe, the stalwart rock. A good father...

* * *

"It's time, Babe," Joe said. Jess started awake from deep REM sleep. One minute dreaming of tropic seas, of perfect waves crashing on a beach the color of pure cane sugar, and her husband inexplicably surfing on a bright pink inflatable flamingo while her father, Martin looked on in amazement – and in the next, opening her eyes in a dim-lit hospital room. It was that kind of dream – logical and surreal. "It's five to eight – you have just enough time to wash up and get back into bed before Nurse Silvia gets here."

"It saves time, not having any breakfast," Jess groaned, as Joe helped her waddle the short way to the attached bathroom, with the shower enclosure set at floor level. "You should have just enough time to pop down to the cafeteria for your own."

"Already done, Babe," Joe replied, and handed her a towel and a fresh hospital gown. "I wasn't that hungry, but I was treating that coffee urn like it was a long-lost cousin, even if it wasn't a patch on the Café's best brew. Hurry – you have only fifteen minutes now."

Jess hurried with her ablutions, painfully aware of the dragging weight of her belly, and how clumsy it made it on her feet – feet swollen and tender, ankles even more swollen. That was the thing that made her OB even more anxious – that Jess, when tired, had entirely lost her ankles.

She showered, lavishing the antiseptic gel on her lower abdomen. Almost H-Hour … and she was glad of it, ready for this to be over, done and dusted. The door to the suite opened, a sound to which Jess had become drearily accustomed over the last three weeks of confinement.

"Jess – Silvia is here," Joe's voice, tense and absorbed, chiming with Nurse Silvia's cheerful one.

"Good morning, Mrs. Vaughn – are you nearly ready?"

"I am," Jess hurriedly toweled off and assumed the humiliating hospital gown before emerging from the bathroom with the urine sample cup in her hand, as Jerry had said. Her husband lurked, watching from the suite portion of the room, sensibly not wanting to interfere with the work of experts.

Jess and Joe had been introduced to Silvia several days previously; the nurse specialist expert who prepped patients for obstetrical surgery and metaphorically held their hands and monitored their condition during two- or three-hours post-op, before Jess would be turned back over to the post-natal ward and the care of regulars like Jerry. The girls, upon delivery would be assessed by a team from the neo-natal intensive care unit, in case their condition upon delivery necessitated such care. Jess was guardedly hopeful that the girls would be released to the regular nursery. Jess and Joe had been carefully briefed about all that. It wasn't as if they had much else to do, these last three weeks. At the last assessment by the med-center perinatal experts, the girls were both estimated to be well over five pounds, even though they would be delivered at 37 weeks gestation, instead of the full 40.

Silvia was young, professionally upbeat; it was obvious that she loved every minute of her job. She carried an official-looking cellphone and a small tub of prep supplies, which she set down on the small standing desk at the head of the hospital bed.

"Good morning, Mrs. Vaughn," She nodded cheerfully at Joe, as she took the cup and helped Jess swing her legs up onto the bed. "And Mr. Vaughn – all ready for your big day? Thanks – I'll do a quick blood draw before we start the IV."

"Ready for it to be done and dusted," Joe answered, and Silvia giggled. She handed Joe a folded up overall of the kind that painters wore to protect their clothes, with a hairnet and a pair of shoe covers on top.

"These are for you; go ahead and put them on. It's going to be a good day for a birthday," she said. "Valentine's Day! Easy to remember. Do you have a preference, Mrs. Vaughn – right or left arm?"

"Left," Jess replied. It was simpler and rather comforting to let Silvia carry on both ends of the conversation, letting that cheerful commentary wash over her like the regular waves of bubbling surf, while she tried to set aside the minor discomfort of a tourniquet and the needle sliding into a vein. *Think of the girls*, Jess ordered herself.

Silvia was quite extraordinarily deft with the hollow needle; she hit the vein on the first shot, drew a syringe of dark red blood. Jess closed her eyes at this point. Then the IV hookup, the bag of solution hanging from the rolling stand close by, the clear tube going down to her hand. In the other part of the suite, she could hear faint rustling sounds, as Joe climbed into the jumpsuit.

"This thing was tailored for King Kong!" he commented. "Gimme a couple of tent poles, I could camp out in it with at least two other guys!" Jess smiled at that. Her husband stood six-feet and two inches tall. Imagine a hospital jumpsuit even larger than Joe. She opened her eyes, and caught his, lingering close on the far side of the suite.

"Fuel, check, lights, check, oil pressure, check. We got clearance. OK, Jess – let's get these babies off the ground."

"Aye, aye," Jess replied. More than a month ago, Joe had printed up and attached that Far Side cartoon to the refrigerator;

a mild in-joke for the two of them. *Let's get this baby off the ground.*

Now it was all in the hands of the medical team. There was nothing for her to do, but to ride along, passive, and cooperative. She was not in her body but submissively allowing things to be done to it. Only after this indignity, could Jess reclaim autonomy. *For the sake of the girls.*

"OK, very good, Mrs. Vaughn," chirped Silvia. She had finished with the depilation of Jess's near nether regions, after lifting the hospital gown and considerately placing a sheet over Jess's legs. "Now, I'm going to take you to the operating room, and a meet with Dr. Agostino, the anesthetist. We'll install the Foley catheter, once you have indicated your approval to the procedures and Dr. Agostino administers the spinal block. It'll take about twenty minutes to take effect. Once it does, and Dr. Bagby is ready to begin, I'll bring Joe to the operating room. OK, Mrs. Vaughn?"

"Perfect," Jess replied. She so much wanted all this to be over. She closed her eyes as much as possible and visualized how she and Joe would come home with the girls. Home to the little cottage on Oak Street, with her dear barrel-racing champion horse Sweet Pea out at the back. Pictured the girls in matching cribs in the bedroom adjacent to the master bedroom, the room which had been designated the nursery, and outfitted with all manner of pretty pink toys and accoutrements. She imagined how Little Joe would embrace being the big brother to his little sisters. *The girls.* They would come home to the nursery, sleep in those cribs. Elizabeth would be the placid, undemanding twin, but Alice would be the fussy, frenetically active child. *Mom! Watch me! Pay attention to me!* Jess imagined Alice at the age of six or so, perched on the back of Sweet Pea, or Sweet Pea's successor, galloping through the geometric pattern of barrels... Elizabeth wouldn't be a competitor, Jess decided in her imagining. Elizabeth would be the calm, easy-tempered child, competently doing trail rides.

Jess firmly closed her eyes, once in the operating room. No, she didn't even want to look. Not at the lights overhead, the screen of blue fabric hung below the level of her breasts, although presently there were at least half a dozen other people in the room, sexless and anonymous in blue surgical gowns, caps, masks, and gloves. The rest of her body was an alien, awkward and lumpish thing, no longer attached to herself.

Get it over with. I want to go home.

"We're ready, Mrs. Vaughn," The voice of the anesthetist, Dr. Agostino cut into her concentration.

"Where's my husband?" Jess demanded.

"I'm here, Babe," That was Joe's voice, his hand finding hers, under the sterile surgical sheets drawn up to her shoulders. She opened her eyes, smiled at him – and thought he smiled as well, but the disposable mask covered his mouth and nose. "We're getting these babies off the ground."

"Show them to me, as soon as you can," Jess pleaded. "I need to see them, Joe; bring them to me, just as you promised."

"I will, Babe." He looked over the blue fabric drape, the one which kept her from seeing anything at all. Joe, standing at her shoulder could see over it easily. "They're starting. The NICU team is standing by, too. If we had some music here, we could find partners and dance." He grinned over her head at Dr. Agostino, at her other side, and staring absorbed into a computer display. Dr. Agostino spared a shy grin. He was the only one besides Jess not wearing a surgical mask.

"I can't dance," he confessed. "Two left feet and no sense of rhythm. You can imagine the humiliation of being the only Italian in South Texas who can't two-step."

"My sympathies." Jess said. "I'm not even certain I have feet now, since I can't feel them at all."

"Doing my job, Mrs. Vaughn." Dr. Agostino grinned even more widely and consulted his screen again. "Looking good ..."

Joe squeezed her hand. "Babe, I think the first girl is nearly here."

Jess felt a weird tug on her lower abdomen – a fleeting sensation, and one which she could not entirely feel was real, given that she could feel nothing of her body from the middle of her chest on down. This was so different from giving birth to Little Joe; almost alienating.

"Is she all right? She's not crying!" Jess demanded urgently. There was no noise other than a kind of mechanical slurping sound, "I want to see her, Joe!" Joe let go of her hand, his eyes intent on the view beyond the screen.

"The NICU nurse has her now – they're taking her to the warming unit, and it's OK for me to watch."

"I want to see her!" Jess insisted. "Bring her to me!"

"As soon as I have the all-clear, Babe." Joe disappeared around the screen. After a moment, she felt that odd tug at her abdomen again, and again heard that slurping sound, immediately drowned out by the thin and indignant sound of an infant wailing.

"Child number two is away!" remarked Dr. Agostino. "How are you feeling, Mrs. Vaughn?"

"Faintly sick," Jess confessed.

"Any pain or discomfort?" Dr. Agostino bent over his keyboard controls, instantly watchful.

"Not so far," Jess replied, all other thought banished, as Joe appeared with a tiny bundle swaddled burrito-fashion in a hospital baby blanket striped in red and green, and laid it on Jess's breast. The baby's head, about the size of a large orange – was topped in a knit beanie, and her eyes were fast closed.

"Elizabeth," Jess cuddled the infant to her, after gently stroking that little reddened cheek. "She's perfect. As the quiet, bigger, placid one, she is Elizabeth. Alice is the screamer."

"She certainly is doing that," Joe agreed. "Little Liz is a whole six pounds, six ounces, and with an excellent APGAR score – hey, that's what the NICU nurse said to the other one. Eight of ten, so she doesn't need to go to the NICU."

Jess closed her eyes again, hugging her perfect, beautiful little red-faced daughter to her. Perfect. One out, safe, alive, and perfect. Her sister screamed to beat the band. In Jess's experience, a kid who screamed so indignantly and so loudly, had nothing wrong with her, either. Abruptly, the screaming ceased, and Jess' heart leaped in alarm. But no need, for Joe appeared with another burrito-wrapped infant.

"Alice – six pounds and three," He reported, and laid the second baby on Jess's chest, next to her sister. "Also in perfect fettle. Nine out of ten."

"They're beautiful," Jess' heart overflowed with protective love and pride. "See, they already have long eyelashes."

"In about fifteen years," Joe bent down and kissed Jess's forehead. "They're gonna be heartbreakers. Good that I got the .45 and a shovel, isn't it, Babe?"

"Perfect," Jess answered.

From the Karnesville Weekly Beacon

Celebrity Author Interview – Trish Creighton Doyle, with Beacon Staff Writer Kate Heisel - Part One of Two

I had the unexpected opportunity this week to interview prolific and best-selling author Trish Creighton Doyle. Ms Doyle's thirty-seven historical romance novels include *Those Boleyn Daughters*, (which is set to become a Netflix miniseries to be released next year) the family saga *Durnsford Castle,* the tragic epic romance, *Stateroom C-64 RMS Titanic,* and a WWII romance, *The General's Driver.* Since her first blockbuster, *The Secrets of Durham Place*, which came out in 1978, she has brought out a novel every year to eighteen months over the last four decades, most of which have been best-sellers, and have guaranteed her to be one of the wealthiest American writers making a living purely from their books. Her fans are among the most devoted book fans in America, probably second only to those for J.K. Rowling, although Ms Doyle is famously retiring and rarely grants interviews. I asked Ms Doyle what had brought her to Luna City.

"To do research," she replied, earnestly. "I pride myself on the depth of my research! I started out as a fact-checker at the *New Yorker*, you know. My very first job after I graduated from Smith. I wanted to be an editor, but here I was, just out of college with a BA, not even the Mrs degree, which was really what I was supposed to emerge with at graduation, along with the diploma. Anyway, I married my first husband, Arthur; he was in advertising, and we had a baby due. We could barely get along on his salary and bonuses, living in New York, you know. So, I set down at my typewriter – I still use a typewriter for the first draft; a vintage Olympia that Arthur bought for me. Call me traditional – and I wrote *The Secrets of Durham Place*, in between midnight feedings and changing diapers."

"I understand that your first book was based on your hometown in upstate New York," I said, "You were born and raised in Kinderhook, near Albany. I understand that many of your parent's neighbors were quite unhappy when they read the book."

Ms Doyle giggled like a middle-schooler. "Oh, yes," she agreed. "There was quite the ruckus, even though I changed the name of the town, and the characters. Everyone in Kinderhook still recognized who I wrote about as a character. Oh, so many scandals that they thought had been buried forever! The illegitimate children, the dirty business dealing, incest, child abuse, convenient deaths which were actually murder... bringing it all out as a novel was quite delicious. All the dirty, dirty laundry hung out to dry, in front of a nation-wide audience! That was the most fun that I had since I was an ugly duckling in high school. And on the strength of that one book, I got a literary agent ... you know, there were nibblings from Hollywood, that there would be a movie made from it, but the powers decided that since there had already been a movie from that Metalious' woman's book, so no more water from that well! Anyway, it wasn't worth the trouble to fight about it. I just buckled down and wrote another novel, and I divorced Arthur and married my agent. Really, dear, it seemed like the sensible thing at the time. Since then, I have set myself a strict schedule; a year for research, six months for writing. Sometimes I am writing all day, and into the evening, when the muse whispers to me. I usually juggle three or four book projects at a time, so that I can bring out one a year. I do the necessary publicity, and then I get back to work. The thing is," Ms Doyle added, with an air of confidence, "That having written the book is only half the chore. The other is marketing it. The nice thing is that I am in such a position as that I do not have to slog out those awful publicity tours – fifteen cities in twenty days, with a signing at a bookstore! A strategic appearance here and there, a workshop or a fan convention … and I adore doing book club meetings, because people have read my book from cover to cover."

"You said that you came to Luna City for research," I asked. "Exactly what is your process for researching for a book?"

"I travel to the places that will be the setting for the story under consideration," Ms Doyle replied. "And that is after reading … oh, many, many accounts by historians, as well as original documents. I usually have a notion of my main characters – how they think, feel, react. But it works incredibly well for me to visit the places where the story is set. I need to see … and walk around and take pictures. My camera is my best research tool. I often finish up with a whole album of pictures of scenery, objects, and people. They feed my inspiration. I can visualize my characters, the places they inhabit or travel through, the things they hold in their hands. Sometimes I have given my cover artist pictures of people that I took, so that they have a better notion of how my heroes and heroines should appear. Sometimes the cover artists have a notion completely opposite to how I have visualized my characters.

(To be continued in Part Two; Ms. Doyle talks about her upcoming book projects.)

Lord of the Rings

Two days later, when the morning breakfast rush had calmed down to a dull roar, Araceli approached him in mid-flight.

"I talked to Abuelita," she launched abruptly into conversation. "And she approves. She says that you and Katie will be perfect together as a couple. Your children will be handsome and clever... and she wishes to ..."

"What – preside over the wedding?" Richard was frazzled with nerves, both over the impending yet still uncertain change to his relationship with Kate, with management of the Café, the impending visit of his parents to Texas, and the process of his citizenship application, which looked to have hit another snag since his reliable advisor on that process was most cruelly and unfairly sidelined with her own life-challenges. Like the imminent birth of her two children. Richard was not so self-centered as to blame Jess for having more immediate concerns just this very moment – but his whole future was at stake! *Didn't anyone have consideration for his agony, here?*

"No," Araceli replied gravely. "Abuelita really, seriously approves. And she … well, Uncle Jesus is going to bring her to the Café today at 11. She says that she has arranged for the ring. She says that she has the perfect ring for you to give to Kate. It's a family thing. Not a fancy expensive heirloom at all, but a ring that Abuela Jesus bought for her to celebrate their fortieth wedding anniversary. She never wore it, as it was too small for her fingers. Abuelo Jesus was really not careful about things like that, but she says that Katie always loved it. And it would be perfect for her. It's her birthstone – a garnet in the shape of a heart."

"That sounds perfect," Richard replied, with considerable relief.

The local UPS delivery driver came to the Café, that very day, ten minutes later, just before the expected arrival of Abuelita. A Gonzalez cousin, of course, who parked his brown delivery van in front of the Café and came wandering in with his clipboard in one hand and a small box in the other.

"Hi, 'Celi," he admitted bashfully to his masterful cousin. "I gotta special delivery for Richard Astor-Hall. Can he sign for it now? High value items must be delivered in person to the recipient. Otherwise, I gotta make another trip..."

"Never mid, Hector; Chef is here. He's the recipient. Richard Astor-Hall."

"Oh, good," replied the UPS delivery driver. "Don't wanna make another trip. 'Celi, my schedule is full enough at it is." He handed a small package to Richard, summoned from the kitchen by Bianca. "Mr. Hall? Sign here. Here you go. Hey good luck with it – an engagement ring? Must be a winner since it came all this way from England!"

"Thank you," Richard said, as he signed the receipt with a flourish, marveling at how the Luna City bush telegraph so efficiently transmitted such personal information. He looked at the small package, with anticipatory dread. Now he had two engagement rings in the offing. What would he do with them, and which one should he offer to Kate?

In that feeling of dread, he opened the small box from England. Yes, that feeling of dread was fully justified. He became aware that Araceli was looking over his shoulder, clinically judging the contents, as Richard shook out the heavy contents of a small jeweler's flannel bag.

"Oh ... my." Araceli gulped. "What is that center stone ... it looks like a piece of fossilized chicken-crap, polished and set in gold."

The center bezel was indeed a polished cabochon-cut brown stone about the size of a small marble, a stone topped with an oval blotch of white, set in pure burnished yellow gold; a pattern of intricate tendrils of gold foliage set with tiny blossoms of pearl with diamond-chip petals surrounded the dread object. It was so hideous that one could barely tear one's appalled regard from it.

"Harlequin brown jasper," Richard finally replied. No, he could not wish this hideous, ungainly, knuckle-duster and man-sized ring on his Kate, his adored and cherished Kate. Not unless he expected her to throw the hideous thing back at him. That would mean at the very least, a black eye, if not a concussion, as Kate had starred as a pitcher on the St. Scholastica's varsity girls' softball team, back in the day. "I will have to do something with it. My Aunt Moira said I could have it all re-done, if I wanted ... Araceli, I can't give this awful thing to Kate. It's hideous."

"But expensive," Araceli weighed it in her own hand, holding it up to her eyes to squint at the hallmarks on the inner band. "The pearl and diamond flowers are pretty enough, but that center stone..." she shuddered, in very real revulsion. "Honestly, how could your what ... great grandfather spent a bomb and still come up with something so butt-ugly?"

"It's a gift," Richard replied. "Cheap and ugly is a natural occurrence; expensive and ugly takes an enormously creative genius. My aunt told me right out that I ought to have it remade to fit Kate."

"That might work," Araceli mused, and her expression became infused with enlightenment. "Chef, I have an absolutely brilliant idea! If your people are OK with you having this ugly-ass bit of bling re-done, then maybe I can talk Abuelita into having both rings re-made! Yes!" his chief restaurant administrator and right-hand manager became downright enthused. "It would be symbolic, you see; two rings re-made, two families joined ... there's a ton – ok, maybe not quite a ton of gold in this one, and a bit in Abuelita's garnet ring. I think that there's enough gold to make a ring for our Katie with Abuelita's garnet and your pearl and diamond flowers, and a bauble for you – maybe a signet ring set with that brown jasper? Cousin Sylvester said that you bought a vintage white-tie outfit in San Antonio, and if you're going to be married in it, it would all be perfect!"

"Two families, united through two pieces of recast and bejeweled bling," Richard agreed, rather glumly, and Araceli beamed at him.

"Yes, exactly. It will be perfect, and I'm sure Abuelita will agree." Araceli took on that determined expression which meant that a Gonzalez would most definitely get what a Gonzalez would want. Just at that moment, the antique silver-toned bell on a spring attached to the front door of the Café chimed as the door opened.

Yes, the uncrowned queen of the far-flung Gonzalez/Gonzales clan was without, attended by Jesus-of-the-Garage Gonzalez. Richard was he was almost certain that he was one of her sons, and therefor Araceli's uncle. Richard was comforted by the knowledge that practically no one else was absolutely certain either. The two sons of the original founder of the clan had sired twenty and eighteen children each, through legitimate marriages and additional less-formal relationships way back in the sunset days of the 17th century. Only the straight-line descent of the oldest-son's oldest son to his oldest son was unquestioned, connected as it was to ownership of the remnant of the Spanish grant which had brought the clan to Texas in the first place. Every other Gonzales/Gonzalez family branch had degenerated into an impenetrable and tangled thicket, what with repeated names, indecipherable handwriting on many official documents, and a fair number of productive extra-marital relationships over the subsequent two centuries.

Now, Abuelita Adeliza tottered through the doorway, attended by Jesus-of-the-Garage, and Berto, Araceli's younger brother. The aged and uncrowned queen of that branch of the family beamed approvingly on Richard and took him into a fond familial embrace, kissing him on both cheeks. It rather comforted Richard, reminded once more of how fortunate he was in that Granny Adeliza loved him; mostly for being a cook, a mad fan of his former celebrity self, and only distantly and in third case for appearing to bear a strong resemblance to her late husband, who in the days of his military service in WWII had been a cook for the US Army. Richard now had the approval, unquestioned, of the most socially powerful woman in Luna City ... one of the most socially powerful, of course, in company with Jess Abernathy-Vaughn, Miss Letty McAllister, and perhaps

Patricia Pryor. There were poles of subtle social female power in Luna City. Richard was resoundingly grateful that every single one of them had aligned in his favor. Proof that he had not lost his touch at all.

Abuelita patted his cheek and spoke to him, as Araceli obligingly translated.

"Granny is no-end pleased that you have decided to marry. It is good to marry and have good, handsome, and intelligent children, the more the better. It is what we are required to do by the Church and custom and that you have proposed to a Gonzalez? Granny is ecstatic. Even more that our Katie is your chosen. Granny is convinced that our Katie is the perfect wife for you. Katie is strong and determined, and very, very clever. It is a perfect match. She says that you have (*and here, Araceli looked rather embarrassed*) impure impulses and old habits that are not good for you. A marriage to Our Katie will keep you from those very bad life habits. She will keep you on the good path, towards happiness and many children."

"Thank you for your consideration," Richard brought himself to confess, admitting now that he was total and malleable putty in the hands of certain Gonzalez/Gonzales women. "Tell your grandmother – Abuelita – that I will try my very best to make Kate the happiest woman on earth. At least, the very happiest woman in Luna City, against considerable competition from so many other happy women."

Abuelita Adeliza beamed even more approvingly on Richard, after that message was relayed to her through Araceli.

She fished in her handbag and produced a small ring box which once had been covered in velvet, but which was now rubbed and wilted.

"This is the ring which Katie loved when she was a child." Araceli related. "Abuelita says that there is not a problem to have it remade for Katie. She and Uncle Jesus are not in any manner the same as you and Kate. It is the enduring love and respect which matters most. The form that it takes is a minor thing. So you are OK to redo the rings, then." Araceli murmured. "Abuelita is on board with that. That is good…"

Abuelita Adeliza put the small ring box in Richard's hand, and gently closed his fingers over it, with both of her hands. She went on tiptoe and kissed Richard again on both cheeks, adding some remark which caused Araceli to briefly close her eyes, and Jesus-of-the-Garage to stifle a snort of laughter.

"What was that?" Richard asked, suspiciously, as Abuelita Adeliza and her escort departed the Café.

"Nothing, really," Araceli was a trifle evasive. "Just wished the both of you a glorious wedding night. Only … a little more barnyard. Now," she returned to her more usual businesslike, practical self. "As for remaking the rings, did you have anyone in mind?"

"I was going to throw myself on the mercy of Georg Stein's friend, the one who restored the Gonzaga Reliquary, and hope that he can wang together something respectable that I can present to Katie … oh, lord. I may have to put off our Monday, to give the man time to do a ring for her."

97

"Let me see to that," Araceli took masterful control. "Some kind of emergency on Sunday night. Something that you have to work Monday for. I know; the gourmet food sideline thing. You have to work on Monday to sort it all out. You tell her that, and I'll back you up from my end. And don't worry," Araceli added. "I'll be subtle."

"All righty-oh," Richard agreed with a sigh. A month without Kate and her undemanding company seemed to him an eternity. But it would have to be so, and he texted her that very afternoon.

Sorry, Love – Monday no good for me, demand for Café products way up, must work. See you next Monday? Need to ask you important question.

Her answer came back almost at once.

Ok – no problem. I'm really feeling under the weather still. Went back to work yesterday, think I overdid it. See you on the next. Give Ozzie some catnip and say it's from me.

To The Sticking Point

Georg Stein's jewelry-restoring friend came through in the nick of time. Georg came into the Café Saturday afternoon, a beaming smile across his countenance and a small envelope in his hand.

"It came just now, by special courier! I told Ulrich that you would need the rings at the very soonest possible, that it was not a matter of museum perfection and a simple matter! And he obliged. Don't you wish to examine the work?" Georg asked, hopefully, and Richard put aside the matter of constructing sugar flowers for the wedding of Dr. Mindy and Gunnison-Penn.

Georg had done him a solid service and deserved some small reward.

The envelope was one of those sealed with tape, and additionally, a bit of string wound around a circular disc. Richard slit the tape with a pair of desk scissors and unwound the string. There was the same worn and rubbed velveteen box in it that Abuelita Adeliza had given him more than a week ago. Richard snapped it open and regarded the two rings inside.

"*Sehr schone!*" Georg Stein exclaimed. "Oh, very nice!"

"Very nice indeed," Richard answered, more impressed than he had been prepared to be. The two rings were now more of an equal weight. The enormous harlequin brown jasper knuckle-duster now set in a circlet of plain unadorned gold, and the garnet heart set in a circular filigree of gold leaves and diamond-chip daisies with miniscule pearl centers; as charming and feminine as the jasper was masculine. "Your pal does lovely work, even in a hurry and not to his usual exacting standard. Tell him that I'll send a check for his time…"

"Not to worry!" Georg gave him a clap on the shoulder that nearly launched Richard into the cash-stand and the set of shelves containing Café packaged goods. "Invite us to the wedding, *hein*? That is, if your lady says 'yes' of course. And if she says 'no'," Georg added on a note of brute practicality, "Then we shall all go together to the Vee-Eff-Double-You and drink together, to console ourselves over the irrationality of women."

"I am certain of her answer," Richard responded, gamely optimistic, brazenly confident, although with a sudden cold feeling at the pit of his stomach – what if Katie <u>did</u> say 'no'. *What would he do, then?* "That she will say yes. And I will indeed ask that you, your good lady and your friend Ulrich to be guests. There will be a paucity of guests on the groom's side of the church, otherwise…"

What if Kate did say 'no'? The question continued to haunt him for the remainder of that day, into the next, even as he and the staff prepared for the grand wedding do at the Rincon de los Robles rancho, which was a case of all hands to the deck. On Monday morning, he rose from somewhat troubled sleep in the barely-double-sized bed in the tiny room at the back end of the Airstream which had been his home since arriving in Luna City. Richard was fiercely fond of the Airstream caravan, his tiny home on wheels, his solidary culinary-devout monk's cell, the fortress of his solitude, wherein he and Ozzie communed with the spirit of the great chefs of the past and plotted how to bring a new sense of culinary appreciation to the good people of Luna City. *(Although Ozzie mostly seemed to plot a campaign against mice in the alley behind the Café and his next hit of home-grown catnip, provided by Kate.)* Caviar cuisine at the price of canned tuna fish, as an unnamed wit had once remarked; his mission, should he accept it, and Richard had, with all of his heart and a great portion of his earthly soul.

He fixed himself a good strong pot of tea, toasted some brioche for himself and opened a can of tuna as a special treat for Ozzie, and considered the store in his little pantry and refrigerator, from which he hoped to prepare that very special supper; something simple, as the oven and hob in the caravan necessarily limited things. There was half a bottle of Calvados in the pantry cupboard and some lovely apple cider, and a whole small chicken, a jug of cream and half a dozen apples in the refrigerator. He had about decided on Chicken a la Normande, with fresh green beans, with a plain salad with the last of the salad greens. For a sweet ... well, he considered a plain egg crème brûlée. He had all the ingredients to hand, and nothing made him happier in the world than to fix a meal for Kate, but the setting had to be special.

Still musing on the menu and mentally plotting out the timeline necessary for prep, cooking and final touches, he considered walking up to the Amazing Straw Castle Aquarius. Perhaps Bree and her grandparents, Sefton and Judy could help conjure up the perfect romantic setting for a proposal of marriage. God knows, Richard thought, Judy and her granddaughter were romantically inclined and certainly creative enough. The whole ambiance of the Straw Castle establishment bore testimony to that, hung with banners, sun-catchers, birdfeeders and garden spinners.

On this early Monday morning – mid-morning for both Richard, and the Grants as they were all accustomed to rising and going about their work well before sunrise – the only one in the Straw Castle was Bree, sitting on the shaded terrace with her laptop computer open before her and a tall mug of something hot and milky at hand. It was still cool through midday, although that would not last much longer, and the shaded pergola commanded a view of the stone-studded river, as it swept around the small promontory on which stood the Grant's main house, in a reach of water turned to quicksilver by the morning sun. Two cats slept in a patch of sunlight, and Azúcar, the tame bottle-raised llama stood in a patch of shade beyond the edge of the terrace and regarded Richard with lordly scorn.

"Hi, Chef!" Bree greeted him, as chipper and bright as a tree full of squirrels. "Isn't it nice to have a day off? I'm reviewing my notes for taking the CLEP exam for natural sciences. I think I'm about ready, but there's so much! Can we help you with something?"

"You can," Richard drew a deep breath and took the plunge, taking Bree and by extension, her grandparents into his confidence. "I am going to ask Miss Kate Heisel to marry me ... and I want to make it a special occasion ... over and above our usual Monday supper together. I usually fix her a lovely meal, and we eat it together, but I would like to make this one Monday more than special..."

"Oh, Chef!" Bree exclaimed, closing her laptop and springing out of the comfortable willow-twig chair. "That's so romantic! Don't say anything more! Gramps and G-Nan and I will make it so special! Your place – the little porch outside the trailer? Oh, there's so much that we can do, don't say another word, just leave it to us!"

In an exuberance of unseemly affection, Bree flung her arms around him and kissed his cheek. "Don't say another word, Chef! We will make it so that she can't possibly say no!"

* * *

Seven hours later, as daylight began to fade from the eastern sky and the western turned the color of a ripe peach, edged with purple clouds, Richard regarded their handiwork with a mixture of awe, gratitude, and surprise. The small patio which shared the cover provided by a metal roof on tall pipe legs had been utterly transformed into a bower of romance. Pale filmy curtains were suspended from the edge of the roof on barely visible wires. Richard presumed they were mosquito-netting. The curtains filled in three sides of the shelter, although they were at present drawn back and tied with lavish garlands of white artificial magnolias, lilies, roses, and green leaves. Strands of white fairy lights hung from the edge of the shelter roof, twinkling like fireflies. More garlands of flowers crossed from side to side and corner to corner. From where they met over a small table, a lantern hung, already flickering to life, now that it was in the shade. The table itself was draped in white, with a silver candlestick set in the middle, amid another wreath of flowers, and knots of white and silver ribbons. A pair of elegant straight chairs similarly decked with flowers and ribbons flanked the table.

"Stone the crows, I didn't expect anything like this!" he exclaimed. All that was missing were plates and place settings.

Richard regretted with a pang that all he had in that way was simple melamine stuff and cheap metal utensils seconded from Marisol Gonzalez's resale shop in Karnesville, hardly worthy of this vision from the most romantic Hallmark movie setting ever. He had never cared enough to have his home kitchen things replaced. Anyway, Kate had never before given any indication of minding.

"It's not too much, is it, Chef?" Bree sounded anxious.

"Oh, no, never!" Judy assured her, airily. "I will perform a blessing to align the spiritual flow in the most beneficial direction and burn some incense to banish malign influences. I do the same for those who come together at our quarterly rites to burnish their sex-magickal practices. These are just things that we had around, for special occasions."

"No, it's not," Richard replied. "I don't know how to thank you ... this all looks most splendid..."

"Invite us to the wedding, of course," Judy beamed fondly. "I can perform the binding rituals for you, if you are in tune with the magickal world."

Interiorly, Richard shuddered. What Judy Grant's 'magickal' rituals might involve was a book that to him would best be closed; closed, sealed, welded into a lead box and dropped into the Marianas Trench.

"It's kind of you to offer, Mrs. Grant, but Kate and I are of rather more conventional and orthodox beliefs. I think that we will offer our marriage bans and vows to be announced and celebrated among the Lutherans in Karnesville. But ..." he added, in all honesty, "If my suit and hand are accepted, you are invited, of course."

"Of course," Judy Grant beamed at him, not at all put down. For all Richard knew, her biding rituals were performed under a new moon, in a state of nature, and concluded with a very public bedding. He contemplated the image, suddenly stricken with a vision of critiques from the interested audience. That was a thought to throw ice-water on amorous impulses.

Judy continued, "My Seftie will come around later, and put out and light the tiki torches – a line of light to lead your truest love to the bower. It will be utterly magical, Richard; she will hardly be able to say no."

"So I hope," Richard replied.

Bree took her grandmother by the arm. "G-Nan, I think that we are finished. Best leave Chef and Kate some privacy. We can wait until morning, to hear how it all works out." She gazed earnestly at Richard, and added, "We will be eaten up with curiosity over what Kate will say, but I promise that we <u>will</u> stay away from here tonight. Oh," she added, upon picking up a couple of large and empty fabric bags, which had evidently been used to convey the flower garlands and curtains. "Nearly forgot – the mail came, and this stuff is all addressed to you." She shoved a fat sheaf of envelopes, and a couple of slim mail-order catalogues into his hands.

"Thanks, I'll look at them later," Richard had prep to do, and a custard to whip up, for it was well past four in the afternoon, and Kate would be there soon. He left the envelopes on the bedcover, next to where Ozzie was curled into a neat c-shape. One of them, he noticed vaguely, was from the Immigration and Naturalization service. He would look at it when he had the time, but time which was about to run away from him entirely.

The rubbed and faded velveteen box sat on the little dresser, a portent and talisman. Richard put it into the front pocket of his cargo pants, just to know that he had it close to hand. He had not decided on the moment, but upon consideration, perhaps after the main course. Just sitting in that bower of flowers and fairy lights should warm Kate's heart and incline her affections towards him in a marital manner.

It would be so very pleasant, introducing Kate to his parents, later in summer. He would be able to say to them, *'This is Kate, who will be my wife.'* Perhaps then, they might be inclined to consider him as something more than a reckless teenaged boy with many, many bad habits and antisocial inclinations, whom they were obliged to indulge because he was their only chick and child. Perhaps Mum and Dad might be a little less … anxious on his behalf.

He resumed work in the tiny caravan kitchen, so tiny indeed that he could reach everything in it within two steps, including the miniscule dining table and banquette bench, where they were accustomed to dine, when it was too hot, too cold or too wet to venture eating in the patio. But this evening, this momentous evening, was one of those evenings when it was perfectly temperate out of doors; mild, with just a light breeze to stir the leaves of the scrub oaks overhead and send ripples through the overgrown field starred with yellow wildflowers which served as a campground. In another few weeks, the field would be mown to stubble, when the summer season began, and the old communards, members of the original Age of Aquarius hippy commune would assemble for the reunion and observation of the summer solstice. But that time was not yet; Richard could appreciate the knee-high waving field of tall grass and yellow wildflowers. The beaten-down track of those rare visitors paying regular visits to him and the scant other visitors to the Age campground was now marked by tall tiki-torch stands driven into the relatively yielding ground. Sefton Grant was just now going along them with a long BBQ-lighting lighter, picturesquely clad in his native attire of cowboy boots, hand-loomed loincloth, and straw cowboy hat. Pale flames blossomed where ere Sefton walked. He waved towards Richard in a friendly manner – and at that moment, Richard spotted a rising trail of dust, in the direction of the turn-off for the Age from Route 123.

Kate was here, finally, after a month of Kateless Mondays.

She emerged from her little VW, smiling and it seemed a little breathless. Richard waited for her under the bedecked patio, feeling not a little breathless himself.

"Hello, you!" she exclaimed, as she sent a bright-eyed look around the patio. "I see this is a special occasion – just for me?"

"It is indeed, my Kate of Kate Hall – all for you. It has been four whole weeks since we broke bread together. This occasion is to be celebrated. By the by, I have an important question to ask of you ..."

"Save it until we have eaten," Kate replied. "I'm starving! What have you fixed for us? I have not forgotten Ozzie's catnip fix. I went by Abuelita's house ... and she bustled out and told me that tonight would be a very significant night and gave me an extra-large bunch of fresh catnip. It should be enough to keep him catatonic," Kate giggled at her own wit, "for simply hours."

"Chicken a la Normande," Richard took her hand, "That's chicken, cooked Normandy-style, with apples and Calvados – that's apple brandy, when it's not being pretentious. You'll love it. And for afters, crème brûlée. Meanwhile, as I cook, you can pet Ozzie, and tell me all about your week. Have you interviewed anyone famous this week? Or even just merely notorious?"

"Let me give Ozzie his 'nip' fix," Kate giggled again. "And then I'll tell you all about my scoop of the year! I had a sit-down interview with Trish Creighton Doyle. She's in Luna City, doing local research for her next book, The book club picked one of her books earlier this year, and they invited her to come to their meeting, so they could ask her questions. Did you know she was in town?"

"I did," Richard opened the door to the caravan, and Kate bounded up the two steps. "Staying at the Cattleman. I met her one morning, as she was having breakfast with Lew Dubois and his good lady. She seemed ... interesting. Her next book is going to be set in Texas, it seems."

"From what I hear, very loosely set in Texas," Richard observed.

Kate snickered. "The literary flight of fancy will approach near-orbit and break the speed of sound, but my reading is that she is a good-hearted soul, who can tell a good story, even if well-told previously. She's <u>not</u> a malicious freak-a-zoid who only wants to gross-out the multitudes, like that awful creep misogynist who wanted to do that nasty movie..."

"Don't remind me," Richard bent and dropped a fond kiss on Kate's lips as she settled onto the divan. Unbidden, Ozzie emerged from the bedroom half of the caravan, and leapt onto Kate's lap, purring like a motor, and butting his brindle head against Kate's handbag. "Ah. Your master calls, my dear Kate of Kate Hall, and not before time."

"You've missed me, kitten!" Kate rubbed Ozzies' ears, as the one-eyed cat purred like a mad thing, even louder than the AC unit which kept the tiny Airstream at a comfortable level, even in the hottest of Texas summers.

"He has ..." Richard cleared his throat, upon confessing something which revolted his British stiff-upper-lip upbringing to the very core of his being. "I missed you too, my Kate. My sufferings on your absence were profound. Shook me to the core, it did."

"I missed you too, lover," Kate replied. "And your little cat, too. So I did, Ozzie my little dumpling." She gave Ozzie a particularly energetic scritch. "Well, that was my week and the week before that, and the week before that, when I wasn't being sick with the flu at Mom and Dad's house, being fed broth poured hot over an egg broken onto a piece of wheat toast. That's Mom's sovereign meal for the sick, upon recovering something like an appetite for food. That, and plenty of ginger-ale." Kate added, in the spirit of one vouchsafing a trade secret. "Ginger-ale; it tastes nearly as good coming up as it does going down. And what were you doing with yourself, all last month?"

"Ugh," Richard grimaced. "I appreciate your mother's wisdom, but let's not dwell any further upon regurgitation. I have worked all afternoon to prepare this sumptuous repast and Bree and Mrs. Grant have worked all that same time to make the scene of our revels a memorable one. Vomiting will not work well with that concept."

"Agreed," Kate gave Ozzie's brindled head another good skritch. "Oh, how I missed this – and missed you. Texting at odd hours just isn't the same. We're both too busy during the day and too damned tired at night."

"It certainly does make the relationship easier, when we commit to time together absolutely," Richard reached into the upper cupboard for a pair of wine glasses – these at least were real glass, although from the Dollar Tree store in Karnesville. He poured out a golden glory of Sefton's peerless mustang grape elixir into each glass and handed one to Kate. "I've been busy. Not just the usual kitchen matters, but the staff came up with some notions of prepared Café-brand gourmet sauces and mixes and things, to sell as a kind of extra."

"That's marvelous," Kate beamed. "How is it working out – and is it a lot of extra work for you?"

"Curiously enough – no," Richard gave the stewing chicken another gentle stir, replaced the pot lid, and took a deep swing of Sefton's magical vintage. "The kids – Robbie, Bree and the others ... they were all for it, and god bless them, they've been doing the heavy lifting on the project. I have every confidence in them, actually. If the Café becomes a local brand leader in prepared foods, sauces, cakes, and spice mixes, it will be because they are doing most of the work. I'm enormously proud of them, by the way," Richard confessed. "It's a vindication of my own mission – to acquaint the public with the taste of excellent food. Can't send everyone to do a course at the finest cooking school in Paris ... but honestly, I can show them what the good stuff should taste like, and ... well, this project is showing them by easy steps how to achieve that enlightenment ... Kate, my own, I am considering seeking another employer, now that my mission at the Café is nearly completed..."

"What?" Shocked, Kate set down the wineglass, and stopped skritching Ozzie's head. Ozzie gave a querulous 'mew' and set a paw on her hand. Kate, obedient to the commands of her feline overlord, resumed the caresses. "I thought you loved the Café – that you'd never leave Luna City! What brought all this on?"

"Well," Richard temporized. "I'm about to make some life changes, you see. I have set the Café on the right path, trained up a good staff, who can be trusted to carry on with my standard.

Araceli is a suburb manager. If she had any ambition at all, she would be at the top of the restaurant-management game, but she loves Luna City as well, since her whole life is here. It's not that I plan on leaving for other employment just yet ... oh, dearie me, no. It's just that I must think of a future, in a year or so. I wouldn't be leaving Luna City at all. No. Just ... taking up another enterprise which needs my firm guiding hand."

"The Cattleman," Kate sighed, in sudden comprehension. "You're accepting Lew Dubois's offer to be the executive chef there. Are you certain that is wise, lover? Until this year, you always said 'no' – as if Lew were showing a wreath of garlic and a crucifix to a vampire. You feared to lose your soul to celebrity temptations, you said."

"I know," Richard confessed, and fortified himself with a swig of Sefton's glorious elixir, and a stir of the chicken, now nearly done, fragrant with the soul of the apples, encapsulated in Calvados. "But there are ... considerations, my Kate of Kate Hall. I must soon take on expanded responsibilities. Mrs. Abernathy-Vaughn has advised me that my salary from the Café will tap out. Has tapped out, as of this year. I hold the place in dear affection, and respect Miss Letty and Doctor Wyler, no less for giving me a chance when all other opportunities turned dark and I had not a true friend in the world. Look, let's not dwell on this, my Kate. Supper is nearly ready; it is near sundown ... and the bower prepared for us will be at it's best. Let me pour another glass for ourselves, plate the first course ... and appreciate what has been done for us at the most perfect hour."

"Of course, lover," Kate acquiesced, and Richard wondered if she already knew what he was going to ask. Wouldn't surprise him in the least if she did: he just wished he could be absolutely certain she was going to reply in the affirmative.

The sun had already vanished behind the treeline to the west, leaving a bright apricot glow behind. The strings of tiny fairy-lights winked on, and brief sparks of light from fireflies echoed them from the tall grass in the abandoned campground. A light breeze stirred the gauze curtains and sent the flames from the tiki torches and the ivory-wax beeswax candles wavering. The candles lent a faint scent of honey to the air; it all looked even more beautiful in dusky twilight.

"This is the most perfect place for a date night that I have ever seen," Kate confessed at last. "There's just enough light to take a picture, to prove that it is really real."

"As you wish, my Kate of Kate Hall," Richard set his own wineglass on the table. "Let me bring out the salad course, and the bread ... and I'll ask you the question that's been on my mind."

When he emerged from the caravan, balancing two plates of salad, and a basket of bread slices, Kate had already put away her camera, and was sitting in one of the decorated chairs, looking at him, expectantly. Richard set down the plates, the breadbasket, and felt the small lump of the ring box in his trouser pocket.

Get to it! His inner voice commanded. *You've been putting it off for long enough. Not a minute longer.*

"Well, this is it," His own voice sounded high with anxiety to his own ears, and he fumbled the box out of his pocket and set it on the table, next to the butter dish. "The question I've been meaning to ask you ... I think ... I'm ... Kate, will you marry me?"

"Of course, I will," Kate replied, completely unruffled. "Is that my ring?"

"Of course ... well, sort of." Richard opened the box. "It's the one that..."

"Abuelita's garnet heart," Kate replied, still completely unruffled and prosaic. "She told me that she had given it to you, and 'Celi said that you would have it remade, 'specially for me. It's beautiful, Richard. It really is, and I adore it as much as I adore you. Here – I suppose that traditionally, you are supposed to slip it onto my finger."

"Quite," Richard could barely find his voice, overcome and nearly fainting under a great wave of relief, as he did so, slipping the gold circlet onto Kate's capable and slightly printer-ink stained hand. A perfect fit. *Why, this was almost painless!* If he had known how easy it would be, and how promptly Kate assented – he would have proposed to her weeks, nay, months ago. "Well. Then. You haven't given any thought to when and where, and all that?"

"Since I was in eighth grade," Kate picked up her fork, and began tranquilly to eat her salad. "When all my girlfriends were planning their weddings, although most of us had no notion of whom the groom would be. Except for Jasmine Mooney, and everyone knew she had the hots for Brian Colbert. She was pregnant by him at graduation, I'll have you know, although she got tired of his drug habit and divorced him a couple of years later. As for me; Mom and Pop's church in Karnesville, of course. And the party afterwards at their house. Nothing really fancy and expensive. Just invite all our friends and have a nice party. I'm more of a *'barefoot in a meadow in an embroidered Mexican folk dress'* kind of girl." She looked very straight at Richard. "I have a theory that the more elaborate and expensive the wedding, the sooner it all goes crash."

"Not high maintenance at all," Richard picked up his own fork, washed by a second wave of relief. "All right, then. Any notion as to when? It's not like there's any hurry ... my parents will be visiting at mid-summer..."

"I'll tell Mom," Kate replied, not sounding particularly worried. "She'll take care of everything for us. All I'll have to do is have that stupid dress that my grandmother wore altered to fit me. All you have to do is show up on the date or else risk my brothers beating the crap out of you. All sorted, Richard. Don't look so worried ... oh, this is magnificent! Did you put something new in your salad dressing? I could swear that you did..."

"Experimenting with a new signature dressing," Richard explained. "With an eye to another flavor of the ready-made in our battery of goods. Tarragon, steeped garlic cloves and white-wine vinegar, and grape-seed oil."

"Nice." Kate replied, judiciously. "Another winner for the Café. What does everyone think of it so far?"

"Guarded approval, at this point," Richard took a bite of his own salad, oddly comforted that they were back to a more usual topic of conversation, now that the insurmountable mountain pass of proposing marriage had been gotten over. He and Kate were on the straight glide path to a day in the near future when she would wear a white dress, and he the formal white tie ensemble, and both sets of parents would look on approvingly.

Only at one point was the matter of the wedding discussed, and that was over the main course of chicken a la Normande.

"Have you given any thought to where we will live?" Kate mopped the last of the savory cream sauce and last bite of chicken with a piece of bread, roughly torn in quarters. "When we're married. I wouldn't mind moving to Luna City, honestly – I'm bopping all over the county anyway. And I love your little trailer, but it's honestly too small for the both of us, all my stuff and Ozzie, too."

"I have, my sweet Kate," Richard replied. "And agree. It's been hinted to me that part of my generous renumeration for taking on the Cattleman job involves company-provided staff quarters, either at the hotel itself, or on Mills Farm."

"It would be cool, living at the Cattleman," Kate mused. "But it would be a bit like government quarters. It wouldn't really be ours, would it?"

"It would do for a time," Richard agreed. "Time enough to sort out something bespoke to suit."

"The perfect house for us both," Kate set down her fork, suddenly animated. "With the perfect gourmet kitchen and pantry for you. An office and library for me. A sheltered catio – a screened porch for Ozzie. One where we could all sit together and watch the sun go down ... something like the Straw Castle Aquarius."

"Only larger," Richard agreed, utterly content. He was finished with his own portion of chicken a la Normande, appetite sated, at peace with the world, now that Kate, his glorious Kate, had accepted his proposal. Their future was bright, even brighter than the twinkling lights from the strings of fairy lights strung with abandon around the patio. "A perfect gourmet kitchen, designed to my preferences! I like the sound of that, my Kate. Are you ready for the dessert course, now?"

"Perfectly," Kate twinkled at him. "But I have to use ... your facility, first. Do you mind?"

"Mi casa, su casa!" Richard waved an indulgent hand, following her as he carried the main course plates into the tiny caravan, where he left them in the sink, and put the small salamander iron to heat over the hob, the better to caramelize the delicate sugar crust over the twin custards, now at a gentle room temperature.

Kate was taking an unconscionably lot time in the facility – he had just begun to wonder where she was, when she emerged from behind the little privacy curtain that hung in the opening between the bedroom and bathroom portion of the caravan, and the kitchen/lounge part. Her face was pale and set like stone.

"I have to go," she said, abruptly. Richard, with the iron salamander in hand, watched, utterly astounded as she took up her purse from the divan.

"But dessert is almost ready ..." He protested. "Is there some kind of emergency, that you have to go now."

"An emergency," she replied, still terse, abrupt. "Work thing. I have to go."

"Will you be back tonight?" Richard asked, stunned – they hadn't even gotten to desert.

"I don't think so," Kate said. "I really have to go. Right now."

And go she did, without another word, leaving Richard standing in the middle of the caravan with a salamander in one hand, and a single crème brûlée custard ramekin in the other.

What had gotten into Kate? His adored and level-headed Kate. Richard could imagine some kind of family emergency – but surely, she would have said something. A breaking news story? No, the *Karnesville Weekly Beacon* was not the sort of publication to front that kind of story. It was a weekly after all. Richard finished caramelizing the second crème brûlée sugar crust and wondered what he ought to do now. It was a deflating end to what had been a splendid, indeed, triumphant evening.

In the end, he ate his crème brûlée, sitting alone at the lavishly adorned table, still deeply puzzled. He sent a text message to Kate before he went to bed that night but got no answer. He did note, as he crawled into bed, that Ozzie had disarrayed the pile of mail and catalogues left in the middle of the bedcovers.

* * *

"Good morning!" he said to Araceli, the next morning, as he came through the back door of the Café, pulling on the Café-branded chef's jacket, which had been a Christmas present some years past. "And how was your day off? Hope it wasn't eventful."

There had still been no reply from Kate, and he was becoming steadily more unsettled about last night. Even as the wedding at the Gonzales rancho loomed, almost to the exclusion of all other concerns. Araceli, sitting on a tall stool at the main worktable, was deftly assembling silverware in napkins for the morning table settings, working as deftly as a machine, as she rolled knife, fork and spoon in a stiffly starched napkin, securing each with a band of paper tape.

"It was very pleasant, thank you for asking, Chef," his right-hand management replied. "It was quite uneventful, until our Kate sent me a message at about eight o'clock – that you had finally asked her to marry you. She posted a picture of the ring on her hand and another of the supper venue on her personal FB page. Very nice. Romantic to the max – all of her friends know now how much trouble you went to, in order to make it so special."

"Not me," Richard confessed with a sigh. "It was Judy Grant and Bree. They brought over the lights and flowers and all, to make it special, they said."

"It looked fantastic," Araceli assured him, although he detected a tiny frown-line of worry between her brows. "She posted all those pictures and sent out a blast message with a link to all of us. Honestly, Chef, we've all been waiting on tenterhooks for you to pop the big question, these last couple of weeks. She posted that she said 'yes', of course. Abuelita will be so pleased. Berto was going to download and print out the picture of the lovely garnet heart ring on Kate's hand for her. Abuelita," Araceli added, as if in explanation. "Is old-school. She doesn't do the internet or social media. She only believes in cold, hard, printed factuals." Now Araceli shot a disturbingly acute look in Richard's direction. "Was there something that happened? Did something go all wrong, later in the evening?"

"I think that there was," Richard confessed. "Although for the life of me, I can't think what it might have been. I was doing the last touches, caramelizing the exquisite sugar crust on the crème brûlée. The dessert course, to a meal carefully planned. Kate claimed the need to use the necessary. We had drunk a lot of wine, you see. In celebration. Natural urge and all. And when she came out of the necessary, suddenly she said that she had to leave. Not another word. Only that she had to leave at once. I thought it might be that she had received a sudden report of a disaster, which she might have to report upon, in her capacity. But sudden disasters and the *Karnesville Weekly Beacon*?"

"No, not exactly what one thinks of, when one considers rapidly-breaking news," Araceli agreed. "News 4 San Antonio is more like it. Even the *Beeville Bee Picayune* breaks the odd story here and there. I haven't talked to Katie or had any messages since last night. But that's not odd. Today she'd be busy with work, and we've got Mindy's wedding to sort."

"I've messaged her, myself," Richard confessed. "Last night, and again, first thing this morning. I haven't gotten an answer. Usually, when I send her a text after our supper on Mondays, she sends me a reply, letting me know that she got back to her place safely. It's all very odd, and it's starting to worry me. We were having a lovely supper and we were sorting out what to do about the wedding, and where we might live afterwards ... then suddenly. No communication at all. It's as if she were angry with me, but I can't for the life of me think why."

"She'll be busy all day today," Araceli consoled him. "Likely won't have time for personal stuff. Wait and text her again tonight."

"I'll do just that," Richard promised, as it was now all hands to the deck to prep for the breakfast rush, and after that, the last mad scramble for the lavish catered wedding supper for Professor Mindy and Xavier Gunnison-Penn. "Still, I wonder what happened in those few minutes when she was using the necessary?"

It wasn't until he came home that evening and walked into the bedroom portion of the Airstream that fate put him in the way of a clue. The stack of mail from the day before still lay on the narrow dresser opposite the bed; the bed and dresser which Kate had walked between on her way to use the lavatory. The envelope from the Immigration and Naturalization Service was on top of the pile. Richard's eyes fell upon it, and a horrible supposition began to form in his mind.

What if she ... oh, my God. This is a disaster...

Summer 2019 Newsletter

Summer 2019 Newsletter

Luna City Chamber of Commerce

5 North Town Square, Suite 4

Check out our Facebook Page

Bring your lawn chairs, picnic blankets, drinks, popcorn and snacks for the whole family, and enjoy a good old-fashioned open-air movie double-feature every Saturday evening from June through August at the eastern side of Town Square! This community get-together is sponsored by the Chamber, together with Mills Farm, Abernathy Hardware, and Bodie Feed & Seed, who have generously donated use of a 12x20 foot screen and a professional-grade projector for this summer-long event. The featured movies begin 1/2 an hour after sundown. The schedule of old and new classic family movies will be posted at the Bandstand and on the Chamber of Commerce notice board.

Luna City's Newest Historical Marker

Following unveiling of the newest Texas State Historical marker on June 15th, the Gonzalez family of the Encino de los Robles Ranch will hold a reception at the rancho to celebrate the occasion. Dr. Miranda Rodriguez-Gonzalez will talk briefly on the history of the Rancho. Dr. Rodriguez-Gonzalez' careful historical research and archeological dig at the site of the original ranch proved beyond any shadow of a doubt that the old main house was constructed at least eighty years before the Borgfeld-McAllister House, upon which construction had begun in 1850. A number of relics discovered in Dr. Rodriguez-Gonzalez' search will be on display.

Upcoming Events

May 27

Memorial Day flag-raising at the War Memorial on Town Square at 9:00 AM, followed in the afternoon by a pig-roast at the VFW post. All veterans are welcome.

June 15

Formal unveiling of a new Texas State historical marker noting the founding of the Encino de los Robles Rancho will take place at mile 6, Rte 123 northbound at noon.

July 4

Festivities begin at noon with arrival of a parade led by the Mighty Fighting Moths marching band, and elements of the Karnes County Rangers.

Graduation!

Graduation ceremonies for the Luna City HS class of 2019 will be held May 17th beginning at 5:30 in the Nando Gonzalez Memorial Auditorium.

Hayes & Hayden

Luna City ISD News

Registration for Kindergarten 2019-20

Registration for kindergarten and new students will be on Friday, March 29th, at the Luna City ISD offices on Town Square. All paperwork for the upcoming school year must be completed. Students will be notified in late April regarding placement in classes for the 2019-2020 school year. Parents or guardians must bring a copy of their child's birth certificate, and immunization records.

Summer Job Fair

Local employers such as Mills Farm, Pryor's Meats and BBQ, the City of Luna City, Luna Café and Coffee, the Wyler Game Ranch and the Karnesville Parks and Recreation, will have tables for the fifth annual summer job fair on Friday, April 29th, from 12:00-1:00 in the Luna City HS gym. Applications and information for summer, part-time and full-time jobs will be available for interested students aged 16 and older.

Mighty Fighting Moth Football & Band Practice

Marching Band practice will begin July 23rd, every Tuesday, Thursday and Saturday at 8:30 on Moth Field. In the case of rain, practice will be held in the school gymnasium.

Drill, workout, and practice games for the Mighty Fighting Moth Varsity begin July 22nd, every Monday, Wednesday and Saturday at 8:00 on Moth Field. In the case of rain, supervised workouts will be held in the field house or the school gymnasium.

Community Marketplace

Summer Excursions

Mills Farm offers family excursions on the river, beginning May 25th, beginning at the new landing adjacent to the Tip Top Ice House. Groups and families may ride the river on rafts, tubes, or kayaks, break for lunch at Mills Farm Country Restaurant, or the 1912 Boathouse, continue on to the Route 80 landing near Helena. Transportation back from the landings will be scheduled regularly. Tickets for excursions may be purchased at the main desk of the Cattleman Hotel or through the Mills Farm website.

From Chief Vaughn, Luna City PD

Local drivers are cautioned to keep in mind the speed limit of 30 MPH on Luna City streets and 70 MPH on Route 123, Drivers are also cautioned to watch for pedestrians, especially around the boat landing by the Tip Top. We value our tourists and wish for them all to have a good experience visiting Luna City.

Luna Café Specialty Gourmet Items

Chef Richard and the staff of Luna Café and Coffee have developed a line of ready-made gourmet food items, for sale at the Café and at the Tip-Top Ice House, Gas and Grocery!

The Luna Café and Coffee Gourmet foods include Chef Richard's Blood Orange Salad Dressing, Spicy Mustard, Ginger Syrup, Spiced Apple Butter, and Prize Winning Chili Fixins Dried Spice Mixture. More will be added in coming months, including Chef Richard's own English Wedding Cake, and Spiced Cranberry Confiture.

The Chapel of Love

Richard did have to admit, as the trusty and battered refrigerated van from Pryor's Meats and BBQ bumped around that last corner in erratically-paved country lane which led to the ancestral home ranch of the many-branched Gonzales/Gonzalez clan at Rancho Rincon de los Robles, that the whole place only appeared modestly stately – and a couple of degrees less so than other historic and presumably stately structures went in Luna City and environs. The winning point for the Rancho Rincon was due to age. The Rincon de los Robles manse outscored all local competition in that regard; the magnificent and pillared classical plantation sprawl of the Wyler HQ house *(copied after a famous ruined grand house in Mississippi)* dated only from the late 1870s, the Beaux-Arts late Victorian commercial splendors of Town Square from the decade following, and the modest stone-built McAllister House, firmly dated from 1854. *(The McAllister House was dignified by a metal plaque on a pole by the side of Route 123 designating it as a Texas Historical Monument.)* The Rincon de Los Robles headquarters house now held clear victory in the age competition, as Dr. Miranda Rodriguez-Gonzalez had proved to the satisfaction of the State of Texas authorities who sat in judgement of historical matters. The very oldest wing of the Rincon del Los Robles home ranch house *(the thickest-walled, darkest, and most uncomfortable part, devoid of plumbing and electricity and used principally for storage)* had been proved beyond a shadow of doubt to be of late 18th Century construction, a domestic establishment founded by two sons of the minor Spanish nobleman who had been granted a lavish property on the San Antonio River, a residence continuously lived in by their descendants thereafter. The property had been considerably shrunk by two centuries of subsequent wars' alarms, and economic vicissitudes, but due to Mindy Rodriguez-Gonzalez's tireless efforts, the Los Robles establishment had been awarded the suitable historical plaque which made note of all this.

The formal unveiling of said plaque had been the highlight of the civic and social calendar the previous month in Luna City. That it had been positioned on the verge of Route 123 adjacent to the lay-by and turn for the gate to Los Robles, with only small signs posted half a mile in either direction notifying motorists of the presence of a historical marker was a mere bagatelle. Doctor Mindy was satisfied with the official honor paid to her family. Besides, she had more urgent matters to attend; her wedding to the peripatetic treasure-seeker, Xavier Gunnison Penn, to all appearances now the love of Dr. Mindy's hereto arid academic life. For this event, Richard had been recruited in a dual role; as best man for the treasure-hunting Canadian, and as head caterer for all the culinary offerings aside from the main course – a whole roasted beef on a massive outdoor spit set up over a cookfire of coals which seethed like the crater of a passive volcano.

This main course was the purview of the driver of the van. In his weekday job Andy Pryor was a petroleum engineer employed by various concerns in the shale oil business, but in private the husband of the magnificently demi-royal Patricia Wyler Pryor, doyenne of what passed for a social set in Luna City, director, and president of the drama society. She was also rumored to be the heir of her irascible grandfather, Doc Stephen Wyler, the second-oldest resident of Luna City, owner of the largest ranch property in Karnes County, and of most anything of substantial value going in the immediate vicinity. Fortunately for all, as had often been observed, the old man mostly used his considerable social and economic powers for good, as did his granddaughter. They ruled their demesne with a light and barely perceptible hand. Patricia and her husband, with the aid of their three strapping sons, ran a custom butchering and BBQ business from a nondescript building some distance from historic Town Square. Now, Richard and Andy Pryor were on their way to the Rancho, with the wedding cake, and the various side dishes for the wedding feast all stashed on racks in the back of the van. Andy and Patricia's oldest son, Anson had been overseeing the whole-roast-beef-onna-outdoor-spit since the day before. Richard would otherwise have wanted to know how this could be accomplished – but he was simply too busy with the wedding cake and all the various sides. The Pryors were the experts in this regard, although Richard was looking forward to picking their various brains about the process. Meanwhile, Richard's toque, white chef's coat – with his formal black-tie tuxedo on another hanger, shrouded in a plastic suit bag hanging from a hook in the divider in the van, was more than willing to do his duty in both roles – as caterer and best man.

The ranch house sat in a small grove of ancient oak trees, with a few desultory plantings of shrubbery and some large-leaved thickets of tropical-looking plants. The thickest of those plantings clustered around a small two-tiered stone fountain in the graveled circle before the main front door. The front prospect of the Rancho Rincon de los Robles made an uninspired gesture in the direction of formal elegance, as if designed by someone who had an elegant Southern plantation house described to them, but who had never actually seen a picture of one. The place seemed to be entirely deserted, and Richard viewed the discouraged prospect with mild alarm.

"Did we come on the wrong day?" he asked, somewhat apprehensive, and Andy grinned sideways.

"No, Ricardo – it's all on for today. But the party is around in back."

Andy steered the van along a barely graveled but adequate narrow drive, leading around the side of the house. Richard was immediately reassured. There was the life of the party; strings of lights and those intricately cut, lace-like paper banners, flown with abandon on wires strung across the space in the back of the house, from porches to several ancient and venerable oak trees, to the outbuildings and back again. There was the modest front of the new chapel, at some distance across what looked like a kitchen garden, flanked by an extensive complex of stables, corral, and henhouse, a garage with several tractors and four-wheel-drive vehicles parked therein, and Gunnison Penn's ancient RV, parked in front and already adorned with more balloons, paper lace flags, and a large banner which announced, *"Just Married!"* in two languages.

The area at the somewhat humbler back of the sprawling old farmstead was filled in also with folding tables and chairs, and even some ordinary dining-room chairs – drafted from within, standing awkward, naked and embarrassed in the out-of-doors. Richard thought that he recognized the folding stock from the Catholic parish hall, possibly filled in with loans from the Methodists ... tables now adorned with paper tablecloths and arrayed with centerpieces of fake flowers and garlands of real ivy, as well as droves of candles in ornate holders. The largest and longest table obviously was meant for the buffet, as it sat under a wide pavilion raised on metal legs adjacent to the back door of the old Rancho HQ house. He breathed an interior sigh of relief. All was going for <u>this</u> wedding as was expected. He spotted Araceli in the pavilion, giving orders to several younger members of the clan, who were carrying trays loaded with cutlery. Ah, yes – the Café kitchen brigade had everything in hand. Or maybe it was the Gonzalez/Gonzales clan kitchen brigade. There was his right-hand person in daily command of the Café, a notebook in her hand and a pen in the other, instead of the carafes of freshly brewed coffee and a pitcher of cream with which she usually appeared with, at the front of the house.

"Oh, good," she remarked, as Richard appeared from the passenger side of the van, and Andy swung the double doors at the back of the van all the way open, revealing the shelves within, stacked high with bulk food containers and boxes. "Is the cake OK? Mindy is freaking out about the cake."

"She shouldn't be," Richard answered. "The cake and the topper are perfectly fine. Now that we have arrived, I will assemble them in the appropriate space. Look; I have to tell you what I think happened with Kate and I, why she walked out on our engagement supper."

"Save it for later, Chef. We have to concentrate on this wedding for now, and I have to hand-hold Mindy before she melts down entirely." Araceli managed a parody of a curtsy to royalty. "As for your workspace; the kitchen is through here. I'll tell Andy that it's probably best to wheel everything up the ramp, rather than carry it all up the steps. You might want to take it all to the old butler pantry. Mind you dodge the cousins on the way through the kitchen…"

"The sisters, and the cousins and the aunts. I know," Richard replied, somewhat grumpily.

"All you need do is to scowl at them," Araceli replied, smartly. "You're Richard from the Café! The finest classically trained French chef and the prize of the culinary scene in Luna City, if not in the entirety of Karnes County. They all know you!"

"That's what I'm afraid of!" Richard unsheathed the trademarked scowl from his televised Bad Boy Chef days. It had no effect whatsoever on Araceli, inured as she was through extended exposure.

"Besides," Araceli added. "Abuela Adeliza is in the kitchen, taking command. I would best leave it in her hands. In a bit, I'll have to leave everything and do my maid of honor duty in getting Mindy dressed and made up for the occasion. I think that Uncle Jaimie is rather overwhelmed today. He has never coped well with social occasions. And no one seriously expected Cousin Mindy ever to marry."

Richard had never quite grasped the degree of kinship between Dr. Miranda Rodriguez-Gonzalez and Araceli Gonzalez-Gonzales, much less how exactly Dr. Mindy was kin to the man he thought of as the native laird of the Rancho – granddaughter, or niece, he suspected without much evidence. Richard also knew full well that the combined ancestral trees of the Gonzalez-Gonzalez clan rather more resembled an ultra-complicated

Gordian knot, which had defied for at least a century and a half any attempt by genealogists to map anything other than the direct father-to-son line of descent of the owners of the Rancho De Los Robles. It was a general understanding that Gonzales-with-a-z were assumed to be descended from the oldest legitimate son of the original Spanish land grantee, and Gonzales-with-an-s from the younger son. Each of the original pair; the heir and the spare, sired eighteen to twenty legitimate and less-than-legitimate offspring. Following generations until the 20th century basically repeated the same pattern, with the same score of names. Said names were often recycled upon the death of an infant or juvenile sibling for a subsequent child and parents were often charmingly lax in the official records with regard to marital status and the name of the maternal parent. It all had driven dedicated local genealogists to a frenzy of frustration.

"It's a tangle, indeed," allowed the magisterial Miss Letty McAllister, the oldest inhabitant of Luna City, president emeritus of the Luna City Historical Association, when Richard had mentioned his own puzzlement in the matter, about time of the second year of his residency in Luna City. "But in the long run, best to just conclude that any Gonzalez and Gonzales with a connection to Luna City are cousins, first, second, removed ... any variation thereof. It saves the historians sanity in the long run. Not that sanity is an overrated quality among the truly obsessed, genealogically speaking. Honestly, Stephen is of the

opinion that absolute specificity only matters if you are breeding cattle or race-horses."

"I am certain you are right," Richard replied, and only with an effort, refrained from adding "My Lady, Your Highness, or Your Honor," to his reply. Miss Letty McAllister was <u>that</u> commanding a person.

Now, Richard nodded to Araceli.

"I have the cake topper. It's fragile, so I don't trust anyone but myself to carry it. Andy is in the van. Summon the minions or whatever minions we have available to unload the van. The wedding cake layers are in the big white pasteboard boxes. Be careful with them. Any minion who drops one of those boxes..."

"I know, the Wrath of Chef," Araceli replied. She took up the box containing the second layer of the wedding cake. Richard was keen on on-site final assembly, as a prevention against horrible accidents, and led the way across the screened back porch and into the commodious and retro-style kitchen. *(The box with the bottom layer would require two people, or perhaps a dolly to convey it safely into the kitchen)* Only it wasn't deliberately styled that way; the kitchen was as it had been for the last half a century possibly longer. Tile counters, extensive cabinets ... a lot of old-style pots and pans hanging from a rack over the stove, an enormous old-style enameled gas item, on which several massive pots simmered, pots sufficiently large enough to boil a baby or a small child.

"The sauces for the beef roast," Araceli explained over her shoulder. "The *borracho* beans, and steaming the tamales ... it's what everyone expects, at a BBQ like this."

Richard nodded. "I'm glad that the happy couple agreed that we would supply a buffet of mostly cold or chilled sides, just as we did for the Boathouse opening. It saves a lot of trouble."

The kitchen was crowded with women, most of them of the Gonzalez-Gonzales clan, of all ages and body types, but universally tending in the direction of olive complexions and dark hair, although some of the very youngest sported brilliant magenta, green, or purple locks. Abuelita Adeliza Gonzales-Gonzalez, the absolute ruler of the Gonzales branch of the clan and Araceli's grandmother, beamed upon Richard most fondly, and called a welcome in Spanish across the crowded kitchen. Of all the women in Luna City, Abuelita was his original and most influential local fan, even before his advent in Luna City. Abuelita never had watched much American television other than the Cooking Channel; it was Araceli's opinion that Abuelita's enduring fanship for the Bad Boy Chef was because of his resemblance to her late husband, Abuelo Jesus. Richard smiled back; for himself, he would have been reluctant to admit that he was rather fond of the bossy old trout. Then he looked away from the younger crowd, already obeying Araceli and Abuelita's barked commands regarding the stacks of boxes from the van. Richard deliberately looked away from the youngest set, at work in the old kitchen. Too many reminded him of his eccentric junior chef, with his peacock-colored Mohawk crest and lavish facial piercings.

"You can do the final touches on the cake over there," Araceli nudged him in the direction of a narrow archway giving access into another and much smaller room, a windowless place entirely lined with shelves; obviously storage space for little-used dishes, pots, pans, covered casseroles, and china place settings. A substantial butcher-block-topped table took up most of the center of that small room. A sturdy bar cart sat next to it, already decked out in white draping and bunches of artificial lilies of the valley. "Abuelita said that space was strictly reserved for you, and she will <u>so</u> do something awful to anyone among the ladies who intrudes."

"I've always liked the cut of her jib," Richard replied. "Although I can't possibly imagine what awful thing that sweet old-age pensioner could possibly do to anyone."

"You'd be surprised," Araceli replied, darkly. "Not share with them her special heirloom recipe for rice pudding. Tell them in front of <u>everyone</u> that their *pollo asado* is garbage, fit only for stupid Anglo tourists; Abuelita has means, and some of them are very mean indeed. The vicious seventh-grade clique of popular girls has nothing on our Abuelita."

"Glad to hear it ... or not," Richard replied, and paid no more mind. He had to focus and focus he would. The kitchen brigade, under the direction of Araceli and her formidable grandmother would take care of the rest of the wedding buffet, while Andy and his capable offspring would take care of the main course – the whole roast beef-onna-magnificent mechanical spit. Now his attention must be focused on the wedding cake; assembling those three magnificent layers on the wheeled cart. He had extra ganache, buttercream frosting, all his piping bags and specialty icing tips, a tray of fragile sugar flowers with sufficient extras to cover breakage. The magnificent cake topper replicated the fabulous Gonzaga Reliquary in gold-tinted sugar paste, molded sugar gems, and a central plaque replicating the painting under crystal of the Madonna and Child exiting Bethlehem riding on St. Gigibertus' horse. The tooth was also replicated in tinted marzipan, contained in a column of clear melted sugar. The girls – such was his degree of concentration that he did not even notice the combined party who brought in the first layer, the massive one with the dowel supports already set into it. They unpacked the box and slid the bottom layer onto the foundation tray, already mounted on the cart. The other layers would be carefully maneuvered onto that initial layer; he would trim it out and set the sugar-jeweled topper onto it. Araceli had already taken pictures of the finished topper and uploaded it to the Café's Facebook page. Richard had been astounded to discover that the Café possessed such a thing. Araceli had looked at him as if he were dimwitted. (*"Seriously, Chef ... Jess, Doc and Miss Letty authorized this simply ages ago. Where have you been?" "Blissfully unaware!" he had riposted. In any case, his cake genius had been recorded for the ages, and barring any accident ... well, these things would happen.*)

He would trust Araceli and the other women in the kitchen brigade to wheel the completely assembled and trimmed cake all the way out through the kitchen and down the ramp from the porch to the place of honor set aside for it. The temporary kitchen brigade bustled in, arraying the boxes with the other layers on the old table, and he set to work, losing himself to absolute concentration, stacking and securing the upper layers, and covering the inevitable joins and cracks with ganache, carefully smoothed to match, and then adorned with swirls and galloons of buttercream. Then the careful insertion of sugar flowers and leaves ... he managed this without breaking very many of them, delicate things tinted in the various colors of native Texas wildflowers. All was ready for the crowning glory of the topper. Richard stepped back for a breath, wishing for steady hands and absolute concentration ... *Oh, confound it – what was the fuss now? It sounded like a woman crying.* He so didn't need this, not on a wedding day. This was not a good omen, especially if it were the bride.

"What's going on? Who's that crying!" Richard went to the door into the main kitchen and demanded of the nearest girl, the one arrayed in magenta-colored braids and a totally unattractive eyebrow piercing who cried in answer,

"I don't know, Chef! Really, I don't!" and fled before he could request enlightenment. He regretted unleashing the trademark scowl. But Araceli bustled in; now in a formal long gown, but her hair and makeup still in their natural and decidedly casual state, barefoot and carrying a pair of strappy little sandals in pastel hues to match her dress.

"It's Mindy," she replied, in somewhat of an unaccustomed fluster; definitely unaccustomed for Araceli, who had been rendered emotionally bomb-proof after two decades of front-house service in the Café. "She's been getting all heck from Tio Jaime. It seems that ..."

"I can't deal with this," Richard replied, through teeth griding so intensely that he might have to make an appointment with a dentist in Karnesville. He had to install the cake topper and oversee the delicate business of moving the whole edifice out to the back yard of the Rancho. Meanwhile, the deep niggling worry about Kate continued gnawing at his nerves.

"You might have to," Araceli replied, crisply. "You're also the best man; here to support the groom. Take a deep breath. Mindy needs ... "

"Six inches of good Canadian (redacted)" Richard suggested with a snarl, "Maybe eight, if her good Xavie has indeed been generously blessed by nature in that manner!"

"Really, Chef, you don't need to be so crude!" Araceli snapped. "You <u>have</u> to do duty as best man! Seriously!"

"Oh, Chr..." Richard exclaimed, and intercepted Araceli's scowl. He was as near as dammit going to take the Lord's name in vain, something to which Araceli particularly and frequently objected. "...Christmas! What do I need to do – and be specific, my attention needs to be focused on one ... damned thing at a time."

Araceli took a deep breath and then another. "I think you need to fetch Mr. Penn for an emergency family conference in the parlor with Tio Jaimie. Mr. Penn will be in his trailer, getting ready for his and Mindy's big day. The final assembly of the cake can wait on that for at least a few minutes. The problem is that Tio Jaimie suddenly found out about what Mindy is about to do for her honeymoon. She's going to nuke her career as an academic with tenure and follow her heart and her heart's love ... to work on one of his stupid and fruitless treasure quests! He thought that she was just going to use her sabbatical for this. Now he has found out that she's resigned from the university!"

"Oh, Christmas!" Richard exclaimed. Araceli nodded, in deep understanding.

"They can't see each other on the wedding day. Until the ceremony. It's one of those traditional customs, you know. Not until the bride comes down the aisle, but Tio Jaimie demands a straight answer from both of them, or he won't escort her down the aisle and the Bishop is due at any moment to perform the wedding, and dedicate the chapel, and ..." Araceli sighed in exasperation. "What shall we do, Ricardo? I'm all out of ideas, myself. Mindy is in her wedding dress."

"Well," and Richard thought fast. "They don't <u>have</u> to look at each other, do they? Mindy can stay in the parlor, and her beloved Xavie can be in the hallway, just outside and out of sight while your Tio Jaimie gets his concerns off his chest. Honestly," and Richard regarded Araceli with honest appeal. "This will not cancel the party entirely, if all goes ill?"

Araceli heaved a deep sigh. "I hope not, Chef. Tio Jaimie is horrified, as this is the first that he has heard of it. Has always taken such pride in Mindy's career; she was a Gonzalez and proud Tejano and went on to advanced education and had such a respectable position in a high-class university ... as things go around here," she added hastily. "I know, nothing like those snotty Ivy league dumps. But please – go get Mr. Penn."

Richard looked at his handiwork; yes, all but finished, only the ornate sugar-jeweled topper to be applied. "I'll back with Mr. Penn in a tick, even if I have to drag him by his bow-tie," he replied. Araceli heaved another sigh.

"He won't be wearing a tie," she explained with an air of exaggerated patience that nearly sent Richard spare. "He's wearing a guayabera for the ceremony ... you know that sort of fancy short-sleeved shirt. It's not all that formal an affair."

"I wish that someone had said something to me!" Richard exclaimed, having spent a pittance at Sylvester Gonzalez' favored second-hand outlet in San Antonio for a vintage white-tie ensemble, complete down to the gold shirt-studs, which fitted him to a tee without even the necessity of being altered to his measurements. He had expected to look like James Bond *(the suave and gallant Sean Connery iteration)* in the outfit.

"We did," Araceli replied, indulgently. "But you were so looking forward to being best man and I think you were planning to wear it when you and Katie tie the knot? You didn't pay any attention at all when I told you about Mindy and Mr. Penn and how it would be an informal wedding. You were busy making sugar flowers for the cake."

"Well, that explains it," Richard snarled. "My mind was on higher things than your cousin's academic career in a backwater public uni. All right – I'll go fetch Mr. Penn. In the meantime, think of what you and I ought to be saying to your uncle. And I am still planning on marrying Kate, once I have the chance to explain myself, and she gets over whatever she thought upon finding out that I am applying for full citizenship! What is it with you Gonzalez women anyway? Did someone feed you all a crazy salad with your baby food?"

He barely heard Araceli's reply, as he took off his chef's apron, ditched the towel tucked into the waistband, and cast a regretful look back at the towering and ornamental cake as he stalked out into the main kitchen. *Was this project all for naught, after all? Was this an even bigger and more extensive potential disaster than most every catered event at the Walcotts'? It certainly seemed as if it had that potential.*

"... she thought that you were ..." the rest was lost behind him as he stormed out through the kitchen and across the back veranda of the Rancho HQ house, even as he took a moment to consider Katie and her prolonged ... whatever it was. His lovely and even-tempered Kate was on the outs with him for a stupid reason and wouldn't even answer his text messages and phone calls.

All seemed in order for a country wedding, as he crossed through the venue; the tables, the pavilion, even a temporary floor laid down for dancing, and past a large burly middle-aged chap in clerical black and white, extracting himself by easy stages from behind the wheel of a somber-colored Mercedes sedan.

"God bless the day," that gentleman remarked as Richard passed nearby. He sounded Irish, although the brogue had been softened and tenderized as it was by long residence in Texas. "I am expected, d'y'see. For the blessing of a marriage of this house and consecration of the chapel? I am arrived at the right locality on the correct day?"

"You are," Richard answered, much harried. "Although there is trouble in the wind, I am afraid. Richard Astor-Hall. Caterer and best man for the groom. It seems that the bride and groom have plans which come as a surprise to the bride's guardian and host for this magnificent affair. I have been sent to bring the groom to the family parlor."

"Say no more, indade," the clerical gentleman replied, with a commiserating look. "And if I had a free drink for any contretemps that I have arrived in the middle of, I'd be drowned in a vat of good whiskey. Tommy Mulvaney is my name, Bishop for Karnes County is my station. I'll show myself in, Mr. Hall, as I am expected. I thank you for the warning of trouble. Forewarned is forearmed, as the old saying goes."

The good bishop briskly trotted up the back stairs to the main house, and Richard turned his mind to his errand – that of fetching the blushing bridegroom to a sudden conference. He knocked politely on the door to Gunnison-Penn's aging and travel-battered RV, and upon hearing a response from within, opened the side door and stepped up the rickety metal stairs to the mobile abode.

"Xavier, they need you in the parlor, *tout suite* – your host for this magnificent affaire has just found out about your plans for a peripatetic honeymoon and your darling bride's plans to scarper from her university position..."

"But ... but ... I thought it was all settled!" a shirtless and bare-chested Xavier Gunnison-Penn emerged from a narrow doorway farther down the interior of the cramped and rather grubby-looking RV which Richard assumed housed the WC and associated conveniences, as the former wiped off the last line of shaving cream from his cheek. The usually rather ratty-looking beard was neatly trimmed and shaped for the occasion. Richard was impressed. The most famous unsuccessful treasure-hunter in the western world looked relatively handsome; strong resemblance to a somewhat thinner Colonel Sanders of the chain fried-chicken franchise notwithstanding.

"Apparently not," Richard answered. The eccentric treasure hunter was comprehensively not one of his favorite people in Luna City, but he wanted very much for the wedding to continue as planned. Or else Araceli would be ripping strips off his hide for the foreseeable future, as this concerned her academic and otherwise unmarriageable Cousin Mindy. "And the Bishop is here, so make yourself decent."

"Oh, right," the prospective bridegroom shrugged on a neatly ironed and starched short-sleeved shirt, of the open-necked kind with the elaborate pattern of tucks and stitching down the front and on the sleeves, a style locally popular for a certain kind of casual yet official event. "Thanks, Astor-Hall. How do I look?" he added as he fastened the final button.

"Ready for anything," Richard answered. "Your lady awaits … in the parlor, but you may stand just outside of it, so that you need not actually break pre-wedding protocol."

"It was all sorted, I thought," Gunnison-Penn fussed, as he and Richard left the RV and headed across the yard to the house. "Mindy assured me that it was understood! She was owed a sabbatical or two from the university before her retirement. I thought that had been explained to her grandfather!"

"Obviously, not in words that he comprehends, or perhaps it has not sunk entirely in," Richard replied, though tight lips. Gunnison-Penn continued as if he had not heard a word, as Richard led him through the crowded kitchen and into the dark interior corridor beyond. Richard did not know the Rancho HQ house any farther than that. Fortunately, there were the sounds of voices to guide him: female sobbing, an irate male voice from behind the farthest door, and both Abuelita Adeliza and Araceli beckoning him urgently from the end of that hallway.

"Besides that," Gunnison-Penn yammered at his elbow, "I have definite information as to the possible whereabouts of a great fortune in precious jewels and coin stolen from a Mughal treasure fleet … a treasure of importance to India and to the British Isles, and a solution to a mystery four centuries old!"

"India and the Isles, you say?" That was the interested voice of Bishop Mulvaney himself, now looming up in the doorway at the end of the corridor. "A pirate treasure! God save the day! Among my kin back in Kildare they say that the founder of our own family fortune was a pirate! Long Tom Mulvaney, they called him. There is a long ballad-lament about his hanging in Derry in 1725, for he was a handsome man, and beloved of the ladies. It wasn't that he was that tall, y'see; the 'long' referred to … another physical endowment. Look you – no need to come within. Your bride is there …"

It was completely admirable, thought Richard, that the Bishop kept his bland countenance throughout the following exchange. *Must have been something about those cold showers, vigils in the wee hours, and the discipline of regular ritual.* He and Gunnison-Penn stood in the hallway together, a little removed from Abuelita Adeliza hovering like a censorious Hispanic Ghost of Weddings Future. Bishop Mulvaney stood in the doorway, and Araceli and Mindy stood within the parlor, just in reach. A small pale hand appeared around the doorjamb. Although Richard noted – not all that small and pale, but rather capable and work-roughened from field work of an archeological nature.

"Xavie?" Dr. Mindy quavered. "Are you there? Abuelo doesn't understand about the pirate treasure project. He thinks that I am throwing my whole career away. He doesn't understand."

"No, my darling sweetness. You are just moving on," Xavier Gunnison-Penn took that hand, from the other side of the doorway, as he stood resolute with his back to the parlor. "And you haven't told him about the other matter? You are moving towards better and higher, more meaningful things! The thrill of the search and the finding! Wasn't it glorious, finding the portions of the Gonzaga Reliquary? The legendary and historical treasure of your family?"

"We wouldn't have found it, without your knowledge and determination!" Dr. Mindy replied, fervently and addressed her remarks to the unseen authority within the parlor. "Abuelo, it's not what you think! I'm ready to do the work that I want to do! To work with Xavie! Please, Abuelo, please understand. I'm not crashing my career; I'd be doing the work that I want to do, alongside my husband. I'm done with the university! I want to live in the outside world now! I do have a pension plan with medical coverage and all! Comprehensive medical coverage, which is something I will need, soon enough! I'm just cashing in the last couple of sabbaticals that I never used! Please, Abuelo — I have thought his all out, and I will do it! Darling Abuelo, I will be all right and provided for..."

Bishop Mulvaney backed her up with the assurance, "And you would have, indade! Finding that precious reliquary was a marvel of persistence and a triumph of research. It's a gift you have, the both of you. But what was this that you claimed, regarding a pirate treasure cache?"

"So you say," replied Don Jaimie, from within the parlor — a sorely-tried and perplexed man from the sound of it, Richard wished that he could ask for enlightenment from Araceli, but she was within the parlor, and remaining silent. A wise decision on her part, he thought, considering the ongoing drama.

"Abuelo, listen!" Mindy pleaded. "Xavie has a clue to the whereabouts of a great treasure of India, a treasure stolen by pirates almost four hundred years ago and never found. Listen ... he can explain it so better than I can."

Another great treasure, long sought after, Richard thought with an interior sigh. Out loud, he murmured to Gunnison-Penn, as they stood outside in the dark hallway.

"That would be your clue. Make it good and convincing – put every bit of belief and passion that you have into what you have next to say. Your wedding cake depends upon it."

"My wedding cake?" Gunnison-Penn sent a wild-eyed look sideways to Richard. "What has that to do with it all, I ask you?"

"Everything to me!" Richard snarled in response, while nudging Gunnison-Penn emphatically with his elbow. "Spill all about your so-called treasure of great importance to India: what it is, where it might be, and why you have special reason to think that you are at least warm on the track to finding it!"

"Right, then," The famed *(or notorious, depending on how one regarded him)* Canadian treasure hunter cleared his throat, and addressed his seen and unseen audience; his beloved, her maid of honor, her grandfather, great-aunt, best man, and Bishop Mulvaney in the manner of one accustomed to larger audiences. "I have information relayed to me through private means which I am not at liberty at present to reveal, of the possible location of a master's portion of a great treasure, worth two hundred million dollars in modern currency, at the time it was looted in 1695. A pirate fleet under the command of one Henry Every – or Avery, no one is entirely certain – attacked and robbed at least eleven ships, one of whom carried enormous treasure in the Indian Ocean. That ship was part of a rich fleet returning to India from participating in the Haj ... the ritual pilgrimage to Mecca. Those ships were crammed full of gold and silver coin, precious gems, wealthy voyagers, including – according to legend a granddaughter or grandniece of the Mughal emperor Aurangzeb. There is a well-founded belief that Henry Every considered that one woman the greatest prize of all. It was a very rich haul, for a pirate expedition; possibly the richest on record and made wealthy men of every individual pirate who took part. Wealthy for a short time at least, and Henry Every very, very rich, since he was entitled under terms of the prior piratical agreement to a double share in raiding ships in the Indian Ocean. This attack on the Mughal fleet excited considerable controversy, not the least because it put the British Crown at odds with the Mughal Empire at a time when the East India Company was expanding operations in the sub-continent, and because of the extreme brutality with which the pirates treated the passengers on the main vessel. There was ..." Here, Gunnison-Penn looked embarrassed, and his voice sank to a mumble. "... a veritable orgy of rape, torture, and destruction. But Captain Every's fleet got clean away with their loot. They took refuge first at an African port on an island near to Madagascar, where they divided the spoils. Many of the foreign element – the French, Spanish and Danish sailors in Every's fleet decided to take their winnings and call it a day. As for Captain Every, he may have realized that he and his crew were marked men, having made enemies of the Mughal emperor, the English Crown, and the East India Company alike. He took his single fast ship, the *Fancy*, around the Horn of Africa and made for Nassau in the Bahamas. Probably wise of him to do so, for he was now branded as an outlaw, an enemy of the whole human race, with a substantial price on his head for capture... a price doubled by the East India Company. I do not think that all his rich takings could have availed him much," Gunnison-Penn added honestly. "Much of it was in peculiar foreign coinage which would excite comment, no matter where they tried to spend it. Every changed his name to Brightman, or Bridgeman, and made the pretense of being an unlicensed slave-trader with a cargo to sell. He bribed the English governor of the Bahamas with his ship, and a quantity of ivory elephant tusks, gunpowder, firearms, and usable anchors. The English and the French were at war at that time, and the French had just taken Exuma. The Governor was in a perilous position, needing the support of the *Fancy*'s crew as a garrison against French invasion, almost as much as he needed the money which Brightman or Bridgeman offered him. It is thought," and Gunnison-Penn cleared his throat, "That the Governor of Nassau allied with the bold pirate commander. In any case, when he was forced by his superiors in England to issue warrants for arrest of the Fancy's captain and her crew, it is said that he tipped the word to them, in advance. Only twenty or so of them were captured, but for all intents and purposes, Captain Every vanished from the face of the earth. Oh, there were stories; that he went to Ireland, returned to England and died there in either prosperity or misery under another name. My new information suggests that he went to New England and settled in Portsmouth, Rhode Island, under the assumed identity of Captain Nicholas Bridge – a retired merchant and ship-owner of moderate station and irreproachable respectability."

Richard listened to all this, much diverted in spite of his overwhelming concern with the wedding cake. It all seemed very *Boys Own Paper*, or at least an old-fashioned black and white movie adventure starring Errol Flynn with a score by Erich Wolfgang Korngold.

"And what basis have you for that theory, indade?" Bishop Mulvaney rumbled. "I know of the pirate Henry Every and his exploits, being interested because of our own family connection to Long Tom Mulvaney. There were books and books written about them all – which I read as a boy, being fascinated by the subject, y'see."

"In specific details, I am constrained by a Non-Disclosure Agreement, which I signed with my informant, a direct descendant of Captain Bridge, and owner of the townhouse in Portsmouth, which was built by Captain Bridge, and wherein it is surmised that the remainder of the Mughal treasure is hidden." Gunnison-Penn sighed. "I violate the terms of that agreement with extreme reluctance and hold you all to extreme secrecy."

"But what is it, about your Captain Bridge who settled in Portsmouth in something seventeen-whatever." Richard administered a verbal nudge. "What leads you to think that he might be the piratical Henry Every?"

"Not so much for unexplained wealth," Gunnison-Penn replied, all in earnest. "Although he was of the approximate age that Henry Every would have been, when he established his household in Portsmouth, fifteen years after vanishing from Nassau. This Captain Bridge claimed to be a retired officer of the Royal Navy and having dallied a bit in trade with China, India, and Africa. This afforded him leisure to build a fine mansion and invest in a warehouse and various shipping enterprises in Portsmouth, and to be elected as selectman by his neighbors. He was a popular, and well-respected man, from all accounts."

"And no one recognized him as the infamous pirate Henry Every?" Richard asked, somewhat skeptically. "Surely he was known to a great many people who would recognize him and shop him to the Crown for a reward?"

"It is possible that he managed to substantially change his appearance," Gunnison-Penn replied. "Although aging fifteen years might have done the trick with all but those who had known him very well. It was a hard life in that century, even for a ship-captain. Henry Every was said to possess great powers of charm and persuasion; that quality alone might have bought him influential friends in New England."

"But how might one be certain that this Nicholas Bridge was actually Henry Every, at this late date?" Inquired Bishop

Mulvaney, in his soft Irish burr. "A deathbed confession, concealed at the time?"

"Not as such, but several things suggest the correlation," Gunnison-Penn fished out his cellphone from his pants pocket with some difficulty, as the cellphone was large, the pocket small and the pants rather tight. "A number of finds; quantities of very old coins, discovered in and around Portsmouth; ancient silver coins with Islamic lettering, from India and various other localities in the Middle East. Curious finds, one would think – but in the aggregate, I believe this to be significant. The most significant indicator is the appearance and character of Mrs. Bridge. She was an elegant lady, considerably younger than her husband. There was a pair of portraits painted of them both by the itinerant artist Robert Feke, which have been preserved as family heirlooms," Gunnison-Penn thumbed through the pictures on his cellphone. "This is the Captain Bridge portrait."

Richard looked down at the picture on the phone; a plump and late-middle-aged party with a hooked nose and an enormous and elaborately-curled wig. There was an equally elaborate lace cravat tied under the double chin of the subject, detailed with almost more care than the detail which the features were delineated. All but the eyes. The eyes were alert, shrewd, calculating in how they regarded the portraitist.

"No telling if that is any sort of likeness," Richard remarked, as he passed the phone to Bishop Mulvaney, who passed it within the parlor, from which it returned some moments later by the same route. "I don't suppose that there was a wanted poster with a true and accurate portrayal of the piratical Captain Every for comparison ... no?"

"It was an age considerably before reliable images of the criminal were distributed by law enforcement," Gunnison-Penn admitted. "It would seem that apprehension of Henry Every as a suspected pirate would have depended on someone in Portsmouth authoritatively and with personal knowledge identifying Captain Bridge as the felon in question. It appears that no one ever did, throughout his long career as a respected leading citizen of Portsmouth."

"Besides the coincidental discovery of silver coins of a medieval Islamic derivation in a Colonial American locality, what other evidence is there for your Captain Bridge having been Henry Every, the notorious pirate captain?" That was the bishop, obviously convinced, but aware of the necessity for further and convincing evidence.

"This!" Gunnison-Penn thumbed the gallery of images on his cellphone to another. "See ... this is Mrs. Bridge! Supposedly painted from life. Do you not see?"

This image was clearly painted by the same artist, with the same loving attention to the details of lace and personal adornments; the lady, a dark-eyed and dark-haired charmer with the pale ivory complexion favored in that century looked out over a rose held in indolent fingers, a faint half-smile on her lips, lips which nearly matched the delicate pink of the rose.

"I am trying, but I do not see the significance of Mrs. Bridge's appearance," Bishop Mulvaney ventured at last. "A verra attractive woman, of any age including this – a lovely black Irish colleen, or perhaps she is Spanish, of the old noble blood. Your Captain Bridge married advantageously, regardless." It sounded as if the bishop was puzzled.

So was Richard, who nonetheless was moved to poetry. "'*She walks in beauty like the night, of cloudless climes and starry skies. And all that's best of dark and bright, meet in her aspect and her eyes.*' Neither can I," Richard added with a sigh. "Even allowing for the conventions of portraiture three centuries ago."

"She is the woman who was Henry Avery's greatest prize, which he claimed to have plundered from the Mughal treasure ship!" Gunnison-Penn exclaimed in exasperation. "Can't you picture her as a high-caste woman of India, the Emperor Aurangzeb's granddaughter or grandniece?"

"She could be," Richard replied, after a moment of startled thought, mentally reclothing the woman of the portrait in a diaphanous embroidered sari, notable head necklaces and elaborate earrings and realizing that such would be a very natural fit. "I could indeed picture Mrs. Bridge as the star in one of those Bollywood song and dance extravaganzas! I suppose that at this late date, there is no way of making certain through a registry of marriages. I imagine that they <u>did</u> regularize the connection, but under what name and in which parish or country is indeed a conundrum. There isn't, is there?"

"No, alas," Gunnison-Penn truly sounded disappointed. "All there is among my informant's information is a family legend that Mrs. Bridge was of noble blood, or even royalty in some degree or other. But that is not the single most important element in our search. The major portion of Henry Every's share of coin and gems was never recovered. It was a considerable sum! My informant is convinced that it was hidden somewhere about the family townhouse in Portsmouth, a grand and historic but rather decayed mansion. Extensive termite damage and wood-rot to the timber foundations, y'see. My informant is convinced that the remainder of that treasure is hidden somewhere within it. He has asked for my expert help in searching and retrieving that cache, so that he might rebuild it in a fitting manner. And that was the intention of our honeymoon..." Gunnison-Penn added, in a tone of voice which indicated fading hope. Within the room, Mindy added, in a rather desperate-sounding voice.

"It's true, Abuelo. I did the dive into the historical archives. There is a treasure for sure, at least if Captain Bridge is indeed Henry Every. I'm convinced that he was, just by the evidence..." Within the room, Don Jaimie retorted curtly in Spanish, and Mindy began to sob; Richard's heart sank. No, this was not going all that well.

"Being identifiable as loot from the Mughal treasure ship," Bishop Mulvaney cleared his throat gently, "Would have excited comment – and pointed comment, as he was a wanted man, even if a very rich one. I see, then. As a clever man, a long-sighted man, and one w' a well-developed sense of self-preservation would have been extremely circumspect in his life. A gem here or there, disposed to a trusty purchaser, with a verra convincing story of how he came to be in possession. That was all that he could spend. Enough to make a good living, but not so much as to attract unwelcome attention. Indade, I begin to see the sense of his living a quiet life, with his lovely Shakespearean dark lady, in an out-of-the-way part of the world, as it was then."

"Exactly!" Gunnison-Penn beamed, apparently relieved at how quickly the message had gone across to at least one influential listener. Richard could only hope that it had made a positive impression on Don Jaimie. Otherwise, the wedding was off, and there went all the work that he had put into the cake, the catering of this party and heartbreak for Mindy. More importantly, the wrath of Araceli.

The voice of God emerged from the parlor, and Richard's heart sank all the way down to his sensible trainers. "I cannot approve of this," Don Jaimie rumbled, to the accompanying thunder of shrill protest from the female element. "You will be hazarding your professional future! The wedding should not go forward, Miranda! I forbid it!"

"But you can't forbit it, Abuelo!" Mindy cried in anguish. "We must be married, today! Immediately – or as soon as possible!"

"Why is that?" Don Jaimie sounded utterly implacable, and Richard's heart sank. No, this was a disaster in the making; all his hard work would go for naught, as well as the hard work of the Pryor family. It would have been hard labor, turning the crank of that massive, improvised grill device, which flipped the whole spatchcocked beef roast back and forth over the massive fire which had barbequed it to a fair turn over the last two days.

"Because, Abuelo – I'm pregnant!" wailed the desperate and near-to-heartbroken Dr. Mindy. "Xavie and I are having a baby! We <u>have</u> to get married!"

And that, as anyone agreed, comprehensively resolved the whole situation, right then and there.

* * *

Very late that evening – by the clock it might have actually the next morning – Richard sorted out the last of his cake-decorating tools, stands and platform bases and carried them out to the Pryor's van. All were neatly scoured clean by the kitchen crew under the gimlet eye of Abuelita Adeliza.

He confessed to Araceli, "That was certainly the winning move, I must say; your cousin Mindy pleading her belly! Game, set and match. Are they really going to have a baby, or was it just a ruse?"

"No, Mindy <u>is</u> pregnant; almost three months along. Since she is over forty, she is going to be monitored very carefully, throughout." Araceli replied. "I've known for a month or so. They already have the schedule worked out, all the way along."

"Penn looked ridiculously pleased about the whole matter, I thought," Richard commented, as they paused on the back verandah and looked over the scene of the late revels, lit by strings of fairy lights strung between the trees, and the dying glow from the barbeque pit. Vacant tables had already been cleared of the debris of the grand feast, although a handful of epic holdouts still lounged about under the trees, with the last of their drinks in a companionable fashion. The bishop himself was among them, genial and nursing a small whiskey and talking to Andy Pryor, Don Jaimie and the artistic reformed and previously illiterate lowlife, Reuben Sifuentes.

Mellow golden candlelight shown through the rose window of the small chapel, now duly consecrated and blessed by performance of the marriage sacrament. Through the open double doors, Richard could see the mural which Reuben had painted across the altar end, of the Holy Family on their Journey to Egypt with local flavor. He earnestly hoped that Reuben was about to take up a profitable new career, that of providing artistic embellishment to religious establishments throughout the diocese, rather than the low-grade and spectacularly unsuccessful criminality which had heretofore formed the lives of Reuben and his partner in crime. Anyway, such a career ought to be more remunerative than petty and impulsive criminality.

From the overheard conversation as Richard and Araceli drifted past, it sounded as if Bishop Mulvaney was pitching new artistic opportunities, or at least, offering welcome career advice to Reuben. Richard devoutly hoped that such would stick, as the formidable and exacting teacher, Miss Letty McAllister had spent at least eight months of effort in bringing Reuban's formerly nonexistent reading abilities up to the fourth or fifth form level. Perhaps Miss Letty and the Bishop between them would haul Reuben Sifuentes over the threshold of respectability and into a rewarding career. Maybe now, Reuben could marry a fine and upstanding girl from the ranks of the many-branched Gonzalez/Gonzales clan, one which would authoritatively steer his fragile ethical bark away from the shores of alcohol-fueled temptation.

But then, it was really none of his business. Gunnison-Penn's down-at-heels RV had already departed, leaving a curiously open space at the back of the Rancho. Richard calculated, since they had already departed in a flurry of thrown rice, confetti, and old shoes some hours ago, that they must be almost to San Antonio now. Unless they had pulled into a handy lay-by for a bit of a honeymoon…

"All right," he said." Fine. Done and dusted. See you in the morrow."

"Of course," Araceli replied, as sturdily as Richard knew that she must. "And then you can tell me what's going on with Katie."

The Trouble in Paradise

As was Richard's wont in time of absolute crisis, he unburdened himself to Araceli, early the next morning.

"Did you hear from Kate at all, yesterday?" He demanded as soon as his chief waitress and manager walked in the back door to the Café on Wednesday morning, resplendent in an old-style pastel pink shirtwaist dress with a small tidy apron tied at her waist, her thick-soled athletic shoes tied with matching pink shoelaces.

"No, not at all," Araceli replied, unconcerned. "She's likely busy, just as we were with Mindy's wedding. There was a huge fire at one of the oilfield locations last night. Could have been arson, and on the other side of the county, three good old boys got into a mad punch-up at a country music concert and the resulting all-hands brawl did thousands of dollars' worth of damage to the sound system and the bands' instruments. There may have been a celebrity involved. Massive quantities of alcohol were, undoubtedly. Katie will have her hands full, getting the straight story on both incidents. News-wise, that's the most exciting time they've had in a long time. Add in a three-car pile-up on the 35, and that would be the trifecta." She eyed Richard with a slightly concerned expression on her face. "Why so worried, Ricardo?"

"She hasn't yet answered any of my text messages," Richard confessed, finally glad to be able to unburden himself. "Although she has viewed them. I tried to call directly – and her phone just went to voicemail. I left messages, but she hasn't returned them. It came to me the night after that when we finished supper on Monday, and I was putting our dessert together ... she might have seen the letter from the Immigration and Naturalization Service. I fact, I'm almost certain she did. It was on the top of the pile on the dresser unit."

"Oh, damn," Araceli went slightly paler with alarm and concern. "That must have been it ... you didn't happen to mention that you were applying for citizenship?"

"No, it was to be a surprise," Richard stammered. "I decided on it, at the moment I decided that I should ask Kate to marry me. Jess had warned me about Kate's brother Matt having a run-in with a bar wench who only wanted him for his citizenship, so I thought it best not bring it up. Not tangle the two lines. <u>Have</u> you heard anything more from Kate since she sent you all pictures of the ring and everything?"

"I haven't," Araceli answered, slowly, as if she was thinking. "And I kind of thought that I would, you know. We've been best friends forever since ... well, forever. She seemed so happy, absolutely thrilled to the max – that you had finally asked, and that the supper was so lovely, and how beautiful your little dining area looked. Like a bower of flowers, she said. She couldn't wait to tell all of us and show us the pictures. Look, I'll message her myself, later on this morning. I'm wondering if Jess has heard from her as well. Jess is home now, but pretty well taken up with the babies, so at the best of times, she's about sixty percent conscious, but I'll message her, too."

"Thanks, Araceli," Richard replied, unexpectedly buoyed in his mood for having shared his concern with his best gal pal in Luna City, after the stress of the day before at Rincon de los Robles. There had been no time to worry any more about this matter the day before, and very little space to worry about it now, for it was well past time to prep for the breakfast rush: coffee to set to brew, trays of cinnamon rolls and orange pecan rolls to slide into the oven, the grill to prep. Bree appeared through the back door, yawning slightly, to set about prepping the fruit sides and the garnishes for the various plates. She was alone this morning, as Robbie had classes on Mondays, Wednesdays, and Fridays. But she was followed through the back door by Luc, sporting his usual luxuriant Mohawk crest of hair, rainbow-hued as was now the high fashion among what passed the scattering denizens espousing punk culture in Karnes County. Richard eyed him closely. It looked as if Luc had gotten another tattoo. Richard made a mental note to speak to his junior cook about that. Tats were a money sink, and the new one on his neck was just a bad notion overall, when it came to the usual customers at the Café.

All the staff as one hunkered down to deal with the breakfast rush at the Café; a constant relay of hot-from-the-oven fresh-baked cinnamon and pecan-orange rolls, simple sausage and scrambled eggs, fruit compote for the observantly healthy, and the full lavish-with-protein English breakfast for that solid workman element who had a day of hard physical labor to go to, after hoovering up a substantial plate of fried eggs, Canadian bacon, sausage, beans, fried tomatoes and mushrooms, and toast with a side of marmalade. In the interests of continued good health among the most dedicated early morning Café patrons, Richard also included a small glass of orange juice as a lagniappe. Sometimes the lonely glass of orange juice was even consumed, mostly as a last-minute gesture before Roman the builder's crewmen left a lavish tip and lumbered away from the table to pay the tab and dedicate their day to a long haul of pouring concrete, framing up a building, installing drywall, setting tile or nailing down tarpaper and roof tiles. Introducing the sheer gustatory joy of a full English to a far outpost of civilization counted as one of his culinary victories in a new world.

Richard liked the customers in the building trade. They ate like heroes, tipped lavishly, returned often, and lent the early morning hours a kind of rough *joie de vivre.* The more delicately middle-class patrons drifting over from the Cattleman for early breakfast relished this, as they were experiencing a genuine and authentic small-town working-class culture most usually observed in their own world on TV shows.

When the breakfast rush had quieted to the usual desultory mid-morning pause, Araceli finished overseeing setting up the tables for luncheon service and took out her cellphone out to the back, where Richard's raised beds full of herb plants had the full benefit of morning sun, and shelter from the hottest of the afternoon. She returned, scowling; always a dangerous sign.

"Did you get ahold of Kate?" Richard couldn't restrain himself from sounding anxious. "What did she say?"

"She didn't answer, either text or voice message," Araceli herself now sounded worried. "It's not like her. She usually calls back in ten or fifteen minutes or so, unless she's on the road. I called the Beacon office, just to make certain she hasn't been in an accident or something and talked to Rita, the receptionist. Rita says that Kate is fine, she's at work, hyper-busy as usual, didn't seem to be sick or anything. Not as chatty as normal, Rita said. She thought it was because Kate was really very busy. She did ask about how Kate's dinner date went, and Kate just said *'fine'* and left it at that. Which Rita thought was odd, because she usually gives Rita a full account of her Monday suppers with you. Rita likes to cook, too ... but this time she thought it was just because Kate was dashing out the door to cover the oilfield fire aftermath. I honestly don't know what's going on, Ricardo," Araceli conceded, wearily. "Maybe Jess has an idea. She'll be here in a bit. Her grandmother is going to mind the girls and Little Joe for a couple of hours."

"I certainly hope someone has an idea of what's going on," Richard confessed. "I'm out of all ideas. If Kate is angry with me ... I don't know how to go about telling her she has got the wrong notion, if she won't even answer her phone. And why she isn't talking to you, either ... I haven't the foggiest notion how that came about."

* * *

"Embarrassment," explained Jess Abernathy-Vaughn, immediately when that question was anxiously put to her by Araceli the next morning. Jess, in appearance still a little pudgy from a pregnancy with twins, still looked fit and fresh, although there were certain shadows under her eyes which suggested sleepless nights. Araceli brought out the usual light luncheon, of fruit cup, and a glass of the Café's signature cold sweet tea. *(Richard had never been able to prevail against the abomination of pouring perfectly brewed tea over ice cubes ... although he had been able to gain a certain enthusiasm for his own concoction of it, which included mint and lemon verbena, gently crushed and added to the tea leaves, for a spritely and refreshing summer drink. The junior staff were already researching the means by which such could be dried and packaged commercially and added to the Café's brand of gourmet products.)* "And hurt, even if it wasn't your fault, Richard. Oh, thanks, 'Celi. Can I have a toasted ham and cheese panini to go with it? Need the protein, I'm merely a milk cow at present supporting two infants and a toddler."

Jess unshipped the files from her business briefcase, as Araceli bustled off to put in the additional order. Meanwhile, Jess finished spreading out the various files and eyed Rich with sympathy. "Congratulations, Rich … I know, it's a bit of a disaster at the moment. But Kate honestly loves you. I swear that she was thrilled no end that you got to the point of proposing, with such style and verve. She shared the moment with all of us – her friends. Pictures of your little patio, so beautifully decorated. The ring – everything. It was like a Hallmark movie moment."

"Embarrassment?" Richard stared at Jess in complete bafflement. "I don't understand; enlighten me."

"She was so happy," Jess explained patiently, as if to a slow child. "That she went and told simply everyone about the engagement. Then, I think she saw the envelope from Immigration, and assumed the very and most absolute worst. Now, I am absolutely certain that Katie is trying to sort out what to do about it all. Look, I'm an old hand at boyfriend-girlfriend romance dramas. I swear, that's all that I had to cope with, on active duty. I'm 100-percent certain that's why she isn't answering any calls or messages. I've tried getting ahold of her myself, and she's not responding to me either. Her job makes it easier to just duck us all and shove the matter of your proposal aside. Honestly, I don't know what you ought to do, Richard, except maybe wait for her to calm down and return your call ... or for one of us to explain that you weren't proposing just because you are processing an application for citizenship. I know absolutely you were going through the regular process, not trying to take any shortcuts through a hinky marital arrangement." Jess sighed. "And I can swear on the usual stack of Bibles that you are. I will do so once I have a chance to talk to her."

"Is there anything you can advise me to do?" Richard considered the present disaster, after a short and depressed silence, appalled that his otherwise level-headed, tantrum-free Kate should have been so uncharacteristically angry over this simple misunderstanding.

The family drama over Matt Heisel's gold-digging buy-me-drinkie girlfriend must have been simply epic to leave such a lasting scar on his younger sister.

"I confess ... I am almost afraid to do anything, at this point, for fear of making things worse. I had considered begging Chris for a ride to Karnesville and putting the matter straight with Kate's parents. But that might definitely make matters worse, and I can't risk that. I'm all out of ideas, Jess. I'm throwing myself on your collective female mercy."

"Better yet," Araceli suggested, as she appeared, silently on crepe-soled trainers, bearing Jess's ham and cheese panini on a small plate. "Appeal to Abuelita. If anyone can bring sense out of all this, Abuelita can."

"What a splendid notion!" Richard was instantly buoyed up with hope, out of the absolute depths of despair. "Abuelita – why did none of us think of her first? If anyone commands instant attention and obedience from the clan ..."

"Well, Kate is only half a Gonzalez," Araceli temporized. "Still, Abuelita has her ways. And Kate would absolutely have to listen to her. She's very fond of Abuelita."

"But that Kate is ignoring every one of her friends, at least temporarily," Jess warned. "Still, it's a better shot than me packing up Little Joe and the girls and driving Ricardo to Karnesville to plead his case with Kate's mom and dad."

"I'll talk to Abuelita tonight, after work," Araceli's mouth tightened into a thin, determined line, which usually meant that whatever mischief was building to a head, was about to come to a screeching stop. "Don't worry about it, Ricardo. She'll talk sense to Kate, make her see reason, before she does anything reckless."

"Reckless?!" said Richard, greatly alarmed. "Not something suicidal, I hope."

Araceli heaved a deep sigh. "No, nothing like that, Ricardo. You're a prince among men, although hardly to the level of Prince Harry, but neither of you is worth killing yourself over, and our Katie is too level-headed for that kind of idiocy anyway. No, I was thinking that if I know Katie, she would for certain return the ring and break your engagement. Honestly, I don't think her heart would be totally in going that far. She loves you and she's always adored Abuelita's heart-garnet ring. So that's something to hope for. She's hurt and embarrassed and simmering – not boiling-over angry."

"I agree. Right, then," Jess gathered up the contents of her briefcase, making it bulge even more, as she snapped the catches closed. "She's hurt and embarrassed and burying herself in work until she can think straight. I agree with Richard, in not making it all worse.   Make it so, 'Celi. I'll come over tomorrow for breakfast, as soon as I've nursed the girls. Little Joe is wanting a 'tcookie' in the worst way, and the only way I can shut him up about it is to give him one of yours. See you tomorrow, then?"

"Absolutely," Richard agreed with a somewhat relieved heart, just as the old-fashioned silver chime hung from the Café's front door jingled musically once again.

A fresh installment of customers, two of them, agreeably middle-aged, prosperous, and nicely kitted out in the sort of gear that well-off English tourists wear, when venturing to that rebellious former colony of America. Richard looked up and was gobsmacked.

"Mum ... Dad!" he exclaimed.

"Darling!" Exclaimed Mum, exuberantly rushing up to Richard, and flinging her arms about him – really, it was most uncharacteristically English of her. Not for dear old Mum the undemonstrative upper-class stiff-upper lip. *Must be all that French influence*, Richard thought, as he returned the embrace. And the prior influence of Gram, working-class, opinionated and fiercely proud of that, too. "I'm so happy to see you, at long last! You look so well! Is this your dear little restaurant! Everyone says that the menu is so absolutely scrumptious, and that you have done a marvelous job with it! Are you happy, darling? We so worried for you, early on, but we thought it best not to interfere... you didn't <u>want</u> us to interfere, did you, Richie? Your father said no, it was best that you find your own feet. You <u>have</u> found them, haven't you, dear?"

Mum looked up at him anxiety clouding her eyes, and the fresh fair countenance, the English rose look, hardly burnished by a suntan in all of her half-century of life, although her hair was gone to a faded blonde, intermixed with grey. Obviously, there was no decent hairdresser in Saint-Didier.

"No, Mum – I'm fine," Richard, initially stunned. He hadn't expected to see his parents for another couple of months, at least. "I'm at a crisis at present, though ..."

"And is this your Kate?" Mum smiled brilliantly at Araceli. "How marvelous to meet you at long last. Richie left us absolutely stunned when he announced that he was going to propose!"

"No, that's my cousin Kate," Araceli replied, sturdily. "I just work for Ri – for Chef. Pleased to meet you. Araceli Gonzales-Gonzalez. Excuse me, we're still working the breakfast rush. Can I show you to a table?"

"Of course, dear," Mum replied, with a charming laugh. "That would be marvelous! We were so done in by traveling all this way, we missed breakfast at the hotel. They're quite awfully strict about hours, even for room service. Dorothy Astor-Hall, but everyone calls me Dottie."

"Dottie by name and nature," Richard's father added, with a look of tried affection which took out any malice from his words. Araceli gestured them toward the small couples table, just out from the door into the kitchen, and handed them a pair of menus. "Alfred Astor-Hall. So pleased. You haven't introduced us to your other lady, Richard." There was a slight tone of reproof in his voice, and Richard sighed. Dad was so very much the Englishman, the *pukka sahib* of legend, tall, lanky, imperishably polite, and completely unshockable, a lean and angular face graced with a neatly trimmed mustache. No wonder he had gotten on so well with the wine-growing denizens of Saint Didier. He was the archetypal imperturbable upper-class Englishman of song, story, and movie, come to life.

"Jessica Vaughn," Jess replied, switching her briefcase to her other hand. Richard wondered briefly if she would render a proper military salute. Jess had that '*noticed by a worshipped senior officer*' expression on her face. "CPA. I do the financial management for the owners of the Café. Rich and I have worked together for almost five years."

"An accountant!" Alfred Astor-Hall's expression warmed and lightened, as Araceli vanished into the kitchen. "How very marvelous, and what an interesting coincidence! I started out as an accountant. Been in finance for more years in the City than I like to think! Moved on, now I make fine wines – so very much more relaxing."

"I've been guided by Mrs. Vaughn's towering efficiency and competent good sense in money matters for the last few years," Richard interjected.

"What a refreshing change," Alfred murmured, and Richard winced. Dad still had the gift of the verbal stiletto, even though he had been indulgent far, far beyond the tolerance of normal parents when it came to Richard's chosen career, and the inevitable, spectacular flame-out of the crash over the disastrous Carême opening. It came to him that his father had mostly been left to cope with the resulting financial disaster, after Carême. There was a hell of a lot about that disaster which Richard didn't remember with any accuracy at all. Through it all, Dad and Mum had been good sports, against every natural human impulse to write off their only son as a dead loss on the human calculation. Richard was grateful, grateful beyond all words for their continued indulgence. For that, he could overlook the occasional verbal jab from Dad.

"Rich, I'll see you tomorrow," Jess replied, and with a polite nod to the gathered small clan of Astor-Hall, she was gone with the silvery tinkle of the bell over the Café's front door.

"What a lovely woman," Mum commented, "I so like her!"

Alfred murmured, "Got a modicum of financial sense, then – pity you couldn't marry her, instead."

"She's happily married already, Dad," Richard snarled, finally provoked. "With three children, and a husband who looks like a tattooed human traffic bollard. The chief of police in this place! Did I mention his extensive gun collection? And that his absolutely fascistic devotion to law and order is legendary? I daresay I did not."

"You didn't, dear," Mum replied, soothingly. "But never mind about all that. We ... your father and I came for the professional tour of wineries in the Hill Country, officially as other wine-involved professionals, you see. A business expense. But our main reason is to see you and your lovely bride. She is lovely, I am certain, knowing of your ... umm, tastes. Don't clear your throat at me, Alf. We both know that Rich has a certain standard. Which is nice, considering the appearances of the resulting children. There is something to be said for breeding, you know. Attractive parents rarely birth unattractive children. This saves the poor little mites so many nasty schoolyard jibes over unfortunate physical features."

"Mum!" Richard exclaimed, exasperated. Yes, Mum was the most charming and possibly the silliest and least-tactful woman in the Home Counties and Saint-Didier combined. The theory that a male was programmed to be attracted to the same kind of personality-type as his mother had caused him many an episode of misgiving over some of his sexual choices. "There is a crisis on. I proposed to my lovely Kate, and she accepted, but for some reason she has become annoyed with me."

"I can't possibly imagine what might have brought that on," Alfred sank another mildly sharpened stiletto into Richard's quivering ego.

"It was because ..." And Richard drew in a deep breath, resolved to spill all, once and for all. "I am applying for American citizenship and Kate assumed that my reason for proposing was an ill-conceived tactic to jump the queue, as it were, by marrying a citizen."

"Oh, Richard, how could you?" Dottie exclaimed, her eyes already welling over. "How could you do such a thing?"

"It seemed most sensible, logical!" Richard protested. "I mean I have lived here for five years, worked my fingers to the bone at all hours, taught people to appreciate fine cuisine, trained up the next generation of cooks..."

"No, I didn't mean that!" And Dottie sniffled a bit and wiped her eyes. "How could you let her go on believing such a thing?"

"Because she won't answer my phone calls!" Richard exclaimed, finally goaded beyond all tact. "Or my messages! Or that of her friends – also my friends, those ladies whom I introduced just now, they are going to plead my case! It's a crisis, Mum! What am I supposed to do?"

"Breakfast," Alfred replied, calmly. He had been perusing the menu. "I think that breakfast would do us all a world of good. Cinnamon buns, one each, I think. Scrambled eggs. And coffee. I have been accustomed for the last few years to have coffee with breakfast. Café au lait if you please. And nothing of this chalk-artificial-muck for creamer..."

"Dad, we do straight cream, half-and-half for the slimmers!" Richard protested. "It's one of my inviolable principles, here at the Café!"

"Oh, good," Alfred waved in a vague manner. "Carry on, then. And come and sit with us if you can and your kitchen duty allows. We need to tell you how you stand, with your current economic situation."

"I can hardly bloody wait," Richard snarled, as he went into the kitchen.

Why was this happening to him, now at all the times possible in the world?

* * *

Fortunately, his parents were about the last of the breakfast rush, and it would be another quarter of an hour before he was needed in the kitchen to assist with luncheon. He brought a cup of coffee for himself and pulled up a third chair to the table.

"It's ... terrific to see you both again," Richard confessed, feeling suddenly quite awkward. "I just didn't think you would be here until late summer, at the very earliest."

"Not to worry, dear," Richard's mother poured herself a cup of tea from the small china teapot which Araceli had set on the table, along with a little matching jug of milk. "We had been planning this trip for so long. Your Aunt Moira told us what a charming little town which you had found yourself in, and how everyone had made her and her pals in the motorcycle enthusiasts feel so welcome!"

"Er ... yes," Richard thought he ought to skip mentioning how very, very, <u>very</u> welcome Aunt Moira had been made by Harry Vaughn, who had treated her to a brief and naughty weekend at the pre-renovated Cattleman Hotel. "It's a lovely place, Luna City. I'm quite at home here, and that's why I've decided to make it my permanent home – just as you did with Saint-Didier," he added, with a faint touch of malice. Just to pay back Dad for all those poisoned stilettos. His mother blinked, slightly baffled.

"Well, of course. Why shouldn't you make it official, since you are intending to marry an American, after all. Dear Moira made it seem so ... so charming and special." And Mum raised her eyes from the cuppa, and the plate with the scrambled eggs and the warm cinnamon roll. "Richie, dear; all of this has made you happy. You have friends here, and supportive allies. Don't deny it to my face, it has. All of that other; the fame, and the bits on the telly, even that top-shelf restaurant. Those were not good for you, really. It was a poisoned sweetmeat, even though all that made you simply pots of money..."

"Not that I have much left of that," Richard commented, and his mother continued, as if she had not heard, while Dad shot him a simply telling glance over the table.

"Tasting good in the mouth and curdling in the belly. But as your Gran said, you were a silly boy, taking what you were offered with both hands and never considering the consequences."

"I'm considering the consequences now," Richard replied, with some asperity. "At a late date but considering them."

"Well, simply bloody hallelujah," Alfred grunted. "You've grown up at last. Accepted responsibility. Wish that we'd sent you to work all hours in some seaside caff in off-terms from school. Gotten all that out of your system before you got sucked into it for good and all. As it happens, your financial disaster has been somewhat mitigated."

"Your father has worked very hard on your behalf," Mum pointed out. "It turned out to be a fortunate thing that he was registered as your enduring power of attorney."

"I don't remember having agreed to that," Richard replied, after a moment of wracking his memory.

"Not surprised," his father stirred a round of cream into his own coffee. "You had a lot on your plate. The power of attorney was supposed to cover your various business accounts and properties, when you did that travel series, and were unavailable for weeks at a time."

"That I do remember," Richard acknowledged in a guarded fashion. He did recall the three seasons of the traveling cooking show, mostly as a long dull slog through strange foods, and even stranger drinks and other interesting and mind-altering substances, most of which were not, strictly speaking, completely legal.

"At any rate," Alfred continued. "In the aftermath of the Carême matter, and you having gone out of the country, it was left to me to manage your various business concerns and properties. The debts and resulting lawsuits for damages were astronomical and remain a dreadfully tangled affair, although I have done my best to remediate them. Income on the lease of your London flat and sale of the restaurant freehold mitigated the worst of the matters. It will take another five years to so to resolve them to everyone's satisfaction. It was most providential, too, that I invested the residuals from your final season in profitable securities. As it stands, at this moment, Richard, much work still remains before you can clear the remainder of the debt. I have done all that I can do, at this point."

"Well," Richard considered his father – whom he had never known to be wrong when it came to matters financial. "I'm grateful, Dad. I really am. Mrs. Vaughn will be overjoyed to hear this; that I don't owe quite as much as I thought I would. Still… it's a good thing that I am considering another offer of employment. It will be a chore to pay off what I thought I might owe, as part of processing for citizenship…"

"We wanted the best for you, dear," Mum patted his hand. "It's all that we have ever wanted for you. It's important that you and your Miss Heisel can start off on an even keel …"

"You really need to start sorting out these matters for yourself," Alfred grunted. "I won't be around forever, you know."

"About that, Mum," Richard cleared his throat, and tried to ignore Alfred's expertly placed verbal stiletto. "There's something I have to tell you…"

4th of July!

Celebrate the Glorious 4th of July on Town Square!!

Reading of the Declaration!

Parade of the Karnes Company Rangers!

Encampment of Historical Reenactors under the Oaks

Special Showing of 1776 on the Outdoor Movie Screen

Carnival Rides for the Kids!

Food Trucks Around the Square

Equestrian Demonstrations by the Rangers

All Day Fun for the Entire Family!

The Last Word

It was with a relatively light heart that Richard cycled home to the Age, on the Sunday after meeting with his parents. Sunday dinner service was always relatively light and wrapped up early. Tomorrow, he would spend the day with his parents, showing them around Luna City. And definitely, he would introduce Dad to Sefton Grant, and that small wine-making industry which Sefton maintained, along with woodworking rustic Texas cedar furniture, the goat herd and the campground. There was still a pale rim of light along the western horizon as he pedaled slowly up the rutted gravel driveway to the Age of Aquarius, and a handful of lights gleamed in the Straw Castle Aquarius, and in a pair of RVs parked down at the very far end of the campground.

There were no lights on in the little silver Airstream caravan which had been his home for the last five years.

"Almost home, Ozzie," Richard said over his shoulder to the brindle cat riding along in plastic crate strapped to the back of his mountain bike. He felt reasonably cheerful, the matter of Kate notwithstanding. The debts in London, following upon the catastrophic failure of Carême ... which would have been such a game-changer on the restaurant scene! Now he came to realize that perhaps it was not to be. There were four and five-star restaurants in the capitols and big cities of the world, on every corner, if one could believe the media accounts. But a superior restaurant in a small and out of the way town; a medium-sized fish in a small pond surely had a better audience than a medium-sized, or even a large fish looking for attention in the most impressively-sized ponds. It was only good sense – a sense that he could see clearly now. Some kindly interference had sent him to Luna City.

He came around through the gate in the hedge around the campground and saw that there was an automobile parked around the side of the Airstream, veiled in dark shadow, but he thought it was the same general shape of Kate's little VW bug, and his heart lifted. It was her, sitting quietly in the dark, under the shade of the metal roof that sheltered the Airstream and the patio in front of it.

"We have to talk," she said quietly, as Richard leaned the bike against the support post.

(To be continued, of course.)

Luna City 11th Inning Stretch

We Have to Talk

"We have to talk," said Kate quietly, sitting almost unseen in the shadows under the awning which sheltered the Airstream caravan which had been Richard's home for almost five years. "Hi, kitten," she added, as Ozzie leaped from the basket strapped on the back of Richard's bicycle, and in another bound, landed heavily in Kate's lap, purring extatically and butting his head in Kate's face. "Ooofff! What have you been feeding him! It feels like he has gained weight!"

"Well, I haven't been feeding you," Richard answered. Kate's appearance was ... unexpected. Unprepared for. And he hated surprises. His parents showing up out of the clear blue was about all the surprise that he could stand for one day. Although it was perhaps a good sign that she was not throwing heavy objects and death threats ... or launching her engagement ring at him. "So Ozzie gets the full gourmet culinary benefit. Are you hungry?" he added, hopefully. Feeding Kate was one of the simple joys in his current life.

"A little," she replied. "But we still have to talk."

"I know," Richard sighed heavily and unlatched the door to the Airstream. "But I'm not prepared. I always prepare when we have a supper together..." he added, rather pettishly. "All I have is some eggs, a bit of cheese ... the usual herbs, and some of Sefton's incomparable white ... will a simple omelet do, Kate-of-my-heart?"

"It will," and it seemed to Richard – unaccustomed as he was to be divining the motivations of the female of the species – that Kate was ... uncomfortable. Embarrassed, even. It came to him that he ought to sit down and talk to Kate, rather than evade the issue by fossicking about in the tiny kitchen.

"Look, I can fix the omelet later," he declared, sitting down in the other chair. "You said that we have to talk. Let's talk. I'll start: my parents appeared in the Café this morning. You know – my parents from England. Though they live in France, now. I was surprised no end. I didn't expect them to appear until later in the summer. You'd like them, Kate. They're nice. Although my father has a skill at subtle verbal sadism that would be the envy of any interviewer on the telly. Mum's a charmer, though. They do want to meet you, when they return from touring the wineries in the Hill Country in July. That is if we still are engaged to wed, at some future point?" As Kate hesitated, petting Ozzie in her lap, Richard pressed his advantage. "This was your notion, Kate-of-my-heart. That we should talk. Your turn."

"Yes, we are still engaged," Kate replied, after a long, fraught moment. It seemed to Richard that moment had lasted half a decade. He hoped that his sigh of relief was not visible.

To Kate.

Who continued, petting Ozzie in a distracted fashion. "I ... well, you see. I have to apologize. And I'm not used to doing that. Well, not very often. I ... made a stupid assumption. That you had proposed to me in order to expedite your application for

186

naturalization as an American. I was! And now I'm completely sorry." Kate sniffled, and in the faint light under the awning, it seemed to Richard that her eyes were close to overflowing. "And I was so happy, so extatically happy that I told simply everyone ... and ... and then it was like a wonderful treat grabbed away..."

That ended on a sob, and Richard was horrified. Tears! His whole being revolted against witnessing female tears, especially from Kate, who was the most level-headed ... well, one of the three most level-headed women of his acquaintance. He hated female tears, above almost everything else, to include greasy and salt-laden junk fast food.

"Look, love," he protested, taking her hand – the one what wasn't clutching Ozzie. "The whole misunderstanding is my fault, you know. I should have told you that I was planning to apply for citizenship, honest and straight-up. I just didn't want to tangle my lines, you see. I thought that I would surprise you. Jess told me about your brother's encounter with his ... um, lamentable former girlfriend, so I thought best not to say anything until I was farther along in the process. Don't blame yourself, Kate – it's my fault for not telling you about my plans."

"But I was awful to you!" Kate wailed, and Richard cringed inwardly.

"It's just one of those misunderstandings!" he begged, truly distressed now. "Don't start crying, Kate-of-my-heart. It was just a simple failure to communicate ... but it's all over and done with now. Please, you're dripping tears all over Ozzie, and he abominates getting wet ... let's just put this behind us ... and let me fix us a quiet supper."

"All right," Kate sniffled again, and mopped at her eyes with the back of her hand as Ozzie had jumped down from her lap, indignant at being sprinkled with saltwater. "Ugh ... I was so upset this afternoon, I quite forgot to be hungry and now I am...."

"Omelet, a light salad, and let me get you a glass of wine," Richard, relieved beyond all imagining, dropped a brief light kiss on her forehead and hopped up the steps to the Airstream, feeling as light as a feather.

Everything was going to be fine, now. More than fine. He and Kate were still a thing, were still going to be married. He could feel it in his bones; the Almighty Power in which he maintained a slight and conventional belief remained safely ensconced in His non-denominational paradise, and all was right with his own personal world. Kate was going to marry him, he wasn't nearly as deeply in debt as he had feared, and the process of applying for American citizenship was, according to Jess Abernathy-Vaughn, going about as speedily as could be expected. (*It'll be finalized about the time of the birth of your second child, Jess had commented mordantly, the last time that they had discussed the matter.*) He was hungry, and so was Kate. Ozzie was hungry, too; he looked reproachfully at Richard, as he sat, tail curled around his haunches, in front of the pair of dishes which normally contained his water and a meager handful of dry kibble.

"Slave driver!" Richard commented to Ozzie. He topped up the kibble dish and poured two glasses of Sefton Grant's incomparable mustang grape wine. He was tired; he would sit with Kate in the twilight and have a glass … or two … even three. Then he would assemble the salad, and concoct an omelet… but for now, sit next to Kate. She scooched the folding patio chair close enough that she could lean her head on his shoulder, as the apricot glow behind the trees at the edge of the Grants' rattletrap campground faded. A brief spark of light blinked against the shadowy hedge and the unkept grass that straggled against it.

"Hey! A firefly!" Kate exclaimed. "Gosh, I haven't seen fireflies for ages… oh, another one!"

188

"A wet spring," Richard said. "Miss Letty said so. They come out just after dusk. I'm usually too late to see them, most evenings."

"It's a good omen," Kate declared, and they sat silently for some minutes, sipping wine as the tiny white sparks flickered against the shadows. Finally, Richard cleared his throat, and ventured,

"There was another thing I was going to tell you. I have accepted Lew Dubois' offer to be the executive chef for the Cattleman. He's offered before, and I always held back. But everyone and everything has conspired to change my mind. We'll have to work out where to live. We both can't move into the caravan, and I can't possibly move into your place in Karnesville, not if I work here. I don't drive. I can't drive..."

"Well, I could teach you," Kate replied, in a bracing way. "But you're right – we'd have to live in Luna City, if that is where your work is. Mine is all over the place, and I can drive. I'll ask 'Celi and Jess, if they know of any places looking for a tenant or a buyer; some place that will suit for a bit. I am hungry now, Rich – really. Are we going to eat soon?"

"Soon," Richard sighed. He really hated to get up from the lawn chair; he was bone tired anyway, possibly slightly drunk, and it was curiously comfortable, sitting with his arm around Kate, and her head resting on his shoulder. "I'll start the salad ... another?"

"Yes, please," Kate replied, and with a sigh, Richard loosened his embrace, and went to pour another round. The inside of the caravan seemed very cozy, with the small lights in the kitchen and banquette area casting a warm yellow glow. He set out the eggs, and the salad greens, washed and wrapped in a towel to drain. Absentmindedly, he thought of how comfortable and homey it was to be doing this, after the week of tension and fraught nerves, his worry over Kate and their future. He felt like his nerves had been stripped out, soaked in something soothing, and then wrung dry and reinstalled. He couldn't help thinking that Kate must feel the same way. Just then, she tapped at the screen door.

"Hey, lover – I'm getting cold sitting there all by myself ... and I could use another glass of this."

"Excellent – and so can I!" Richard hooked out the gallon jug from where it sat underneath the miniscule sink and drainboard and dealt out another glass for each. Kate settled onto the banquette and regarded him somewhat owlishly. It came to Richard that they were both the tiniest bit squiffy. "Supper will be ready in a tick. Are you sure you'll be fit to drive home after this?"

"No," Kate replied, and hiccupped slightly. She gazed at Richard in bewilderment. "I'm absolutely ravenous ... I haven't eaten all day; I've been so wrought-up over having to drive out here and make it up with you."

"And I thought you had the hardest head imaginable, being raised on your grandfather's home-brewed beer," Richard marveled, and Kate hiccupped again.

"Yes, but it's nothing compared to Sefton's wine," she allowed.

Richard sighed, yet again, and reached for Kate's voluminous handbag. He fished out the keys to the 'Bug and jingled them at her. "For your own safety, Kate-my-heart, I am confis-confisticating your car keys. You'll have to stay here for the night. Ozzie will guard your keys. I'll put them with his catnip mouse, which he protects with tooth and claw, and I will myself guard your virtue. You can have the bed, and I'll sleep on the banquette ... or maybe go throw myself on the Grant's mercy and ask for the use of one of their little guest huts for the night ..."

"Not necessary," Kate replied, and regarded Richard with even wider owl-eyes over the wine glass. "I'll share the bed with you. It's big enough for two We're going to be married, after all. You won't really do anything … make advances of a sexual nature, then?"

"No," Richard confessed. "'Pon my word, Kate-of-my-heart, I'll be too tired for any shagging after they day that I have had, and all of Sefton's elixir that we have drunk together. All I want is supper, a hot shower, and a good long kip."

"Damn," Kate murmured, and hiccupped again, appearing mildly disappointed that making mad passionate love wasn't part of the program. "I'll settle for that sch.., sch … skedd-duly. We can sleep in tomorrow. We did the print job early…"

"Right, then," Richard yawned, and put his favorite small non-stick pan on the tiny stove burner to heat. "Supper, a wash and then a good cuddle before we sleep … I think that I may stay awake long enough to finish supper without falling face-first into my plate."

Somewhat later that evening, Richard lay chastely next to the sleeping Kate, spoon-fashion in the double bed in the Airstream, his arm around Kate, and Ozzie purring at their feet, and felt more deeply content with life, the universe and everything, than he could recollect feeling in decades. If this was what it was going to be like, married and sleeping in one bed with one's beloved snuggled close, and the other beloved – the feline one – at the foot of the bed – then he was enthusiastically all for it.

Yes, God was in his heaven, and all was indeed right with the world – or at least that part of it encompassed by Luna City.

Of Science, Spies, Saboteurs and Thieves

"Did you know what I saw last night, on my way home?" Richard ventured one morning, as he brought out another plate of signature Café cinnamon rolls to the stammtisch – the large table at the front window, where the regular early morning clientele gathered, along with any wandering visitors who felt sufficiently assured to take a seat. "I saw one of Roman's work crews hard at work with a post-hole digger and a couple of bags of concrete! They were setting a new post in front of this otherwise undistinguished little cottage just around the corner from the Catholic church. They told me it was for another state historical plaque, but they could not tell me why that little cottage was so dignified. It's owned by the Wyler family, so they said – been a rental for as long as anyone can remember. Can you enlighten me, Miss Letty?"

The regulars this morning included the venerable Miss Letty McAllister, the oldest resident of Luna City, impeccably dressed even to a hat and gloves which matched her handbag, Annice and Georg Stein, who ran the antiquities establishment next door. Opposite them sat Mrs. Anne Dubois, whose' husband was one of the notable C-suite powers at the international corporation who now ran the newly renovated and updated Cattleman Hotel, and Anne Dubois' author friend, a dreamy woman of middle-age with an absent-minded expression on her countenance which suggested that she barely noticed the plate of cinnamon rolls placed in the center of the table, as she thumbed through entries on her cellphone.

"I can indeed," Miss Letty replied warmly, and with a certain expression of triumph. "That house was where Professor Pavel Markov lived for almost a decade while he was developing a number of his theories and working on their application with working prototypes. Certain of his inventions were subsequently turned into working weapons during the War..."

By the way in which Miss Letty managed to install a verbal capital letter to that mention, Richard knew that she meant the big war of her generation, after which all those other international conflicts were small and paltry armed conflicts. The Second World War – although she might also have referred thusly to the first of that ilk.

Georg Stein looked astonished; he breathed reverently. *"Ach du meine Güte!* You mean Herr-Professor Pavel Markov, the inventor they called the Thomas Edison of Russia? <u>That</u> Pavel Markov? I did not know this, Miss Letty!"

Miss Letty coughed gently. "Well, we in Luna City didn't know who he was for the longest time. I was just a girl then and I only found out about the Professor much, much later. He was in hiding, with his wife and family. My father told us at the time that they all were family. The Professor was a political refugee at the time, you see – he was an adherent of the moderate faction in Russia; an ally of Kerensky. I believe he was even elected to the Duma, in pre-revolutionary days. When everyone thought that the overthrow of the Czar might mean a translation for

Russia into being a proper parliamentary democracy, as we understand the concept in the West. Professor Markov was a new and modern representative of Russia, educated, widely famed and feeling an obligation to interest himself in political affairs. Everybody wished for his endorsement – scientific and political."

"Well, that must have turned out really, really well," Richard observed, somewhat acidly. Miss Letty nodded, sadly.

"Yes, after that brief essay in civic responsibility, Professor Markov decided that discretion in the political regard was much the better part of valor. Especially when Josef Stalin declared him to be an enemy of the people and sent a Cheka death squad after him. This would have been... in the late 1920s, I think. The Markovs were in exile in France at the time. They didn't talk much about that – or at least, Dym didn't talk about it much. Dym – that was the youngest son. Dimitri. He was my age... and we made friends with him. My brother and I, Stephen, and the Vaughn boys. We let him join our club, as it was. The Markovs approved of Stephen as a playmate. We had free-range on the ranch property; you see. A relief for Dym. The rest of us were part of the package, as it were. Dym was suffocating from over-protective parents. His oldest brother Sergei walked him to and from school almost every day at first – so he didn't get out much to wander with us. But he was in the same grade at school as Stephen and I, and Artie Vaughn. He was a very clever boy," Miss Letty sighed in reminiscence. "He spoke three languages! Can you imagine how impressed we were, in our little town, where none of us had traveled very far outside of Texas, ever? Stephen could rub along in Spanish well enough because of all the Hispanic ranch employees, but Dym spoke French and Russian as well as English. Dym had gone with his parents to nearly everything there was a picture of in our history textbook! Castles and cathedrals and monuments, oh my!"

"He didn't get his arse kicked every day, out behind the lavatory block, and twice on Sunday, just for being an insufferably superior git?" Richard inquired, skeptically, recalling his own schooldays.

"No," Miss Letty replied, mildly. "For one; Sergei would have prevented that. And if he wasn't on the spot immediately, Sergei had taught Dym some very interesting and effective methods for discouraging such attempts. Oriental tactics in hand-to-hand defense. I believe that they call it 'judo' or martial arts these days. The Vaughn brothers were most impressed. Harry was always a dirty fighter, even back then. He was taller and heavier than Artie, although nearly four years younger."

"Harry Vaughn is <u>still</u> a dirty fighter," Richard admitted glumly. How he was bullied by the elderly Harry Vaughn into going out in a cockleshell tin boat with a wonky engine on a flooded river was still a humiliating memory. The OAP Harry remained an overwhelmingly formidable force; what he must have been as a grade-school tyke didn't bear thinking about.

Miss Letty vouchsafed a tiny smile, as she consulted the equally tiny gold old-fashioned ladies' wristwatch. "Oh, my – I am late. I know it is an interesting story, but I didn't know half of it at the time. Chief Magill wrote up a thorough account of the murder in his memoirs, though. I must run. The historical association has a complete transcription in the newsletter. Tomorrow, Richard?"

She rose haltingly from the stammtisch, gathering up her handbag, gloves, and cane from the table, and the silver bell over the door chimed as she departed. Outside the big window of the Café, the big pickup truck with the emblem of the Wyler Ranch embossed on the doors waited for her'

Richard sighed, glumly.

"She teases us with an amazing story... a murder, another murder here in Luna City! Then she loves and leaves us all, wanting more. Just like a woman!"

"My wife has the email newsletter of the Luna City Historical Society on her computer at home," Georg Stein gulped the last of the peerless Café coffee in his cup. "I had not read it, yet – but I will review. And print out a copy for you, Richard. This is a *sehr-interessant* story! How a man of the intellect such as Herr-Professor Markov came to be here... Here in Luna City. And associated with murder! We are teased. Richard, teased, indeed!"

An excerpt from the untitled memoir of Alasdair Duncan Magill, late of Fife in Scotland, long-time police chief of Luna City, published now with permission of the family in the Luna City Historical Association Newsletter. The extensive memoir was found among his private papers by his family, after his death from natural causes at the age of 98 in February 1987. It appears here with the generous permission of his family.

Chapter 53 – The Matter of Political Murder

Of course, we assumed – my chief investigator, Detective Sergeant John Drury and I both – from the very start that the brutal and mysterious death of the young man was more than it had seemed. Luna City was a peaceful, quiet place, through the efforts of citizens and law enforcement alike over time. Both John Drury and I had done our best for decades to assure this happy state of existence. In my tenure as a member of the constabulary, as street officer and as chief of the Luna City Police Department, we had put an end to the antics of local bad-hats such as the unsavory Charley Mills. Charley Mills now lived almost as a recluse in his tumbledown wreck of a homestead. The Newton Boys robbery gang ran afoul of other law enforcement agencies. All the disruptions which these miscreants and others threatened to bring to our little town had been dealt with. None the less, it was a perilous time, those decades of which I write. The Great Depression had bitten hard and long; many were those desperate souls who sought to make a living by thieving, either through stealth and petty crimes, or by outright robbery. Still, Luna City was an oasis of calm and obedience to the rule of law, all during those years. Of the four recorded murders in Luna City during the 1930s, one was domestic; a woman aggravated beyond tolerance of a drunkard husband beating her without mercy. The second was the result of excessive consumption of alcohol – a dare regarding relative skill at marksmanship after a particularly rowdy fandango at the Gonzalez Rancho. The third was committed by an outraged farmer, upon discovering a transient whom he had hired to help harvest hay attempting to rape the farmer's eight-year-old daughter. The transient was dispatched by the farmer, wielding only his bare hands *(Charges were dismissed by the jury when that case came to trial, as rightfully they should have been.)* Only the last murder, in the year of our lord 1934 was judged to be premediated and deliberate.

But I am getting ahead of myself, in outlining the circumstances, which were indeed peculiar and with international implications. My involvement began with an interview in my own office, with Mayor McAllister and Mr. Albert Wyler, the owner of the ranch enterprise which was the largest of that sort in all of Karnes County. That these gentlemen condescended to meet me without fanfare in my own office in the new Police Department building indicated

197

to me the matter was of some significance. At the time of setting the appointment, they only told our sergeant of police, Sgt. Grigoryev that it was a matter of small import, and they wished to meet with me alone, without any other person present. This, I sensed, was a matter of delicacy as well as importance. That two of the most prominent men of the town should require a meeting with me, stressing absolute privacy ... well, I might have been born at night, but it was not last night.

The new department building had incorporated a separate office for the chief of police, and another smaller cubby for the head investigator; just as the old building had. My own new office was commodious, with two windows; space sufficient for my own desk, a smaller one for a secretary (*against the day when the budget allowed for a dedicated secretary-typist, save a single woman clerk who did all the typing and filing for the department, including that of John Drury, who was still my chief investigator.*) John's presence was not requested, on the occasion of this interview, as I sensed that this was not merely a courtesy call on the part of the local nobility – but I intended to confide in him at earliest opportunity, for he was a trusty man.

My new office allowed space for four leather-upholstered club chairs, a few framed botanical prints on the adjacent walls and a small occasional table with a plant on it, to comfortably facilitate informal meetings such as this one. Sgt. Grigoriev, promoted from constable following upon his heroic conduct in defending the former jail building against an outraged but misinformed mob several years previously, showed the gentlemen to my office. Sgt. Grigoriev was a man inclined to do things emphatically: saluting, stomping, and slamming doors. After several years as a member of the police force, we had managed to tone down his enthusiasm for performing the role so enthusiastically. But he remained emphatic – not to say loud – on the occasion of showing important visitors into my office

"Sah!" he opened the door and shouted into my office. "Grazhdanin Wyler and Gospodin MacAllister! They told me it is a matter of importance and discretion, sah!"

"I am certain that it is, Sergeant," I replied. "And so the matter must be rightfully discussed in whispers. Or at any rate, in a lower voice."

"Sah!" Sgt. Grigoriev replied, fervently, as he held the door open for Mayor McAllister and Albert Wyler, and then closed it ... not with the resounding slam which I had expected. So progress was being made.

"So, gentlemen, I take it that the small matter you bring to my attention is something of major import, and involves my department," I gestured the two men to the chairs, and took my own seat as they did.

"It is, Chief," Albert Wyler admitted, with a glance of confirmation toward Mayor McAllister, as they settled into their chairs. "But we must ask you to share this intelligence with only those few in whom you repose trust. A man's life is in our hands, our several hands,"

"An exaggeration, surely," I ventured, and both men shook their heads.

"No, in absolute earnest," Albert Wyler replied, his countenance set and grave. "As of last week, the government of Soviet Russia has set a bounty on this man's head, declared him to be outlaw and criminal. You may have heard of him – Professor Pavel Markov, the inventor. For no better reason than for having been a member of the pre-Revolutionary government and for being a prominent man of science in his own right. After many attempts to entice or force his return to Russia, they have ordered his execution, for no more than opposing the rule of Stalin, a brutal criminal, long before he dispatched his various political enemies. The Soviet Cheka murder squads might reach far, but it has been in our minds that they cannot reach far into Texas, into a small, obscure town – which honesty compels me to confess that Luna City is. Not New York, or Boston, Los Angeles or St. Louis. Professor Markov is a decent man and a most clever one, too. I have extended my sympathies and support and rented him the small house on Pine Oak Street, behind the Catholic church, for him and his family. I don't put much into the political nonsense that goes around these days, but I do recognize a decent, intelligent man when I meet one. And Professor Markov is a decent man, indeed."

"They say that he was the Thomas Edison of Russia, in the days of the Czar," I replied, after a moment of astonishment. For even I knew of Professor Pavel Markov and his mechanical inventions. "One of their most brilliant scientists, and a patriot, as well."

"Not that brilliant," Mayor McAllister remarked, with a touch of asperity. "One should learn that discretion is the better part of valor, in politics as well as war. Professor Markov as a scientist was too accustomed to speak frankly on matters of import and of state generally, little reckoning that such a habit might turn out to be just a teeny bit unpopular among the Reds. But that is neither here nor there."

"He is going by the surname Marcus," Albert Wyler took up the explanation. "A scholar of botany as we have so arranged as a ... what do they call this in spy-craft? A cover story. Semi-retired and interested in our local flora. I have a reliable friend on the faculty of the University of Texas in Austin, who has set up a kind of paper alibi in that name. Marcus – I think we should be in the habit of calling them by that name – and his family are posing as Czechoslovakian. Mrs. Marcus is of that nation, originally, so that guise should be fairly convincing. Only the three of us in this room know his true identity. Chief, it is imperative that the Professor as well as his family be protected from assassination, which is why we are informing you, as the head of our police department."

"Hmm," I took the opportunity to say something noncommittal, while I thought about this situation. Yes, it was a great honor, to be trusted with such knowledge as this, but still a challenge. My force consisted then of myself, my chief investigator, John Drury, late of the Texas Rangers and semi-retired, Sergeant Grigoriev, our lady secretary, Miss Avery, and six ordinary constables; all local lads and unmarried, save the most senior of them, Henry Vaughn, who had lost his farm property near Beeville to foreclosure, and took the job to provide for his wife and boys. "So, who among us in Luna City might not be fooled by this particular subterfuge of Marcus the Czechoslovakian scholar-botanist?"

"There are no Czechs settled any closer than Beeville, I reckon," Albert Wyler replied thoughtfully. "There are Poles – but they're in Panna Marie. Of Russian; only your Sgt. Grigoriev, and he's a White, or so we assume." And he bent a skeptical look upon me.

201

"He is, most assuredly," I replied. "When he gets drunk, which does happen, under circumstances which I do not inquire regarding, he insists that everyone present drink a toast to the late Czar and his family, and to his exiled commander, Colonel-General Deniken."

"Ah." Albert Wyler rubbed his chin, in a thoughtful manner. "Then I suppose it might be safe to let your sergeant know of Professor Markov's presence here. He's a bright lad; Perhaps he should be informed from the start, rather than figure it out later and assume the worst or be resentful regarding a lack of trust. Of a certainty and as a Russian, he would recognize the famed inventor. In any case, Professor Markov is not completely without a layer of protection. The young man posing as his oldest son, Sergei, is actually a dedicated bodyguard. The middle son, Mikhail, is really Professor Markov's scientific assistant. He has been with him in that regard for several years. Only the little boy, Dimitri is his child, Madame Markov being so very much younger than her husband."

"How old is the boy, then?" I asked. "I presume that he will be kept at home for lessons, for his own security."

Alfred was already shaking his head. "School age; the same as my boy Stephen. Part of their reason for settling here for the foreseeable future is for the little lad to have a chance of a normal life, now they can no longer be assured of safety in Mexico City, where they have been for several years. There are too many Communist sympathizers there. Madame Marcus insisted on coming to the United States. It is planned for Sergei to keep a watchful eye on the boy, in any case."

Mayor McAllister cleared his throat. "The essential part required of your department, Chief, is for your force to continue maintaining that commendable degree of vigilance that you have always kept ..."

"I take great pride in my ... in our record," I returned, and Mayor McAllister nodded.

"Of course, but with the presence of the Marcus family, and the threats posed to them, it is essential that your people keep a watchful eye on any strangers, especially foreign strangers suddenly appearing in Luna City and exhibiting an unseemly interest in the family. We leave it to your discretions as to who you take into your confidence as to their identity, or the nature of the threat against them."

"I'll keep that intelligence to the smallest number possible," I said, "Always remembering the axiom regarding a secret; that two may keep it, if one of them is dead."

Albert Wyler snorted with a suppressed laugh. "I hope you do not intend to go to that extreme. But we should all keep our eyeballs peeled. I've given my word to the Marcuses that they should feel safe enough in Luna City, and I do not like to think that my word is not my bond. They will be arriving sometime next week"

"Your word is a bond on all of us, Mr. Wyler," I assured them, and both gentlemen looked pleased. I showed them to the door, and then sat at my desk for a long while, considering how best to manage this grave addition to my already heavy responsibilities.

The New Boy in School

On the first day of school in the autumn of 1934, Letty McAllister and her older brother Douglas rode their bicycles from their home – the old stone house standing in a garden on the outskirts of Luna City – into Luna City proper. The big red brick consolidated school building sat on the far side of Town Square, which had once been intended to accommodate a courthouse. Luna City was once supposed to be a station on the San Antonio – Aransas Pass Railway, and be the county seat, but that had never come about. Town Square was now a lovely green park, with a bandstand in the middle. All the tall town buildings; the Cattleman Hotel, the old fire station, Abernathy Hardware, the Luna City Savings and Loan, the McAllister's Mercantile Building, and the school itself overlooked that space. The steeple of the First Methodist Church hovered a little away from one corner, like a tall and slender girl too shy to join the crowd.

Letty would be starting the seventh grade. Her brother Douglas, who was clever and bookish, was in the nineth grade. The pair of huge sycamore trees which shaded the paved school playground in front of the school were just beginning to shed

204

their crunchy autumn leaves and prickly round seed pods over the areas marked out on the asphalt in painted squares and circles for games. Letty looked ahead, as she and Douglas wheeled their bicycles through side gate into the playground, looking for friends. Douglas had a new pair of long trousers; his first pair of grown men's trousers for school, and Letty a pretty blouse with puffed sleeves, worn under a plaid jumper with a pleated skirt. They both had new leather shoes; Letty had her hair cut to a neat bob, and Douglas had his hair cut at the barber shop on Town Square – as he was nearly grown up now, and too old for a home-done trim with their mother's sewing shears. The first day of school was an important day for the two, even if they expected no real changes.

The first real surprise waited for them, just inside the gate; their good friend Stephen Wyler, who was four months younger than Letty, stood there, with his hands insouciantly in his pockets. He was a wiry, compact boy, who had yet to get his growth Artie Vaughn, who normally tagged along with Stephen and Douglas's gang, stood jiggling from one foot to another with suppressed excitement. With them stood a third boy, a slightly taller lad. Letty had gotten her growth and stood half-a-head taller than Stephen and Artie, which she found obscurely embarrassing, looming over the boys her age. This new boy was exactly her height. though. A tall, heavy-shouldered man in a suit of a vaguely flashy and foreign-looking cut lingered just outside the school grounds, looking through the railings and watching the group with intense interest. Letty wondered why: the young man didn't look quite old enough to be a father.

"Hi, Stephen," Douglas nodded toward their friend. "Ready to be lectured by Miss Horrible for not understanding an algebra problem?" Miss Hornby, an aged and gray-haired spinster with an uncertain temper taught math, algebra, and geometry to the upper grades. She was notorious among Luna City school students for her impatience with error and the furious tongue-lashings which the smallest error or carelessness on the part of a student would trigger.

Meanwhile Artie Vaughn was hardly able to contain himself. "Letty, there's a new boy in the 7th grade! Can you believe it!"

"No, but Miss Horrible is like a blue norther; just bundle up and get through it," Stephen replied, as if he had not heard a word. "Dym, these are my friends, Doug and Letty McAllister. Letty'll be in the same class as us. Dym's the new kid this fall. His family moved to town last week. His Pop's a scientist ... and Dym has even ridden in an airplane! He's been to all those foreign places in Europe!"

Dym, with gray eyes and angular features, stared at the ground, appearing to be wholly embarrassed. "Wasn't my fault," he replied when he brought his gaze up from to meet theirs. "Pleased to make your acquaintance. Dym is just short for Dimitri. Papuch an' Mama took me. I didn't care – just another moldy old building."

"Dym lived in foreign places," Stephen explained, unnecessarily. For Letty and her brother knew right away that the new boy had, for he didn't talk quite like they did; but careful and precise, without the customary drawl.

"You should tell us about them in class," Letty offered. "I'd like to hear about foreign places. Maybe I can travel to them myself, someday."

"Maybe," Dym offered a shy, yet wholly charming smile. "But Sergei ... that's my big brother," and he gestured toward the heavy-shouldered young man who was still watching them from the sidewalk. "He says that I shouldn't start folk talking about our business, lest the wrong people hear about it."

"What kind of wrong people?" Douglas was intensely interested, but just then the school bell rang, and it was time to go inside; Douglas to his class, and Letty, Stephen and the new boy to theirs.

Dym shrugged and replied, "Just wrong people. Bad people." He turned to wave to the young man watching from the other side of the wrought-iron and brick fence which marked the boundaries of school grounds. The young man returned the wave, and then strode away as the group of children mounted the stairs toward the main school doors – a portico held up with four tall white pillars, and the words **"Science – Religion – Patriotism"** engraved in gold letters across the entablature.

That night at supper, Letty's father said the blessing over supper dishes, and Mama got up to bring in a basket of fresh hot biscuits straight from the oven. Mama set down the biscuits, wrapped in a clean cloth, and Papa unrolled his dinner napkin and looked at Letty and Douglas.

"And how was your first day at school, then? I understand that Letty's class has a new student."

Letty wasn't startled that Papa knew everything. He was the mayor of Luna City, and knew everyone and everything, so it wasn't a surprise at all that Papa knew of the new boy, Dym.

"He's nice, Papa," Letty replied. "I like him, lots. He's been to all kinds of foreign countries. And he said something about not talking too much about it, because of bad people. Why, Papa – is it dangerous to talk about bad people?"

"In a way," Papa replied, with a most serious expression. "It's called political persecution and your friend Dym's father is a refugee from political persecution. His family thought that they would be safe, here in Luna City. And so they shall be, as long as we all do our part to keep them so. Never talk about him and his family to strangers. Say nothing about them to anyone that we do not know – to outsiders. Professor Marcus and his family are all good people. And we don't want to see any kind of harm come to good people as they are, do we?"

"No, Papa," Letty and Douglas chorused, and Papa took a biscuit from the basket of them, split it and spread it with butter.

"Good." Papa took a bite from the biscuit and helped himself to the casserole which Mama had set in front of him, at the head of the table; a layered casserole of potatoes, onion and rice, interspersed with a little bit of ground beef, over which a quantity of tomato sauce had been poured before being consigned to the oven. "But if you see or hear about any strangers in town, asking about Professor Marcus or his family, you must tell me at once, or go straight to the police station and tell Chief Magill or any of his police officers. Promise me that you will."

"Of course, Papa," Douglas replied, and then Mama scooped out a generous spoonful of the casserole to everyone's plates, and they talked then of other things.

If anyone, such as Dym's mother, worried that the boy would be the odd one out among his new schoolfellows, such fears were allayed within the first week of school. Of course, the sponsorship of Stephen Wyler, son of the wealthiest landowner in the county, and the ready friendship of Douglas and Letty McAllister, might have had a lot to do with it. But left to himself, Dym Marcus was adept at ingratiation; intelligent, charming and with wide-ranging enthusiasm. Madame Katya Marcus should have nothing to worry about, and the walnut-shaped and sweet-cream-filled cookies, and the many-layered jam-filled pastries that she made for the children would have ensured a welcome among his peers for a child considerably less socially-skilled. Within the space of that week, he was accepted as one of the unofficial club, even though their established meeting place and club-house, the teepee constructed out of river wrack had been demolished a year or two ago in a spring flood, all the bits and pieces that had made it their little refuge washed away. If they couldn't go to that place anymore, there was always the wide acreage of the Wyler ranch. Then there was Dym's house, with Madame Marcus, Pilar Gonzales, the Mexican housekeeper, the hovering older brothers, and Professor Marcus.

"Mr. Hyde told us all about ancient sieges," Douglas remarked one day, as the four of them walked from school to the Markus house, tagged along by Artie Vaughn and shadowed by Dym's older brother. "Back in the old days, they built enormous machines to batter down walls. The ancient Romans had all kinds of keen stuff to break into enemy strongholds and throw stuff at their enemies. I never heard about all this. Have you ever seen any of them, Dym?"

"No," Dym admitted, sounding regretful, but his face brightened. "But I've seen pictures in books, and Papuch says he built scale models of them, when he was a boy. A battering ram, and a ballista! I'll bet he and Mikhail would help us build ones that would really work."

"That would be a keen school project for Mr. Hyde's history class!" Douglas sounded terribly excited. "And we could bring them to school and demonstrate how they really work! Do you really think your Pop would help us build them?"

"Oh, for sure," Dym replied, and Stephen enthused,

"There's an old shed at the ranch with the roof all busted in. Pop's been talking about knocking the rest of it down since forever! We could try out the battering ram on a real wall, if we can make it big enough!"

Letty sighed, to herself. Boys! All about building things and bashing things down. But still, she was intrigued at the thought of building something historic and mechanical. She and Douglas often built model airplanes together: Letty was exceptionally skilled at painting the tiny details. Sometimes Letty wondered about herself; why she wasn't really interested in doing girl-things, like embroidery, fussing with her hair and clothing, giggling about the attentions of boys, and trying inexpertly to get the attention of a certain boy. Letty already had the attention and respect of the boys that she knew; she liked doing the things that they did, and was interested in a lot of the same things they were interested in. She didn't want to be a boy; she just wanted to go places and do things, adventurous and exciting things, just like her brother and Stephen and Dym did. Mama often sighed and said that Letty would be a confirmed bluestocking, whatever that was. But Papa chuckled at that, saying that Letty knew her own mind very well, and that he always liked women who knew their own mind and spoke in their own words. Which made Letty feel so much better. And she really did want to see how a life-sized model battering ram, or a ballista would really work.

It turned out that Dym's father was just as interested in the project himself, although Madam Marcus tut-tutted under her breath. Professor Marcus was lean and gnomish, almost the age of Letty's grandfather as she remembered him, but with a turn of enthusiasm for projects of a nature such as the one to build an almost-full-scale battering ram and ballista which seemed to transform him into a boy hardly older than Stephen, Dym, Artie, and Douglas. Upon hearing about this latest enthusiasm over lemonade and those sweet walnut-shaped cookies, the professor announced,

"Then we shall make it so, my lads! To my workroom! I have some books! Katya, bring me the book from the study! Folio-sized, red cover, second from the left on the bottom shelf under the window ... yes, yes – it's about siege warfare in the medieval era..."

The Professor hustled off to in the direction of his workshop, leaving Letty hesitating, as Madam Marcus rang a small silver bell, resting on the table in the cluttered dining room. In a moment, Pilar appeared from the direction of the kitchen, wiping her hands on a dishcloth.

"Pilar, you may clear away the tea things," Madam Marcus sighed. "I will bring the book to him. His library is organized on methods that are only apparent to his closest. My husband has been overtaken with yet another enthusiasm."

"Yes, Madam Marcus," Pilar replied, although Letty sensed that the younger woman's countenance was carefully blank, even as Madam Marcus put her own napkin on the table, and rose to her feet; obviously intent on the search for the particular, red-covered folio in her husband's study.

"Let me help clear up the tea things," Letty suggested. The McAllisters didn't have servants of any sort, although there was a woman who came to help with spring cleaning, sometimes. She and Mama always worked side by side. Madam Marcus looked faintly shocked, but Pilar nodded an assent, as she tucked the towel into the waistband of her apron, and took up the tray upon which the teapot, milk pitcher and sugar bowl sat, with the empty plate adorned with crumbs which had contained cookies and little squares of frosted cake. Pilar added the empty cups to the tray, and Letty stacked the abandoned plates and added the dirty silverware to the top plate and followed Pilar into the kitchen.

Letty was intrigued by the Marcus' housekeeper. She didn't look like a housekeeper or a maid at all. Instead, Letty thought she seemed more like who Letty imagined to be the something-heroine in the opera *Carmen*. Pilar was young, slim, with her dark hair pulled back into a bun high on the back of her head. Pilar had hazel eyes and a fair complexion; she didn't look in the least like the Gonzales and Gonzalez kin in Luna City. Perhaps she was a distant cousin since Pilar looked ... exotic. Letty could imagine her, with a bright red flower tucked behind her ear, singing in a vibrant contralto about her many lovers; soldiers, smugglers and bullfighters alike. Letty's parents loved listening to radio broadcasts from New York on Saturday afternoons, from the Metropolitan Opera company. Stephen's parents had even gone to the opera house there and told them all how splendid it was to see in person! The spectacle and the music! Letty's parents could never in their lives afford – or even want to travel all the way to New York for anything, let alone to see the opera. But they loved listening to the radio; a touch of the wider world, Papa often said, and what a blessing it was! When he was a boy, he often told Douglas and Letty; all they had was the magazines and newspapers which might be anywhere from a week to a month late! What a miracle, the modern age and technology!

As Letty set the stacked crumby plates down in the kitchen sink, she turned to Pilar, and inquired in all seriousness, "Are you really kin to Don Antonio, of the Rancho? Everyone here in Luna City called Gonzales with an s or a z hereabouts is kin to them. They have been here forever, my Papa says."

"Your papa is correct in that," Pilar answered, as she took the various elements of the tea service and plopped them down in the metal sink, careless of whether she chipped the fine china or not. "I am indeed a very distant cousin to your Don Antonio. My father is Don Pedro Rodriguez of Morelia. He was the alcalde there, for a brief time. It was all very complicated…"

"I know complicated," Letty replied, and then she heard someone calling her name from the little yard in back of the house. "I have to go, Pilar. The boys want to show off to me … or have me help work something complicated, I think."

"A familiar feeling, *hija*!" Pilar responded with a smile, as Letty went off, tracking the excited voices to the garden, where the younger boys and Professor Marcus were pulling odd bits of lumber from behind the sturdy shed which seemed to serve as his workroom/laboratory, while her brother and Stephen were intensely studying a picture in an enormous, red-covered book.

John Woodlief Drury

From the Texas Handbook of History –
Texas State Historical Association

Drury, John Woodlief – 1859-1944. John W. Drury, Texas Ranger, and soldier was born in Brownsville, Texas, the oldest son of John Ambrose Drury, and his wife, Sarah Woodlief. The senior John Drury was a cattleman and sometime storekeeper, who had moved to Texas from Kentucky with his family sometime during the early 1850s. Both John Ambrose and Sarah Woodlief were of Scots-Irish extraction, and sternly Presbyterian as to religious beliefs. John Ambrose Drury had served in the same unit at some period during the Civil War as Captain Leander McNelly; the two men reputedly thought very highly of each other. Sidelined by a near-fatal wound sustained late in the war, John Ambrose returned to Brownsville to recover. Some years later, when Leander McNelly was charged to raise a Ranger company for service in support of law and order in the hotly contested and bandit-haunted Nueces Strip, McNelly thought of his old friend, John Ambrose Drury, and wrote to him, asking if he would consider service in his company. John Ambrose wrote back, tendering sincere apologies. He was not fit for service in that vein, he wrote, having never entirely recovered from those crippling injuries sustained during the war. However, his oldest son, John W. Drury was aged 16, a skilled rider, an excellent shot with rifle or pistol, and eager to serve under the command of his fathers' old comrade. Captain McNelly somewhat reluctantly accepted John D. Drury into his company on that recommendation.

John W. Drury continued to serve as a Texas Ranger during McNelly's campaign in the Nueces Strip, including in the episode known as McNelly's Red Raid. In 1879, he married Alice Marks, in San Antonio. She gave birth to a son, John Marks Drury, in 1881, and died shortly thereafter from complications of childbirth. The infant was sent to live with his maternal grandparents for several years, while John W. Drury continued serving as a Ranger, excelling as an investigator into various crimes across South Texas. He was credited with many useful contributions to the so-called 'Book of Rogues' as the registry of criminals and offenders across Texas was then informally known. In 1885, John W. Drury married for a second time, to Juana Mendez-Segovia, a native of Brownsville, by whom he had three children, Leander John Drury, Samuel Houston Drury, and Sarah Alice Drury. In the same year, John A. Drury had invested in a speculative venture, in the form of a town lot in a prospective planned community in Karnes County, Luna City, which at the time was expected to become the county seat and a profitable stop on the San Antonio-Aransas Pass Railroad. That property was left to John W. Drury, in his father's will when John A. died the following year. After a brief service with Teddy Roosevelts' Rough Rivers in the Spanish American war in 1898, during which conflict he served as a senior sergeant, he retired from active duty as a Ranger. Sometime around 1905 (the exact date cannot be determined) John W. Drury took up residence in Luna City, and subsequently was hired on an ad-hoc basis as a sergeant of the local police force and chief detective in which capacity he served for nearly twenty-five years until his final retirement. During this period, he was associated with many locally prominent citizens in Karnes County. These included Alistair Duncan Magill, the chief of police of Luna City, rancher and fellow Rough Rider veteran, Albert Wyler, notorious bootlegger Charles E. Mills and the famed Russian intellectual, politician and inventor, Professor Pavel Markov. John W. Drury died of natural causes on April 21, 1944. He was interred in the main city cemetery in Luna City, where his grave is marked by a particularly fine example of monumental statuary, depicting a riderless horse.

The Two Bodies of Evidence

Another excerpt from the untitled and unpublished memoir of Alasdair Duncan Magill, 1987. Chapter 53 – The Matter of Political Murder

Miss Amory, our clerk-typist, called my attention to the telephone on a chilly spring morning, early in March, 1935. It was already past 8 o'clock, and I was uncharacteristically late, as our youngest son was teething, and had kept my dear wife and I awake for most of the night before.

"It's Mrs. Mills," Miss Amory said, covering the receiver with her hand. "Calling for you, personally, Chief. She says that she has just found the body of her husband, out by the alligator pond."

"God save the mark," I exclaimed. "The old reprobate is dead at last! What are the odds, hey? Bludgeoned, stabbed, or shot by a jealous rival or fellow miscreant, do you think?"

"Really, Chief," Miss Amory sniffed. "That's not Christian of you to say such an unkind thing! The poor man is dead!"

"It may not be Christian, Miss Amory," I replied. "But it is most brutally realistic; Charley Mills was a thief, a pervert, and a blight on the community of Luna City. Those were his good points! I'll take Mrs. Mills' call in my office."

"Yes, Chief," Miss Amory still sounded disapproving. On my way to my own office, I looked into the chief investigator's small cubicle next to mine, to see if John Drury had arrived; he had. And he was in confabulation with Sgt. Grigoriev, whose countenance bore a worried frown upon it. John looked up at my rap on the door frame.

"Chief, it's bad news," he said with a grave expression on his own face, "There has been a message from the Marcus place. Sgt. Grigoriev has just been briefing me. The Professor's oldest son has been found dead this morning round in back of their house; his face bashed in with especial violence, bashed in with a stone! No idea of who did the foul deed, although the household seem to believe he was attacked sometime in the early morning. The blood is hardly congealed on his body and on the murder weapon. Mrs. Marcus called us, just now. This last week the Professor was helping his son and some of their friends build a working ballista and it's one of those stones they were stocking up to throw with it which killed Sergei Marcus."

"Oh, my god!" I exclaimed. "The professor! Is he in especial danger, do you surmise? This is appalling news! We were charged with keeping him and his family secure!"

"I don't think so, Chief," John replied. "And we don't know for certain if this was just some random mischance ... or malice on the part of an assassin. They say in the newspaper this morning that Stalin made an especially fiery radio speech a few days ago, calling again for the deaths of his enemies – and specifically mentioned Pavel Markov! In any case, I ordered Constable Vaughn to remain on guard at Marcus's house, until we can sort out the situation; if it is murder or merely an accident. Have there been any reports of unexplained strangers in town? We were charged with keeping track of that kind of thing..."

"Kapitan," Sgt. Grigoriev spoke up. "There is one stranger in town ... a young man riding on a ...what-do-you say ... an Indian motorcycle. With a sidecar. That is a brand of motorcycle, sir – not one made by Indians. A very nice motorcycle. I wish for one of my own, Kapitan-sir. This young man, he has a dog with him, a splendid large dog. No, I do not wish for a dog. But this stranger in town; he is camping in the field by the Mills place since last week."

"Most interesting, Sergeant," I said, having come swiftly to a decision, knowing that Mrs. Mills was waiting to speak to me on the telephone. "John, I believe that I will go and speak to this person first while you and Sgt. Grigoriev begin investigating the death of Sergei Marcus since I will need to go out to the Mills property anyway." At his interrogative eyebrow lifted, I added an explanation. "It seems also that Charley Mills has also been found dead, out at his place. Miss Amory just told me. I still must speak to Mrs. Mills. We should compare notes this afternoon, upon completing a preliminary review of our respective corpses."

John Drury whistled in astonishment. "It never rains but it pours, Captain! Two dead bodies in a single day! Some kind record for Luna City."

"I know," I sighed. On the rare occasions when my police were lumbered with dead bodies, they usually arrived singly, and it was usually a matter of simple observation and deduction to arrive at the reason for their deceased state. The great *(and purely literary)* detective-sleuth Sherlock Holmes would have little in the way of exercising his deductive skills in Luna City; in fact, were he real, he would perish of sheer boredom, unless he took up the profession of deducing which dog or coyote was killing chickens. Once in my office, I picked up the receiver, a little astonished to still find Mrs. Mills still waiting.

"Mrs. Mills," I said, by way of apology. "I am so sorry to have kept you waiting. It seems that we have experienced another sudden death in Luna City – but let me extend to you my sympathies on the loss of your husband ..."

"It is of little import to me," Carolina de San Pedro Mills replied, sounding as if distraught with grief were the farthest thing from her mind. "We were married as a matter of convenience only. For the business, you see."

"I hope that he did not suffer," I ventured. I privately hoped the opposite very much. Mrs. Mills snorted, in a somewhat derisive manner.

"No, I rather think he did not," she replied, decisively. "There was no mark upon him, save where he had lain heavily as he had fallen to the ground. He went down to feed his disgusting *caimán* – those three giant lizards in the pond – at sunset last night, and never returned."

"And you did not think it strange that he never returned? And raised no alarm? Strange that would be, for a married couple..." I swear that I could almost feel her shudder of revulsion, at a distance and over the tinny-sounding telephone line.

"*Dios mia!*" Mrs. Mills exclaimed. "Think you that we shared a bed?! A room, even! No, my husband had his place, and I had mine. And that is all that you need to know."

"One thing that I should ask, Mrs. Mills; have you touched or disturbed your husband's body. It might complicate the investigation, so I should be informed if you have done so."

"I did turn his body over," Carolina de San Pedro Mills confessed. "For I thought that he might still be alive. I did not wish my husband dead, Senor M'Gill. But at the hour of sunrise this morning, he was quite cold and stiff. I ... brought a bedquilt from his quarters to cover him. It seemed a decent thing to do. Besides," and Carolina de San Pedro, late the wife of Charley Mills sounded brutally practical. "Those dreadful black scavenger birds were already circling over the pond."

It seemed only good sense that John Drury, our most experienced investigator, should be the one dispatched to survey the most immediate crime scene. That the disreputable Charley Mills had perished of old age and the accumulated weight of his many crimes against the laws of God and Man? Only to be expected. I felt myself equal to making pro-forma visit to the scene, just to make certain that the black-hearted b*stard really was dead, and to authorize the call to the county coroner to come and remove the body. So I drove my trusty Ford to the old Mills place, a short distance down the dusty and much-traveled rural road south of Luna City. The turn-off to the Mills place was as obscure, and the homestead as desolate as ever; the current economic Depression had not been kind to the old farmstead, although the larger part of the unkindness had been due to the decades-long carelessness of the inheritor to a property which had once been the pride of Karnes County.

The gates to the place were not even maintained any more but sagged open at the side of the dusty drive under the weight of overgrown weeds and their own decrepitude. In what had been once a hay paddock, there was a small tent set up under a straggling hackberry tree, with a large Indian motorbike with sidecar parked by it. There was no sign of the camper with the motorbike, whose presence Sgt. Grigoriev had noted to me. The main farmhouse had burned down several years since: local rumor had it that Charley Mills had attempted unsuccessfully to collect on the lapsed insurance on the structure. The house remained as a burned and blackened shell, with morning glory vines already shrouding the mound of charred remains in strangling green vines and purple flowers. There was a barn still standing, leaning perilously to one side, with what had been a shed of some kind attached to the side of it. At a little distance from the house was a small outbuilding in considerably better repair, with a thread of smoke trickling from a tin chimney. I think it had once been a summer kitchen, then the quarters for the hired hands when Mills Farm was in it's glory days.

Carolina de San Pedro Mills waited for me there, leaning elegantly against one of the porch posts, doubtless having heard the engine of my Ford coming down the rutted drive through the desolate, abandoned farm.

Carolina de San Pedro: aye, what can I say? She was a bonny woman of about thirty at the time of which I write; elegant and forceful, for all that she wore trousers and men's shirts commonly. Old Spanish blood, said John Drury – aristocratic and proud as Lucifer. Why she had tied herself in marriage to that disgusting old reprobate Charley Mills for almost fifteen years was a riddle for the ages. John Drury speculated that it was because her kin had come out on the wrong side of the latest Mexican civil war, and marriage to Mills on our side of the border was as safe a harbor as the poor lass could manage. Well, at least she would be free of him now. I parked in the open space which once had served as a dooryard to the old house and clambered out from behind the wheel.

"Good morning to you, Mrs. Mills," I said, as I noticed that there was a very large dog, sitting in the doorway to the little outbuilding, regarding me with intelligent dark brown eyes. A young man with a large coffee mug in his hand, lounged in one of the simple chairs on the porch. The dog was covered in fine, kinky fur the color of butterscotch candy, the young man was dressed like a tramp. Like the dog, he was also regarding me with the same mixture of intelligence and curiosity. "Are you going to introduce me to your friend, then?"

"But of course," Carolina de San Pedro Mills replied, not a bit put out. "This is our guest of some two weeks; Perry Woodstone, and Françoise. John, this is Chief McGill, captain of the police in Luna City."

"My traveling companion is a pure-bred pedigreed French poodle, you see, so she has a French name," Perry Woodstone drawled. He had an educated manner about him. Yes, he was one of the gentry, I thought. He put his coffee mug in his other hand and shook mine with a firm grip. "Pleased to make your acquaintance, Chief McGill. Just call me Perry if you would be so kind. It's short for Percival, which I have been trying to live down for simply years. Mumsy was a fan of the King Arthur legends." He paused to sip his coffee. "I see you are wondering what I am doing here. I have a stipend from the Federal Writer's Project – to go forth and collect local material and reminiscences from aged citizens. It's not a particularly generous stipend, so I make the most of it by taking to the tramping life in making my funds stretch like elastic rubber bands."

"Oh, aye?" I replied, extremely skeptical. "So, what exactly was it which brought you to Mills Farm, Mr. Woodstone?"

"It was the opportunity to talk to Mr. Mills which was my primary impetus," young Woodstone replied, with a shade of regret. "I thought that he might have some interesting tales to tell of his days with the Dalton and the Bent Cactus gang; tales which the FWP might find worthwhile to include in an upcoming project."

"It sounds like you have an interesting project on hand," I remarked. "Was Mr. Mills forthcoming?"

"No, he was not," Perry Woodstone admitted. He sounded regretful. I wondered if young Woodstone had ambitions as a novelist. "What I had heard about him, made it sound like a fascinating character, but he was not willing to talk about himself. A pity, as his yarns might have made an interesting addition to the prospective visitor's guide which the FWP has in mind."

"Mr. Mills' yarns might have been a tad too spicy for a guide to this part of Texas," I said, rather annoyed. "And the spiciest of them might have opened him up to criminal prosecution. The late Mr. Mills was a particularly scabrous customer, with a criminal record as long as your arm. He was always able to afford the services of an effective lawyer, though." Here was this aristocratic lay-about, being paid by the government to scribble tourist guides; I was offended. "And how long have you been camping here, and who else have you conversed with in the time that you have been here?"

"Hardly anyone, aside from my good hostess and her late husband," Woodstone admitted. He didn't sound particularly distressed. "Am I being interrogated? And if so, on what grounds? I daresay the FWP has a lawyer on retainer, and I should let you know that my stepfather is also lawyer of a very combative nature and Mumsy dotes on me. Which is embarrassing, in it's own way ..."

"There has been a murder in Luna City during the sometime last night; a murder which might possibly have political connections," I replied. In retrospect, I should not have been so indiscreet, but I was rather rattled. I did not care for precious Perry, slumming through the country on a government stipend. But if he had a cast-in-iron alibi for his whereabouts during the previous night? We would have to scratch him from a list of suspects with an animus against Professor Markov.

Young Perry Woodstone nodded and exchanged a significant look with his hostess. "Mrs. Mills can vouch for my whereabouts yesterday afternoon and evening. I was interviewing Mr. Mills until about the hour of five o-clock. Then I conversed with Mrs. Mills until about half-past, and we drove to Beeville to meet some of her friends at around six. We ate supper together at a quaint little diner in Beeville. We did not leave the diner until two in the morning, as Mrs. Mills' friends can verify, if it comes to that."

"I hope they were of a reputable class," I suggested dryly, shifting my gaze towards Carolina Mills. "And would have no problem confirming your presence, should our inquiries lead us in that direction?"

"Of a certainty," Mrs. Mills affirmed, with an edged and dangerous smile. "Now that sense has returned to this country and the prohibition on consumption of alcoholic beverages has been revoked, my friends and associates are all law-abiding and respectable citizens. They have no problem with ... as you say ... assisting the officers of the law with their inquiries."

"I should hope so," I conceded defeat on this front graciously enough. "Now, if you would conduct me to the body of the late Mr. Mills, so that I might satisfy myself that his mortal end did not involve anything suspicious?"

"Of course," Mrs. Mills replied, still smiling that edged smile. "My pleasure ..."

Well, I reflected; *That must have been the most pleasure that the late Mr. Charley Mills had ever given to his last in a series of wives and carnal connections. In that case, she was well-entitled to a bit of satisfaction at having outlasted the old b*stard, and to have a young admirer dancing attendance must have added to her pleasure on that account.*

I followed her down through the ruined meadows and paddocks of the Mills place, to a sullen muddy pool down on the hillside below the collection of shabby buildings which were all that was left of the place. Three alligators of middling size lived there; their pond being surrounded by a ramshackle fence; the only thing keeping the alligators from departing as fast as their crooked legs could drag them. Local legend had it that Old Mills was in the habit of feeding the dead bodies of business rivals to the alligators, although local experts insisted that such was not an efficient means, given the relative size of a dead human body and Old Charleys' pet alligators. Pigs, on the other hand, I was assured by the same experts, were the most efficient means when it came to disposing of an unwanted corpse, but I digress.

A long form shrouded in a ragged bedquilt lay on the ground just outside the fence, a pair of dusty boots with worn-out soles showing at one end. I lifted the quilt from the other end and regarded the unlovely, whiskered countenance of Charley Mills; clay-cold, and pale, save for a blue shadow over one cheek where the blood had settled. His hands lay at his sides, the fingers loose, already relaxing from rigor mortis. A quick survey of his lifeless form revealed no obvious wounds, or signs of violence

"He was stiff, as one frozen, when I found him at first light this morning," Carolina de San Pedro commented, over my shoulder.

"Ah, then," I said. "I think it would be safe to say he has been dead for more than six hours, possibly close to eight. And there are no obvious marks of violence anywhere that you could see? I shall wait for a final verdict from the country coroner if you wish it, but it is my initial finding that your husband is dead of natural causes. Had he complained of feeling ill or palsied, of late? Light-headed, or a weakness in his extremities?"

Carolina de San Pedro Mills frowned, considering. "He had complained of a persistent ache in his right arm, and of being short of breath. But that was all, and he had complained of aches and pains often before."

"Probably his heart finally giving out on him," I said, mustering a bit of sympathy for her. "He was of the age when something like that would have been expected. Well, if you do not entertain any doubts about the nature of his passing, then make whatever arrangements that you need to make for the body. If you have any suspicions of foul play, then do call my office. My sympathies, Mrs. Mills."

"Thank you, Chief Magill," she responded, although her eyes were quite dry.

I was about to bid her farewell and take my leave when I was struck by a further thought. "Mrs. Mills, I assume that you will inherit whatever estate Mr. Mills has left. Will you choose to remain here or settle elsewhere?"

"This?" Carolina de San Pedro Mills looked around at the derelict property. "My... husband had other children by his ... women. His relatives may also have rights to this place as well. For myself, I care nothing. I have my own income, and certain resources. I have my own plans, which are no concern of yours, Chief Magill, but thank you for asking. You have no need of concern for me."

"That is good to know," I replied, and took my leave with considerable respect. She was indeed a wholly capable and admirable woman, who had made her bargain with the late Mr. Mills and escaped from that situation on her own terms. Not that I would have recommended her method to any woman whom I held dear ... but never mind.

I drove next to the Markov/Marcus house, suspecting that I would find John Drury still there. He was, and accompanied by Sgt. Grigoriev. The two of them were contemplating another body; the body of a much younger man, and one of much more use to humanity in general and to the family of Professor Markov in specific than the late and spectacularly un-mourned Charley Mills. There was no doubt that murder was involved; that much was chillingly obvious.

The body of Sergei Marcus or such was the young man's official identity, lay sprawled at full length in the tall grass at the bottom of the garden. Any identification which might be made through his facial features had been obliterated by the roughly rounded stone which appeared to have been the means of effecting his demise. Said stone lay in the tall grass, a short distance from the body; a rounded granite stone about the size of a grapefruit, generously clotted with dried blood and other ghastly materiel. There was a stack of similar stones, unblemished by gore, a short distance away from a peculiar contrivance which I readily identified as a quarter-scale reproduction of a medieval siege machine.

"So, what do you think, John?" I asked, as I came upon the party contemplating the dead body. This included Professor Marcus, who was standing at a slight remove.

"He was killed by someone whom he trusted to get close enough," John Drury replied. "Someone whom he did not consider to be a danger to him, who then had the element of surprise."

"This is unconscionable!" Professor Marcus exclaimed, turning an accusing eye on John and myself. "We trusted that we would be safe here … and now! My … son … someone whom I regarded as a son, who was our first protector, has been piteously and foully murdered! How can we think ourselves to be safe now? My wife is most distraught!"

"Calm yourself, Professor," I replied. "This is a sad development indeed, but my department is not without resources! Until we catch the miscreant who has done this awful deed, Sgt. Grigoriev will be detailed as a guard, twenty-four hours a day. He is one of your countrymen, a loyal White, in spite of his resemblance to the Red dictator, and as such, has been in our confidence regarding your peculiar situation since the very first. You have your orders, Sgt. Grigoriev," I added to that gentleman, who rendered a more than emphatic salute toward John Drury and me. Sgt Grigoriev directed some remarks in his native language to the professor, which we did not understand, but which Professor Marcus seemed to find reassuring.

We made arrangements for the body of poor Sergei to be removed for close examination by the coroner, as this was obviously a murder, unlike the natural death of Charley Mills. Leaving Sgt. Grigoriev with instructions to secure the safety of Professor Marcus, day, and night, even if he had to sleep across the doorway of the Marcus bedroom, John Drury and I returned to the police station, considerably vexed, reminding myself to put in a trunk call sometime in the afternoon to the so-called Federal Writers' Project to verify the existence of the adventurous Mr. Woodstone. Even if he had been vouched for by Mrs. Mills, and her Beeville friends, I wanted to assure myself that he was whom he claimed to be. Such vexation increased when Miss Amory informed us that Mayor McAllister had hurried over from his offices in City Hall. She had shown him into my office, where he was waiting upon our return.

"He looked mighty distressed, Chief Magill, so he did," she assured us. "I didn't know what to tell him; just that you would speak with him immediately."

I sighed heavily and turned to John Drury. "I was hoping that you and I would have a chance to review the situation just between ourselves. Well, let us confabulate together with the Mayor and count ourselves fortunate that he is himself an able and intelligent man."

"If we are doubly fortunate," John Drury replied, as we climbed the stairs. "He may have something of import, or at least, some insight to contribute."

"We live in hope, John, we live in hope. Good morning, Mr. Mayor; I take it that you have been informed of the dire news, regarding the Marcus' dedicated bodyguard?"

"So I have," Mayor McAllister replied, grimly. "And it indicates to me that an assassin is stalking our refugees. How much easier to murder the Professor than first to remove his most-dedicated protector?"

"For the nonce, the Professor does have a most-dedicated protector," I replied. "Sgt. Grigoriev. In the meantime, Mr. Drury and I will bend every effort toward apprehending this nefarious assassin. I assure you, Mayor, there has been no threat toward the Marcus family from outsiders in Luna City. To the best of my knowledge, there has only been one notable outsider in recent days, and last night, he was in Beeville. Poncy-looking chap on a motorcycle with a big dog in the sidecar. He has an alibi, and in any case, I just don't fancy him as the murdering type, although I will have to check on that with the office that he purports to work for."

Mayor McAllister nodded in agreement. "One of your effete intellectual types. I saw him with the dog when he came into town. Stopped at the Icehouse and asked for directions to the Mills place. To be frank, gentlemen, I have not seen any other strangers in town, only the usual drummers and traveling salesmen doing business with the grocery store, the hardware ... guests at the Cattleman, most of them. Darius Bodie says that all the guests this last week are regulars with good and solid reasons for being here in Luna City. Nothing that would raise any alarm in their purpose for visiting."

Darius Bodie, a member of the Bodie clan who owned the feed mill and the Cattleman, was the regular manager of the place; he was also a lodge brother of mine, and like John Drury, a member of the Methodist congregation. Our social connections wove such a tight spider-web across Luna City that plucking at a single strand would have aroused our professional interest. Interest for being without overt purpose, for being a certain kind of outsider or obvious foreigner, or for asking impertinent questions about the Professor and his family.

Now John Drury cleared his throat. "As I pointed out earlier, Chief," he ventured in a most thoughtful manner. "Sergei Marcus was the long-time bodyguard for the Professor and his family. He would have been too experienced, too wary, to allow a stranger within reach of a heavy stone with which to bash out his brains. I cannot see it, Chief. The situation suggests treachery to me, treachery among the household, or their circle of friends and associates. Someone whom Sergei Marcus otherwise knew and trusted."

Mayor McAllister bent an interrogatory regard upon me. "Have they had any visitors of late, other than Dimitri's school playfellows? I am not aware of any. As Mr. Drury suggests, the secret assassin may be within the household. Someone trusted, even intimate; how many adults of either sex are there within that household?"

"Three," I admitted, reluctantly. "The Professor's wife, of course. Pilar the housekeeper. And Mikhail, supposedly the second son – but in reality the Professor's long-time research assistant. If we are considering all possibilities, even the unlikely ..."

"As the great detective, Mr. Holmes remarked," Mr. McAllister said, "'When you have eliminated all which is impossible, then whatever remains, however improbable, must be the truth.'"

"We must eliminate the impossible," John Drury concluded. "The impossible are all the long-time residents of Luna City. The recent visitors are being investigated and eliminated, even as we speak. This leaves us with the three intimate members of the household: Mrs. Marcus, Pilar Gonzalez, and Mikhail."

"The first, I think must be eliminated," I said. "She has been married to the Professor since before his banishment from Russia. I cannot think that a woman might cherish and nurture a murderous grudge for two decades..."

"Ah, but you have been happily married yourself, Captain," John Drury replied. "I have known of married women who cheerfully murdered their husbands for very trivial reasons, but I do agree with your estimation. Mrs.

Marcus has always struck me as a devoted wife. After all, she has a child by the Professor, and gives every evidence of caring deeply for the man. I think that we should examine the other two in the household most closely; Mikhail Marcus, or whatever his name might be in reality, and Pilar Gonzalez, the housekeeper."

Mayor McAllister frowned, as if he ruminated on a sudden, inconvenient suspicion. "Mikhail. If memory serves, has been with the household nearly as long as Mrs. Marcus. Miss Gonzalez is a more recent addition to the household. If I recall correctly, she came to work for them shortly before they moved from Mexico City – claiming that she wanted to return to her Gonzalez kinfolk in Luna City."

"Then she would be a connection to Don Antonio, of the Rancho Encino?" I asked.

John Drury replied, thoughtfully. "There might be a connection. Perhaps Don Antonio can vouch for her."

Mayor McAllister had an abstracted expression on his face. "There is something that my daughter said about the Gonzalez woman; that she was a cousin of some sort, through a relation of Don Antonio's in Mexico. But the conversation with Letty was weeks ago, and I was not paying complete attention at the time."

"Then we should confirm this with Miss Letty," John Drury suggested, as he made a note. "As part of our investigations. And ask Don Antonio to verify the connection."

"Let us break here for an hour or so," I replied, mapping out the course of our inquiries. "Mr. Albert Wyler might wish to be a part of this investigation, as he has been instrumental in offering a safe refuge to the Marcus family. The Wylers are on the telephone exchange, but the

Rancho Encino is not. I myself will drive out to the Rancho Rincon de los Robles and invite Don Antonio to consult with us. A man who rates matters of honor and loyalty to clan is not one to be interrogated like a common suspect."

"Wisely diplomatic, Chief," John Drury advised, with a grin which quite removed the sting of the words, "For he is not only of the old Spanish nobility, but as proud as Lucifer. Take care that he might be offended on the part of his kinfolk being accused of being a murderer."

"Exactly, John, and I shall take every care," I replied, and I did, for when I drove out to the Rancho, I was presented to Don Antonio after a short wait in the parlor. The grandee of the Rancho Rincon was, I was given to understand, overseeing the matter of an amatory encounter between a prized female goat and a ram of note, and would be present shortly.

This was the new house, which had been grafted onto the old adobe structure not a decade before, incorporating many new and pleasing features; a tall house with a wide veranda on the ground floor and another on the second. Don Antonio's sister Aïda received me in the parlor; a lady with a most distracted expression, who soon excused herself, saying that the kiln was already cooling, and that she must go to see if her latest batch of pottery had been successfully fired. Don Antonio's sisters were artistic, you see. They dabbled in all those fine and womanly arts, save that of marriage. The eldest of them, Dona Carmen, had long been an invalid and died of complications to her main malady several years before, but her sisters, Aïda and Leonora were still in fine fettle and inflicting their various handiworks on all who came within range. *(Their father was an aficionado of grand opera, afflicting his daughters with the names of his favorite heroines. Frankly, I think his lady wife ought to have objected, strenuously. What those poor girls must have endured during their schooldays didn't bear thinking about. But never mind.*)

"Don Antonio," I said, as soon as that gentleman came into the parlor. "I excuse the urgency of this errand, but we have the investigation of a murder on our hands. We are looking into the background of any who might have reason and motivation for that murder, and one of them is a person represented to be a Gonzalez kinswoman."

"Who is this woman?" Don Antonio demanded, all lordly wrath. Frankly, even at his advanced age, the man was a worthy and substantial opponent. All of those who bore the name of Gonzalez or Gonzales in Luna City were related in some degree to Don Antonio, the laird of the second-largest ranch property in the locality. He was a proud and worthy keeper of the dignity of the name and clan, as John Drury had observed.

"Pilar Gonzalez, who is currently employed in the household of Professor Marcus as a housekeeper and maid-of-all work," I replied. "It has been suggested that she is a distant cousin of your family, from Mexico. We are meeting in my office for a consultation on this matter within the hour. We would be honored and enlightened also if you would attend. It is a matter of urgency, otherwise I would suggest a time of your convenience."

Don Antonio nodded, magisterially. "I understand, Chief Magill. I will, of course, be present if the matter is as urgent as you say."

"It is," I replied, and he gave me a severe look. Oh, he was the undisputed clan-chief, no mistake at all about

234

that, not in the slightest. "I have heard that the Mills man – Mr. Charley Mills – is dead. Is that true?"

"It is," I agreed. "For I have just come from examining the body, this very day."

"Ah," Don Antonio replied, with an inscrutable expression. "Interesting, indeed. Well, then, my nephew Ambrosiano may proceed with a proposal of marriage to his lady now that she is free. He is a lad afflicted with an over-developed sense of honor, Chief Magill. Divorce was never possible, for a man as devout as he is. But an honest widow? That is acceptable to Ambrosiano and the Church to which he has given all loyalty and devotion. Sad as a death might be, it certainly provides an acceptable solution for Ambrosiano! However, I do not think any of my ancestors bothered with such scruples, any more than my goats."

"Ah … and that is why this county is strewn thick with your clan, even as your pastures are covered thick with pedigreed goats," I replied, and Don Antonio agreed with a bark of laughter.

One of his hands drove Don Antonio in his own Model A, following my own back to the police station. It was then a little past one in the afternoon. I saw that Mayor McAllister's Hudson was parked in front of the station, and that John Drury was climbing the steps to the front door, in company with Albert Wyler.

We gathered in my office; John and I, Don Antonio, Albert Wyler, Mayor McAllister, and young Miss Letty, who didn't seem abashed or intimidated at all by the dignity and importance of the company. She was about fifteen or so, that year, if I recall correctly: a very composed and prim young lady. John brought in a chair from his own office, so that she could sit down, next to her father.

"Now, Miss McAllister, we have some questions to ask you, since you have been a frequent visitor to the Marcus house. It seems that there has been a murder there; of Sergei, the oldest brother."

"Yes," she answered, readily, her eyes up and level. "I know about Sergei. I'm dreadful sorry. Dym is our friend; mine and Douglas and Stephen's. The boys were building a ballista as a class project. Sergei helped, sometimes. And he walked Dym to and from school, every single day."

"How often were you at their house, after school?" John Drury took over questioning at a nod from me.

"Almost every day," Miss Letty replied.

"And you spoke with Miss Pilar Gonzalez, the Marcus housekeeper?" John prodded, and Miss Letty frowned slightly.

"Not very often," she replied, after a moment of consideration. "Pilar was usually busy in the kitchen, while we were with Professor Marcus and Dym, out in the workshop. Sometimes she served us tea, sometimes – with Mrs. Marcus's walnut cookies. We liked the walnut cookies," Miss Letty added, irrelevantly. "They were baked in this special iron, which made them in halves, like walnut shells, and then filled with buttercream and pressed together. Mrs. Marcus showed me how they were made. I had never seen the like. But they are foreign, you see..."

"You spoke to Pilar Gonzalez, though," John Drury persisted, and Miss Letty returned to the immediate concern. "When she told you that she was related to the Luna City Gonzalez family. Try to recall her exact words, your exact conversation on that occasion, Miss McAllister, as this is a matter of murder, now."

Miss Letty frowned again, completely absorbed in recollection. Her father kept silent, but patted her shoulder, and both Don Antonio and Albert Wyler waited breathlessly for her reply.

"That was the day that we – the boys, that is – decided to build a ballista for a class project, and Professor Marcus and the boys went to his workroom. He asked Mrs. Marcus to bring a book from his study, and when she went to look for it, Pilar came in to clear away the china and tea things. I think I surprised her, offering to help," Miss Letty confessed, honestly.

"What did you think of her?" John Drury sounded so casual, but that was part of his art, to lead the investigatory conversation subtly, in the direction to which he wanted it to go, so that the person being interrogated would be at their ease, frank and unconcerned ... and bubbling information like a fountain.

"I thought she didn't seem much like a maid at all," Miss Letty replied, her small face serious and thoughtful. "I thought she was like Carmen, in the opera. You know, bold and brazen, with many boyfriends, singing about who she wanted most to flirt and kiss and dance with."

Here, Don Antonio stifled a snort of laughter. Miss Letty continued. "I asked her if she was kin to Don Antonio at the Rancho, as all the folk named Gonzalez with a 'z' or Gonzales with an 's' hereabouts are kin in some degree. Papa says so, since they have been here, practically forever. And she said that she was; a distant cousin from Mexico. She said that she was..." and Miss Letty frowned in concentration, calling to mind the exact words, and names. "... the daughter of Don Pedro Rodriguez of Morelia. He was the alcalde there, she said. The mayor, I guess. But only for a brief time, she said, and it was all complicated."

At that moment, Don Antonio's countenance darkened, and he frowned, dangerously. John Drury looked from Don Antonio to the slim young girl, with her father's hand on hers.

"You are absolutely certain that is what she said? A daughter of Don Pedro Rodriguez, the sometime mayor of Morelia? John Drury's voice was calm, level, steady, but he was alert to the charged atmosphere in the room.

"I am, Mr. Drury," Miss Letty replied, her voice absolutely level, certain. "That was exactly what she said. Papa will say that I don't forget what people have told me."

"She does," Mayor McAllister affirmed, with an affectionate glance toward his daughter. "Like a baby elephant. She does not forget. Ever."

Our glances crossed, like upraised swords; Mine, Mayor McAllister, and John Drury. I said then, "Thank you Miss McAllister, for confirming what you were told. Mayor, I think that we are finished with this. You may take your daughter home, or to go fetch an ice-cream, as a reward for having been a good citizen, in coming forth and cooperating in this investigation."

Mayor McAllister nodded; a good and responsible citizen, and better yet, a good and responsible father. Whatever was to come next in this, he had his daughter to consider.

"Keep me informed as to the results of your inquiry," was all that Mayor McAllister said, and as they departed, little Miss Letty regarded me with that serious and level gaze.

"When you see him, tell Dym that Douglas and Stephen and I are awful sorry," she said. "Sergei was to Dym what Douglas is to me; my big brother."

And they were gone, the door to my office closing after them. We heard their footsteps on the stairway, Miss Amory showing them out, and when the silence in the room had gone on for some moments, John Drury looked to Don Antonio, still scowling, and nodded.

Don Antonio cleared his throat. "My cousin, Pedro Rodriguez, the alcalde of Morelia? He had only sons to lived to the age of adults. He and his wife had a daughter, who did not live past a year. I am certain of this, as we corresponded on the breeding of goats for many years. It was a grief to him, the death of that daughter. The woman in the household of this Anglo Marcus..."

"Not an Englishman, but a Russian, fleeing political persecution," I added.

Don Antonio scowled, even more darkly. "She is an imposter. My cousin, the alcalde of Morelia, has no living daughter, and his sons have not yet married and brought wives to his house. He often wrote of his sorrow on that account. If you are seeking an assassin in the household of this Marcus, I would seek no farther than this woman."

"Indeed," I agreed. It did make it all rather plain and logical. Pilar Gonzalez or whoever she might be, had insinuated herself into the household, perhaps to spy upon them, and waited until she had the opportunity to kill Sergei, the dedicated bodyguard. And now that she had killed once, Professor Markov must be next. And our Sergeant Grigoriev must be in terrible danger.

"I think that we should ..." I began to say but was interrupted by the urgent ringing of the phone on my desk. I picked it up, and Miss Amory exclaimed, "Antonin – Tony! Sgt. Grigoriev is on the line, Chief! He says that the matter is urgent!"

"Put him through, Miss Amory," I commanded. I had never heard Miss Amory become so emotional. *As it later emerged, she and Sgt. Grigoriev were, as the saying once was, walking out together. They married later that year. The Police Department presented them with a gift of a set of silver Apostle spoons, on the happy occasion. She left the job upon marrying, as was the custom, since his pay was sufficient to support them, and the family which subsequently developed.*

Now I waited for Miss Amory, with several false starts, to complete the connection. "Chief," I finally heard Sgt. Grigoriev say. "You had better come quick. That b***h has got the boy."

"We're on the way, Sergeant," I said, struggling for calm. "Try and keep the professor safe."

"*S'delayu, kapitan,*" he replied. *Will do, Captain,* and then the connection was cut. I looked at John Drury, at Don Antonio and Albert Wyler. I had guaranteed the safety of the Markovs to Mr. Wyler, and he had assured them that they would be safe in Luna City. Safe to lead a normal, ordinary life. That it had turned out otherwise was a deep and never-to-be sufficiently regretted stain upon our honor and our word as gentlemen. "Sgt. Grigoriev says that Miss Pilar Whatever-her-name-is has taken a hostage. The boy Dym, I judge. He has called for assistance."

"And he will have it," John Drury exclaimed, as Don Antonio swore such oaths in his native tongue as would have set my office furniture on fire, and Albert Wyler smiled, grim and determined. There was no one in the office downstairs save Miss Amory. Our single duty constable was out serving summons for a court trial in Karnesville. There was only myself and John Drury.

"We are coming with you, then," Albert Wyler announced, perfectly level and assured. I only noticed then that he had a holstered revolver at his side. So, of course did Don Antonio. That gentleman's readiness for gunplay had never been reduced since he fought a duel with a family rival in the street outside the ice-cream parlor a decade previously.

"A matter of family honor," Don Antonio added, in a voice which sounded like a mountain landslide gaining gravely velocity.

"Gentlemen, it is a matter for sworn police ..." I protested, even as I secured my own side arm from the lower desk drawer, and John Drury snorted.

"Captain, in the early days in Texas, it was every fit man with a horse and a weapon, sworn into the Rangers, against a threat. Consider Don Antonio and Mr. Wyler sworn into law enforcement, for the term of the emergency."

"Agreed, gentlemen, agreed." I replied, and we headed down the staircase in a thundering rush. We did not bother with the automobiles, since the Markov/Marcus residence was just around the corner, a brisk five-minute walk from the new police station. We did it in a bare two minutes, although I confess to puffing slightly. Albert Wyler and Don Antonio, being of my age yet accustomed to a strenuous outdoor life, were not in the least discommoded by our haste, or the emergency. Sgt. Grigoriev and the Marcus couple met us, just at the corner where Pin Oak and Church streets met at the parish church of Saints Margaret and Anthony. At some distance, several congregants and a black-robed priest gathered on the church steps, watching our approach. Mrs. Markov was near to hysterics, begging us to rescue her child.

"She has a knife at my boy's throat!" Mrs. Markov wailed. "She has promised that she will cut his throat, unless my husband surrenders to her!" It was heartrending, to witness her panic and distress, although Sgt. Grigoriev seemed more embarrassed and annoyed by her display of motherly emotion. Don Antonio raised his voice, and called out in Spanish to the priest, obviously explaining the situation.

"Sonia, I will do what that *сука* wishes," exclaimed Professor Markov, "And give myself up..."

Mrs. Marcus dissolved into a fountain of weeping.

"You should not," Stephen Wyler said, calm and stalwart. "She *(although he used a cruder descriptive for a female of our species)* will not escape, whether she murders you, or the boy. She knows this, for certainty. I gave my word that your family would be safe, Professor, and I keep my word."

"Where is she, with the boy?" John Drury did not waste time.

"In the kitchen of the house," Sgt, Grigoriev replied.

I came to a decision. "John, go around to the yard and prevent her from leaving with the boy from the back door. Meanwhile, we'll go through the house ... how many doors into the kitchen are there?"

"Three," replied Albert Wyler, as the owner of the house in question. "A door to the hallway, one to the dining room, and another to the butler's pantry, but that's a blind end, as there's only a window to the outside in the pantry."

"Sgt. Grigoriev. Since you have made yourself familiar with the house and are the youngest and fittest; you climb in through the pantry window. Mr. Wyler and Don Antonio; we'll go in through the hallway and the dining room. Five minutes – will that be sufficient time?"

"*Da, Kapitan,*" Sgt. Grigoriev snapped a quick salute and hared away, following John Drury toward the back of the Markov house. Good lad, that; now that reinforcements had arrived, and there was a plan devised, he was afire for action. Albert Wyler and Don Antonio hurried with me, while the priest and a scattering of lady parishioners clustered around the Professor and his wife.

The house was eerily silent; a radio was on in the parlor, sounding tinny and unreal. Albert Wyler, Don Antonio, and I entered silently through the half-open front door, moving with our best efforts at stealing noiselessly on cat-feet like Indians. In spite of our best efforts, we did make some small noise, as the wooden floor creaked with age and there was no carpet. There was a scrape of a window being forced farther open, as Don Antonio and I approached the door at the end of the hall. I unholstered the revolver that I was accustomed to carrying only when absolutely necessary. At a nod, Albert Wyler detached himself from our small group, and vanished into the dining room, just as a woman's voice, sweet and poisonous, called from the kitchen.

"Markov, you traitor to the proletariat; are you surrendering to me, in exchange for the life of your spawn?"

"No, he is not," I announced, square in the doorway, with Don Antonio at my shoulder, his pistol also drawn. "Miss Gonzalez, I am arresting you for the murder of Sergei Markov, for conspiracy to commit murder, and for kidnapping. Put down the knife and let the lad go."

She stood with her back against the sink. A long butcher knife in her right hand was pressed against the throat of the boy. Her left hand holding him fast across his chest and shoulders, a dangerous smile on her lips. She was gloating at the thought of blood; a wicked woman she was, glorying in her wickedness and lust to shed blood. There was a narrow thread of red gore on the boy Dym's throat and dripping onto his white shirt-collar, but the lad seemed unnaturally calm. A curious thing, under the circumstances. He looked across the room at me, seeming to wait for a sign, tensed to react to the right signal.

"Running dog of the vile capitalists!" she spat, "Who suck the blood of the proletariat, the working people! This spawn of the criminal Markov will die, and so will you; all who thwart the will of the working classes!"

"Lass, you'll never get away," I took my most conciliatory tone of voice, although I feared that it was wasted on this fanatical bit of skirt. "My men have the house surrounded, Leave the boy go..."

"No!" she screamed, suddenly, irrationally enraged. At that moment, the back door swung open, so violently that the door banged against the wall. John Drury stood silhouetted against the bright daylight, his long-barreled Colt revolver drawn and leveled. She couldn't help but look around at this new threat, and in that moment the lad Dym took action; he grabbed at the arm which held the knife and bit hard like a savage on her hand. He drew blood, as he squirmed out of her grip, kicking out at her legs as he dove to the ground. She shrieked again as she lost her grasp on him. The lad was away, rolling on the kitchen floor. John Drury's Colt crashed a single shot, Don Antonio's long, old-fashioned revolver a second after. A red cicatrice bloomed in the center of Pilar Gonzalez' forehead; a second shot rocked her head backward, and she fell like a sack of old clothes, instantly stone dead. Sgt. Grigoriev appeared in the pantry door, also with weapon in hand. He looked vaguely disappointed that the murderer and hostage-taker was already dead, although a cloud of expended power still hazed the room.

"Good shooting, gentlemen," I remarked, upon recovering my hearing. My ears rang for some minutes afterwards. "I cannot say when I have appreciated some timely marksmanship more than today."

"The honor and good name of my family," Don Antonio returned his own pistol to his holster, with an expression of steely resolve. "This woman impugned it and I do not forgive such transgressions readily."

"A murderer and a liar," John Drury was as calm as if this kind of affray happened regularly. Perhaps in his long-ago youth in the wild days of Texas it had. "And well sorted. Karnes County is spared the cost and trouble of a trial, not to mention the international embarrassment. You OK, young fella?" he added, as he helped Dym Markov up from the floor.

"I am, sir," Dym Markov replied, with remarkable aplomb. "Thank you. I knew that Sgt. Grigoriev would bring help at once."

"That was a brave move," John Drury mused, most respectfully. "Biting her hand and then kicking her legs as you fell. Did someone teach you that and how to pick your moment, or did you just make it up on the spur of the moment."

"Oh, Sergei taught me," Dym replied, his expression briefly sorrowful. "He was good at fighting tricks. I know he wasn't really my big brother, but I thought of him as if he really was."

It later emerged that the woman that we knew as Pilar Gonzalez was a long-time dedicated Communist, whose duty was to spy on the Markov family, and until the death sentence was declared on the Professor, that her assignment was to facilitate, if possible, their kidnapping and return to Russia. It was only when the Cheka higher-ups lost patience at the end, that she was ordered to assassinate Professor Markov. A fortunate escape for the Markov family, for she might easily have poisoned them all, without anyone being wiser.

* * *

"And that was the resolution," Miss Letty replied, the next morning, when Richard and the regulars at the stammtisch all chorused for the final chapter in the saga of political murder. Everyone had read the excerpt from Chief Magill's memoir; the email newsletter with the account had flown on the wings of the internet to people normally not interested in the goings-on of the Luna City Historical Society. "Hardly a mystery at all, in the end. Professor Markov and his family lived in peace and quiet in Luna

City until ... I think 1939. Dym and Stephen and I had graduated from high school that year, and Professor Markov was offered a position at the Chicago Institute of Technology, and from there into some high governmental position, to do with secret weapons development, or so everyone said. He and his wife were protected by our government from then on. Eventually, Professor Markov worked for NASA."

"What about your friend, Dym?" Richard asked. "What happened to him?"

"He had a very adventurous life," Miss Letty replied with a small sigh. "He learned to fly, as he was passionately interested in air power, and everyone knew that a war was coming. When it did, Dym went to Canada and volunteered for the RAF; he always said that it was to uphold the honor of all White Russians, after Hitler allied with Stalin in 1939. He fought in the Battle of Britain as a member of the Eagle Squadron, you see. Douglas and I were very fond of Dym."

"He sounds like a dangerous man to be fond of," Richard replied, assuming that Dym Markov must have had a short life but a merry one and that he likely hadn't lived for very long, given the War and all.

Miss Letty smiled sweetly, obviously intuiting his thoughts. "Oh, he was a caution, Dym. When America joined the War, he transferred to our Army Air Force. I met him in London, in 1944. We went for supper at the Strand and had a marvelous time, talking over old times. He retired as a major-general in the Air Force. We exchanged Christmas cards for decades. They settled in Colorado Springs, eventually. His wife was very nice, and they had seven children."

"There is no ending like a happy one," Richard replied.

A Change of Management

"You know, Richard – you will have to tell the Café staff soon," Jess remarked, at the end of their usual Tuesday budget and management confab. Richard sighed.

"Given the speed and accuracy of the bush telegraph around here, I think they probably already have an idea," he replied, glumly. Richard's heart ached at the thought of leaving the Café. He had trained staff and built up a money-sink of a business. He had taken it from a simple coffee-and-breakfast place into a full-service six days a week lunch and supper culinary destination for discriminating foodies across Karnes County and even as far as San Antonio and Corpus Christi. But the fact remained that it was small, barely seating more than forty at a time, even if the outside tables under an awning on the wide sidewalk were in play. And with summer temperatures in late afternoon flirting with if not actually consummating triple digits – those tables were not popular for evening dining for at least four months out of the year. The kitchen was on a modest scale, although he had done his professional best to make the absolute most of those limitations.

He had instilled perfection into every aspect of the Café and was already feeling alternate twinges of boredom and mad envy of the palatial dining room, up-to-the-minute newly renovated and modernized kitchen, and all the culinary possibilities offered by the Cattleman. Boredom for him, he already realized, was the first step on that seductively attractive paving which led straight to hell.

"They may have heard rumors," Jess explained, patiently. "But they all would like to hear it straight from you, although Araceli already is pretty certain."

"I have never been able to keep anything of import from Araceli," Richard was glum. "And since you and she are besties with Katie, who already knows of my plans ... you are correct. What do Miss Letty and Doc Wyler have in mind when it comes to replacing me?"

"They don't," Jess grinned. "You are irreplaceable. One of a kind. Doc and Miss Letty figure that what with Luc, the kids — that is Bree and Robbie as alternating backups in the kitchen, with Araceli to ride herd on them all, and boss the front staff — the Café can toddle forward into the next decade."

"I suppose they can," Richard grumped, feeling at his most ungracious, and then hoped that he didn't really sound all that sullen. "It's just ... I suppose this feels a bit like sending your spawn off to boarding school..."

"Or college," Jess agreed. "Or enlisting. You want the best for them, you worry like heck ... but in the end, you must accept that they are going on with their life and let go."

"Right," Richard scowled at Little Joe, in the front seat of the simply Brobdingnagian-sized triple-seat stroller. Little Joe scowled right back. His sisters, the twins Lizzie and Alice, were fast asleep in their seats. Richard often wondered how on earth

Jess managed to steer the darned thing. It was half the size of a small car, a Morris mini, at the very least.

"So, when is the date that you have committed to start working for Lew Dubois?" Jess fished in the oversized diaper bag and pulled out a zip-lock bag filled with graham crackers. She handed one to Little Joe, who began gnawing at it with messy enthusiasm. Richard regarded the spectacle of Little Joe, with his mouth and chin covered in graham-cracker colored paste with faint revulsion. Should he and Kate ever be rewarded with spawn, he hoped that such revolting spectacles would never be presented to his view. He had the excuse of work…

"End of June, I told the man. And that's what it said on the contract."

Jess brought out her calendar notebook, being sufficiently old-school that she didn't keep that kind of thing on her phone. "Right. You have three weeks to break it to the peeps. A word of advice from an old ROTC hand … tell 'Celi privately first. She's been your right-hand manager all this time. As inimitable and irreplaceable as you are, she's the one that Doc and Miss Letty really couldn't replace for any consideration."

"I wonder if I ought to be insulted," Richard ventured, "That the head waitress is more irreplaceable than the formerly-internationally-famous Cordon Bleu-trained celebrity chef…"

Jess grinned. "Commanders come and go," she answered. "But the NCO corps remains eternal and invaluable. 'Celi has worked at the Café since she was sixteen and in high school. She pro'lly won't ever leave, but if she did, the place would collapse in a week. You leave? Well, the Café is still viable, even if the original gourmet cooking goes all to heck. And with the kids, and that tatted fry-cook freak doing his magic at the grill… no, the Café will carry on. But tell 'Celi, and then tell the kids about your lateral career move. Don't just pack up your toque and apron one evening, and not appear to oversee breakfast the next morning."

"I suppose that you are correct." Richard admitted, realizing that Araceli, the senior waitress was still hovering on the other side of the great picture window at the front of the Café, with coffee carafe in hand, shooting him meaningful looks. It was time to begin prepping for lunch. "OK, word of honor, honor bright. I will tell Araceli about my imminent career change – and pass the word to her that the baton of management is passing into her supremely capable hand. May I suggest," he added, with a touch of malice, "That such an honor to her involves an increase in the pay-packet? It's only the rightful due to the person whose departure would mean the Café would collapse in a week."

"She'd never do that!" Jess exclaimed, with an expression which mixed horror with dawning realization. "Oh, God, you are right, Chef. At that value, she is worth the candle. I'll tell Miss Letty and Doc and get their approval."

To Richard's mean satisfaction, Jess seemed truly rattled. It seemed to never have occurred to her, or anyone else, that the most experienced and adept front of the house manager in the history of the Luna Café and Coffee should be worth more than the paltry sum she was paid as the head waitress.

"If I might be so bold," Richard continued, "I would suggest to Doc and Miss Letty – that the amount allocated to pay my own salary, or a substantial portion thereof – ought to be awarded to Araceli. That would be fair. She's an uncut gem when it comes to restaurant management. And if management of this place is to be left in her hands, Araceli ought to be worth the candle, as well as the bell and the book."

"Point taken," Jess nodded. "And I should have thought of that. 'Celi always seemed to be completely happy as a waitress. It was curious," Jess mused, with a reminiscent expression on her face. "Everyone thought that she ought to have done better for herself, instead of marrying Pat straight out of high school. She had such good grades. The career counselor was heartbroken, that she didn't want to go to college, seeing how well she did at school."

"Well, in the long run, it has turned out well," Richard nodded, as Jess gathered up her folders and paperwork, indicating that the session was done. "I'll confab with Araceli, as soon as you tell me that her raise has been approved by Doc and Miss Letty – agreed."

"I'll talk to Miss Letty today. Doc is in San Antonio for the week, but I'll message him," Jess assured him. "Expect to hear from me tonight, tomorrow morning at the latest."

Jess texted Richard late that evening; his phone pinged as he was cycling home, the moon rising over the line of trees along the river and making the tower of the Aquarius home place glow as if it were an enchanted castle. *Pay increase for A is approved per Doc and Miss L.*

All right then, said Richard to himself. *Sorted.* He felt a kind of lightening of his sour mood. Yes, he would be leaving the Café in good hands. The insight occurred to him that he had avoided even thinking about his departure from the management, because it was easier just to avoid thinking of uncomfortable realities. Perhaps it was better to face them full-frontal and take charge. It hadn't actually been that difficult, insisting that Araceli get rewarded for being left holding the metaphorical baby. He put those regrets about leaving the Café aside – actually, tucked them in tenderly and covered them warmly with a sense of satisfaction. He was moving on, without any but modest and mild regrets, all sorted.

At the break after the breakfast rush was done, he beckoned to Araceli, who was refreshing the big coffee machine. "A word in private, if you will," he said, and Araceli nodded, and wiped her hands on the towel tucked into the waistband of her apron.

"Sure, Chef," she replied and followed him out to the back of the Café, where three substantial raised beds set out on the decayed paving boasted a bumper crop of gourmet salad greens and herbs; beds lovingly cherished by Richard during his tenure at the Café. As soon as the door closed behind them, she turned and faced him, hands on her hips. "So, what is it that you want to tell me? I know that you've signed a contract with Lew to take over the Cattleman restaurant."

"I have, indeed," Richard sighed. "I'll be managing the Crystal Room and the catering functions at the Cattleman as of the beginning of June. I will have a family to support, you see, support in the manner to which I would like them to become accustomed. Katie as well as Ozzie. I can't possibly ask Katie to live with me at the Age..."

"Of course not," Araceli agreed. "She has too many books to fit in the trailer."

"I've consulted with Jess, and she has the approval of Miss Letty and Doc Wyler," Richard had no gift for diplomacy, subtle or otherwise. "And here's the offer as regards the Café. You will be the overall manager, and work with Jess as to the budget and any expansion. You will have supreme authority. And you will also have a substantial increase in wages, which is only meet, right, salutary and your due ... in all honesty, Araceli," Richard confessed as he took in Araceli's expression of boggled surprise. "You're one of the best managers in this demented line of work that I have come across, ever. I would have come a cropper a dozen times in a week, ever since I came to work here, if it hadn't been for you. Watching my back. Telling me whenever I put a foot wrong. The kids trust you ..." Richard confessed his deepest fears. "I want to know that I'm leaving the place in good hands." He added, addressing the doubts that he saw in Araceli's hesitancy. "Your hands. I thought you'd be ecstatic about the increase in salary, you know. Food management isn't notorious for earning a princely income for the wage slaves..."

"It takes a bit to get used to," Araceli mused. "You know that I also have a family; Pat, Matty and Angelika. I'd like to see them oftener than for a couple hours a day. Management is a demon; that's what Jess has always said. Always on call, always thinking of the place, being on call every hour of the day and night when you are not there... Being a wage slave is not so hard, you know. Once you walk away at the end of the day ... not my problem. Not my circus, not my monkeys. Take the paycheck and think of something else – anything else until the next shift."

"But you love the Café," Richard pointed out. "You know that you want the Café in good hands as much as I do. Who else but you? You were the sole survivor there, washing dishes, and straightening up, when Doc Wyler and Miss Letty gave me the job ... for my various sins."

"I suppose so," Araceli sighed. "And you are right. I know the place, every stick and pot and dish." She looked at Richard, and it seemed to him that a sudden resolve came upon her. "It's part of Luna City – an important part. I'll manage, Chef. I guess it's time that I had a real job," she added, irreverently. "All my other woman friends do. I just wanted to stay home and raise the kids."

"They're all but raised," Richard pointed out, and Araceli laughed. He added, "The thing is – deputize. You don't have to be there, twenty-four and seven. I know you can do it. You've been doing it for years. You're the best bit of restaurant management material that I have seen in years. If it weren't for the Café, and that there is already a front house manager at the Crystal Room, I'd poach you to come work for me."

"Oh, I wouldn't go that far," Araceli fixed him with a firm look, and Richard knew that he had won. She would take on managing the Café. "I have standards, and the Café suits them fine. OK, then. When do we tell the kids that you are moving on, and I'm the boss, now?"

"Right now," Richard replied. Best plunge ahead, take the bull by the horns, get it all sorted. "This very minute. I waited until I had conferred with you."

"Right," Araceli nodded, her expression determined and her eyes level. "Let's do it, Chef. I'll take it on."

"Excellent," Richard nodded. "You won't regret ... or at least, I hope that you won't. The kids are good, and Luc is a solid cook. He just needs careful handling."

"I can do it," Araceli replied. "I have handled toddlers."

She followed him inside, at his elbow as he called for attention to orders from the kitchen staff, and Beatriz and Blanca, who were busy straightening the tables after the morning rush, starting another urn of coffee, and ferrying in pans of dirty dishes to be shot through the restaurant dishwasher. Luc was scraping down the grill, and setting all in place for the lunch rush, his mind obviously on higher things, such as whatever evening engagement that the desperately unsuccessful garage band OPM had. Robbie and Bree had their heads together at adjacent stations – Robbie stirring a cauldron of Café brand BBQ sauce on the enormous Wolff stove, a substance eventually to be bottled and sold at the front desk, and Bree prepping salad ingredients for the lunch crowd. They all looked up as Richard repeated in a louder voice,

"Oy! I've got something to tell you all! Can you please just drop what you are doing for the moment, and listen up?"

"I can't stop stirring, Chef," Robbie replied, in a reasonable tone of voice. "This stuff will scorch on the bottom of the pan, and we'll have to throw the whole batch out and start all over. It will cost ..." and he named a figure. Richard sighed. Obviously, someone had been paying attention to the cost-to-profit ratio. He supposed that someone had been paying rapt attention to Jess's lectures, or they were really teaching Robbie something useful at that public uni of his.

"All right then," Richard took a deep breath. "As of the end of this month ... Mrs. Gonzalez-Gonzales will be your boss. I am leaving the Café, to take up another position – executive chef at the Cattleman."

For a moment, he thought that he had set off a small bomb in the Café's kitchen; one which had rendered everyone speechless. Then Robbie went back to stirring the cauldron concoction with focused attention.

"Oh, that's OK, Chef. We're on it. You've taught us everything important that we need to know. I'm sure we can carry on, like you have trained us. No problem," Robbie added, with a sunny and confident smile

"We got it, Chef," Luc mumbled. "'s OK. Follow your bliss, ya know?"

"I think it's romantic!" Bree burbled, chorused by Beatriz and Blanca. "And the Crystal Room is fantastic ... you'll be famous again, won't you, Chef?"

"I hope not," Richard exclaimed, almost involuntarily. "Fame is a bitchy and demanding mistress, whom it is better not to pursue, not if one wishes peace of mind and a quiet, happy life. No, the real mission of our kind is to feed the multitudes ... feed them excellent and nourishing food, teach them what is best in life..."

"Sort of like Jesus, then, Chef?" Blanca observed, pertly. "Feeding the multitude with bread and fish..."

"Kind of like the ideal chef," Richard agreed, "Under pressure at a mass event, and making the very best of some leftover cold fish and some small bread rolls..."

"Chef, that's getting perilously close to blasphemy..." Araceli murmured, and the girls all giggled.

"Look, Chef," Bree set down her knife, and regarded Richard intently. "We understand. Totally. That you finished up here, and made the Café into what it is, and gave us all a good start; we understand. You need to make enough in basic salary to get married to Miss Heisel and that's not possible here – we get that. Everyone else ..." and she waved the knife in the general direction of the other staff. "We all work for a living. Grandpop and Gee-Nan made it clear to me, early on. There may be people on this dirtball who get a princely salary and economic security handed to them just for breathing and having been squeezed out of the right uterus – but there's none of that set here. We'll go on, making good food for Luna City; depend on that. And besides," Bree added, as he bent back to work, slivering up salad ingredients. "We like working here. Robbie and I and Luc – we have some ideas..."

"As long as you don't get too grand about them," Richard replied, heartened and warmed by the equable manner in which his – no, the staff at the Café – seemed to be accepting the news.

No, they would be all right. The Café was in good hands.

The Glorious 4th

"It's a very significant holiday," Richard explained to his attentive parents at mid-morning on the 4th of July, as the three of them stood in the foyer of the lavishly-renovated Cattleman Hotel. This establishment was an ornate monument to Belle Epoque taste when first constructed with no expense spared at the command of a wealthy Italian hospitality entrepreneur in the sunset years of the 19th century. "I had to learn all about it for the citizenship exam. It marks the issue of the American declaration of independence. The mayor of Luna City will read the whole bally thing, after the parade, from the steps of the bandstand — including the series of vile accusations against our late sovereign, George III."

"Ah," drawled Alfred Astor-Hall. "You have been applying yourself, academically. I always thought you would go far, if you had chosen to apply yourself to a serious profession."

"I have, Father," Richard barely kept himself from snarling. "And application to such studies as I found interesting have led me to the position of executive chef in this exceedingly respectable and up-scale establishment – a second chance after the Carême disaster."

"Now, now, Alf," Richard's mother Dottie took his hand into her own carefully manicured ones. "Stop teasing the boy. You know how he takes all this so awfully seriously – and this hotel is absolutely splendid. We love the view from our suite!"

Alfred merely grunted in reply. He had been left sorting out the wreckage of Richard's previous essay into restaurant ownership and management, for which Richard was grateful. Now Richard's mother continued. "Now, dear, why don't you take us around the Square and introduce us to all of your lovely friends! I know we have already met Mrs. Abernathy-Vaughn, and Mrs. Gonzalez-Gonzales, but when shall we meet all the rest of your dear chums – and your adorable Miss Heisel?"

"Today and within the hour," Richard replied glumly. "Everyone – absolutely everyone turns out for the 4th of July celebration in Luna City. The parade begins at noon, and the doggie patriotic costume contest is at two. They'll all be somewhere on the Square, save maybe the kids in the Café. Who, if I have succeeded in training them properly, will all be hard at work providing nourishment – sustenance of high quality to the elite of Luna City and the visitors alike. Kate messaged me that she will be here by noon."

"A parade?" Dottie looked like a small child promised a personal visit from Santa Claus. "Oh, I wouldn't want to miss it – such fun, these little town celebrations. They have a parade in Saint-Didier on Bastille Day, and the fountain in front of City Hall is filled with wine, instead of water, and the dear little children all dress like characters from *Asterix and Obelix,* while everyone cheers the aged heroes of the Resistance ..."

"So, not much difference then, Mum," Richard replied. "All except for the fountain running with wine. I think that our locals would rather see it running with beer or BBQ sauce. The Pryors who run the local bespoke butcher and roast meat concession roast a whole pig for the occasion."

"Fascinating," Alf Astor-Hall remarked, rather in the manner of an English Spock upon considering quaint native customs.

Richard sighed. "Come along, then – let's walk around the Square so I can introduce you to everyone before the parade begins."

He led his parents out through the monumental entrance to the Cattleman, adorned as it was with flags and banners, and a pair of topiary longhorn bulls, clipped out of enormous box bushes planted in planters the size of bathtubs on either side of the doorway. The landscape expert who had created them had finally gotten the box bushes grown out and trimmed to the point where they actually did look more like bulls than the blobby walrus shapes they had resembled early on. The three walked around the Square, clockwise.

"This is Stein's Wild West Emporium," Richard said of the first storefront they passed. "Annise will be in the shop, of course, but Georg will be with the reenactors. See their tents and teepees over there, among the trees? He has an affection for dressing as an authentic Comanche warrior, although he looks more like Otto Von Bismarck's great-grandson. I can't imagine a man who looks less like a Comanche than Georg, but he is the local expert on their weapons and such crafts as they practiced."

"Singular," Alf mused, looking into the window of Stein's, where a wealth of woven Navaho blankets, an old ox-harness and a saddle ornamented with silver plaques depicting rattlesnakes and buzzards held pride of place among an array of smaller items of similar provenance and vintage. "Stein – sounds German."

"They are," Richard hastened to assure his father. "Originally, but now Americans in general and Lunaites in particular. I met Annise Stein almost the first day that I arrived here: she favored me with a generous gift; a copy of *Larousse Gastronomique*; a rare edition, which is nearly my favorite possession. If my home ever caught on fire, it's the one thing – aside from Katie and Ozymandias-King-of-Kings that I would risk my life to preserve. They deal in rare books, relics, and Western art, and they have three enormously fat and spoiled cats who terrorize the place and lavishly pee on the antique carpets. Bach, Beethoven, and Mozart; I don't think that Ozzie is besties with the musical trio, but they are guardedly respectful."

"I think that I will pay a visit," Alfred announced, "Just a brief one, to see if they have anything particularly Texan which will intrigue visitors to the vineyard..."

"We'll wait outside for you, darling," Dottie Astor-Hall announced. "Such lovely plants! I adore the way that they have hanging baskets. So quaint and old-fashioned. It is so nice to see traditions honored. A shame that so many of our own high streets have let down the side when it comes to beautifying with flowers." As Alf vanished within the shop – the bell on a spring attached to the door announcing his presence with a silvery chime. Richard and his mother sat, relishing the elusive cool of a morning in South Texas, waiting for Alfred to return.

After a few moments, Dottie ventured. "Richard, are you truly happy, here? It seems like such a charming place, but you know that you have never really seemed content, save when you visited Mam's little country cottage, when you were just a little 'un... is this a good fit for you at long last? Are you really happy?"

"I am, Mum," Richard assured her. "No, really. We can sit here on this bench, while Dad has his fun. I am more than just content. I have good friends here ... and the project of putting the Cattleman on the culinary map, now that I've done the same with the Café. And then there is Kate. Mum, I love Kate to bits. And we have made up. After that tragic misunderstanding – we're good now. Kate and I haven't set the exact date yet – but when it is set, we will be married officially and move into one of the new staff cottages at Mills Far. Sometime in the autumn, I think. Kate says that these things do take time to arrange, even if she is a woman of simple tastes."

"That's good, darling," Dottie sounded much relieved.

The door to the Stein's Wild West Emporium chimed a musical herald to Alfred's return, significantly with a wrapped package under his arm, and the three of them moved on, in the direction of the Café, with all the outside tables filled with customers, including the familiar figure of Clovis Walcott. Clovis looked to be just finishing up a late-morning brunch, with his military saber looped over the back of his chair.

Richard said, in the manner of a tour guide, as he waved in the general direction of Araceli and her ever-present coffee carafe. "Now, here is another member of the keen reenactor fraternity..."

"I never would have guessed," Alf Astor-Hall murmured, for Clovis Walcott was arrayed in all the splendor of 1830s martial glory; a high-collared blue jacket adorned with gold frogs, much braid, and epaulets, over buff-colored trousers and knee-high cavalry boots. This tasteful ensemble was accessorized with a brace of *(replica, or perhaps, knowing Clovis Walcott's pocketbook and quest for authenticity, they were authentic antique)* pistols tucked into a brilliant red silk sash, and a saber belt with scabbarded saber buckled over the sash which would clank resoundingly with every stride. Richard knew this well from previous encounters with Clovis in his 19th century persona, although the military arms were temporarily laid aside while Clovis Walcott ate breakfast.

"Colonel Walcott," Richard replied, as they approached the range of tables and chairs set under an awning under a wide awning over the front of Luna Café and Coffee; an area comfortable only when the temperatures were mild, which in July meant for an hour or so around sunrise before a rising sun baked everything in Texas to a toasty brown. "He is really a colonel – reserve and mostly retired from active service. He designs and builds things of extraordinary complexity; a refreshing change from his previous career of blowing them up. In his misspent youth, he played in a garage band, and he owns the ugliest MacMansion anywhere in the vicinity. His youngest son – God knows how the youngster came to this – is currently working as sous-chef in the Café. I can only suppose that I taught the boy correctly, and that the good colonel doesn't bear an abiding grudge over that development, proof positive of his generosity and good public spirit. Colonel Walcott is another of Luna City's leading citizens, all of this, despite the temper of his missus, the fire cat Mrs. Sook Walcott, the tiger mother from hell … good morning, Colonel."

"Good morning, Richard!" Colonel Walcott looked up from his fruit salad and croissant breakfast. "Ready for the Glorious Fourth; our celebration of the independence which is the rightful inheritance of every man and woman in this blessed land?"

"Yeah, verily and forsooth," Richard replied, "Father and Mother, may I present Colonel Clovis Walcott of the … something-or-othereth. A gentleman of the first water. Sir, may I make known to you my parents, Alfred and Dorothy Astor-Hall."

Clovis Walcott chuckled. "The tongue and vocabulary of the old century does have that hold on you, doesn't it?" He stood up and bowed in an exaggeratedly courtly manner over Dottie's hand, raising it to his lips and kissing it in a way that made Richard's mother almost simper. "This most handsome lady –

hardly to be of an age to be your mother, Chef Richard? And the most gallant gentleman; I regard myself as the most honored in making your acquaintance at long last!"

"How d'ye do, Colonel," Alfred replied, with a stiff and most formal nod, in the best olde stiff-upper-lip manner. "Alfred Astor-Hall, at your service, my good sir, My son speaks most highly of you."

"Charmed!" Clovis Walcott responded. "Charmed to make your acquaintance! Are you planning to take up residence in our Texas? I assure you, there are many opportunities for an entrepreneurious gentlemen such as yourself. I can introduce you to my good friend, Colonel Bowie, if you are so inclined as to take up a grant in our fair country."

"I regret that I am already committed to a substantial property in another land, my good sir," Alfred replied, while Richard goggled at how readily his father fell into this kind of make-believe. He had never suspected his father of entertaining such theatrical leanings, let alone a facility for improvisation.

"Our loss, indeed, good sir," Colonel Walcott rendered another formal bow, and went clanking off across the street to join his fellows at the reenactor camp, who had been gesturing him from across the pavement for him to get a move on and lend his theatricality to the festivities.

"Oooh, I do like him!" Dorothy sighed and fanned herself theatrically with her hand. "Such a gent!"

"He is, that," Richard agreed glumly, and encouraged his parental units to move on. Miss Letty, Doc Wyler and Harry Vaughn sat at another table. Richard sighed, upon seeing that trio, for the two gentlemen were looking daggers at each other, while Miss Letty sat, prim and elegant in her shirtwaist dress, wide-brimmed summer hat, matching gloves and a handbag which matched the colors of the modestly flowered summer hat. *(Which also matched her dress. Miss Letty had always been detail-oriented.)* "Mum – these are some of the people I've told you about before: Doctor Stephen Wyler and Miss Letty McAllister; they jointly own the Café and hired me to run the kitchen when I first came here. The two are the highest degree of aristocracy and what they don't know about Luna City could be put into a thimble."

"Know where all the bodies are buried, then?" Alfred grunted.

"Likely, they assisted in putting them there," Richard acknowledged. "The scowling gentleman with the impressive mustache is Harry Vaughn, another old resident. It was he who insisted that I accompany him in a reckless venture on the river in flood, to rescue some luckless tourists, a couple of years ago."

"Ah," said Alfred. "The occasion when your school enthusiasm for rowing finally served a useful purpose."

"Not quite how I thought of it, Father. All the county river rescue boats had already been called out. I was prevailed upon as a trainee member of the volunteer fire department, with a presumed familiarity with small boats. Harry Vaughn threatening to brutally belt me about the head and shoulders with an oar had nothing to do with it ... good morning, Doc, Miss Letty ... Mr. Vaughn."

"Good morning, Chef," Doc returned, looking over his glasses at them. "I heard that your folks came to town."

"Indeed. The bush telegraph is as active as always." Richard answered, and Doc Wyler and Harry Vaughn both grinned; Harry Vaughn a bit evilly, as befitted a former federal marshal, and Richard sighed. "My parents, Alfred and Dorothy Astor-Hall – Stephen Wyler, but most everyone calls him 'Doc', Miss Letty McAllister." Mis Letty nodded regally, and Doc Wyler growled. It seemed as if Doc Wyler had not had enough coffee yet. "And this gentleman is Mr. Henry Vaughn. Father and Mum are here, doing a tour of the wine country, such as it is, and meanwhile have come to observe the rituals of celebration."

"Charmed, I'm sure!" Dottie trilled, as gentleman half-rose from where they were sitting,

"There will be merriment and dancing tonight, before the fireworks display," Harry Vaughn rumbled, with a significant look at Dottie. "May I claim a dance with your charming mother?"

"Only if you don't plan on seducing her, afterwards," Richard replied, rather nettled. Dottie giggled and Harry Vaughn settled back in his seat, looking rather smug. Miss Letty frowned; levity regarding sex outside of the marriage contract was a matter of which she sternly and Methodistically disapproved. Meanwhile, Harry Vaughn grinned, under his magnificently drooping soup-strainer mustache, and Richard hurried his parents on. When they were out of earshot of the Café, Dottie remarked, artlessly.

"Oh, was that dear Moira's gentleman friend? I had no idea!"

"My sister Moira has a finely developed sense of duty," Alfred replied. "I am certain that Mr. Vaughn held information necessary to completion of her mission,"

"No, Father; it was purely a naughty weekend," Richard answered, and Dottie upheld him.

"Dear Moira is entitled to whatever romantic romps she can indulge! The places that she travels to, the intrigues she encounters; a nice relaxing weekend with a handsome gentleman who isn't trying to plant a knife in her back! Well, that's her chosen career, and I do not judge – do I, Alfred?"

"No, you do not," Albert replied, the very image of the austere Englishman. "Much is required of an intelligence operative in their line of duty."

Richard thought he had better not pursue that topic any further. It was perhaps the closest that his father had ever come to admitting that Aunt Moira was a kind of distaff 007, with an official license to kill, seduce, or subvert, as the specific mission required.

"Everything happens in the park, or around the edges of Town Square," he explained, as the ever-popular miniature train ride trundled slowly past; a train of recycled oil drums set on their side on wheels to make the carriages, and an engine also cobbled out of oil drums and powered by a motor which once had powered a ride-along mower. Clem Bodie of the Bodie Feed Mill had constructed the miniature train some fifteen years ago, for fun and to exercise his welding talents – and also to dispose of a number of items of metal scrap and put them to good civic use. All the streets which fed into Town Square had been blocked to vehicle traffic, for the convenience of the little train, the parade at noon, and for the drifting of pedestrians back and forth, like the gentle washing of a wind-blown tide at a mountain lake shore.

"The heart of the community," Dottie Astor-Hall remarked, with unexpected sagacity. "I do like this little town, Richard ... oh, look at the little dogs! How charming, and how clever! Do you know their owner?"

"I do, as a matter of fact," Richard confessed, as they crossed the street in front of the Café, where the Hanging Oak brooded over the sidewalk, as it had for decades, *(less the one decaying branch from which Charley Mills had nearly been lynched in 1926).* "Anita Blake-Silva, with Oscar and Felix – the dachshunds," he added, as the dogs greeted him with a chorus of barking. "Good morning, Judge. I see that you have entered the dogs in the patriotic costume contest."

"I have, if they can keep from ruining their wigs before judging time," Judge Anita Blake-Silva replied. She was a pleasant-looking woman in her fifties, clad in jeans and a sort of gauzy embroidered peasant top, accessorized with Navaho silver jewelry and cowboy boots.

Richard performed introductions. "Judge Blake-Silva, my parents, Alfred and Dorothy Astor-Hall. This is Anita Blake-Silva, one of the local magistrates, and Oscar and Felix."

"How very pleasant to make your acquaintance!" Dottie exclaimed, as the one of the dachshunds laid his nose on her right shoe and looked up adoringly. "And the costumes are so very clever! Did you make them yourself?"

"I did," Anita Blake-Silva confessed. "With the help of a niece who is a costume designer, and very fond of the boys."

"Who obviously don't mind cross-dressing," Richard commented. One dachshund was dressed in a blue coat with buff facings over a buff weskit and lace cravat, a tricorn hat *(over a white curled wig)* and a small sword-belt, and the other gazing up at his mother so worshipfully was gotten up in an elaborate dress with panniers, a mobcap, and a white wig.

"Well, you see," confessed Judge Anita Blake Silva, "They are representing General and Mrs. Washington. Total hams, both of them, and they don't really mind at all, as long as everyone pays attention to them."

"Good thing," Alfred commented, as soon as they had moved on, past the Judge and her excitable duo. "If I were a dog, dressed up in a ridiculous costume, I'd want to bite the next person who held down a hand."

"Well, come along, Father," Richard urged him, "You and Mum wanted to meet everyone. Now, this is Pryor's Meats BBQ; their food truck, which they run for special events. They open the BBQ on weekends. Honestly, the place has all the ambiance of an industrial warehouse, but no one really cares. They do meat processing during the week. They make the most amazing sausages and supply the Café as well as Mills Farm and the

Crystal Room. I have always preferred to purchase locally sourced goods, and the Pryors can't get much more local than this." He gestured towards the food truck, around which a small crowd had gathered, and his mother giggled.

"Darling, are you going to introduce us to all the local aristocrats to day?"

"Certainly, Mother," Richard answered. "Mrs. Pryor, who looks most amazingly like the late Princess Di, is also the granddaughter and heir of Doc Wyler ... whom ought to be known as Duke Wyler, as he owns the largest ranch in Karnes County and just about anything else of value that isn't already nailed down or owned by the Bodies of the Feed Mill. The other remaining local aristocrat would be Don Jaimie of the original Spanish holding, but I don't believe he comes to town very often. If you have a hankering ... sorry, I have been immersed in the local vernacular ... if you have an urge to sample original Texas BBQ, you should taste it from here, before they run out."

The Pryor's BBQ food truck was parked along the Square, under the branches of a particularly towering oak tree, under whose shade were set a series of folding tables and chairs, for the convenience of those diners, partaking of an early lunch. The enormous metal smoker and BBQ unit sent up a lazy stream of smoke, which twined around the overhanging branches like a species of aromatic fog. Patricia, Andrew, Anson, and the younger boys were at work, either tending the Brobdingnagian BBQ grill and smoker, working the serving window or clearing away the brief disposable trash of paper plates, plastic cups and wads of napkins left in the wake of satisfied diners, who mostly left satiated, belching comfortably, and if careless and enthusiastic gourmands, with smears of the Pryor's various degrees of home-made fiery sauce on their outer garments.

Richard waved toward Patricia, framed in the delivery window of the truck, dealing out heavily laden platters of sliced brisket, sausage and perfectly smoked chops. She returned the wave with a somewhat abstracted expression.

"I'm only slightly peckish now," Alfred declared, "But I think that we will be, by the time that we make another circuit of the Square and become acquainted with all of your good friends."

"Don't leave it too late," Richard advised. "Their BBQ is very good, very popular, and once they have been cleaned out of the goods, there is no more, until the next day, or the next weekend."

Alfred consulted his watch. "Ah, then. I think that we should get in line, Dottie."

"You won't regret it, Father," Richard assured his parents, and they joined the line of about twenty people before the order window, where Anson Pryor took orders and rang up sales. Another twenty or thirty stragglers stood around, waiting for their orders or taking up a place at one of the tree-shaded tables. "This is something that would rock St. Didier to the foundations, if you could import authentic Texas BBQ like the Pryor's. Best to snag a seat, before the luncheon rush truly begins. Over there – the large darkly-tanned gentleman is another friend of mine. Alan Lee Mayne, former footballer and the host of *Ala Carte With Quartermayne*. Alan Lee is featured on the Food Channel, but we never encountered each other until I came here."

Alan Lee had already spotted Richard and his parents, and waved enthusiastically, his countenance beaming with delight. It looked as if he and the older gentleman with him were almost finished with their meal – so that end of the table would be free, shortly. Richard waved back.

"He's very ... large," Dottie observed, somewhat dubiously. "For a footballer ... aren't they usually rather wiry and fast?

"American football," Richard sighed. "Weight counts – apparently, he played as a kind of human pile-driver. But I understand that he is very nimble, and did a turn on *Dancing*

With the Stars, the American knockoff of *Strictly Come Dancing,* before becoming a traveling food critic and all-around appreciator of small-town restaurants. I'll hold a place at the table for you, Father, if you and Mum want to go stand in line. He's very jolly company and did an excellent turn of service for Luna City last year when they found a skeleton in a most inconvenient place. It turned out to be the mortal remains of an old serviceman, and Alan Lee was instrumental in identifying the body. I think we consider him an honorary citizen." *Although no one ever thought of presenting him with a key to the city,* Richard added to himself, as his parents joined the end of the line, and he wended his way to the table where Alan Lee and his elderly companion sat, their plates of BBQ brisket and other smoked delights already almost scraped clean. *I don't even think there is a key to the city. Maybe a key to the power system under the bandstand for the Christmas lights...* "Mr. Mayne, how wonderful to see you again!" he added in normal tones, as he slid onto one of the folding benches.

"Same here!" Alan Lee looked as if he had been given a most wonderful Christmas present, in the form of Richard's company. "Ricardo – good to see ya, pal! I brought my ol' Daddy here on a road trip! No better place than Luna City for the 4th of July! Daddy," he turned to the elderly gentleman. "This is Richard Astor-Hall, the cook and chef that I done told ya about. He was the one who gave us the first clue to unraveling the Walters story." The older man sat on a walker with a seat; his grizzled hair testified to his age and the hardships which life had dealt him, and his severe expression to his time as a Marine; also testified to by the ball cap with Vietnam Veteran embroidered across the front, with a set of years and a smaller row of ribbons.

"We never leave one of ours behind," Mr. Mayne, Senior, extended a flint-hard handshake with Richard. "Good to meet ya, Chef. Alen Lee tol' me all about this li'l town. Tol' me about everyone who did the good work of finding out the ID of that poor soul and seeing him laid to proper rest. You are blessed, indeed."

"We like to think so," Richard mumbled, wholly embarrassed, while Alan Lee explained.

"We just came from the cemetery. Daddy wanted to leave some flowers for Lance Corporal Walters, on the 4th. Seemed only fittin'. I hear that you got hired on to manage the kitchen at the Cattleman! Daddy an' me have the RV parked out at Mills Farm for the week, but the word does get around. I guess that Lew Dubois made a better offer!" Alan Lee grinned, completely without malice. He had once offered Richard a job as traveling co-host to his food show, an offer which Richard had fled with the alacrity of a hemophiliac offered an intimate date with a thirsty vampire. He had been there, done that, and realized the myriad unhealthy temptations which such a lifestyle offered. It did appear that Alan Lee had been able to avoid them, doubtless due to his early conditioning in professional sports

"I accepted it because I'm getting married in the autumn," Richard explained. "It was indeed a splendid offer which would allow me to stay in Luna City, since I will have need of a solid income, once that Miss Kate Heisel and I are committed in holy matrimony."

The senior Mr. Mayne beamed approval. "Marriage is a sacrament and a blessing. A good woman is a worth a price above rubies, so it says in the Good Book!"

Alan Lee also radiated approval. "She's a fine woman, your Miss Kate. A fine woman, an excellent woman; you could not do any better, in my opinion."

"She loves me for my cooking, and my cat," Richard answered, wryly.

Alan Lee grinned. "I'm sure there are other qualities," he replied genially. "Let me know when the blessed day is set, and I'll send a present for you both. Hey, Daddy – let's go get us a good place for the parade. See ya around, Ricardo! Congrats on the new job, and on the wedding!"

"Thank you," Richard replied, in unaccustomedly humble gratitude for the consideration which Alan Lee had shown him and also that the departure of the very large Alan Lee and Daddy Mayne had left three places at the end of a table. The range of tables by Pryor's food truck was becoming more and more crowded. In a few moments, Alfred and Dottie appeared with a pair of heavily laden plates; brisket, sausage, and chicken, a few wodges of pillowy bakery bread to sop up the fiery sauce, and sides of spicy baked beans and coleslaw weeping cream dressing into it all. Richard sat with his parents as they ate, Dottie exclaiming over and over again between mouthfuls, how very tasty it all was. Father said very little, which was also promising, since he was not a demonstrative kind of man, but he polished off the brisket with an appetite and every evidence of mild enjoyment, leaving Richard with a distant impression that his aged paternal parent was planning to import a genuine Texas smoker-BBQ to St. Didier and to importune Andy Pryor for his secret rub and sauce recipes.

"Oh, my – that was so good!" his mother bubbled, not being made of the same stoic material. "I declare, I will not have any appetite for simply hours!"

"Well, it will be hours and hours until the festivities are concluded," Richard allowed. "So consider it fuel to take you over the long haul, until the dance at twilight, the outdoor theater showing of the movie *1776* ... and then the fireworks display, for those who are still awake..."

"Such wonderful fun!" Dottie burbled, with undiminished enthusiasm. "Oh, such a sweet young couple! Are they friends of yours, too?" she added, as Berto Gonzalez and a dark-haired young girl with whom Berto held hands with every evidence of shy devotion, approached along the shaded promenade which

273

led to the cynosure of Town Square, the fabulously ornate bandstand.

"Indeed," Richard admitted, with a deep sigh. "Berto Gonzalez; younger brother of Araceli Gonzalez-Gonzales. He was working his way through college by driving a limo for his uncle in Elmendorf – which is a little town to the south of San Antonio, although it sounds Austrian, like a location for *The Sound of Music*. Through an amazing turn of luck for us both, he was the one who collected me from a charter flight, when I was in a somewhat ... incoherent condition. Out of the goodness of his simple and charitable heart, he brought me to the Age of Aquarius Campground and Goat Farm. Judy Grant, the proprietress, is known the length and breadth of Karnes County for her charity to the halt, lame, and lost of all species. Berto's grandmother, whom all the clan reveres and obeys without question was perhaps my most devoted fan in the days when I was famous. I owe him almost everything, gormless though he usually appears, and what I don't owe to him, I owe to his fearsome and autocratic gran." Richard raised his voice and waved. "H'lo, Berto. Nice to see you again! I'm showing my parents around. Mum, Father; this is Berto Gonzalez and Miss..." Richard couldn't for the life of him remember the name of Berto's girlfriend. He was certain that he had met her before, although exactly when remained a quandary.

"Marigold," replied the dark-haired maiden, with her hair pulled back in a ponytail, and a pair of heavy-rimmed dark glasses perched on her nose. "Marigold Yasbeck. Nice to see ya again, Chef." She shook Dottie and Alfred's hands in a firm, masculine grip. "H'lo ... isn't this the greatest? I'm always hoping to come back to Luna City for the 4th of July. I was here for that stupid zombie movie, remember, Berto?"

"I know," Berto regarded her with fatuous fondness. "We danced and watched the fireworks. Now that you're back in

Texas, you can come every year. It's not that far from Houston. And I can always come and get you..."

"Silly," Marigold giggled. She kissed Berto lightly on his cheek. Turning back to Richard and his parents she explained earnestly, "I just finished at Cal Tech this year, and I'm interning at JPL in Houston for a year or so..."

"How very nice for you," Alfred returned, starchy as always. Richard sighed. Obviously, Cal Tech, JPL and all were unfamiliar to his father, so wrapped up as his parent was, first in the financial world, then in the world of vineyard management in the South of France. Marigold and Berto didn't seem to notice the manner. Marigold giggled again, and Berto took her hand into his again.

"Sylvester was supposed to bring Abuelita, later on," he explained. "And I promised to drive her home, once she got too tired. She wants to see the doggie costume contest most of all. The movie's in English, an' she don't understand that all too well. See you 'round, Chef."

"See you around," Richard replied.

As they walked away, Dottie mused, "I could swear that was Amy Butler! You know, the actress, but so much older and serious looking. But with those glasses... so unattractive for a girl. They used to say that boys never made passes at girls..."

"I know," Richard interrupted hastily.

Katie sometimes wore reading glasses.

At the next turn of the path, they encountered a faded 10 by 10 pop-up canopy, underneath which were piled an array of goods on makeshift stands made of old crates, drums and freight pallets; vegetables, herbs, eggs, and jars of honey; goods nearly swamped by displays of aromatic home-made goat-milk soaps and herbal potions, the purpose of which Richard couldn't even begin to guess. Some of the soaps were cast in more than interestingly erotic shapes. Those were the ones sold already packaged, the precise Certificate X details tactfully half-hidden by shredded paper.

Charming and canny, Sefton and Judy had also included a small enclosure next to their stand, containing a pair of infant goats; bewildered at being removed from their normal habitat, but displaying the charm available to all immature species of mammal. The pen with the baby goats in it was surrounded two and three deep by shoppers upon whom that charm had been effectively exercised. The goats were timid, but obliging, and Sefton and Judy were at the center of a throng of shoppers, Judy running credit cards through an apparatus attached to a cellphone, or taking in cash, while Sefton packaged up the goods. They looked to be doing a roaring business.

"My landlords, at the Campground and Goat Farm," Richard explained. "Sefton and Judy Grant ... and some of their nearest and dearest among our animal friends. Sefton and Judy are possibly the last breeding pair of authentic 1960s hippies left to wander untrammeled in their natural habitat. Their granddaughter, Brianna, is one of the younger generations whom I trained in the strict traditional manner. She now works in the Café, her enthusiasm for the profession curiously undimmed by brutal experience in a restaurant kitchen."

"Oh, they seem like such nice people!" Dottie fanned herself. "So kind of them, to take you in!"

"Me and all kinds of other strays," Richard admitted, glumly. "Both animal and human. Strange as it might seem, they are − eccentric as they are in their habits and attitudes − held in affection by their neighbors. Their wrecked homeplace was entirely rebuilt in a week and a day by volunteers, a couple of years ago."

"That was so nice!" Dottie beamed approval, as Richard waved to Sefton, who seemed to have a moment between packing and wrapping erotic soaps and lord knows whatever else Judy had taken in her head to sell to customers. Meanwhile, the crowd was pressing close, and Richard decided that it was best to move on.

"I still want to consult with Sefton Grant," Alfred announced. "At his leisure, of course – a leisure that he does not seem to have at this moment. A later time will suffice, I think. I wish to see what he might know, regarding the source of a peculiar stand of grapes ... there was a local distillery here which produced a particularly legendary brandy in the 1920s. Carolina San Pedro – perhaps you might have heard of her."

Richard regarded his father with astonishment. "I have, as a matter of fact, but I didn't know that she was supposed to have used anything special for that brandy."

"It was part of her legendary technique," Alfred replied. "There was also supposed to be something special about the wild grapes from which the original low wine was made, and then distilled and aged."

"After almost a hundred years, though," Richard ventured. "Could there still be a remnant of wild grape vines somewhere close by – that you can be certain were the source?"

"I don't know," Alfred clasped his hands behind his back. "But I assure you that I have every intention of finding out and Mr. Grant is the acknowledged expert. Producing fine brandy would offer a fine challenge, commensurate with my current establishment in St. Didier. I have always relished a new challenge, you see."

"He does, indeed," Dottie backed him up loyally. "It's where you get it from, Richard."

"Er ... I never thought of it that way," Richard replied. It had never occurred to him that he had any qualities inherited from his father. Maybe he should ask Kate for her opinion. She was very good at figuring out humans and how they ticked.

Richard and his parents wandered on, through the increasingly crowded Town Square. Most of those so gathered on this day of celebration were strangers, but a few were friends and acquaintances.

"There's another very important person in Luna City," Richard said, upon seeing Adeliza Gonzalez making a slow and stately way along one of the avenues connecting the bandstand. She tottered as if her feet hurt her, leaning on the walker which supported her and provided a seat when she was too tired to proceed. Sylvester Gonzalez hovered at her elbow, resplendent in his signature Buddy Holly dark-framed glasses, khaki slacks, and a vintage Hawaiian shirt in patriotic shades of red, white and blue. Richard had often wondered if there was a retail outlet somewhere, which provided this kind of outerwear to American males for patriotic occasions.

"'lo, Ricardo," Sylvester waved, cheerily, and Abuelita Adeliza's face lit up in recognition.

"Ricardo!" she followed that with a gush of Spanish, which Richard didn't understand. Neither did his parents, who listened with expressions of polite incomprehension until Sylvester interpreted.

"Granny is pleased beyond anything that you and Katie have made up, and she is also pleased beyond mentioning that she can finally meet your parents. Granny has always thought the world of you, and she was certain that your parents must be also very superior people to have brought forth such a clever and hard-working son. And that she is certain that you and Katie will have marvelous and genius-class children. Blood will tell, Abuelita says..."

"She's dreadfully old-fashioned," Richard whispered frantically. To his relief, Dottie kept a sympathetic expression plastered to her face. "Sylvester, say something to your grandmother; that Kate and I will be married, and that my parents appreciate the sentiments..."

"Sure, Ricardo," Sylvester sent him a sideways glance of sympathy and humor mixed. "Old folk – they say what they will, right?"

"We're too old for hypocrisy," Alfred replied, and taking Abuelita Adelizas' age knotted hand in his slightly less-aged-knotted one, bowed courteously over it. "Tell your aged grand-P that we appreciate the loyalty, friendship and generous support that she has given to our son ... occasionally unworthy of such that he sometimes has been."

"Ouch, Father," Richard murmured, as Sylvester relayed the message. Yes, Alfred's stiletto of sarcasm was as well-honed as ever, and his aim with it just as unerring. With another final burst of Spanish, Abuelita Adeliza moved on, leaning heavily on her walker.

Sylvester added, over his shoulder. "She expects to be invited to the wedding, or the reception, at least – that is, if your marriage is celebrated here in Luna City."

"Of course," Richard replied. He would hardly dare not invite Abuelita Adeliza. She ruled the Clan Gonzales/Gonzalez with an iron hand and a degree of autocratic authority that Ivan the Terrible probably would have envied, and even Don Jaimie, the authentically aristocratic head of the clan would hesitate to contravene.

They passed the little booth for tickets to ride on the oil-drum train, which was just coming in – at a stately pace dictated by the reworked lawnmower engine which was pulling all eight carriages. A little thread of smoke came out of the welded chimney-stack; eight small children, shrieking with excitement, scrambled out of the carriages, to be replaced by another installment of passengers, all just as excited.

"They are having so much fun!" Dottie exclaimed, almost as thrilled as one of the children. "It does your heart good, Alf. doesn't it, to see them all so happy and excited. I'm certain," she added, "That I have never in one day seen so many cute children and darling dogs as I have today!"

"And the day is not nearly over," Alfred added. "Is this another one of your friends, Richard? He seems to be waving to us."

For Roman was waving, clad in the old-fashioned garb of a train conductor, with an ostentatious pocket watch. He was directing traffic to and from the miniature train, with all the gravity and authority required in that office.

"He is indeed," Richard replied. "Another of the Clan Gonzalez; Roman of That Ilk. A considerable power in these parts, as a construction contractor. I owe him for making the current residence livable when I first moved there."

"Hey, Ricardo!" Roman enthused, in between handling – or man-handling small children in and out of the small rail cars. "How's it going, guy! These must be your parents! Hey, welcome to Luna City. I understand the wedding is on! You know, Conchita and I expect to be invited, along with Abuelita." Dottie and Alfred exchanged mild pleasantries with Roman, as the latter shifted children in and out of the drum train carriages.

"Yes, it is," Richard confessed; knowing that marriage was now an absolute in his future, like a date with the headsman in Elizabethan times, for a favorite who had fallen out of favor. "You and your good wife, Araceli and your esteemed grandmother are at the very top of the list of those meriting an invitation. One thing does occur to me, though. Which side will you all be sitting on? The bride's side of the aisle, or the groom's ..."

"The chapel at the Rancho is so small, it will hardly make a difference." Roman laid a finger aside his nose – an affectation picked up during his turn on the dramatic boards in that presentation of Dickens' *A Christmas Story*, which was such a wild success for the Luna City Players over the previous holiday season. "A little bird hinted to Conchita and me, that the chapel will be Katie's chosen venue. But you didn't hear it from me, of course."

"A little bird named Araceli Gonzalez-Gonzales whispered it in your ear, of course," Richard acknowledged, while Roman grinned. Out of the corner of his eye, Richard noted that Trish The Author was taking pictures with her serious looking professional-grade camera. Ah; Lew had said something to the effect that Trish The Author loved taking pictures; inspiration and guidance for her characters, and eventual marketing of her books.

"Ask me no questions, I'll tell you no lies," Roman replied, and then Otis Bodie, at the command of the riding-lawnmower turned train engine sounded the horn. The train trundled off on a circuit around Town Square, every little car full of excited young Lunaites. Richard and his parents walked on, in the direction of the dunking booth.

"What a charming gentleman!" Dottie burbled. "And is he a relation of the elderly lady that we met previously?"

"Nephew, I think," Richard replied, although he was not entirely certain of the Gonzalez-Gonzales family tree, with all it's many-tangled branches. Of course, no one else was, either. Such was the clan's propensity for distant-cousin-marriage and other less formal relationships, many, many, many children generated from them, and a tendency to recycle the same names, unto the many generations that the Gonzalez-Gonzales family had been settled in the vicinity of Luna City. "But he is one of the notable ornaments of a lush and many-branched family tree. At the bidding of his aunt, grandmother, he and his people made the Airstream caravan where I have lived since arrival a cozy and livable little place. I am honored by their friendship and support, to a degree that I really can't ever be sufficiently grateful for. On the other hand, Roman owes me, and has generously never forgotten that I saved his company almost 20 million dollars, when a bent decorating sub-contractor tried to walk off with eighteen priceless antique Lalique platinum and glass chandeliers, from a refit of the Cattleman..."

"Indeed?" Alfred observed dryly, and Dottie clutched her hands to her chest.

"Ooooh, they didn't! How brave of you, Richard!"

"It wasn't brave at all," Richard admitted. "I merely mentioned to Roman, that I had been told the chandeliers were Lalique. He, with a mind-boggling grasp of detail, noticed that said chandeliers were missing from his worksite, in spite of having been refurbished at great expense by his client. He connected the remaining clues, with the aid of our crack police force. I do believe that the chief of our police is about to complete his scheduled round in the dunk tank at the top of the hour. Such is the devotion of our citizenry and public employees that they are willing to undergo this humiliation ... the Mayor was the feature last hour. But it's all in aid of the local food pantry, you see. And it's all in good fun, and Mayor Bodie and Chief Joe are all amazingly good sports about it." They continued their slow progress along the Square, until Richard paused. "Oh, now there's another of my good friends. Chris Mayell, with Stephanie Royce. His lady-friend is the public relations expert for Mills Farm and the Cattleman Hotel; as brainy as she is beautiful. You may gather from the outset that he is – in the vernacular – not from around these parts. He is yet another stray, taken into the hearts of the good citizens. I should tell you," Richard added, "That he is a disabled war veteran. He was the best friend to Doc Wyler's grandson – a Marine. Chris was a medic in the Naval service. He has a disability pension, and for now, he runs the little petrol stop and grocery on the outskirts of town."

"Oh, the poor lad!" Dottie's eyes filled with sympathetic tears.

Richard cringed. "No, Mum; don't say anything to him about all that. Chris is a good bloke, and one of those things that he doesn't want is pity. He's been a good friend to me! Oh, hi, Chris – Stephanie! Having the usual good time on the Glorious Fourth!"

"You know it, pal!" Chris replied. "Hey; these the 'rents? Good to meet y'all!" he shook hands energetically with Alfred and Dottie after introductions were performed, adding confidently, "Just wanna say that your boy is solid! Best of the best, out of all us adopted sons of Luna City!"

"Refreshing to know," Alfred replied, in that cuttingly austere tone which Richard knew so well, and they walked on.

Dottie observed, "She's such a pretty girl; Stephanie. They make a perfect couple, don't you think, Al? Do you think they will be getting married?"

"I have no idea," Richard replied. "Not my business. Now, you remember Mrs. Abernathy-Vaughn?"

"Well, of course," Alfred replied with austere courtesy. "You introduced us when we first sought you out at the little Café. The accountant for the enterprise. A very charming and sensible woman. I thought. If Miss Heisel had not already been honored by your affections, and Mrs. Abernathy-Vaugh were not Mrs. Abernathy-Vaughn, she would have been a most acceptable match for you. I would have approved."

"Alas, that you are not a medieval monarch, waving your royal scepter and negotiating a marriage alliance between royal houses," Richard commented glumly. "I am certain you would have done it, forsooth, no matter what the two of us felt about it."

While Dottie giggled, "Oh, Al, you do go on! You are so naughty! You're embarrassing the boy!"

"I protest, Father!" Richard said. "Most indignantly! I have never considered Mrs. Abernathy-Vaughn in any other role than in her professional capacity! She is an attractive and intelligent woman, but ... really! She has three children, and a devoted husband, so please put your monarchial ambitions aside. Please ... Hullo, Jess – Small Joe, and girls..."

Jess Abernathy-Vaughn had paused the huge three-seat stroller on the outskirt of the crowd waiting in line to pitch baseballs at the target; a target which if hit fair and square and with sufficient force, would empty the person sitting on a perilous perch over a small tank of water, into that body of water. The current occupant of the perch was Joe Vaughn, bare-chested and clad in bathing trunks, behind a heavy screen of mesh which protected the object of the dunk from errant pitches. He was already dripping wet; evidence of many successful and energetic pitches at the small target. But his enthusiasm was unabated – he continued with abusively creative taunts against those in the crowd who were having their chance at five dollars for three throws, especially those who were missing the target by a wide margin.

"Ohhh!" Dottie cooed, bending over the occupants of the enormous stroller. Little Joe, some two years old and some, was scowling at all comers, but his expression melted into something more ... well, calculated charm was how Richard read it. "Such little darlings, my dear! What are their names, so that we can be properly introduced?"

"This is Joseph James," Jess Abernathy-Vaughn replied, with an air of fatuous fondness. "Shake hands, Little Joe, like you have been taught!" She admonished her offspring, and to Richard's mild surprise, Little Joe put out his tiny infant hand, and gripped Dottie's first fingers. "And these are the girls – Lizzie, who is asleep, and Alice who is not. They're twins," Jess added, unnecessarily, for both were exactly the same size, with the same feathery dark hair and dumpling unformed features. They were also dressed in identical pink rompers and ruffled lace blouses and bonnets. Alice's face creased in a delighted grin, her eyes almost squinching shut, as her tiny starfish pink hands closed on Dottie's fingers.

"What a charmer!" Richard's mother exclaimed. "Oh, I simply cannot wait until you and your Kate have a trio like this of your own! I do so want to spoil grandchildren!"

"Mum, really!" Richard closed his eyes and waited for the humiliation to pass, while Jess chuckled. "Give us a moment – we've only just decided to get married! It takes a while to start up the kids."

"Nine months, on average," Jess commented, trying to conceal a sympathetic grin. "But it has been known to take considerably less for first children."

"Thank you, Mother of the Year," Richard commented, in tones meant to be cutting, and Jess merely giggled. In the meantime, the minute hand of the clock in the tower of the old Luna City Savings, which now housed the city offices, moved one last tick to the top of the dial.

In the dunk tank, Joe Vaughn moved easily and athletically from the collapsible seat and climbed out, taking the towel that was offered to him by the ticket-taker for the dunk tank – an earnest young Boy Scout doing his civic duty, and being no end amused at the spectacle of Luna City's major power players being repeatedly dunked in water. (*Of all Luna City's notable citizens, only Don Jaimie of the Ranch, and Monsignor Evans, the senior priest at Saints Margaret and Stephen Catholic Church, had declined the opportunity for repeated baptisms in the interests of charity. As elder citizens, they were inclined to stand on imperishable dignity and respect. In Monsignor Evans' case, he had already done enough for charity, in organizing the handicrafts sales at the church's thrift shop.*)

Joe toweled off, and came barefoot and bare-chested to embrace Jess, who reached up and deposited a brief kiss on his cheek, and in that moment, Trish The Author snapped a picture – a single passing moment on Town Square, one of scores or hundreds of snapshots taken on the day of the Glorious 4th. That single picture of Joe and Jess passed almost unnoticed. Until six months later, when practically the entire English-speaking world took an intense interest.

"Well, that was so amusing," Dottie exclaimed, as they walked on. "Meeting so many of your good friends, Richard. And your lovely bride to be – oh, I say – is that the band?" She was as happy as a child at a birthday party.

Richard replied, after a glance at his cellphone. "I do believe it is. Let's go find a good position for the parade and the reading of the Declaration, Mum. Kate just sent me a message – she'll be along in a bit, to cover the event for her newspaper. I said that we would meet her by the war memorial."

"Lovely," Dottie burbled. "I can hardly wait – she sounds a lovely person, from her stories on that newspaper blog of hers. Much better than that actress woman you were living with in London -what was her name, Alf? Sunny? Bunny? Something like that. She was purely not good for you, Richard, although I held my peace at the time! If you were happy..."

"Sammy," Alfred said, with austere disapproval "Samantha, I believe. Didn't she take up with another of your friends, after you left London?"

"Tactful way to put it, Father," Richard admitted. "But yes, Sammi took up with most of the Premier League. I'd rather forgive and forget..."

"And rightfully so!" Dottie, as a mother, was stout in defense of her young. "Ohhh ... is that the mayor?"

A brisk and brassy Sousa marching tune grew louder, as the first of the parade came into view – one of the original Luna City

Volunteer Fire Department ladder trucks slowly advanced around the corner, Mayor Bodie waving to the cheering crowd. The fire truck was followed by two mounted ranks of historical reenactors, led by Clovis Walcott.

"Oh, but he looks so handsome!" Dottie exclaimed. "Like a movie hero!"

Then there was the high school marching band, who had won in band competitions the length and breadth of Texas, the teenagers sweating in the heat, clad as they all were in their teal-green and blue Mighty Moth regalia. The band members did their best to avoid droppings on the roadway from the horses. It was a splendid turnout as always, concluded by a straggling body of elementary school children waving patriotic banners; the smallest of them led by their mothers holding their hands.

"Such darlings!" Dottie turned to Richard, as pleased as a small child herself. "Richard, darling ... is that your Kate that I see, over there – the woman with such a large camera?"

"Yes, that's my Kate," Richard replied, his heart lifting, as he spotted her across the street and waved to catch her attention. His lovely dark-haired Kate in her neat skirt suit, taking a last picture of the smallest child, waving a small American flag in one hand, and apparently sucking the thumb on his other hand. She saw him and waved in reply, before walking slowly across the street towards them.

Richard knew her well enough to see that she was nervous; that she was steeling herself for the introduction; a fixedly pleasant expression on her face, and her left hand clenched on the shoulder strap of her camera bag so hard that he could see when she got closer that her knuckles were white.

"Hi, love," he said, as soon as she stepped up onto the sidewalk. He dropped a brief kiss on her cheek and set a reassuring arm around her shoulders. "Mum and Father ... this is Kate. Kate – my parents; Alfred and Dorothy Astor-Hall."

For a moment which seemed to last an eternity, Kate and his parents looked at each other in fraught silence.

"Hello," Kate for once, seemed to be at a loss for words.

"Very pleased to meet you at last," Alfred said, finally, and Dottie shot him a reproving look.

"Oh, Al, you do go on!" Dottie enveloped Kate in a fond embrace and kissed her cheek. "We're so very, very pleased – aren't we, Al! I knew when I saw you, just this very moment, that you would be perfect – and every one of Richard's friends that we have met today have asked about the wedding and said such pleasant things about you! Everyone is so pleased about it all, that I just knew that you would be!"

Under his arm, Richard felt Kate's shoulders relax. Yes, it would be all right now. In fact, it would all be perfect.

Liquid Treasure

Richard had been in two minds, at finally accepting a management position from Lew Dubois, to be the executive chef of the Cattleman Hotel by the end of June. He regretted, but in a minor way, handing over management of Luna Café and Coffee to Araceli, since the Café had been his life and reason for living for five years. But on the other hand, he was experiencing twinges of acute boredom, having turned it into a profitable, popular enterprise, renowned for the in-house cinnamon rolls, and the line of gourmet edibles, sauces and condiments which had been developed by his junior staff. It was, he sensed – and a decision confirmed by the clear head and hard business acumen of Jessica Abernathy-Vaughn – time to move on, now that the 4th of July holiday was over. Richard also had the feeling that becoming bored professionally could have unfortunate results for him, as such boredom might tempt him again into self-destructive habits. In any case, management of the Café was now in the frighteningly capable hands of Araceli – who had been a reliable constant in the front of the house since coming to work at the Café when she was a teenage waitress nearly two decades previously.

"You may wish to make use of a staff suite in the Cattleman," Lew had waved an airy hand in the direction of the grand staircase, "Until the private enclave at Mills Farm for senior staff and visiting management is complete – you and your intended are entitled to one of the cottages there. It's part of your compensation package." This had been on Richard's first official day of employment as an upper-level minion of Venue Properties, International, managing the kitchen and the hotel restaurant, now christened as the "Crystal Room" in recognition of the splendid antique Lalique crystal and platinum chandeliers which adorned it. They were sitting in Lew's office; the smaller of two adjoining offices, 19th century marvels of fine wood paneling and plasterwork. The offices were wedged into the space adjoining the gloriously ornate main bar, accessed by a small, discrete door adjacent to the monumental front desk. Richard had been given to understand that the larger of the two would be his, shared with the hotel's duty concierge, and Mr. Georges, the maître d. Mr. Georges boasted a Gallic mustache to rival Poirot's, and unfailingly greeted Richard in the slangy French patois which Richard remembered from his days training in Paris. A short hallway behind the second office connected with the kitchen, which made it handy for both chef and maître d.

"Oh, really?" Richard confessed to being somewhat gob smacked. He hadn't read that far into the sheaf of documents which Lew had conveyed to him for signature, Jess would surely have administered the gob smacking, for signing documents without closely and carefully perusing every line. "In that case … Miss Heisel and I will be thrilled at having a residence as part of the deal. For myself, though – I shall continue living at the Age until the marriage. I've become very fond of the place, you see.

Sefton has agreed to continue renting it to me as a pied-à-terre, a kind of get-away refuge."

"As you wish, *mon cher* Richard," Lew acknowledged by way of dismissal. "You may wish now to conduct your own review of facilities and staff. In the meantime, welcome to the family of Venue Properties ... oh, tomorrow there will be some slight disruption. The workmen from the security firm will be installing certain additional devices and connecting cables. They will need to work in your office and mine, for about a day, but I am assured that the mess and disruption will be minimal."

"Thanks for the warning," Richard replied, and withdrew to his own shared office, where Bianca Gonzalez – one of the numerous Luna City Gonzales-Gonzalez clan – was already on the phone at her side of the antique partner desk which dominated the windowless room. Bianca was a rising star in the Venue Properties firmament, an elegant young woman who had obviously taken Audrey Hepburn as her sartorial role model: she wore a simple black dress, pearl earrings and had her dark hair rolled into a simple chignon.

"Of course," Bianca was saying into the receiver. "White orchids in the suite, and a reservation for four in the Crystal Room at eight o'clock that evening. The guide for the boys' kayaking excursion will call for them promptly at seven the next morning ... he will have your number, in case of a delay... thank you, Mrs. Sheldon. I'm certain that you and the family will enjoy your excursion... see you next weekend, then ... 'byeeee...Good morning, Chef!" Bianca beamed at him. "Welcome to the Cattleman. Let me know if you have any questions, 'k, or can't find anything."

"Thanks, Miss Gonzalez," Richard replied. "Mr. Dubois was very thorough in briefing me..."

"Isn't he the total sweetheart?" Bianca twinkled at him. "He knows everything about everything, and gosh, you'd best stay on your toes, if you work for him!"

"I know," Richard replied. There was a small closet next to the door to the kitchen. He opened it, to find there were ten or a dozen identical chef's jacket already hanging in dry-cleaning bags, all with the logo of the Cattleman Hotel embroidered over the breast pocket, and his own name – Chef Richard Astor-Hall below the logo. A stack of flawlessly starched and fluted toques sat on the shelf above the hanger rod. No, there was no detail too small for Lew Dubois to overlook. He shrugged a jacket on. It fit perfectly, of course, donned the toque and went to survey his new domain.

An absorbing business, as it turned out: in his new situation, he commanded a sous-chef, a dozen junior chefs and apprentices, a pastry and bread baker, and a pantry supervisor, plus several kitchen porter-cum-dishwashers. The front house staff fell under the stern but kindly rule of Mr. Georges. Most of them were young, hired from schools and culinary training institutions across South Texas; they had not had time, the space, or the energy to acquire bad habits. Richard could barely recall all their names, serially introduced as they went about their duties in a pleasingly professional manner. Fortunately, with Lew Dubois' customary attention to detail, every one of the kitchen staff wore proper kitchen garb with the Cattleman logo and – most importantly – their name and office embroidered over the left front pocket. Richard had not had such a large staff since his abortive glory days in London, launching Carême, the towering failure of which had sent him first on a blackout drunken bender, then on to Texas. He promised himself that the Cattleman's Crystal Room was not going to be a similar disaster. In any case, he was a hireling, not an independent, frantically juggling a dozen flaming balls while tap-dancing on a tightrope.

Richard had only to oversee the restaurant and catering functions and do it to the satisfaction of customers and of Lew Dubois. He was part of a team, not the one whose neck was a hundred percent on the line.

He passed the remainder of the morning, reviewing prospective menus for the Crystal Room, consulting his personal well-thumbed copy of *Larousse Gastronomique* and the availability at a reasonable price for commodities which might eventually be turned into amazing and appealing menu selections. Any match of those qualities would eventually turn a tidy profit for the Cattleman's restaurant. Such research absorbed his interest for the remainder of the day, only interrupted around midday by one of the junior female kitchen minions bringing him a tray with a beautifully composed Salad Niçoise upon it. Barely recalling his manners, he complimented the minion, who fled with the empty tray, blushing beet-red.

"Nomi's very new," remarked Bianca, with some amusement. "At least you didn't make her cry or pee in her underpants. She is so very thrilled to be working here, and she worships you, after watching your YouTube series *Captain Kitten in the Kitchen*. That's why she decided that she wanted to be a chef and work in a real restaurant."

"A cousin of yours?" Richard replied glumly. Of course — one couldn't throw a brick in any direction in Luna City without hitting a round dozen of Gonzalezes and Gonzaleses. Bianca giggled and flapped an airy hand in the direction of the kitchen. She had her own plate, with a small green salad upon it, also arrayed with exacting precision

"Of course. Our family has Luna City in the palm of our hands, Chef."

The remainder of the day passed in the same absorbing fashion; Richard engrossed in plans, cost estimations, and Larousse. When he lifted his head from the various piles on the desk, he was amazed to discover that it was nearly dark outside, well past sunset. The pleasant clatter of plates and silverware, and the low hum of conversation trickled out from the Crystal Room. Feeling that his day had been sufficiently full and tomorrow he would do serious work in the kitchen, he did the rounds of the immaculately out-fitted Crystal Room, briefly exchanged remarks with Mr. Georges, another with the kitchen staff, which hummed along like a well-oiled machine, and stuck his head into Lew's office. That gentleman was just closing up his desk – or more importantly, the computer which sat upon that graceful example of 19th century office furniture – for the day.

"Tomorrow, *mon cher*? I thought you had gone already." Lew remarked.

"Ah well, we in the trade commonly work long hours," Richard replied. "All part and parcel of the game."

"Indeed," and Lew bent a look of near-to-fatherly concern upon Richard. "But one must set limits, *cher* Ricard, especially as one intending to marry and commit to a family. Work, if one is not careful, will expand to consume all of one's time and energy, and that is not conducive to a contented marriage or a happy family life. There is no one, ever, who has on their deathbed confessed that they wished they had spent more time at the office. If you would walk with me, Richard, I will impart some of my hard-won knowledge of management. Successful management of an enterprise such as this; you must not think that it requires your presence at all the hours of the day and the weeks. That way lies madness and despair, if not for yourself, then for your loved ones. No. The way to success is to carefully select your subordinates and train them up most exactingly to the manner in which you wish things to be done. Once accomplished, allow them the authority to conduct matters in your absence." Lew added, in a practical manner, as they walked out of the staff entrance, where Richard's trusty trail bicycle was chained to a handy railing. Lew, who had the advantage of a staff suite in the hotel, had no such convenient transport waiting for him. "Only then might one live what they call a balanced life. It is my secret to success in management, as I have found – train and encourage your subordinates in the way that one might wish – and then when that is done, one might take the time to have a full life. I should write a book, do you think? *Management Secrets of the Lazy Manager*. It is then a matter of the quality of time spent, training quality subordinates, not the quantity of time. Good night, *cher* Richard. Tomorrow, dedicate your time in acquainting your kitchen staff with the standards and principles which you wish them to achieve and maintain. And then," Lew bestowed a beatific smile upon Richard, "Allow them to go forth, dedicating themselves to achieving your standard, while you pick daisies in the field with your estimable and delectable Miss Heisel."

"I don't know if I am up to that, Lew," Richard confessed glumly, "I just don't know if I am that kind of good management materiel. I boobed the job pretty catastrophically, the first time out of the gate. You knew about the Carême disaster? I think everyone does by now, what with all the videos, although it was five years ago. A century in internet time."

"Ah," Lew replied. "But you had a second chance with the little Café, you see. Which was that which inspired my interest in you, Richard. You had the management of a tiny café, and what with one thing and another, you brought in or encouraged a splendid team. You brought in new customers, recruited a solid team to serve them ...Made the little Café famous and popular ... and profitable."

"It was more chance and good luck than good management on my part," Richard confessed, and Lew smiled.

"Ah, but didn't Napoleon himself ask of a prospective marshal for his *Grand Armee* – is he lucky? I myself am not

Napoleon," Lew laid a finger along his nose and looked wisely at his latest recruit. "But I have a sense of who is able … and lucky."

Richard could not readily shed his established habit of rising well before sunrise – with the chickens, as Judy Grant cheerfully said it – or at least with their several roosters, all of whom were given to serenade the setting of the moon with an acapella chorus of cock-a-doodle-dos at five-thirty AM. He secretly rather enjoyed the brisk pedal along the darkened country road, as sunrise paled the eastern sky. He relished the quietness of the streets, and the dimming gold of the old-fashioned gas lamps which lit the margins of Town Square and the area around the bandstand which was the ornate center of the Square. The lights would flicker out just as the sun rose in a glory of apricot and rose – very occasionally trimmed with crimson and purple clouds.

There was a van parked around the side of the Cattleman, with the logo of a national security firm emblazoned on the side. Richard paid it hardly any attention, save for noticing that there were a pair of genial gentlemen in overalls, messing about with drills, rolls of cable and some really impressive toolkits. The workmen bustled in and out of Lew's office, the larger joint office and in the splendidly ornate and paneled bar, which was almost the crown jewel of the Cattleman. He did a tour of the kitchen, which was mildly busy preparing breakfasts for a scattering of early-rising hotel clients, and then retreated to the office to continue his research of the previous day. He pondered Lew's advice, and considered it good … but still, the obsessive habits of a lifetime thus far niggled at him. Was it entirely cricket to spend less than eighty hours a week, in the object of his employment … or was that taking devotion to duty just a little too far in the pursuit of what Lew called a well-balanced life?

He was interrupted shortly before eleven by one of the overalled technicians, lurking hesitantly in the doorway of the office.

"'Scuse me, Chef," the technician ventured. "D'you know where the big boss is? We got a bit of a problem with running the new line."

"Mr. Dubois is around here somewhere," Richard answered, just as the great man himself appeared. That Lew was also wearing a groundskeeper's Carhart jacket and a pair of heavy leather work gloves went without mentioning.

"Hey, Lew," the technician confessed with relief. "There's a problem with running the new cable. It just goes and goes and goes into the wall. Doesn't come out where it's supposed to. Stevo and I think there is a void in the wall between the office and the bar. Can we have a squint at the blueprints again, just to make certain."

"Of course," Lew went to a tall, old-fashioned wooden cabinet, one fitted out with a series of shallow but large drawers. He pulled out several, before finding the one oversized envelope containing the diagrams of the ground floor offices of the Cattleman. They were done on outsized sheets of heavy paper in ink which had faded to a sepia shade; heavily-detailed plans of each room, some adorned with sketches of the architectural adornments. Which, as far as Richard could see from a cursory glance over the shoulders of Lew and the tech, had been faithfully carried out, more than a hundred years ago. All three of them studied the linked plans for the various spaces on the Cattleman's ground floor, joined presently by Stevo, the other security install tech, and Bianca, concerned as a good concierge would be.

"Hmm," Remarked Lew thoughtfully. "I am not an architect, just someone who has had to become familiar with old buildings and their peculiarities, but it seems to me that there might be something anomalous, just there. Your cable should come from my office and emerge in that wall to the left of the back-bar, but it seems to me that there might be a space unaccounted for."

Both technicians agreed, solemnly and with a degree of puzzlement.

"A secret compartment," Richard ventured, with an air of insouciance. "Hardly an old mansion or listed pile in England is without a secret passage, staircase, or priest's hole. They usually hide the door catch somewhere in the woodwork."

"I wonder if you can find it, *cher*," Lew frowned in concentration. "As you appear to be the expert in these matters." There was nothing for it, but that all but to agree with Lew, and all, followed by an increasingly intrigued Bianca, trooped after Richard into the hotel bar.

The barroom in the old hotel had been kept open, maintained, and functioning long after most of the other facilities had been closed up and allowed to molder away, so the renovations in that area, performed by Roman Gonzalez' construction crew under contract from Venue Properties had not been nearly as extensive as they had on the upper floors, to the offices, kitchen and ballroom. The barroom itself was a wonder of elaborate woodwork, with a long bar of Circassian tiger-striped walnut. The whole place was adorned with every possible ornate wood and brass frill that the late 19th century Beaux-Arts designers could imagine, hired at great expense by the Italian hotelier who hoped to make another small fortune in catering to the guests visiting the hot-water spa on the outskirts of Luna City. (*He did end up with a small fortune, but alas, he had started with a large one.*)

Richard, seeing that all were watching him consigned his credibility to the gods, and began feeling his way around the carved panels to the left of the stupendously ornate bar. The woodwork was certainly comprehensive. God only knew how many secret catches could have been hidden in all the curlicues, whorls, and flourishes. Richard ran his fingers over the edges of all the panels, paying particular attention to those where the carving was most ornate, feeling for anything that might move, just a bit, under light pressure. He was feeling a bit under pressure himself, watched by an audience; Lew, both the security technicians, Mr. Georges, Bianca, and a couple of waiters drawn by the unusual nature of the proceedings, on a boring morning after the breakfast rush. To his utter astonishment, a particularly ornate bit of carving at the upper left corner of the panel just to the right of the back-bar, gave under slight pressure.

A small crack appeared in the floor-to-head-height paneling. Richard let his breath out, in astonishment – an astonishment shared by the audience. A segment of paneling the size of an ordinary door swung open, with a faint metal groan of protest, revealing a closet-sized space behind. That space was lined with shelves and row on row of bottles, and several small barrels on the bottom row. Everything was covered in a generous layer of gray dust, dust so thick that it looked for all the world like grotesque fur. Through a small hole at the back of the closet, a long length of clean cable coiled like a snake on the dusty floor.

"Holy cow!" breathed Stevo the tech. "A no-shit Sherlock secret compartment! He fumbled out his cellphone and snapped a picture. "I gotta share this with the boss, Lew! We've never found something like this before! What's in it? Looks like the secret booze store, back in the day!"

"Those are quarter-casks," intoned Mr. Georges, casting a professional eye upon them. "Used to age various brandies, fine whiskeys, and other liquors in bulk. Depending on how long they have been aging, that is – if they have not leaked or evaporated."

"My friends, there might be a fortune, concealed for how long..." Lew mused. "And did no one, not even our cher Roman, who oversaw all the renovations of this place ... ever detect the presence of this secret cellar?"

"I guess not," Bianca was already dialing on her cellphone, "As far as I know, he did most of the work on the ballroom, the restaurant, and the upper floors. There was no need to do much more than paint the plaster and polish up the paneling in the barroom."

"Indeed," Richard agreed. "As far as I recall, the bar was the one space in the Cattleman that was kept in pretty good nick, all the way along. There was no need to do anything more than a lick and a promise and dust the lights as far as the renovations went."

Lew nodded in agreement. "Yes, this is a most unexpected bonus ... Cherie, my dear Mademoiselle Bianca, would you be so good as to dial ..."

"Mademoiselle Stephanie," Bianca replied smartly. "Already on it, boss ... Hello, Steph? You should come to the Cattleman, *tout suite*! We have just made the most amazing discovery!"

Lew, with a smile of beatific pleasure, turned to Richard and Mr. Georges and remarked, "Ah ... I have the most expert staff, do I not? They do what I want done before I can even voice the orders."

Meanwhile, Mr. Georges had already stepped gingerly into the closet, carefully avoiding the coil of cable on the floor, and gently pulled out one of the bottles into the light, handling it as carefully as if were a particularly fragile infant. He blew the remaining dust from the bottle, and the faded sepia-tinted label. He adjusted his glasses and read carefully from the label.

"San Pedro Five Star Gold Brandy ... Luna City, USA ... vintage 1924. *Sacre bleu* ..." and he went off in a long babble of agitated French to Lew.

"What is it?" Richard whispered to Bianca, who had finished the call on her cellie, and put it away, meanwhile looking into the dusty compartment as if the door to the sacred tomb had just had the rock rolled away from the opening.

Bianca murmured in holy awe, "It's a cache of Carolina San Pedro's brandy, Chef. The last bottle of it to come on the open market sold at auction for $25,000. A single bottle! It was distilled from a brew of local grapes, just after Prohibition went into effect. It's almost a hundred years old. How many bottles are there, Mr. Georges?"

"At least a hundred," Mr. Georges reverently considered the dark bottle in his hands. "And six quarter-casks, which should hold approximately fifty liters each. That is, assuming that much has not evaporated over time. The profit for the hotel and VPI will be incalculable."

"Good god!" Richard exclaimed. "This is the stuff that my father was talking about, just the other day! I must let him know that more of it has been found! He wanted to expand his operation in St. Didier, by duplicating it as much as possible!" He also was considering how a very small quantity of such an amazing distillation could be made to serve the cause of haute cuisine, although some experts felt that using a rare liquor in cooking was blasphemy.

"The matter of ownership will be a question of the most complicated to unravel," Lew conceded. "For Venue Properties has only leased the hotel from the municipality, which is the owner of record. Ownership of this cache must be adjudicated, since it's existence predates our agreement to lease, renovate and manage. I have always conducted business with the highest of ethical consideration ..." he turned to Bianca, who was already dialing her cellphone.

"Mayor Bodie," Bianca said into it. "Bianca Gonzalez, at the Cattleman... Good morning – are you sitting down? We have just made the most interesting discovery ... and Mr. Dubois thinks that you should come and see it, right away..."

Lew smiled again, and whispered to Richard, "See, *mon ami*? Before I might even say the words, my staff knows what should be done."

From the Karnesville Weekly Beacon – July 24, 2019

An Amazing Discovery!
Katherine Heisel – Staff Writer

Last Wednesday, workers from GCTV Communications, installing a new security system in the venerable Cattleman Hotel made an astounding discovery – a secret storage area, concealed behind a paneled wall in the 19th century main barroom. The secret room, about the size of an old-fashioned telephone booth was packed with a fortune in bottles and barrels of fine aged brandy. The bottles all bore labels, identifying the brandy as having been distilled in the early 1920s by Carolina San Pedro Mills. It is assumed that they were concealed in the secret room during Prohibition. Carolina San Pedro Mills was at that time the wife of notorious bootlegger Charles E. Mills, although it has been acknowledged by historians that she was the mainstay of Mills' enterprise, as she was an immensely skilled distiller of fine alcoholic beverages.

The cache of century-old brandy has not been assigned a monetary value, although it is assumed to be in the millions of dollars, as a single bottle of similar vintage Mills brandy sold at auction for $25,000 in 2015. Ownership of the cache may be subject to adjudication; while the building itself is currently owned by the city of Luna City, it is now leased by Venue Properties, International, and was owned by the Bodie family of Luna City during the time that the brandy was deposited in the secret storage room.

The Hunt Is On!

Two mornings after the glorious liquor find in the Cattleman Bar, Richard came to work at the crack of dawn as always, relishing again the coolness of the morning, only to find that his parents – and *mirablu dictu* – Sefton Grant gathered at one of the tables set for breakfast service for early risers in the Crystal Room.

"Mr. Grant!" Richard exclaimed, upon seeing his landlord, appearing unexpectedly dapper and neatly barbered, sitting at a table with Lew Dubois, and his own father. "What a surprise! I would have asked for a lift, if I had known you were heading this way this morning! And Dad," he added, "I thought you and Mum were still doing the round of the Hill Country vineyards!" On second thought, he couldn't decide which was the most startling: Sefton Grant appropriately clad in an immaculate white shirt, tie and sports jacket, or that the three gentlemen appeared to be sharing an amiable early breakfast.

" 'S all right," Sefton replied. "It was a late-arranged thing. After reading Miss Heisel's story in the *Beacon*, I had to come and talk to Lew an' your dad, seein' as how I been searching for the San Pedro stand of mustang-muscadine grapes for near on forty years, now."

"Mr. Grant is the unsung expert on just how Miss San Pedro created that marvelous elixir known as the Five Star Gold," Richard's father explained. "Yes, Richard; we were going to explore some of the other wineries, but our schedule is flexible."

"It seems that there was an unusual stand of grapes extant in the area, more than a hundred years ago," Lew Dubois explained. "Which produced the original materiel for Miss San Pedro's distilling. We were just coming to the point where Mr. Grant was about to share with us that which he has deduced, regarding the historical sources for the grand Gold Star Brandy."

"Well, see here, I've been making my own prime vintage – red and white," Sefton set down the fork, with which he had been consuming mouthfuls of delicately-seasoned streaky bacon. (*Sefton was an unabashed carnivore; a vice which he had been able to conceal for almost as long as his marriage to his devoted spouse, dedicated as Judy Grant was to every -ism going, including the vegan variety. How she had never detected the scent of meat on his breath was a miracle passing understanding, even if Judy was one of the most cheerfully oblivious-to-reality women in Karnes County.*) Sefton continued. "Y'see, I started back in the day when we established the commune. One of my pals among the old originals was the son of Czech settlers, from around about Beeville way. He knew all the old ways, of making wine from mustang grapes ... my own folk, they were hard-shell teetotal, they didn't know nothing about the demon alcohol an' didn't want to learn. But Hank knew all the old methods and taught them to me. Pity ... I miss that ol' bastard!" Sefton sighed, sorrowfully reminiscent, and Richard thought that he had to make a sympathetic comment."

"Sorry for your loss," he said, and Sefton snorted in laughter.

"Hank? That ol' son-of-a-gun invested in one o' those internet start-ups in the 1980s, one that really paid off in a big way. He has a family compound in Montana, another in New Zealand, and a mansion on Lake Como; he ain't hurting for anything, these days. We get a card and a letter from him, regular every Christmas. Anyway, he had stories from his granddad of some ol' farmer with a lil' teeny vineyard somewhere between here an' Charco – along the river – with the mos' amazing grapes. Something halfway between wild muscadines and mustang grapes ... tender, sweet, nicely acidic ... and it was from that mutant stock that Carolina San Pedro got the wine that she distilled for that prime brandy. We tried to find that farm, back in the day," Sefton added sorrowfully, "But it was forty years, at least, since Hank heard those stories..."

"With careful tending," Alfred cleared his throat, "A vineyard grapevine can live and go on producing grapes for a hundred years. The Great Vine of Hampton Court is over two-hundred and fifty years old and still bearing copious amounts of fruit – but that vine is sheltered in a greenhouse, and produces table grapes, rather than wine grapes. A special case, really. But none the less, Mr. Dubois and Mr. Grant and I are going into partnership, establishing a new vineyard of those special grapes, should we be successful in locating any vines remaining."

"Did Madame San Pedro leave any record of the location of those splendid grapevines?" ventured Lew Dubois, and the other two gentlemen shook their heads, sorrowfully.

"She was operating during Prohibition," Sefton explained. "And she was real careful about writing stuff down. She kept it in her head, mostly – near as we can figure out."

"Couldn't you search along the riverbanks, then? If you know for sure that this little vineyard was along the river?" Richard suggested, and Sefton shook his head.

"Me an' Hank went searching, in '69 and '70, all the way to Charco. Found us plenty of wild mustang vines, an' a lot of angry cows, but nothing like what we were looking for."

"It is altogether possible that such a small vineyard may have been uprooted or otherwise destroyed in the interim," Alfred admitted. "Particularly if a property passed into other hands. But it would help the search immensely, if somehow, we were able to narrow down a more precise location ..."

"I wrote an' asked Hank last year, if he remembered his granddad being any more exact," Sefton replied. "And he thought – only thought, mind you – that it was his impression that the vineyard was somewhere near to the road to Helena. Which cuts down the search area some..."

Lew Dubois nodded, magisterially. "Such would have been much more accessible to Madame San Pedro, at that time. The automobile allowed so much more range for travel... but only over a horse and buggy, or even a bicycle..."

"A pity," Richard sighed, "That Mindy Gonzales-Rodriguez-Penn is off on a doubtlessly fruitless treasure hunt with her husband. It seems to me at this point that you all could do with the services of a tireless researcher. Of the archaeological or even the archival sort ... hang on, I have an idea!"

"Did it hurt?" Alfred inquired gently, and Richard scowled at his parent.

"That was uncalled for, Father," Richard replied. "No, it occurred to me that Katie, who has chosen to adorn my life, marry my lack of fortune to hers, and to bear your grandchildren - if such a program of such propagation is agreeable to her - works for a local newspaper ... one with an admittedly decaying archive going back at least a hundred and thirty years. I suppose that I might be able to impose and ask her to research through the *Beacon* back issues. Perhaps..." Richard became more enthused as he considered the possibilities, "This was something which might have inspired local media interest! You cannot believe how gratefully a small-market media outlet falls upon anything which might fill in the weekly or daily publication. Anything at all in the nature of the unusual and of fleeting interest which would make a news story! Anything! Anything to fill the unforgiving page! Katie told me once of a small-market newspaper which made a local-section front page story of an enormous and invasive willow tree root pulled out of a domestic sewer outfall ... almost thirty foot long, the monster was – and there was a picture of the two service technicians who had extracted it from the pipe and the champion root, all laid out along the parking lot of the company. Now, any small-town media outlet which needs to make a top story of a massive root in a plumbing line ... might be so desperate for news content as to make a story out of a vineyard. I can ask her to venture into the archives – she has done such searches before..." he added hopefully, and while his father and Lew Dubois looked doubtful, Sefton was already nodding.

"It's a start," Sefton agreed. "We're open to about any suggestions." he looked so very wistful. The quest for the incredible grapes had obviously set hooks into him, hooks of the sort which could only be extracted with much pain, or resolved through complete investigation.

Now Alfred cleared his throat. "Perhaps there might be records kept through the agricultural agency – of what kind of crops were planted on private acreage?"

Sefton was already shaking his head. "No, deal – these old-time guys were always about privacy when it came to the government. 'Specially during Prohibition. Cagy about what they had, what they planted. Look, ol' Hank and I got chased off a good few properties at gunpoint back in the day. 'Course, it was because we looked like your typical hippy-types. Which we were, back in the day. Can't really blame all those good old farmers an' rancher folk not taking a shine to us. Don't blame at all, given what was on the TV back then. I prolly looked like one of those Manson-family dudes ... even though my family ranched out by Noodle, Texas..." Sefton looked earnestly at them all. "Can't really blame those folks ... hey, I was nineteen and dumber 'n dirt, back then. Should have recognized that I was a lot more like them, than not... but superficial appearances, y' know. A lot of us just can't look past them. Not that there's a lot of clues out there..."

"Rest assured, *mon cher*," Lew replied. "We will follow up on all the clues that have been scattered before us. Now, it does occur to me; could we appeal to the local extension agent? Search property records through the county courthouse, of all properties along the river, for any mention of an established vineyard?"

Sefton nodded, already brightening. "Say, I never thought of the extension agent angle. What say that I give him a call, and then all three of us drive over to Karnesville look at old property deeds? Three of us can cover a lot of old files in a day or so."

"In light of no better plan," Alfred finished off the last of his cup of tea and set the cup in the saucer with a brief clink. "I concur. While I am not familiar with this part of the country – I am accustomed to the minutia of bureaucratic documents and winkling out relevant answers from the merest mention in them."

"I'll call Kate and ask her if she has the time to burrow through the Beacon archives," Richard promised, and hoped that Kate would be able, on top of all of her other duties to do with the newspaper and their social media sideline. It sounded like it would be a thankless chore, as the *Karnesville Beacon* had been published since 1875 or so. And in the early days, it had been a daily. He as much as apologized to Kate when he tendered the project to her.

"Well, actually, I wouldn't have to go through the whole archive," she said, over the cellphone connection. "Listen, if it to do with something like a prize vegetable or a pedigree animal – something outstandingly notable ... I'd look for it to have been a prize-winner at a county fair. So, I would only have go to the issues for the week or so in September that the Karnes County Fair and Rodeo was on."

"It still sounds like a lot of work," Richard temporized, and it made him inexplicably pleased when he heard Kate giggle.

"Oh, likely – but I'm getting to be the maven of the archives. Besides, it's kind of cool, going back and looking at the old issues. Gosh, it's like seeing history through a keyhole, just seeing what anyone would have seen and known, day to day. Besides," she added thoughtfully. "You know that Carolina San Pedro was my great-grandmother, right?"

"Miss Letty said something of the sort, once," Richard answered. "She was quite the woman, so everyone seems to think... did you ever meet her?"

"Oh, no," Kate replied. "She died years before I was born – but my mother remembers meeting her when she was a little girl herself. She was very old, Mom says, although that might have been because Mom was a kid and everyone looked old to her. Pure white hair and blazing blue-green eyes. Mom had the weird thought that Carolina was really the queen of someplace or other. Maybe England; Mom didn't know for sure. But Carolina and Great-Granddad were living in Saltillo, then – a big mansion, Mom says, almost a palace she thought, since it had been safe for both of them to go back to Mexico. Great-Grandma Carolina stood as straight as if she was always balancing a book on her head. That really struck Mom, I don't know why. And she had amazing, awesome skills at distilling, even during Prohibition!" Over the cellphone, Richard heard Kate give a rapturous sigh. "She was so awesome, she got hired, straight out of the box, by a big Canadian distillery! Can you imagine what that would have been like for a woman, back then?! I'm right along with Sefton Grant and Lew and your dad, trying to find that amazing vineyard that grew the grapes that Great-Grandma Carolina made into thousand-dollar bottles of brandy."

"I will fix you all the most fantastic supper in the Crystal Room with all the bells on, if you do find it," Richard promised. "Maybe even appeal to Mayor Bodie and Lew, and enter a plea for cracking a bottle of that fine hundred-year-old brandy from the stash, just so that we can all have a taste of that pure amazingness. And just for you and only you, a double-amazing private supper on another evening. Just for the two of us and Ozzie..."

"Promises, promises, lover!" Kate giggled, deliciously, and Richard felt himself go temporarily giddy with pure lust. *He wanted Kate, all for herself and for himself, embracing in the bed of the Airstream, in a clothing-optional condition. Although the vision of Ozzie, perched on the dresser and observing with one-eyed and clinical interest the strange conduct of his human familiars ... that cooled the romantic ardor like an arctic blast.*

"What you can find," Richard said, "And if you can find – text the results to Lew, Sefton and my dad, as soon as you find it. You have their numbers, I presume?"

"I do, indeed. Sure thing," Kate promised. Richard hung up the phone, for some reason now feeling inordinately pleased with himself.

The Vinal Word

Richard had his duties in the hotel kitchen; that kitchen which now ran smoothly, thanks to his earned reputation striking a degree of terror into the juniors, and Lew Dubois's masterful management technique. Truly, Richard only now began to appreciate Lew's advice, regarding training subordinates to one's own philosophy, and allowing them a certain degree of autonomy. Yes, it was unnecessary to spend twenty hours a day, seven days a week, haunting the kitchen. Best to take a page from Lew's book, and work intensely with one minion at a time: 'Show me how you do this, how did you learn this technique, why do you do it this way, did you know that ...what do you think might be done more efficiently?" By afternoon a degree of amity had been reached with that member of staff, and Richard feeling absurdly content with himself. The afternoon would be devoted to matters administrative and reviewing potential additions to the menu. There was also a message concerning a catering event – and he would have to consult with the potential client. The Cattleman operation could certainly do bigger and grander events, with less disruption to normal service than the Café ... and he would have to visit the Café sometime soon, just to ... no, Richard realized. His presence would tangle the new lines of authority being forged in the Café. Better to just go to Patrick and Araceli's for a Sunday BBQ, and catch up that way.

He bicycled home early in the evening, wondering how the quest for the elusive vineyard was going. As he pedaled up the rutted track that led by fits and starts to the Age of Aquarius, his cellphone buzzed. It was Kate. Richard propped the bicycle against the sagging fence that bounded one of the Grant's goat pastures, and answered.

"So, did you find something?" he asked, suddenly recalling the urgency with which Lew, Sefton and his father had departed on their quest that very morning. He didn't know which of the two search teams he envied the least – the trio searching records in the grand Beaux-Arts three-story and ornamental towers style Karnes County courthouse, or his beloved, leafing through the dusty leaves of newsprint in the dim and mold-ridden basement of the Karnesville Beacon. Probably poor Kate, since the courthouse probably had sufficient light, and a pleasingly modern lack of mold.

"I think I did!" Kate sounded thrilled and triumphant. "I went through a decade of coverage of the county fair, just to be certain, once that I found the first reference in 1912. A Mrs. Elfriede Holdenkamp, who won or placed for her grape jelly, cordials, and sparkling grape juice, on a regular basis every year that she entered them. Her husband, Fritz Holdenkamp also placed for his prize yearling calves, intermittently for cabbages and root vegetables ... and most notably for table grapes! Mrs. Holdenkamp also won several first- and second place wins for needlework, lace-making, and panoramic pictures made with seeds, for whatever that might be worth." Kate added.

Richard let out his breath. "A clue, my darling Kate – a very palpable clue! Have you let Sefton and Lew know of this? Was there any clue as to where the Holdenkamps lived? Was it anywhere near Helena, perchance?"

"A clue? Not so far, lover," Kate replied. "I did call Mr. Grant and let him know to investigate properties held under that name. But the Holdenkamp name absolutely drops from anything in the Beacon archives after 1919. I don't know – maybe they sold the home farm?"

"Or changed their name by deed poll, to something less identifiably German," Richard replied, as he racked his memory of what he had been taught or gathered from his residence in Texas. "Look; from things that I have gathered, German surnames were not especially popular in the wake of reported frightfulness committed by the Kaiser's troops, and a lot of German families in the United States found it as expedient to change their names … much as our own dear Royals did, after the start of the Great War."

"That would account for it," Kate replied, thoughtfully. Richard could imagine her – his glorious Kate, in her prim skirt suit, the thoughtful expression on her face, chewing on the pencil which was often thrust through the sloppy bun at the back of her head. His darling Kate, with the oversized trench coat flapping like the cape of a cartoon super-hero. She had so many useful tools of her trade, stuffed away in the pockets of that trench coat. It served as her portable office, as she dashed hither and yon, all across Karnes County, pursuing the elusive beast of news.

"It would," Richard replied, into the silence of thoughtfulness on the line. "Look – be careful, Kate. I love you."

"I love you, too," Kate replied, insouciant and blithe. "Gotta go! Are we still on for supper at your place, Monday evening?"

"Always," Richard replied. Monday was the day that the Beacon went to print; he and Kate were long in the habit of meeting at the Airstream for supper, once Kate had, so to speak, put the newspaper baby to bed. He gloried in being able to fix a classic, delicate something on the tiny cooker and toaster-oven sized stove; something just for the two of them, and Ozzie of course.

The following morning, Richard spotted the three searchers; Lew, Alfred and Sefton Grant in the Crystal Room, huddled over coffee and a large map, unrolled over half of the table. Breakfast had not yet been served, and Richard made a mental note to ask Mr. Georges – why not?

"Were you able to make any use of what Miss Heisel found in the newspaper archives?" Richard asked, and Lew beamed cheerfully.

"*Certainment*! That information was most rewarding; it seems that the family Holdenkamp, as Miss Heisel suggested, changed their name to Holden, in 1920 – and in the following year, a portion of the property was sold to an adjacent landowner, and the remainder inherited by what we presumed to be a son and heir. In 1934, alas – the property was sold at public auction, when the new owner went bankrupt in the Depression."

"That happened quite a lot," Sefton nodded. "My grandparents barely scraped by, for near onto fifteen years; what they called 'the hungry Thirties'. They held onto their place all right, but my grandmother used to say that during all those years, they didn't eat a bite of food which they didn't grow themselves or that Grandpa and the boys didn't hunt, until well after the war began and markets began looking up for cattle."

"We are attempting to deduce the location of those properties which were once part of the Holdenkamp property,"

Alfred explained. "In the hope that some portion of the vineyard, or even propagated cuttings might have been retained. It must have been common knowledge among locals for at least a decade or longer that the Holdenkamp grapes were something special. It is our hope that others were cognizant of such superiority, and that even though the vineyard which Sefton's friend had heard of had been destroyed decades ago; that cuttings might have been taken from it. I know vintners, and those who compete for prizes in such matters," Alfred swept the table with a piercing gaze. "It is only a matter of searching among those who now own that land, or their nearer neighbors. We have worked out the likeliest of those places, and Mr. Dubois has been kind enough to engage a vehicle and a knowledgeable driver for today's expedition. Would you care to join us? I believe there will be sufficient room in the mini van."

"I..." Richard caught a significant glance from Lew Dubois. "I would be pleased to join you on this expedition. Truly I would. I have ... well, there is nothing to do in the kitchen today which cannot be put off to tomorrow..."

"Very good, *mon cher* Richard," Lew Dubois breathed, a comment hardly to be heard over the arrival of a waiter bringing a tray with everyone's tastefully composed breakfast selections, and additional plate for Richard himself. "You are already appreciating the management techniques of the lazy manager!"

Oh, good; the light breakfast of fruit and a small cinnamon roll which had been established as his favored mid-morning nosh. Richard made another mental note to compliment Mr. Georges. Really, he would now have to exert himself and learn the names of every one of the front house staff. Maybe even take a leaf from Lew's book and do a stint as a waiter, even as a dishwasher. After all, it worked for Lew, whose knowledge of his VPI enterprise was encyclopedic, while the personal devotion of his staff was legendary and even unto the death. A thought to bear serious consideration.

Richard put that thought aside for later. He ate his breakfast, while listening to his father, Lew, and Sefton, plotting the most convenient course. It seemed they would spend the day wandering along all those narrow back roads, to small ranches and holdings, centered around the San Antonio River. The river itself wended a torturous way across the landscape, doubling back on itself repeatedly like a particularly drunken snake. When the last cup of coffee was drained, Lew ducked into his office to let Bianca know where he was off to, and to collect an insulated carrier bag.

"I will be available by cellphone, should any emergency arise," he assured Bianca. "And Chef Richard will be with me as well. We should return by mid-afternoon, in any case."

"Nothing to worry about, Lew," Bianca assured him. "Good luck in finding those marvelous grapes! Are you really certain they are still out there, somewhere? The grapes that Carolina San Pedro used for that wildly rare brandy?"

"I am," Lew assured her. "From what Miss Heisel was able to discover, and Mr. Astor-Hall have deduced, there is a high probability that the vines may have been preserved."

"Good luck, then," Bianca replied. "And don't worry about a thing."

Richard followed Lew out through the Cattleman's ornate lobby, noting that the man spoke to the woman working at the reception desk, exchanged a few remarks with a porter steering a wheeled rack of luggage to the discretely hidden elevator, and greeted a guest enjoying a quiet cigarette just outside the main doors – all as if he was an excellent good friend of everyone, and as if he had all the time in the world. It was a masterful display.

Sefton and Alfred were already waiting when Lew and Richard emerged from the Cattleman, blinking in the bright and merciless sunshine. It was already warm, although a few puffy clouds floated in the faultlessly blue sky overhead, falsely promising rain. Within a few minutes, a white Ford SUV swooped around the corner, and pulled to a stop before the Cattleman's main doors. The driver climbed down from behind the wheel, saying bashfully,

"H'lo, Lew – sorry I'm a bit late. Traffic was murder, getting out of the city."

Berto, and one of his uncle's hire-cars; Richard might well have known. Berto the guileless and gormless, who was Araceli's little brother, interning with Clovis Walcott's engineering firm, now that his structural engineering studies were completed, but apparently, he still was driving for Uncle Tony's luxury taxi business.

"Not to worry, Berto," Lew assured him. "We have all day. Did M'sieu Tony brief you on what we are looking for?"

"Sure thing, Lew," Berto assured him. "I stopped in at the Tip-Top for water and drinks."

"And I had the kitchen pack us sandwiches and snacks," Lew handed Berto the carrier bag. "So we shall not suffer the pangs of hunger, as we search."

"You sure do think of everything, Lew," Berto accepted the bag, as he opened the front and rear doors, for Alfred, Richard and Sefton to climb in.

"Nice ride!" Sefton remarked, in honest appreciation, while Alfred passed a neatly printed list to Berto. "Mr. Astor-Hall here, he made a list of all the addresses we want to check out. Some of them we got to talk to on the phone, we know they'll be around. Most didn't really know if they could help us or not … but they said we were welcome to come around and look over whatever grapes they had growing on their place. Likely most of 'em are just your plain ol' mustang grapes… but…"

"We would not know for certain until we check them out with an expert eye," Lew said, as he settled into the passenger seat. "Which means Mr. Grant and Mr. Alfred Astor-Hall."

"Not Ricardo?" Berto cast a worried eye on his passengers, and Richard sighed, admitting,

"I'm just along for the ride, Berto."

"And the pleasure of his company," Alfred added, and to Richard's mild surprise, his father didn't sound the least bit sarcastic.

"Ready for takeoff!" Berto put the SUV into gear, and they were off, threading through Luna City's narrow streets, and then down even narrower country lanes, directed by the mechanical, faintly bitchy-sounding directions emitted by the GPS unit.

It was an interesting morning, all things considered. Richard, as a back seat passenger, realized that he was seeing so much more of Karnes County than he had in the previous five years. His orbit had been so very limited by his inability and disinclination to drive an automobile. He had bicycled every day to and from the Airstream into Luna City, punctuated with occasional forays to Karnesville, to the Wyler or Gonzalez ranches, several times to the Walcott house, and once all the way to Marble Falls. There was so much more here than he had ever thought; pastures interspersed with stands of oak trees, thickets of hackberry and cedar. Gates to properties, ornate or plain, opened at irregular intervals, sometimes adored with a row of mailboxes mounted all in a row on a length of pipe. Most houses were set back a good way from the road, sometimes entirely out of sight. They were modest places, in the main; not half as appealing as country farmhouses in rural England would have been. A good few were merely double-wide trailers with sagging roofs, sometimes with a shed or a deck tacked onto one side. Not many boasted much in the way of ornamental flower gardens, although most had fenced vegetable gardens and patches of standing corn.

On the whole, their party of searchers were cordially, if casually received by the residents or workers. Berto and Sefton seemed to be well-known, which Richard found mildly surprising. Even more surprising was that Alfred hit it off with almost everyone; many were the deep discussions on gardening, to the point where his father had almost to be dragged away.

They worked their way down the list of properties which had been either part of the Holdenkamp ranch, or which had belonged to Holdenkamp neighbors, a century previously, but all they had to show for it was a bag of early garden produce and a jar of home-made mustang grape jam, pressed on Alfred by the wife of a rancher who had sympathized deeply with the quest, and dragged them all to a stand of grapevines tangled in a stand of trees … which were not the grapes that they sought.

Noontime brought them to a lay-by on Route 123, a couple of concrete tables and benches underneath a particularly large and shady oak tree. They pulled over, got out the cooler bag with the sandwiches and drinks and settled there to dine, mildly depressed as to the lack of positive results.

"Take heart, my friends," Lew was up-beat. "If Miss Heisel was correct – and I am certain that she was – and Alfred also, regarding envy, grapes and prize-winning articles; such of their neighbors would have preserved such a marvelous planting."

"We've only gone halfway down the list," Berto also was optimistic. "Something like this is always in the last place you look."

"That's because … oh, never mind," Richard sighed. Berto was as immune to sarcasm as he was to grasp the banality of what he had just said.

"Because you stop looking for something, as soon as you have found it." Alfred explained carefully. Berto's expression brightened.

"Oh, so that's how it works."

Richard took another bite of his sandwich and decided not to comment. Presently, they resumed the search, although Richard did note that even Lew's optimism was beginning to flag. Three more places visited, without any sight of what they sought, and Richard was on the verge of suggesting that they give it up and return to the hotel, when Berto steered the big SUV through an open gate and rumbled across a cattle guard.

"This place seems to be in better nick than the others," Richard commented, as they came round a low hill, and saw the home place; a small white house of early twentieth-century vintage with a deep verandah on two sides, held up by stout stone-faced columns topped with wooden pyramids. The front of the house was adorned with a small patch of sparse lawn and half a dozen rosebushes. Berto honked the horn, as soon as they came in sight of that pleasing prospect, rolled slowly up to the patch of gravel which served as a driveway and parking place, driving carefully as there were a couple of hens and guineafowl using one of the bare patches as a dust-bath. Presently a woman came from around the back of the house, a middle-aged woman in battered jeans and a t-shirt with pictures of chickens on the front. She had a friendly look to her. Berto parked the SUV, carefully avoiding the birds, and everyone got out, prepared for yet more polite conversation and ultimate disappointment.

"Hi, Miz Murtagh," Berto said, shyly. "I brought these gentlemen. They called yesterday about this grapevine they're looking for."

"I got your message," she replied, "Hi, Sefton – these your friends? Pleased to meetcha; Greta Murtagh, y'all. It was so late at night when I got in and listened to your message on the house phone, I didn't want to bother ya. But yeah, my Grandma Maria got a cutting of one of the Holdenkamp's vines, back in the day."

Richard could hardly believe his ears. Success within their grasp, after so many disappointments!

Meanwhile, Mrs. Murtagh continued, "They were friends. Grandma Maria got second place for her jellies, every time that Miz Holdenkamp got first at the county fair, Ya wanna see it? Round in back. She started it by the back door, and we got it trained over an arbor. Marv cusses that ol' vine out, every time he has to build another extension to the arbor, but I tell him it's worth it all, just for those grapes."

"Show us," Alfred's voice was mild, scholarly, even, but Richard sensed that his father was quivering with suppressed anticipation, like Lord Carnarvon upon being told of an unviolated royal tomb in the Valley of the Kings.

They followed Greta Murtagh around the side of the little white cottage; it was a charming building, very well maintained. Richard couldn't see how it had escaped the clutches of Venue Properties, International, for moving onto Mills Farm, subsequent renovation and fitting out as a high-end resort suite.

But the best part was at the back – the fitting conclusion to their quest. A magnificent and sprawling lathhouse, entirely grown over with a thriving grape vine, the parent root of which was as thick as Arnold Schwarzenegger's thigh. The vine was hung with small, and elegant bunches of luscious purple fruit, every orb as large as a small marble. The arbor supporting it all went the length of the small yard and around two corners, veiled along most of the way in bird-netting.

"Behold, the Holdenkamp vine," Lew Dubois breathed, reverently, even as Alfred asked for a taste of the grapes, which were ripe to the point of bursting out of their dewy purple skins.

"Sure thing," Greta Murtagh replied, fishing out a small pair of garden clippers from her trouser pocket, reaching up to shear the nearest small bunch from it's mooring. "Here, have a taste, OK? We're about to start cutting down the bunches. I'm gonna start making grape jelly, and Marv wants to try his luck at making wine ..."

"God save the mark," Albert addressed the sky, and popped a single grape into his mouth. Sefton did the same, and the two of them looked at Greta Murtagh.

"Ma'am, can I trouble you for what you don't want of these grapes?" Sefton asked, just as Alfred said, "Would it trouble you any further, if I could have some cuttings from this vine? We are establishing a new vineyard, in addition to the one I presently own, and it would add an incomparable gift, having these grapes to grow."

"Of course!" Greta Murtagh beamed impartially upon the questors for her magnificent vine. "It's a prime bearer, don't you think? Just name the vintage after Marv and me – all I ask. We're neighbors, after all. Us and Grandma Maria, Miz Elfrieda, you an' Sefton's place ... we all grow stuff together, don't we?"

"Certainly, we do," Lew Dubois replied, seriously. "We plant lovely vines ... and hope that we live long enough to see them give a splendid vintage."

All the way back to Luna City, the conversation concerned pounding out the details involved in setting up the new vineyard on the Grant's property, with starting costs and upkeep to be paid through by Lew Dubois, and by Alfred Astor-Hall in a joint venture with Sefton Grant, who would contribute his own expertise as well as the use of half an acre of his and Judy's land.

Luna City

Fall Newsletter

Luna City Chamber of Commerce

5 North Town Square, Suite 4

Check out our Facebook Page

Celebrate the holiday season in the heart of Luna City, beginning with the weekend after Thanksgiving, when the lights in the trees of Town Square and the decorated Christmas tree across from the Cattleman hotel are officially lit. This year, the streets will be blocked off for the weekend craft market during the day. After sundown on Friday, there will be a nighttime parade led by Santa himself, riding on the vintage fire engine, and a fireworks display. Luna City hospitality continues all through the month of December, with special events, live theater performances, and music concerts scheduled every weekend on Town Square. A complete listing of special events will be posted on the Chamber of Commerce's Facebook page.

Founder's Day Celebrations – 22-28 September

Founder's Day celebrations kick off this year with a presentation dinner and dance in the Cattleman Hotel's splendidly restored ballroom, beginning at 6 PM, on Sunday, September 22nd. The original architect's scale model of Luna City, as proposed by Arthur W. McAllister, architect and city planner, will be on temporary display in the hotel lobby. Tickets for the dinner and dance will be available at the Cattleman Hotel's front desk or at the Chamber of Commerce offices, beginning September 1.

Upcoming Events

November 5

Election Day, in Luna City and across Texas. Consult our FaceBook Page for a list of polling places

November 29

Formal lighting of the community Christmas tree and Town Square, at sundown.

December 21

Luna City's annual Christmas Parade and Santa's arrival, beginning at 5 PM. The Luna City HS Marching Band will be performing seasonal music at the bandstand all afternoon, beginning at 3 PM

Evenings at the Opera!

The Luna City Players begin their season of performances at the Koenig Opera House, with Friday evening and Saturday matinee performances. See the LCP website for more information.

Luna City, Texas – Home of the Mighty Fighting Moths

Luna City ISD News

Holiday Food Drive

The Luna City Independent School District is collecting donations for the holiday food drive. Non-perishable foods such as pasta, mixes and canned goods are being collected at a donation box in the lobby of the High School, and in the entryway of the Elementary school. Perishable foods such as frozen or fresh fruit and vegetables will be accepted during limited periods immediately prior to the Thanksgiving and Christmas holidays. See the LCISD website for dates and locations where such donations may be accepted.

Halloween Parade

Students of the Luna City elementary school will parade in their Halloween costumes on Thursday, 31 October at noon. Students will go around Town Square, showing off their creativity. First, Second and Third Prizes will be awarded for both individual and group costumes.

Homecoming Queen Election

Nominations are open for the office of Homecoming queen and six duchesses of her court. Nominees must be a junior or senior, with a B or better grade average. The Homecoming Queen and her court will preside over the Luna City High School Homecoming game, which will be played on Moths Field on September 28th at 3 PM against the Falls City Beavers. The queen and her court will be announced at a Pep Rally on Friday, September 27th at 3:00 in the gymnasium.

Community Marketplace

Holiday Orders!

Make your holiday special, by ordering that whole smoked turkey, beef tenderloin, crown roast, or whole smoked ham from Pryor's Meats & BBQ. Order a week prior to Thanksgiving or Christmas and receive your choice of a free one-pound package of our home-made jalapeno pork breakfast sausage, or half a pound of our spiced smoked beef jerky.

From Chief Vaughn, Luna City PD

The hunting season for Texas statewide begins on September 28: local hunters are reminded that the bag limit for deer is four, (no more than two bucks) while the bag limit for pronghorn is two. The bag limit for quail is 15 with the same for doves. The bag limit for turkey is two. Hunters are reminded that grazing horses and cattle are not game animals and that shooting them not looked well upon by their owners, or the officers of the Luna City PD.

Luna Café Holiday Dinner to Go

Can't cook? Your oven suddenly doesn't work and can't be replaced until after the holidays? Have no fear for the holiday feast! Luna Café and Coffee to the rescue! Order an entire Thanksgiving supper, with a whole or half roasted turkey, with stuffing, mashed potatoes and gravy, baked yams and roasted sprouts with a choice of pumpkin or pecan pie by November 25th, and it will be delivered to you on Thanksgiving Day! The Café will offer complete cooked suppers for take-out, beginning in December.

Roland, The Silver-Tongued

From the unpublished memoir by Alistair Magill, one-time Luna City chief of police – Chapter 55: Roland d'Avila Shaw, The Gentleman About Town

This most amusing contretemps occurred, if I remember correctly, some months following the attempted lynching of Charley Mills, in the fall of 1927. The first that I became aware of it, was when I drove my trusty Ford sedan from my house to a building on Town Square which was temporarily housing our police department. We had moved our activities to the original town fire station, as that facility was no longer adequate to house our fire engines. The original man-pulled steam-powered water pumps had been replaced by a pair of engine-powered pumper and ladder trucks. The old firehouse, still owned by the city, had been put at our disposal, pending construction of a new and more secure, modern police station. The previous building having been utterly wrecked and rendered useless by a mob intending to lynch Charley Mills, the City Council was prevailed upon *(largely from civic embarrassment over this signal failure)* to fund a new building. In the meantime, we were making do, as it were, with the old fire station. Which was small, but adequate, and conveniently located right on Town Square.

As I passed by the bridge over the river and turned toward the road which led to the heart of Luna City, I noticed that there was a wrecked vehicle – a sporty green roadster, turned on it's side, and with the bonnet crumpled against the bridge abutment. There were fragments of glass, and scraps of metal far scattered, as well as puddles of radiator fluid and oil seeping from the wreck. The contents of the roadster – including sets of female unmentionables and an empty tomato tin with a length of twine threaded through each side – were scattered around on the macadam paving, paving blackened by fire or perhaps by rubber.

One of our duty constables, Officer Vaughn, raised his hand as I pulled over on the verge. It looked like Officer Vaughn had the aftermath of the accident well in hand. Several men in rough clothing, including Mr. Shaw, the proprietor of the Tip-Top Icehouse, Gas and Grocery, were heaving away at the side of the roadster, tipping it upright and back on it's wheels. In the distance, a plume of dust rose from the wheels of another automobile, making all speed to Karnesville, by the look of it.

"Officer Vaughn, what happened here?" I inquired, as the former saluted briskly and prepared to give an account of events.

"A single-car accident," he replied. "Shaw was out pumping gas for an early customer and saw it all. He says it seems like the accelerator got stuck, and the driver tried to pull off on rough ground to try and slow down but missed it clean and smacked into the bridge abutment instead. Tipped the car over."

"What happened to the driver?" I had noted that there was no body with a pool of blood around it, hastily covered by whatever had been handy.

"Knocked silly when he was thrown clear," Officer Vaughn replied. "Mayor McAllister came right away, seeing that he lives opposite – and he's taking the poor chap to the hospital in Karnesville. Faster than calling for an ambulance that can't go any faster than the Mayor's Lincoln."

"Indeed," I replied. "Anyone we know?"

"A drummer on his regular rounds of smaller towns," Officer Vaughn replied. "Roland d'Avila Nelson, by name. He travels in ladies' underwear,"

"How very singular," I commented, and Officer Vaughn laughed.

"I mean, he travels and sells for a line of ladies' things. Menswear, too – things like handkerchiefs, ties and socks. I don't think that he has any customers here in Luna City, save Mr. Milhouse at the dry goods store."

"Was Mr. Nelson hurt very badly?" I asked. "To the point where his survival is a matter of luck combined with timely medical intervention?"

"I dunno," Officer Vaughn shrugged. "I guess we'll find out soon enough." I was about to drive away, when I had a second thought.

"You might want to gather up those garments," I suggested, referring to the intimate silken garments scattered across the pavement, where they had been strewn when Mr. Nelson's sample cases were shattered in the crash. "Those camisoles and brassieres and things. Mustn't give any of the young lads about any unwholesome notions."

"Yes, Chief," Officer Vaughn saluted smartly, and I drove on.

When I arrived at the temporary police station, there was already an agitated woman, sitting in the reception area – which had once been dedicated to Steam Engine #1; a well-dressed lady of certain years and respectable appearance, her gloved hands folded on the reticule in her lap. A handsome woman, I noted, as I inquired of her purpose is coming to the police station. She clasped her hands together, in an agony of concern and replied, in great agitation.

"My husband has been injured in an accident! Perhaps fatally! Driving his car – this very morning, by the bridge over the river..."

"I know only of one accident by the river," I replied, considerably taken back. "A Mr. Nelson. Roland d'Avila Nelson."

"My husband!" The lady brought her hands to her breast and burst into tears. "Lives he still? My beloved, my darling Roland! The father of my children ..."

"Er..." I replied. "I believe that Mayor McAllister was conveying him to the hospital in Karnesville. We have no intelligence regarding his state of health at this moment... may I..."

And at that very moment, another lady rushed into the reception area – like the first, of respectable appearance, similar years and of equally pleasing appearance.

"What has happened to Roland?!" she exclaimed to the first lady. "An accident – they tell me – but it was no accident, I am certain! They intended to kill my husband! Sabotage of his automobile! I am certain of this!"

At that, the first woman burst into tears, and to my utter astonishment, fell into each other's embrace. I had no words to adequately express my astonishment. This Mr. Nelson, the traveling drummer, the agent for an enterprise purveying ladies' undergarments to retail establishments throughout South Texas … had two wives, who were moreover, not only acquainted with each other, but seemed to be on terms of most sisterly affection? This had not previously been my experience of situations where bigamy was discovered by the ladies most intimately and inadvertently connected. In fact, the hair-pulling, screamed accusations and general brawling usually commenced at that point.

"Ladies … be assured that we will do our best to uncover any such deliberate damage…" I insisted, but the two ladies continued their lamentations, until Miss Avery, our newly-hired professional clerk-typist and the only female member of the Police Department, emerged from behind her desk with a little flask of smelling salts and a handful of disposable tissues.

"Leave it to me, Chief," she murmured. A level-headed young lady, and familiar both with female megrims and crime alike, I yielded the floor to her, and retreated to my office on the second floor. Which was formerly the domain of the chief of the fire department, a small cubicle at the back of the building, with a small window overlooking the small yard where the good volunteer lads of the fire department had been accustomed to unroll and drain their water hoses, before returning them to service on the steam engines. The upper floor of the old firehouse, which had formerly been given over to a dormitory and common room for the duty volunteers, was generous enough to accommodate our various offices in comfort, if not exactly in privacy. My chief investigator, John Drury, late of the Texas Rangers, had a small cubicle marked off by tall filing cabinets, next to that of the newly appointed Sgt. Grigoriev, he who had been so stalwart in defending the former police station against a mob of justifiably outraged but mistaken citizens some months previously.

At a rap on the doorframe of my office, I looked up to see John Drury regarding me with an expression which mixed mild malice with considerable sympathy. At my bidding him entry, he settled himself in the one of the comfortable chairs designated for guests and grinned.

"I see you have met several of the Mrs. Nelsons," he remarked, and waited for my reply with anticipation.

"Good lord, so there are more than those two ladies downstairs?" I exclaimed, and John Drury's grin broadened to an outright chuckle.

"Ah, Captain – you haven't encountered Mr. Roland Nelson; the pied-piper of lonely ladies in this part of the world. As it stands now, he has at least a dozen on his marital dance card. He's a phenomenon – the man with a silver tongue, a silver pen, and a silver ...."

I will not sully this manuscript with the last descriptive of Mr. Nelson's physical qualities.

"Surely, you jest, Mr. Drury!" I exclaimed, and John Drury chuckled again.

"M' name's John, not Shirley. Ah, he's a one of a kind, regardless and fortunately. Women adore him; he's a charming b____rd, and to do him credit, he's never done any of them the least unkindness, and he supports every single one of the children he's got from them. At least thirty, on last count," John Drury added, parenthetically. "Although there may be more. He was seen regularly at the Rialto Theater in Beeville this last spring, sparking with a certain young lady, and the rumors have it that she is expecting twins by mid-summer."

"Good lord!" I exclaimed. "However does he find the energy – thirty children!"

"At the very least," John Drury replied suavely. "Nevertheless, Mr. Nelson is a curious character, and I shouldn't be surprised that an angry father, a resentful brother, or even a jealous former boyfriend might have taken it in hand to sabotage the accelerator or the brakes of Mr. Nelson's flivver."

"I suppose that we will have to investigate," I sighed deeply. Crime in Luna City very rarely rose to the level of murderous mayhem on offer in the large cities. It was usually confined to thievery from chicken coops and cattle pastures, drunken antics among the local farmhands following payday, and reckless driving on the rural route which bypassed Luna City itself. Impetuous youth, drunks and the fraternity of itinerant travelers looking for work or any unconsidered trifle formed the bulk of our criminal class, with the occasional startling exception. "What manner of man is this Mr. Nelson – and who are those most especially considered to hold a grudge against him for his romantic exploits among the fair sex? Of what nationality and background? What do you know of him for certain, John?"

John Drury cleared his throat. "Well, he's a curious one, Captain, and no mistake. A fine-looking man, with good manners, about forty-odd, I reckon, and a way with words in two languages that I know of. He ain't a Mexican, that's for certain, although he speaks Spanish – the Spanish of the aristocratic class, which does allow him to cut a swath. He speaks English like a Yankee, mebbe from up in Canada way. He's been in these parts for near on twenty years – mostly traveling between San Antonio and the Border, in a high-class kind of trade. Legitimate trade, I would say," John Drury added hastily. "And nothing to do with alcohol or armaments." For Prohibition lamentably was still the law of this land, and revolution was the constant diversion of Mexico.

"So an international man of mystery." I considered the picture thus sketched by John Drury and suggested hopefully. "I don't suppose that he has a record of being brought up on charges?"

John Drury shook his head, most regretfully. "No, Captain – he does not appear as a wanted rogue in any of our books, although he might just possibly have a criminal record in some other state. But honestly, I do not see how he would have the time or the energy between drumming in a commercial capacity and sparking susceptible and not-quite-so young ladies."

"As I see it," I said, with equal regret. "We must have the vehicle examined for signs of deliberate sabotage. I imagine that Mr. Gonzalez at the garage will be happy to assist... you have some objection?"

For John Drury had cleared his throat in a particularly meaningful manner. "Well, Captain – one of his many nieces – and I am not certain of the precise degree of relationship – is one of the dozen or so women favored with Mr. Nelson's romantic attention. Has been for at least fifteen years; she has three children by him. She is one of the ladies downstairs with Miss Avery at this very moment."

"Well, that is a quandary," I exclaimed, and considered for a moment. "Although, Mr. Gonzalez cannot be all that resentful, if the situation has lasted this long. Perhaps, just to keep the investigation from being utterly compromised, we should arrange with a mechanic from Karnesville to make the examination of Mr. Nelson's vehicle. Make a suitable arrangement, if you will, John. See to having his car towed to a mechanic there. I think we should drive to Karnesville to interview Mr. Nelson, always assuming that he has recovered full consciousness."

"A satisfactory plan today beats all hollow out of a perfect plan the next day," John Drury made a note in his ever-present memo book, and we departed the office area in good spirits – using the staircase for our descent, instead of the temptation posed for the younger constables by the sliding pole which had been installed as an original component for the use of the fire fighters to descend in a hurry, in the days when the steam engines were pulled by horses stabled on the ground floor.

"Remind me," I said, as we rattled down the stairs. "We ought to have that pole removed and the hole in the floor stopped up. One of our men might hurt themselves, demonstrating to Miss Avery or some other young lady their daring and expertise in using it."

"Noted, Captain," John Drury replied, just as we came around the bend in the stairs to the ground floor. Oh, what a dramatic scene was being played out there – at least half a dozen young or not-so-young women, attended by a veritable Greek chorus of small distraught children had mobbed poor Miss Avery in the interim that we had been upstairs. A handsome teenaged lad of about fourteen years of age stood to one side, his cap pulled down over his eyes. What I could see of his countenance bore an expression of acute embarrassment.

"Micky!" John Drury exclaimed upon seeing the lad. "What are you doing here, lad? Is it your father, then?"

"It is," the boy replied, in tones of abject misery. "Mom thinks that someone has tried to kill him."

"And why do you think that?" John Drury inquired gently. The man was a genius when it came to interrogation, I always thought. No verbose language, no threats to the person being the focus of his inquiry, only a gentle and inexorable request for enlightenment on that small, puzzling matter of vague interest to law enforcement. If John Drury could have bottled and sold that manner, there would have been no market for so-called truth serum in all the police stations in the world, for John brought results, every single time.

Now the boy Micky, shrugged his narrow shoulders, and replied, "No reason – really. Except that the car crashed, for no reason. Dad was at our house last night, as usual. It was fun – and I love it when Dad comes to Luna City. He was teaching me an' Jared how to drive his car. Jared's my little brother," Micky added. "He's only twelve."

"Well, Micky – we're going to go see him at the hospital in Karnesville..." John Drury said, which the boy seemed to find oddly comforting.

"K'n I come with you?" Micky pleaded. "I want to see that Dad is OK,"

"Sorry, lad," John Drury replied, with infinite sympathy. "But we're on official business, this trip. This ain't something that a young 'un should have any business doing."

"Were you a young'un, too young to have any bidness, when you went with Capn' McNelly's Ranger company, into the Nueces country to go after cattle bandits?" the boy replied, not any put down, and John Drury looked as if he had been hit with one of my roundhouse blows, when I was briefly famed as the Fife Bomber in my early pugilistic career, although he covered up the fact that it had been a fair hit almost at once.

"That was then, lad and this is now. I was at least two years older n' you are now. An' I had my Daddy's good word to Cap'n McNelly that I could ride an' shoot every bit as well as he did hisself. He was crippled up with the rheumatism and his old war wound, else he would have gone himself ... what have you got in the way of testament, boy?"

"That you'll deal with me fair," Micky replied, looking straight at John Drury, level and firm. "An' I want to know about Dad."

John Drury chewed his lower lip for a long moment, before he looked down at the lad, and replied,

"Sure, Micky. You can come along with us. But mind; this is an investigation into the possibility of a murder attempt, so that you must keep your eyes open, and your mouth tight shut. You will follow my instructions, boy, as I obeyed the instructions of Cap'n McNelly! For he was the captain and knew what he was about, when I was a boy only a little older than you are now. I was sure then, that I knew everything. I was just as sure as you think now that you know everything, but I didn't. God is my witness that I didn't! And you do not, so no matter what you think of our methods, boy, keep your tongue between your teeth, watch and learn. Now get in the car – the back seat, mind, and say nothing to distract Cap'n Magill from our thoughts."

"Unless it is really serious and to the point, mind." I added, seeing that the lad appeared mildly crushed. It was in my mind that an observer with an alert eye and an open mind might yet come to some original observance on the matter under consideration.

We conversed very little on the way to Karnesville and the county hospital there. John Drury and I had our own thoughts, as my trusty Ford rolled along that country road, raising a rooster-tail of pale dust behind us, and I dare say the boy Micky had his own thoughts. On the outskirts of Luna City, we saw that Mr. Nelson's wrecked roadster had been towed away – as John Drury had made the arrangement for it to be towed to a garage in Karnesville for later inspection by an uninvolved party. Although, as John Drury remarked, there was no guarantee that the garageman in Karnesville had no female relations who were part of Mr. Nelson's coterie of wives. We arrived at last in Karnesville, which boasted the county seat and railway station; the hub of industry and commerce which position would have fallen to Luna City, if Albert Wylers' Aunt Bessie had not fallen tempestuously in love with a handsome engineer on the San Antonio-Aransas Pass Railway and thereby earned her formidable fathers' undying enmity against all matters to do with railroading.

The county hospital was a grand old limestone building in the center of Karnesville, some three stories tall, in the shape of a U, with a paved courtyard in the middle. A small pool with a trickling fountain in it ornamented the center of the courtyard. One walked past the little, lily-grown pond, into the stone-floored main entrance and foyer. Corridors went off to the left and right, and a long staircase curled down from the upper floors. To our astonishment, the foyer was crowded with women, and bouquets of flowers, gift-baskets of grapes and edible dainties. Many of the women were weeping, expostulating with the hospital receptionist and telephone operator. Behind the young woman at the desk, the switchboard buzzed frantically for attention, much as the women thronging the foyer begged and plead for attention.

The receptionist/switchboard operator – a very young woman, I must admit – appeared as if she were about to weep herself. I elbowed my way ruthlessly through the throng and presented my credentials to her.

"We are here to investigate a possible murder attempt," I said. "On the life of one Roland Nelson – we understand that he is a patient here, after an automobile accident..."

The crowd of women in the foyer set up such a chorus of wailing and lamentations, as to have raised the roof.

The poor girl at the reception desk appeared as if she were about to join them in their grief and lamentations.

"On the top floor," she said, and gulped back a sob. "The second bed on the male ward – to the left at the top of the stairs."

We climbed the stairs and found the male ward. The second bed was surrounded by a veritable garden of flowers, even more than were downstairs around the reception desk. The man who lay on that bed, propped up on a stack of pillows, had a pristine white bandage around his head, and a white-coated doctor listening to his heart with a stethoscope, before peering into his eyes with the aid of a small battery torch.

Observing the three of us advancing from the doorway, the doctor glared at us.

"This man needs rest! Why are you bothering him when he is recovering from his injuries!"

Obviously, the doctor was a stranger to us both.

"We're here to investigate a threat to the life of this man," I said, firmly. "Alistair Magill, chief of the Luna City police, and we are present here since the accident which incapacitated this man happened within my jurisdiction. Sgt. John Drury and I wish to ask Mr. Nelson a few questions about the accident. One of Mr. Nelson's sons was desirous of accompanying us, also – so we brought him with us to assure Mr. Nelson of our good intentions."

"It's against medical advice," the doctor looked indignant. "This man has experienced a concussion ..."

"It's all right, Doctor," Roland D'Avila Nelson spoke from the bed, It was hard for me to make any judgment regarding his good looks or legendary charm; he seemed to me to be an ordinary-looking but well-set up chap of between thirty and forty years of age, with dark hair – that which could be seen between the bandages, wrapping his head. He winced against the brief light which the doctor shone into his other eye. From behind us, the lad Micky spoke tremulously.

"Hi, Pop," he ventured, and what we could see of Mr. Nelson's countenance lightened.

"Michael, my boy!" he exclaimed. "How did you come to be here!"

"I wanted to see that you were OK, Pop," the boy replied. "Mama is frantic, and so is Jared…"

"We think that someone has attempted to murder you, by sabotaging your automobile, in some manner," John Drury explained. He sought out and settled himself into the single straight chair at the bedside of the sufferer. I stood back, as the doctor finished his brief examination, but the man hovered at the foot of the bed, just as I and the lad did. "Mr. Nelson, is there anyone … anyone that you can think of who cause might have to bear a murderous resentment against you for anything you may have done? A business or political disagreement, perhaps a quarrel over a game of chance? Anyone who might chose to take revenge by sabotaging your automobile?"

"As for those with a murderous grudge," Roland D'Avila Nelson replied with a deep sigh. "I have loved many a fair lady in this country, loved them truly and well…"

"And so very well that he left not a good dozen or two, giving birth in the maternity ward…" commented the hovering doctor, and Nelson added, somewhat resentfully,

"They wished for what they weren't getting otherwise. I saw a need, and why shouldn't I fulfill it, gentlemen?"

"So ... enthusiastically?" John Drury shook his head in a skeptical manner, and Roland Nelson replied, "I've yet to hear any of the ladies complain of my treatment of them; nor any of my children, either. What say you, Michael? Am I not a fair and provident parent to all my boys and girls?"

"The best, Pop!" Micky replied fervently.

"So ... should it be a matter of attempted murder, who d'you think would be at the top of your list of suspects?" John Drury pressed the matter home, and for almost the first time, Roland Nelson seemed taken back a pace or two.

"I can think of no one ... well, other than my first wife's older brother. But he is presently confined in Huntsville, having been convicted for the crime of shooting at his neighbor's prize milk cow..."

"So, he's off the hook, then," John Drury pressed his advantage, and Roland Nelson sighed and for the first time, looked as pale and ill as if he actually deserved to be in a hospital bed. "Were there any other male relatives of your ... assorted ladies, who bore you a grudge; a grudge sufficient to risk a hanging sentence by making an attempt on your life?"

"None that I can recall," Roland Nelson replied, with a wince, as if his head throbbed.

"Can you recollect what exactly happened, in the moments before your automobile went off the road?" John Drury had his little spiral notebook out, his pencil at the ready.

"The brake was jammed, somehow," Roland Nelson frowned, as if pulling up small memories from a deep well, with considerable effort. "It was as if ... the brake pedal had been welded into place. That was most disconcerting, suddenly not being able to stop the car. I could think of nothing better than to steer onto the softer ground and hope that the muddy ground would slow my speed…"

"Until the bridge abutment got in your way. We will have your automobile examined by a mechanic," I assured him. "If it was deliberately tampered with, that should become evident."

"It is a pity about the car," Roland Nelson admitted, with another sigh. "I quite enjoyed driving it … teaching the boys how to drive. It was fun, last night – was it not, Michael?"

"Yes it was, Pop," Micky agreed. "I had 'most got the hang of shifting gears, but Jared …" Suddenly the boy fell silent. After a long moment, he added, "When you get better, Pop – will you have another roadster, just as nice, an' go on teaching us?"

"Sure thing, Michael," Roland Nelson closed his eyes.

The hovering doctor interjected, firmly, "I think that's enough of the questioning for today. This man has suffered a concussion, and complete rest is required for a total recovery from such an injury. If you continue with this interrogation, I cannot be held responsible for the adverse consequences!"

"I think that is enough for our purposes," I signaled John Drury with a significant glance; we were being given the bum-rush out of the hospital ward, so best to go quietly, in the interests of preserving dignity of our office and the integrity of our investigation. The boy Micky lingered behind, for a moment, casting an anxious gaze at his father.

"You gonna be OK, Pop? You know, you gotta teach Jared to brake and shift, once he's grown a bit taller."

"I will indeed, Michael," the pale patient returned from his bed of pain, without opening his eyes. His face had gone almost the same shade as the bandages around his head. "You shouldn't worry – and neither should your mother. You all are so very dear to me."

"I know, Pop," the lad replied, and then he was following us down the stairs. I noticed that when I looked back at him, the lad seemed disconsolate, in the way that his shoulders drooped, and his countenance was the very picture of woe.

"Are you all right, young Micky?" I asked, and when he shrugged in a noncommittal way, I suggested that we all go and have a luncheon at my expense (since it could be counted as a business expense) at one of Karnesville's many inexpensive eateries. I thought of cheering the boy up, since I had long noted that a boy of that age could be soothed and reassured by the prospect of something to eat. A lot of something to eat. We retreated to a luncheon counter near to the railway station – a station which John Drury (and many other Lunaites) never failed to   point out to me on every conceivable occasion, should have fallen to the lot of Luna City. That and the splendid county courthouse.

"Aye well, there's no loss without some small gain," I pointed out. "Think of the criminal offenders that it would have fallen to our lot, should Luna City have been the county seat!"

"Well, we would have had a larger budget to deal with them all," John Drury grunted.

We sat in a row at the counter, as the few tables were all occupied at midday. I opted for the blue plate special of meatloaf and a side of mashed potatoes for myself and the boy, and John asked for chicken fried steak.

"You should be happy, lad, that your father was not badly injured in the accident," I said, by way of making conversation, after the girl behind the counter took our orders. The boy merely looked down at the scarred countertop and answered,

"Yeah. Mom will be glad." He sounded defensive, as if he didn't want to go any farther, and I was at that time, not unaccustomed to dealing with the young of our kind.

"After lunch, we'll go and see if the mechanic is finished with going over your father's car," John Drury assured him.

"I'd rather go home," Micky replied, and I shook my head.

"We had a purpose in coming to Karnesville, and consulting with the mechanic was one of them," I said. "We'll deliver your home as soon as that has been accomplished."

"Ok," Micky said, with a distinct lack of enthusiasm. He picked at his blue plate special when it arrived, which I thought most curious. A growing lad of that age generally was hungry enough to wolf every bite and then lick the pattern off the plate. I exchanged a questioning glance with John Drury, who divined my own puzzlement, and shrugged.

The garage to which Mr. Nelson's wrecked roadster had been towed was conveniently on the edge of town, just off the road which we would take on our return to Luna City. The owner met us in his shabby office, unsuccessfully attempting to wipe black grease from his hands.

"Hey, Chief – I got a good luck at the wreck," he said. "Jeff McCormack. Don't mind not shaking hands – I gotta lotta work to do and not much time to do it, not with all these jamokes riding my back. How can I help ya? Whattya wanta know?"

"If there was any sabotage to the brakes, that you can detect, since you have the eye of an expert," I replied, barely aware that the boy Micky was effacing himself, almost shrinking whenever anyone glanced in his direction.

"Sure – easy-peasy," Mr. McCormack replied. "Say, my folks say they came from Scotland, too – by way of Kentucky, years ago. We might be kin, whattya think?"

"Unlikely," I replied. "I am from Fife; the McCormacks and their ilk from Ireland. But that makes no difference, in the pursuit of truth and justice. What have you found with regard to Mr. Nelson's automobile? Any signs of sabotage to the brakes?"

Mr. McCormack shrugged – I might almost have thought he looked regretful. It might have been that I rejected his query regarding possible kinship, or more likely because there was nothing to be found with regard to the wrecked automobile. I suspect that he hoped for notoriety if it came to an investigation, an arrest and subsequent trial.

"Nope, Chief. Nothing in the least suspicious. Everything mechanical was as it should be, save for being a bit banged up in the wreck. There was this one curious thing, though – found it under the driver seat."

"What was it?" I asked in the spirit of idle curiosity, while Micky looked down at his shoes.

"This ..." Mr. McCormack lifted a small box from the desk, a desk piled high with paperwork, a number of greasy hand-tools. The box contained a number of odd parts, presumably from Mr. Nelson's wrecked roadster... and an item which attracted my attention, as it looked ... familiar. I had seen another such, at the scene of the wreck that very morning; a plain tin can, pierced through on both sides, near one end, and a long piece of twine run through. And now, here was another. What could be the significance of such...

John Drury intuited my question, almost instantly.

"Michael, boy – what was this doing in your father's roadster, this and the other one." He bent his regard on the boy, whose' misery was apparent. The lad moistened his lips, but the interested Mr. McCormack interjected before he could answer.

"Why, my son tied such to his feet, so that he could work the pedals! His legs were too short, you see – and he wanted to learn to drive..."

Micky looked down at the ground; he was only a little shorter than John Drury himself, so I could not see that it was for himself, this contraption of cans and twine ... but for another.

"And last night, you and your father fixed such a pair of devices on the feet of your little brother, Jared – so that he could drive the roadster," John Drury explained softly, an air of dawning insight and satisfaction wreathing his features. "And then, when the lesson was over, the cans got left in the car ... left and forgotten, rolling around on the floor of the roadster. Is that so, Micky?"

The boy nodded mutely. John Drury continued, in his customary gentle manner. "And then, sometime this morning as your father was driving to his next appointment, one of those forgotten tin cans lodged underneath the brake pedal. He said that it was as if the brake pedal was jammed, immovable. That is what happened, wasn't it? And you guessed as much, when you talked about teaching your brother to drive."

Micky nodded again. "Right then – I could see it, clear in my head. Don't tell Pop, though – won't you? That it was just an accident, and not his fault."

"An accident," I agreed, exchanging a look with John Drury. "That's just what it was. No plot against his life – just an accident. And you will tell your mother that. Oh, I suppose that you can skip the details, since it was pretty careless of you all to leave something like an empty can, rolling around in the car... but she should be comforted knowing that it was not a plot against his life."

"All the other ladies should be comforted, as well." John Drury added. "And grateful to be spared the trouble of investigating every father, brother and old spark of thirty women..."

"Thirty-one, if it was true about the girl in Beeville," I added, quietly, and John Drury laughed.

Would that most of our investigations were so readily sorted! Many of them were, of course – but some of those which weren't, like the matter of who had poisoned ten head of cattle and a prize hunting dog. Ah, but that was a mystery for yet another chapter.

The Point of the Exercise

Richard might have been loath to admit it to anyone but Kate –
but he rather enjoyed guest night at the VFW. Even before he had
accepted Lew Dubois' offer to manage the kitchen and catering
function at the Cattleman, and he was still working at the Café, he was
in the habit of taking a break at mid-evening. When the first rush of
diners eased off, and all was safe to leave in the hands of his capable
staff, with Luc in full command of the grill and sauté station, Richard
could meander down several blocks to the VFW building. The VFW
was a converted temporary building seconded from the Luna City High
School upon completion of a new wing. This made a temporary and
ostensibly portable classroom building extraneous to needs. A decade
previously, Roman Gonzalez and his crew had jacked up that classroom
building and rolled it by careful degrees through the streets of Luna
City to a pleasing location in a small grove of sycamore trees on the
banks of the San Antonio River, behind the Tip-Top Ice House, Gas

and Grocery. Richard could spend a brief hour in what was essentially the male hang-out of Luna City; the pub, the regular, all scruffy, familiar and companionable. He would have given up much – not a hand, but maybe a finger or two – to continue enjoying that refuge.

On a quiet evening late in autumn Richard pedaled down the leaf-cushioned path that cut across the clump of woods between Oak Street and the back of the VFW. Early in the spring, he had paused now and again in his journey, hoping to see fireflies – those semi-legendary twilight insects, flitting about their business, flashing like tiny, aerial sparks. Miss Letty had confided to him that back in the days of her youth, they had been so a common springtime phenomenon that she and her friends would capture the little insects and keep them for a time in a jam-jar, with the lid pierced. Spring of the year before had been a grand year for lightening bugs, being rainy and wet, and the new spring grass lush and green … but not this year. This vaguely disappointed Richard; he would have liked to see traditions carried on, with Araceli's Matty and Angelika catching fireflies in the lush garden in front of the double-wide caravan on Oak Street. And he would have liked to have seen the tiny flickering insects in the twilight, himself. *And – dare he think of it; his and Kate's potential offspring doing the same on a cool spring evening.*

Unrewarded by any tiny insectoid flickering among the meadows and groves, he arrived at the back of the sand-pink building and let himself in through one of the doors. There was already a good crowd assembled. Joe Vaughn and Miss Letty, with Sylvester and Chris at one of the scratch tables nearest the window; they waved to him as he came through the door, a gesture of welcome and most welcomed at that.

Chris rose from his seat as Richard approached, "Ricardo, man – what's your pleasure?"

"The usual," Richard answered, settling with a slight sigh onto a chair. "Business is booming tonight – I am on my way home, after an exhausting day, directing kitchen traffic at the Crystal Room. I have time for at least one refreshing draft … say, who are all those chaps in hunting colors at the table with Colonel Walcott?"

"An old friend of his, and a party of his subordinates," Miss Letty replied, with an air of almost arctic self-possession. "An Army Reserve unit. For some reason, the powers which guide that particular command have scheduled a … something they called a team building exercise for the newly minted junior officers."

"Too candy-ass to go for Ranger School," Joe Vaughn allowed, looking balefully into the depths of his beer. "So they come to Mills Farm and spend a week on the river and romping through Colonel Walcott's obstacle course and playing military games…"

Miss Letty looked as if she were about to caution him on his turn of phrase, but tactfully reconsidered. It looked as if Joe's knees were giving him holy hell again.

"Pogues," Sylvester had no such compunction. "Career Fobbits. Hey, Chris, bring me another Dos Equis while you are up. I guess we can't steal their Hum-Vees or make fat jokes. Is it just me, or do they look like absolute babies to you'all?"

"To me, you are all still infants," Miss Letty pointed out.

Joe raised his own beer in salute. "Thank you, ma'am," he said, as Chris returned from the small bar with a beer for Sylvester and a Fever Tree for Richard. "Cheers! Here's to the the single most dangerous guy in the unit; a new second lieutenant with a map and a compass."

"Amen to that," Sylvester responded, and Richard kept tactfully silent, although he did have to agree with Joe. The five young men with Clovis Walcott and the distinguished, gray-haired older man – did look unfortunately little older than Sixth Formers: very pink, and earnest. Miss Letty nodded, as gracious as Her Majesty.

"It is a very curious thing," she allowed. "I might suspect that whoever has authority over Army assignments has a sense of humor; Colonel Walcott's friend has collected an abecedarium for his unit. Up to the letter E. They have a Lieutenant Andrews, Lieutenant Baker, Lieutenant Caneda, Lieutenant Dodd, and Lieutenant Eddings."

"No shit? Sorry, Miss Letty," Sylvester uncapped his beer, by deftly knocking the bottle-top against the table edge, and Chris chided him.

"Hey, Marine – we're a civilized joint, we got bottle-openers!"

"Faster this way," Sylvester answered. "And impresses the ladies. All the new lieutenants in alphabetical order, you say. Well, I'll be…"

Joe snorted. "Wouldn't be the first time. Back in the day, I wondered if there wasn't someone handling classification to an MOS based on the recruit's surname. Knew two guys at my first CONUS assignment. A cook and baker – named Cook and Baker. And an MP – named Copper. Later on – a motor-pool mechanic named Gear. And a medic named Blood. Couldn't have been random."

"Seems all rather appropriate, though," Richard mused, and all at the table nodded.

Sylvester asked, "Hey Ricardo – how is the new job going for ya after four months? A big step, going on to work for VPI. I know you were dragging your feet for a long time over moving up in the world."

"Come men are born to greatness, others have it thrust upon them," Richard replied, somewhat caustically, and Sylvester, Chris and Joe all laughed. "On the whole – I'm very pleased with it all … it's refreshing to have the wider scope, offered by the Crystal Room. The larger budget, also … sorry, Miss Letty." He added hastily, and Miss Letty nodded.

"The Café had but a small and modest mission," she replied. "Coffee. Breakfast and lunches first. It reflects no shortcomings for mine and Stephen's little business. Really, we bought into the Café all those years ago, just to keep Luna City from going moribund entirely. So many of the smaller towns have, you see; in this part of the world. Once there is no place for folks to gather; no school, no local business … the post office closes and all withers away. It has happened before, often enough and in other little towns like this…" Miss Letty looked deep into her well of memories. "We had a bank here, once," she said. "A grocery store, an ice-cream parlor, even a little movie theater. Mr. Milhouse's fabric emporium. It was such a lovely little town, such a busy place, when Stephen and I were children … when everything we wanted or needed was right here in Luna City."

She had her glass of soda in her hand and looked around at the table. "We wanted to keep something of that alive, something to keep the young folk and the businesses from running away to Karnes City or Beeville, in search of jobs and amusement. It seemed to us that buying the Café and keeping it open was a way to keep Luna City alive. Vital. It also helped, with VPI buying and opening Mills Farm… although Stephen will never give them any credit for that. The Café did its part, Richard – and you had a hand in that. It was a wise choice, hiring you for the five years that you worked for us. Never think that we are ungrateful. It has all worked out rather well," Miss Letty added, in her usual magisterial manner, setting down her glass with a decisive click.

"We're a bit of a tourist attraction town now," Sylvester added. "Which makes the traffic a bit of a problem, especially on weekends. Annise Stein told me that there are now more bed and breakfast beds in the buildings around Town Square than there are actual residentials."

"I know," Miss Letty looked pensive. "It is a trial, sometimes. Especially on weekend mornings. Stephen and I merely hoped that Luna City wouldn't go the way of Nixon, or Charco. Most of them are nice people, of course. And we appreciate sharing our little town…"

"We appreciate their money," Chris pointed out, baldly.

Sylvester chuckled. "Ah, well – wait until the weather cools off, and we get the holiday crowd, come for the Christmas tree lighting and the Santa Parade."

"There is predicted to be a cool front blowing in tonight," Miss Letty reported. "And heavy rain tomorrow afternoon."

"Beautiful," Joe Vaughn heaved a deep sigh. "I gotta drive to the VA clinic in Victoria – got an appointment with a therapist there about my right knee. Hope I can beat the rain, coming back."

352

"Serves you right, jumping out of all those helicopters, 'stead of waiting until they land." Sylvester told him, and Chris added, "Motrin – and drink plenty of water. Don't forget to change your socks."

"Assholes," Joe replied, equably. That exchange might have sounded cruelly unsympathetic to a casual listener, but Richard knew them all well enough to know to know how veterans of different military services ribbed each other mercilessly, and that they would turn on an outsider in an instant.

Outside, the sky was darkening; still the color of pale oyster shell in the west, where the sun was setting between a glory of royal purple clouds trimmed in gold. Richard knew that if he departed now, he would reach the Age and his cozy caravan by the time it hit full dark. He finished off the last of his Fever Tree and took his leave. He was tired, tired enough to reconsider the charm of a staff lodging at the Cattleman. But then – the temptation to be on the spot for every minor crisis would drag him in again … and that would play hell with his plans for a quite, rewarding and normal life with Kate. Well, as close to normal as a chef married to a newspaper reporter could ever hope to approach normal.

"Say," Joe drawled as Richard stood up. "I hear that your parents are back in town – does this mean that you and Katie are gonna tie the knot, soon?"

"We haven't exactly set a date at this point," Richard confessed. "But yes, soon."

"I hope that Jess and I rate an invite," Joe replied.

"Up to Kate, I think," Richard said, and Joe laughed.

"Well, we'll send you a really hideous wedding present, at least," he answered, jovially. "But seriously – Jess and I are happy for you both. It's a blessing – marriage is. One which you look back on and think – how the heck did I ever deserve this?"

"I'm pretty certain that Kate and Araceli and Kate's mum have it all in hand," Richard said, as he went out into the humid twilight, and set the bicycle on the path toward home. Or that home which was for the moment, his.

* * *

Late the following day, Jess's cellphone chimed – the brief tune that meant Joe was calling. She was at home, looking out the kitchen window at the sky turning dark gray out to the east – towering clouds that promised … no, guaranteed rain, rain in sheets. She was about to put supper on – a recipe for a beef stew that she had gotten via Richard at the Café, and his Captain Kitten in the Kitchen podcast. The twins were blissfully napping in their adjoining cribs in the tiny back bedroom which was now what Jess called 'the nursery.' Little Joe was in the playpen in the living room, happily burbling baby babble to himself, as he played with the rattling and jingling toys.

"How did it go?" Jess asked. Joe's voice came through, loud and clear.

"Pretty good – got a steroid shot, so the knee feels like original issue. I'm about half an hour out, looks like I'm gonna run into rain, though."

"Take care, Joe…" Jess replied automatically. Joe always took care. That was his way. "See you in a bit…"

And then she heard his voice again, distant, as if something else had attracted his immediate attention. "What the hell … oh, shit!" The sound of something, a crunch and a crash, and the buzz of a broken signal.

Then nothing at all.

To be continued… of course.

A Full Dozen of Luna City

All Hands Search

"What the hell ... oh, shit!" The sound of something, a crunch and a crash, and the buzz of a broken signal. Then nothing at all.

Jess Abernathy-Vaughn listened blankly to that buzz for what seemed to her to be an eternity. Time seemed to stand still, Joe's final words echoing in her ear. Outside, a sudden gust of wind rattled the window, and in the silence, distant thunder

357

grumbled threateningly. There was a storm blowing in from the east.

"Joe! Joe – what happened!" She pressed the redial button on her phone again – instead, the tinny recorded automated message. *Your call cannot go through as dialed. Please hang up and dial again.*

She fought down a rising tide of panic. *No, this simply could not be happening. Joe...*The twins were asleep in their cribs in the nursery bedroom, still, but she could hear Little Joe fussing from his playpen in the front room. She was starting supper – and what had happened to Joe? He was supposed to be almost home by now, returning from an appointment at the Veteran's Administration clinic in Victoria.

Joe must have had an accident, Jess told herself, struggling for calmness. *An accident, on the road. An accident that damaged his phone ... else why wasn't he answering.*

Jess took a deep breath, then another one – the sort of deep breath encouraged by the birthing coaches, before she had Little Joe. She carefully turned off the burner underneath the pan of browning stew beef and sat down at the kitchen table with her cellphone. She called up the number for the main desk at the Luna City Police department.

"Hi, Tina," she said, as soon as the dispatcher sergeant answered. "I think this is an emergency – something's happened to Joe. I was on my phone with him just now, and he suddenly said, *'what the hell and oh, shit'* and then the signal cut off. I heard what sounded like a crash – his or someone elses' vehicle,

I couldn't tell. His phone ... something is wrong with his phone, now. He doesn't pick up ... and I called him right back."

"All right, Jess," Tina Gonzalez replied, her own voice deliberately calm. "We're on it. Do you have any idea of where he was calling from, where he might be, so we can narrow it down."

"He was driving home from Victoria," Jess replied. She ran that brief and abruptly terminated exchange through her memory. "He said he was about half an hour out from home. I'm not sure about which road he was on. I don't think he was coming from Kenedy – too much traffic this time of day. He thought he was about to run into heavy rain, so east of here, I'd assume."

"Half an hour out," Jess could almost hear Tina Gonzalez doing mental calculations. "OK, if he was on Route 81, that would put him somewhere east, between Helena and Runge. If he drove through Gillette, there's not a lot out there, along 80 ... I'm gonna put the call out right now. Jess, is there someone who can come and wait with you? Anyone? You shouldn't be by yourself."

Jess appreciated the heck out of the fact that Tina didn't tell her not to worry. Now she could hear the earsplitting klaxon at the police and fire station blowing three times – alerting all volunteers of the Luna City Volunteer Fire Department within reach to an emergency and report to the firehouse. Those out of earshot would get an automated emergency call on their cellphones.

"I'll call Myrna," Jess replied. "She's at home today."

"Good," Tina replied. "We'll find him, Jess – you can count on that. Joe's a fighter, not a quitter."

"I know," Jess said. Of course, she reflected as she closed the call. Joe <u>was </u>a fighter. On the wall, in all weathers. The tireless scourge of lawbreakers in this part of Karnes County, Hero and father. Her husband. If he was ... not there, a part of her life any longer... Jess gulped and faced the potential possibility squarely ... if he was dead; she would have to cope. She would have to raise Little Joe and the girls herself. Alone.

She turned on the heat under the stew beef again and called up another number from her contact list. By the time Joe's mother picked up, Jess was calm again; unnaturally, eerily calm.

"Mom Myrna," she said into the cellphone, as she stirred the browning beef chunks with a wooden spoon in her other hand. "We think Joe has had an accident on the road ... yes, coming home from Victoria. Just a few minutes ago ... I've already called in to dispatch ... yes, that's what the klaxon was for... can you get here before the rain starts ... I really..."

"I'll be there in a trice," Myrna Vaughn replied instantly, stoic and Spartan.

Five minutes later, one of the LCFD patrol units pulled into the driveway. Fat droplets of rain were beginning to splatter the gravel drive, and the hood of the SUV. Out in the living room, Little Joe sounded as if he were working up to a full fuss – a prelude to a spectacular tantrum. Myrna Vaughn emerged from the passenger side, and Sgt. Milo Grigoriev from the other. Milo had a furled umbrella in hand, which he hurriedly opened and held over Myrna as they ran for the back door.

"I came as soon as I could," Myrna gasped, as a gust of rain rattled against the door, as if the storm was infuriated about the two escaping the soaking wrath of it. "And Sgt. Grigoriev was kind enough to bring me ... oh, sugar – are you OK?"

"No," Jess replied, and just barely escaped bursting into floods of tears right then and there. She would have, save for not wanting to lose it totally in front of Myrna and Milo. Myrna enfolded her in a brisk and reassuring embrace.

"Never mind, sugar ... don't let supper burn! I'm here, and we'll wait it out together!"

Milo added, "We've called out all the guys who are off duty, and the FD search and rescue ... the Karnes County Sherriff, and the Gonzalez and DeWitte departments, too. There's a panic on in Gonzalez; a couple of dirtbag human-smugglers are trying to make a run with a van full of illegals on back roads, and half their units are in pursuit or setting up roadblocks ahead of them ... but don't worry, Jess – we're on it. We'll find Joe before sundown. The trouble is ..." Milo looked awkwardly down, as he folded up the umbrella. "Until this storm lets up, we can't do a search by air. We're gonna have to work on the ground, searching yard by yard. It's gonna take some time, Jess – but don't give up hope."

"I won't," Jess replied, still fighting back despair and tears. Myrna took the wooden spoon from her, as the beef was getting very brown, and Milo made his dash for the unit. The wind dashed more rain against the back of the house. It was now falling in gray sheets, obscuring everything beyond the trees that lined the back of the property.

"Sugar, let me do that – you go see what Little Joe is on an all-mighty fuss about," Myrna commanded. For once, Jess was glad of her mother-in-law's domineering tendencies.

"Joe is normally home about now," Jess explained, "And that clever little monkey can tell time, I swear."

"Go and distract him, then" Myrna encouraged her. "Is this the recipe? Oh, good – I've made *Beef Bourguignon* before. Is this one of the regular dishes from the Café that Richard used to make? I loved that! And it will be something good and filling for when Joe turns up – even if he is late. Beef Bourguignon is one of those things that warms up so very well,"

"Yes, it's one of Richard's *Captain Kitten in the Kitchen* recipes," Jess replied, sunk in misery only a little lightened by Myrna's determined good cheer.

"Oh, excellent." Myrna gave the beef chunks a stir and gave Jess a stern look over her shoulder. "Chin up, Jess – our Joe is a survivor. He'll be all right."

There was nothing to say in reply to that; out in the living room, Little Joe began howling – making any response superfluous, since it couldn't be heard above the hellish music of toddler tantrum.

Richard was halfway through his final pre-supper circuit through the Cattleman's restaurant kitchen when his cellphone buzzed with the urgent message from the VFD; all available volunteers report to the firehouse immediately. He had been a volunteer for the past several years – and this was one of his standby days. He wasn't yet a full-fledged fire-fighting volunteer, due to his erratic attendance at training sessions, but he had scored well enough on the required first aid exams and victim rescue tests to qualify to ride out with Chris in the VFD ambulance. He rushed into the office, to pull his coat out of the closet, and collided with Lew Dubois as he rushed out again.

"You, too?" he gasped, and Lew nodded.

"We'll take my car, *cher*. Mr. Charboneau, from housekeeping has been called as well."

The two men hustled out of the service door, where the old stables used to be, joined in the parking area by a large and normally silent Fred Charboneau, the resident handyman who had married into the sprawling Gonzalez/Gonzales clan. The rain was pelting down in a manner which reminded Richard keenly of a fine summer day in Bickley. Both Lew and Fred hefted duffle bags of turnout gear into the trunk of Lew's late model Lexus and peeled out of the narrow employee lot on two wheels. It was barely three blocks to the VFD station, already being converged upon by an assortment of civilian vehicles.

"Hard to believe that something is on fire in this weather," Fred Charboneau observed. Richard and Lew laughed, hollowly.

"It is said to be most difficult to make something foolproof, as fools are most ingenious," Lew replied.

Richard, recalling the massive flood of the river some years previous, ventured an explanation. "Probably an emergency rescue on the river, or a low crossing ... some kid messing around on the riverbank and getting swept away."

"Could be, *cher*," Lew found a place to park as close to the station as he could, and they all dashed through the driving rain – which now seemed determined to achieve in four hours what it had taken Noah's flood forty days and nights.

There wasn't anything but somber faces in the briefing area, once Milo Grigoriev finished outlining the situation, and setting the search parameters. Every single one of the volunteers in the room knew Joe Vaughn, some of them had even played on the Moths Varsity football team, back in the days when he was the high school football hero. There wasn't a single one who would mind getting soaked to the skin, or worse, scouting along the two most likely back-country roads – just to make certain that he would be found and returned, safe and sound.

"The weather folks predict that the worst of this storm will pass over the search area in half an hour to forty-five minutes," Milo Grigoriev concluded, "There's a hazard in sending out a search while it's still pissing down to beat the band ... but they call it the Golden Hour for a damned good reason – if we find someone injured – badly injured – and get them to medical care within that hour, then there's a much better chance for survival and recovery. We have to risk it, people. It's a matter of life and death. You know the plan, then. Go, people. Find Chief Vaughn – and stay safe out there."

That being said, all but Richard, Chris Mayall, Lew and Steve Gonzales, a full-time FD employee scattered for their personal vehicles. Since the expansion of Venue Properties,

International to include a lease on the Cattleman Hotel and a constant stream of day-trippers and holidaymakers, the VFD had found themselves in the way of affording a second ambulance; vehicle and contents of necessary gear generously funded by the corporate Good Fairy. There were just the four remaining at the VFD to take any calls for EMS and an ambulance from Tina Gonzalez at the police station dispatch desk. Chris tapped Richard on the shoulder.

"You're with me, if they call for Number One Magic Bus. Lew, if you don't mind – you're with Steve on Number Two. You OK with that, Ricardo – Lew?"

"Fine with me," Richard replied. This gave him time to change into his VFD gear, now that he had achieved the dignity of a locker of his own at the Fire Station, in which to keep the issue trousers, boots, and official shirt with his name embroidered over the pocket, against the day when the whole crew of volunteers was called out. Then he rejoined his First Aid fellows in the all-purpose room, where the on-duty firefighters whiled away the idle hour in luxuriously overstuffed Barca-loungers, waiting for various disasters to call them to action. A tall coffee urn perked away on a table in the corner, attended by a stack of heavy china mugs, and a dispenser full of sugar packets and little round containers of shelf-stable creamer.

Chris and Steve were watching an old film noir mystery movie from the 1950s, without much interest. A somewhat intrigued Lew was identifying the scene of the outdoor locations, since he had attended college in Los Angeles. He had once intended a career in Hollywood set design, before diverted by chance into hospitality management.

"Lake Arrowhead was very popular for shooting scenes of mountain lakes and pine trees," He was saying as Richard took possession of an empty lounge chair. "Alas, it looks nothing like the Alps of Switzerland at all ... but in those days, very few people might know the difference, just by looking at a movie screen. But ..."

At that moment, the duty room telephone rang. Chris picked up with a crisp report, "Luna City FD, Mayall speaking."

"Ambulance call, 24 Pin Oak, elderly woman in distress," reported Tina Gonzalez, from next door in the police station. The extension was on the speakerphone mode. Chris gave a deep sigh.

"Thanks, Tina. Sending Unit 2," Chris hung up the receiver and addressed the room at large. "Mrs. Mafilda Potrero. Probably having a panic attack again. She always does when it rains heavy like this. Never got over getting caught in a flooding low-water crossing, ten-fifteen years ago. Steve, you and Lew take it. Ricardo and I'll wait to hear from the search party."

"On it, Doc," Steve shouldered into his rain slicker and hood. He and Lew vanished into the garage part of the station, and the brief wail of the ambulances' siren could be heard until it faded into the sound of rain drumming on the metal roof.

Chris sighed again. "You want some coffee, Ricardo? We may be here for a while."

"Not unless it's from the Café," Richard replied. "I don't trust anything calling itself coffee, unless it came from my kitchen or one that I supervise. Sounds as if you've gone to the dance with the Potrero woman before."

"Frequent flyer, man," Chris sauntered over to the coffee and helped himself. "Nice old broad but still has PTSD from the fright of near drowning in a foot of water over the old road a couple years back. I can relate. A good few puffs of oxygen, some sternly-worded reassurance, and she apologizes for having been such trouble to us, and brings out some butter cookies that her sister made, and brags about her grandchildren. All hunky-dory. But one of these days, she <u>will</u> have a heart attack or something for real ... aannnddd that's why we send the Magic Bus over to 24 Pin Oak. Just in case. You might as well kick back and relax, Ricardo ... by my reckoning, we won't be called for ..." Chris consulted his watch. "At least twenty-five minutes. Sooner, maybe, but only if Joe was exceeding the speed limit, and you know what a freak he was about that kind of thing."

"How do you figure?" Richard was honestly intrigued. He really hoped that Chris was right. And that the rainstorm had blown through by the time #2 Ambulance returned to the barn. And really – if this call-out took too long, could Chris or Lew drop him off at the Age, and spare him the long trek on his bicycle?

"Joe told Jess that he was about half an hour out," Chris explained patiently. "So, even in the rain, it will take almost that long for our search crews to reach the approximate area and begin to search. Longer, if they have to be careful in heavy rain.

So, relax, Ricardo. Have a cup of awful coffee. Sit back and watch a dumb old movie. Betcha anything that Steve and Lew will be back before we get the call. We might even see the end of the movie."

This proved to be one of the very rare times that Chris turned out to be wrong. It was only fourteen minutes, when the call from Dispatch came through; the call they had been waiting for

"I'm going to have to make a note of this," Richard gasped, as he and Chris shrugged into their rain slickers and ran to Unit 1. "It's unprecedented, you miscalculating to that degree. I wanted to see the end of the movie, too – I wanted to see who the murderer was. I'm almost certain it was the lawyer..."

"Don't tell Stephanie," Chris replied. "I gotta reputation as a minor prophet to uphold. No, it was the mistress." The ambulance lurched out of the garage, momentarily blinded by a curtain of rain, until Chris flipped the wipers to 'high'.

"But wasn't the mistress in Lucerne at the time of the murder, shopping for a new hat ... the chauffeur said so..."

"The chauffeur lied for her. She was his lover," Chris explained, as the ambulance sent up a peacock-tail of water as the offside wheel went through a deep puddle. Since they were outside of Luna City proper now, Chris thumbed the siren to 'on' and the ambulance sped north at top speed, towards where Route 123 intersected with a narrow country road, which angled off east towards Route 81 between Helena and Gillett. According to Tina, the call for the ambulance came from a good Samaritan calling from the roadside, just short of Helena, a Samaritan who had found evidence of a vehicle having gone off the road at high speed. Chris, like the other VFD volunteers, knew the county back roads as well as he knew the pattern of the ancient linoleum in his little apartment above the old coach house at the old McAllister place. Richard knew the road maps by heart but lacked actual knowledge of the terrain. Chris did have that granular knowledge and he was gunning the ambulance for every ounce of speed that the boxy contraption could produce, and every skill at high speeds on narrow country roads in his wide repertoire.

"Stone the crows – when did that happen?"

"In the last five minutes of the movie," Chris replied, over the roar of the engine and the wailing siren. "I've seen it before, about a dozen times. It's Stephanie's favorite old movie – she had a crush on Richard Widmark when she was a kid."

"Greater love hath no man," Richard steadied himself against the door of the lurching, swaying vehicle and thought that he might tighten the seat belt a little snugger. "Then to watch his favorite bird's favorite movie ... over and over. Did Sgt. Gonzalez say who reported the accident?"

Chris shook his head, and expertly steered the ambulance around two slower vehicles, who had dodged to the paved shoulder as soon as they saw the red and blue flashing lights of the ambulance in their rear-view mirrors. "A party of young guys coming back from a kayak river expedition. I guess their little adventure got rained out, so they were returning to the Cattleman to try again some other day. As soon as they called it in to Tina, all the searchers converged on their geographical coordinates ... which they had. Wonder if they are the Colonel's set of alphabetical butter-bars. Man, Joe will be so pissed that he was rescued by a set of wet-behind-the-ears baby officers. He will never live down the humiliation."

Richard bit back the reply – *If he lives*. Of course, Joe would live. He was Joe Vaughn and indestructible.

There was no mistaking the scene of the call-out when they came upon it. A section of road was marked with flares, two of the VFD engines, more than a dozen private vehicles parked every which way but mostly on the muddy verges, a pickup truck with a stock trailer attached, every single Luna City Police Department vehicle, a wrecker from Gonzalez Auto Repair and Body Shop ... and a dog. A big handsome yellow hound-type, sitting alertly by the side of the road, like a statue of a proud and noble greyhound. The rain had diminished to occasional splatters. The clouds were ragged grey, and beginning to break apart, although the storm looked as if it were venting all fury out to the west.

"'Strewth, it looks like a convention," Richard observed, as the ambulance slowed to a crawl to negotiate the narrow path between vehicles and uniformed LCPD officers. Milo Grigoriev waved his hands like a semaphore, standing next to the Gonzalez Auto & Body Shop wrecker, a very pink and gawky youth in serious backwoods attire, the dog and a grizzled man of some years in what Richard had come to recognize as the working garb of a local rancher. The trampled grass showed evidence of many footsteps, and at least one set of tire tracks, deeply grooved into the mud from the wrecker.

It looked as if the wrecker was backing a cautious way down the green slope, down through a bank grown with a thicket of spindly bushes, to a point where the gentle slope gave way abruptly to a nearly vertical bank. The back of a pickup truck was just barely visible through the bushes – bushes that had not been damaged by the truck. It looked to Richard as if the truck had sailed over that thicket, as if it had been launched from a catapult. In the driving rain, the truck would have been practically invisible from the road, especially to the sight of someone driving past at moderate speed.

Chris halted the ambulance, set the brake, and flung open the drivers' side door. "Show-time, Ricardo. Grab the rescue stretcher out of the back, we're prolly gonna need it." To Milo, he demanded, "Gimme the sit-rep, Milo. Where is Joe? Still in the vehicle? And is he conscious?"

"In the vehicle and barely," Milo Grigoriev looked pale under his summer tan. "Your guys have put in the stabilization jacks to secure the truck. Don and Frank are working with the combi tools to cut away enough that we can get him out. Don't think he got bones seriously broken, but he did get a whack on the head from the sun visor, when the truck hit down. He's bleeding bad, but the Lieutenant here – he was the first person on-scene – he got some dressing on Joe first thing, before he called it in."

"Good thinking, sir," Chris replied. Richard recognized the youth. Indeed, he was one of the baby junior officers whom Clovis Walcott had brought to the VFW a week previously. The infant officer looked nervous and jittery, in comparison to the dog and the old rancher, observing this exchange with mild and appreciative interest.

"Thank you," the boy gulped like a goldfish and turned beet red. "We stopped and looked because of the dog – we thought it was lost. The dog, I mean. I knew not to try and move the casualty. The truck wasn't on fire, or anything. But the blood ..."

"There's always a lot, with head wounds," Chris replied, with the utter assurance of someone who had seen much, much worse. "You got the rescue stretcher, Ricardo? Give me the kit. I'm gonna assess and we'll extract him before they move the truck. Come with me and look over my shoulder. I'll explain what I'm gonna do, as we go."

Richard followed, obediently – scrambling and slipping down the grass and mud-slick bank in Chris's wake, lugging the awkward burden of the metal rescue stretcher in a nylon canvas bag. Fortunately for him the metal basket stretcher folded in half for easy transport and was not as heavy as it might have been. Still, it was a struggle to manage with both hands, especially when he skidded on the wet grass and arrived at the bottom of the bank sitting with the rescue basket bag in his lap. Milo Grigoriev followed, along with several other VFD volunteers. It would take all of them to heft the basket stretcher with Joe in it, safely back up the steep bank to the ambulance again.

Joe Vaughn's familiar black pickup truck sat upright on flattened wheels at the bottom of that bank. It's momentum had been arrested at river's edge by a scattering of boulders and a quantity of deadwood tangled among them. The front bumper was crunched in around the engine block like so much tinfoil. An odor of gasoline and something else hung in the damp air, and there were puddles of dangerous smelling flids seeping from it and pooling on the sand and rocks. Richard sneezed; that something else was what had exploded the dashboard airbags on impact, which now lay in tattered rags, halfway out the drivers' side of the truck. Two FD volunteers were making swift work of forcing the door out of the way with the combi tool.

And there was Joe, slumped like a rag doll with half the stuffing gone, but his eyes were half-open. Something in the brief flight – or perhaps arresting the truck at the end of it – had shattered the windshield. Crumbs of grass were scattered far and wide, glittering as if they were handfuls of scattered diamonds or ice. The rear left quarter of the truck was also substantially crunched in. Richard couldn't fathom how that had happened unless it was by way of something striking Joe's truck from behind.

Chris set down the emergency bag next to the wrecked truck and put on a pair of hygienic blue gloves and addressed the patient in his usual bracing manner.

"Hey, Army – how many g*ddamn times do I have to tell you about what happens when you don't fasten your seatbelt properly?"

To Richard's secret relief, Joe's eyes widened briefly and there was awareness in them, although partly obscured by smears of vivid red blood and a startlingly white bandage tied around his forehead.

"---- you too, Squid," he mumbled, and added a brief and obscene description of what else Chris could do with himself. "I feel like shit, thanks for asking. Did they catch the scumbag that ran me off the road?"

"No telling, Army," Chris replied, swiftly and professionally assessing what he could reach for additional injuries, broken bones and blood. "Ricardo, make a note – pupils reactive and equal. Above my pay grade. Reckless driving is your department's circus and your monkey. So – Ricardo, make note – patient is conscious and responsive. How many fingers am I holding up? Yeah, good. 'Kay, I'm gonna check you out for a spinal injury and Ricardo here is gonna hold your head and help me put the cervical collar on ya. All righty then – I'm pressing your right hand. Can you feel it?"

"Yes, I can feel my hands. Those bastards totaled my truck!" Joe sounded much more with it and annoyed to a considerable degree. He batted away Chris's grip on his hand. "And it was almost paid for, dammit! Awww, Christ, Squid! That hurts! Do ya have to strap it that tight?"

"Gut it out, Army," Chris returned, heartlessly. "You don't wanna be in a wheelchair the rest of your life, do ya? OK – now your feet. Can you press up against my hand. Good. Look, regardless – you have an E-ticket booked for a ride in the Magic Bus all the way to the Karnesville MedCenter. Just lay back and try and relax. Leave the driving to us."

"Jess!" Joe protested weakly. "Has anyone called Jess! She'll be insane with worry ... I was talking to her when that *(extended explicative)* hit my truck!"

"We'll take care of calling your wife – that is, if Milo hasn't called her already. He just may be waiting for us to tell you that you are your usual ornery self, only a little battered and bruised."

"I can walk!" Joe protested, as half a dozen pair of willing hands shifted him out of the truck and into the opened basket stretcher. "Just lemme out of this thing! I'm fine!"

"Famous last words," Chris replied, heartless and unsympathetic, as he and Richard strapped him in – basically immobilizing him for the short journey to the ambulance, and the longer one to Karnesville. "Usually from someone with half a dozen crunched bones and an oozing chest wound, that we've just extracted from a totaled vehicle. Shut up and enjoy the ride, Army. Let the doctor decide."

Many willing hands helped carry the laden basket stretcher up the bank, with Joe still protesting his fitness every step of the way. When they reached the road, Richard saw Kate Heisel's little VW Bug among the haphazardly parked vehicles with a mixture of joy and mild embarrassment. The love of his heretofore misspent life was deep in conversation with the young sprout of a lieutenant and the older rancher with the dog. Katie was on the job. She had one of her cameras in hand and was snapping pictures of the chaotic scene. He was fairly certain that she got an excellent shot of Chris and himself loading up the ambulance with a still-complaining Joe Vaughn.

Oddly enough, the prospect of being spread all over the media didn't bother him any longer. He was anonymous now; just another dark-haired thirty-something working man volunteer, on an ambulance call in Karnes County. Years of riding the bicycle to and from work, tanned, fit, and living a monastic life with minimum drinking and debauchery had paid off. Also, he appeared superficially like any of the Gonzalez/Gonzales clan males, as Araceli had often pointed out. Practically no one from his old life as the Bad Boy Chef would recognize him, these days.

"Hey, lover," she beamed, when Richard made his presence known, and dropped a brief and affectionate kiss on his cheek. She had been interviewing the old rancher and the dog, who for some reason – probably vulgar curiosity – were still sticking around. "Long time, no see! Doing your bit for the community, I see! I gotta say that I love a man in uniform!"

"I'll bet you say that to all the chaps," Richard replied, and Katie giggled, most unprofessionally, and lowered her voice.

"How is Joe? Can you say anything privately? This is just personal, not for publication."

Richard considered a reply for a brief moment as Chris slammed the ambulance door on the complaining victim. He had occasionally been present when Kate was chasing the news-making machinery behind the popular song, as it were – but almost always as an innocent and uninvolved bystander himself.

"As you can see ... or hear ... not injured badly enough to be stoic and quiet," Richard murmured. "But he still merits a trip to Casualty. You didn't hear it from me, though. Look – there was one thing; he was going on about Jess and had anyone called and briefed her? Could you be a pal..."

"Hey, Ricardo, you coming? Or are you gonna ride your damn bike to Karnesville?" Chris shouted from the driver's side window.

"I will, lover," Katie replied, also in a whisper. "Better than that – I'll call her and offer a ride to the hospital. I know she'll want to be with Joe, but she's probably too freaked out to drive herself safely."

"Good thinking," Richard replied, just as Chris laid on the horn and the siren, and yelled again,

"You wanna finish making kissy-face with your girlfriend and get your ass in gear?"

Richard dropped a similarly brief kiss on Katie's lips and beat feet for the ambulance.

"Yeah, thanks for that tactful word," he snarled, as Chris set the ambulance in gear, and moved carefully away from the vehicular gathering. Because Joe had suffered a blow to the head, he needed to be carefully watched, all during the ride to

Karnesville, lest he slip into unconsciousness. Of course, Joe objected to being treated as if he were lingering at Death's Garden Gate, located a considerable distance from Death's Door. He objected all the way to Karnesville, which really began to wear on Richard's nerves. He vented to Chris, as soon as they pulled under the modern awning which sheltered ambulances in the forecourt of the Medical Center, and a still-protesting Joe was being wheeled away, into the tender care of the Accident and Emergency techs.

"I'd bet you just about anything that's 'cause he is really frightened," Chris enlightened Richard. "Near-death experiences have a way of putting a scare into ya. Hey, if you haven't had supper yet, let's pick up a couple of burgers before we head back to the barn."

"I hate to think of Joe Vaughn being frightened of anything," Richard replied. "Ugh ... fast food. Have I taught you nothing, when it comes to an appreciation of fine cuisine?"

"Probably not," Chris was unmoved by Richard's displeasure. His expression brightened, though. "Hey, isn't that your main squeeze's ride? Looks like she broke the speed limit getting here."

"She said she was going to bring Jess with her," Richard answered. His spirits lightened immeasurably at that moment – not just the sight of Katie, but of Jess, shouldering an overnight bag that she must have packed on the moment, the expression on her face a determined and purposeful one.

"Mos' excellent, Ricardo," Chris looked as if a load had been lifted from his shoulders, more than just the responsibility for Joe. "That's a good woman you have there! Glad you're going to put a ring on her, she's too good to risk being lured away by some conniving Jody."

"Indeed," Richard agreed, although he was not quite certain of what Chris meant. As far as he knew, there were no rivals named Jody for Katie's hand, let alone for the rest of her.

Jess barely gave them a nod and a brief greeting before she rushed into the Med Center's casualty department doors – not that Richard could blame her in the least. But Katie threw her arms around Richard, with a hard embrace, saying,

"Oh, god, I hope you never frighten the heck out of me the way that Joe just did! I'm so glad I could help, though. Jess will be OK – Joe's mother is staying with the children, and she'll have a ride back when she needs it... are you OK? You look like you've been put through a wringer."

"I'm perfectly fine," Richard insisted, although he did feel rather drained, now that the adrenaline of the rescue run in the Magic Bus had worn off. This adventure came on top of the usual hectic day in the Crystal Room, a day which had begun well before dawn. He was now aware that he was very tired and very hungry. The tiny, faultlessly neat aluminum caravan at the Age of Aquarius Campground and Goat farm seemed as far away and as unattainable as a longed-for paradise.

"You're not, you're bushed," Kate returned, as decisive as if the matter had already been settled. "Tell you what ... I'll call my parents and tell them that you both are coming with me for a good home-made supper. Mom's special meatloaf is to die for."

"I'm sure it is, Katie, but I can't – I gotta get the Magic Bus back to the barn," Chris interjected. "And I can grab a burger on the way out of Karnesville. But you go ahead, Ricardo – you're released for the evening."

"Thanks, Chris!" Katie tucked her arm most proprietarily around Richard's waist and added. "Besides … Mom and Dad want to talk to both of us about the wedding plans."

Richard belatedly realized that a fast-food hamburger, eaten in the ambulance on the way back to Luna City might have been a good option – but was too late, now. He was committed.

From the Karnesville Weekly Beacon – Flearoy to the Rescue!
By Katherine Heisel – Staff Writer

Luna City police chief Joseph Vaughn is recovering from a hit-and-run accident two weeks ago, which sent his personal vehicle flying off of a relatively deserted stretch of Route 81 near Helena. Chief Vaughn has been released from the hospital, and is now recovering at home, after sustaining only minor injuries in the crash, which sent his vehicle flying off the road just as a major storm passed through Gonzalez, Dewitt and Karnes County. *(See related stories, page 2, and 3.)* Vehicles from the Gonzalez County Sheriff and US Border Patrol were in pursuit of a fleeing human smuggler driving a Dodge minivan and hoping to evade a checkpoint south of Cuero by taking back roads. It was not until the vehicle was overtaken and detained for questioning just outside of Halettsville, and the driver was being interrogated that several occupants of the minivan mentioned seeing another vehicle driven off the road during the high-speed pursuit.

Chief Vaughn's vehicle sailed off the road and fell at the bottom of a bank without materially damaging any vegetation, so was not immediately visible from the road. Several law enforcement vehicles from the Gonzalez County sheriff's department and two from the Border Patrol passed at high speed and some distance behind the human smuggler without even noting the incident. The accident was only detected approximately fifteen minutes later, when a pair of vehicles occupied by six guests of Luna City's Cattleman Hotel passed the scene.

Lt. Christopher Dodd, driving the lead vehicle, spotted a large yellow hound dog, sitting by the side of the road in the rain. A dedicated animal lover, he insisted on stopping. He and five other junior officers were participating in a field excursion on the San Antonio River, when it began to rain heavily. They decided to return to the hotel and resume their kayaking expedition on another day.

"That poor dog was just there, by the side of the road, with the rain just pouring down." Says Lt. Morris Caneda. "Chris said he didn't want to leave it there, not with no house in sight and that dog just sitting there. We thought it might be lost and injured, besides being wet all through. So we pulled over, and Chris here did everything to try and coax the dog into our vehicle. But that dog – that dog just didn't move. We even tried picking him up – but he whined and struggled so and that bas... er, that dog was <u>heavy</u> ... and then Barry – Lieutenant Baker said, 'Hey, guys ... smell that? Smells like the stuff they explode the airbags in a car with.' He totaled his dad's Ford once, said you couldn't mistake that smell. Morrie said that he could smell gasoline, too, and we couldn't figure where it was coming from. The rain was starting to let up, so we could see ... and that's when we saw the back of that pickup, way off the road."

Lt. Dodd continued the story, "So we all scrambled down the bank! We thought for sure that someone must be still in that truck, the odor still lingering and all ... and we saw Mr. Vaughn

– that is, Chief Vaughn. Thought he was dead from all the blood at first... but Barry said he was still alive, that dead bodies don't bleed – and Barry was rated an Eagle Scout, so he would know ... anyway, we had a First Aid kit in our gear, and Chris called 911 and told them where we were..."

Lt. Peter Andrews continued the story. "While we were waiting for a response from those guys, this old guy in a truck drives up, yelling, *'Flearoy, what you been up to, you silly ol' dog?!'* And that was it. We wouldn't ever have stopped, but for seeing Flearoy the dog, sitting by the side of the road. Everyone reckons that ... well, maybe someone might have seen that truck off the side of the road, what with the search for Chief Vaughn going on ... but any delay might have made things worse."

Flearoy the dog is an 8-year-old German Shepherd-Catahoula Hound cross, owned by Mr. Morgan Furlong, who owns a ranch property near Helena.

Winter Newsletter

Winter 2019-20 Newsletter

Luna City Chamber of Commerce

5 North Town Square, Suite 4

Check out our Facebook Page

This coming January, the Luna City Historical Society will open a new permanent exhibit space in the Old Fire Station, at the south-east corner of Town Square. Early photographs of Luna City and rare memorabilia will be on display, including one of Luna City Volunteer Fire Departments' original Button hand engines. Other relics include the original model of Luna City, as planned to include an ornate courthouse at the center of Town Square. The exhibit space will be open on weekends and holidays, and is made possible through donations from Mills Far, the Wyler Ranch, and many private contributions.

Meals on Wheels – from the Café!

Luna Café & Coffee begins meal delivery service, beginning in January. A choice of two meals nightly, with deliveries beginning after 5 PM, until 9 PM, (10 PM Friday and Saturday) delivered to your door, hot and ready to serve to your hungry family, at a small charge for delivery. Meals offered include a main course, with two vegetable sides, and a dessert, for up to four people, all prepared from the Café's most popular recipes. The menus for delivery meals are available on the Café's new website – *lccafe&coffee.com*. And check out our new line of gourmet sauces, spice and tea mixes and our own prize-winning chili mix, in Mild, Medium-hot and Call the Fire Department versions!

Upcoming Events

December 6

The LCFD yearly fund-raising pancake breakfast will be held at the firehouse 8-11 AM. The new ambulance, donated with funds provided by Venue Properties, Intl. will be formally dedicated at 10:00

December 14

The annual Christmas gift bazaar will be held in the grand ballroom of the Cattleman Hotel! 80 vendors will be present – all this, and Santa, too!

December 31

Ring in the New Year with the traditional dinner and dance on Town Square! Fireworks at midnight, and dance until then to the music of Los Moldanados!

Golf Course Closed!

Mills Farm's golf course will be closed through January for installation of a new irrigation system.

Luna City ISD News

Drivers Needed

The Luna City Independent School District is looking for drivers to assist with delivering groceries collected through the school food drive to needy families throughout Karnes County during the week of December 16-20. Please contact the LCISD main office, if you can help.

Cooking Classes

8th Grade and older students who are eligible for Chef Richard's advanced cooking classes to begin after the Christmas-New Year break must have permission slips signed by parent or legal guardian to participate in the cooking program, as large knives and hot burners will be involved. Students diagnosed with severe food allergies who wish to participate must have additional medical clearance from their health provider filed with the school nurse, and permission for emergency medical aid to be rendered in case of a severe reaction.

Senior Spring Break Trip

The senior class spring break trip is scheduled for March 15-21. Participating seniors must have permission slips signed by parent or guardian turned into the LCISD main office, and all fees for transportation and hotels paid by March 13 at latest. This years' senior trip is to the Texas Hill Country, with private tours of the Fredericksburg Pioneer Museum, and the Pacific War Museum. Students will also attend a concert at Downtown Luckenbach and stroll through the Hill Country's Wildseed Farms wildflower meadows.

Community Marketplace

Christmas Fruitcakes

Order your Christmas fruitcakes now at the Café for delivery the week of Christmas! Our recipe was developed by Chef Richard, from a traditional English wedding cake, full of rich golden raisins, flavorful currents, preserved orange peel and flavored with brandy. Cakes are available in 2.5 and 5-pound sizes, Order now, for a taste of English tradition!

From Chief Vaughn, Luna City PD

Those wishing to indulge in fireworks to herald the coming new year are again cautioned to take extreme care with your choice of ornamental explosives. It will ruin your whole day to blow off a couple of fingers, or to set your shed on fire, and I will absolutely guarantee that the members of my department and the volunteers of the LCVFD will not be the least amused at having to cart you to the emergency room or douse the fire.

The Glamorous Chrystal Room – The Cattleman Hotel

Make that evening special with a champagne supper in the glamorous Chrystal Room! A gourmet five-course traditional French supper for two is available for a simple set price every Friday, Saturday and Sunday evenings from 6-9. Patrons will have a choice of either a beef or chicken main course, with a suitable appetizer, soup, fish course, salad and dessert. Make your reservation as soon as possible for the champagne supper special at the Chrystal Room!

The Ghost of Room 310

Richard was doing the rounds of the Crystal Room at breakfast. He had decided to follow Lew's example (but in the morning at breakfast), of drifting from table to table, and guest to guest, introducing himself to any new patrons, assuring himself that they were superlatively happy with their meals and service, and seeing, as he said (over and over) "if there was anything he could do to make their visit to the Cattleman Hotel and Luna City a continuing pleasure, sir or ma'am?"

The round on this particular morning was otherwise uneventful ... right up until he spoke to the family at Table 4, which overlooked the trees of Town Square, and the barely visible dome of the bandstand. A pleasant young man and his wife – some kind of techie from Austin, he was given to understand – with a baby boy in one of those rocking carriers, peacefully slumbering at the foot of the chair which contained his four-year-old sister, in a booster seat atop one of the ornate gold, glass and gold-brocade upholstered chairs. Richard was obscurely pleased to see that the child had a small spoon in her chubby fist and was applying herself diligently to herbed scrambled eggs, and toast pieces artfully cut into animal shapes and adorned with fresh-fruit jams. Most of the food was getting to where it was aimed at with the spoon – the little girl's bib and face were refreshingly free of jam.

Nothing like teaching the young of our species to appreciate good food from the earliest age!

"I'm glad to see that the children are enjoying their stay!" Richard remarked, belatedly remembering that the couple were Mr. Gerald and Mrs. Katherine Sebold, with Amy and Adam. They were staying in one of the family suites on the third floor – two bedrooms and a miniscule sitting room and in-suite bathroom, artfully crammed into a space originally taken up by a pair of single rooms when the Cattleman first opened before the turn of the century before. (*The second bedroom could be fitted out by Housekeeping with a youth bed or a crib, for a small additional charge upon making a reservation.*)

387

"Oh, yes," Gerald Sebold replied, around a mouthful of Pryor's finest breakfast sausage, with cheese biscuit on the side. "We especially appreciated the resident ghost baby-sitter last night."

"I beg your pardon?" Richard exclaimed, not entirely certain if he had heard that right. "I wasn't ... I didn't think... of course, we can provide you with reference for a local child-minder, if one is required ... but I didn't think that any of them are of a spectral nature,"

Gerald Sebold laughed. "No, just funning with you, Mr. Hall ... but it was the darndest thing. Kat and I, we are certain-sure that we dreamed it all. Adam woke up, fussing and whimpering at ... I dunno, two or three in the morning. Kat was about to get out of bed and go see to him, but we heard someone singing a baby lullaby. After a while he calmed down and went back to sleep. Must have been someone in the suite next door that we could hear through the walls."

"I suppose so," Richard replied. That seemed like a totally logical explanation, until small Amy tore herself away from her complete attention to her breakfast and announced,

"No, Daddy ... there was a lady there, singing to us. She was inna pretty purple dress all over lace. I saw her. She was nice."

"Kids, and their imaginations," Gerold replied, exchanging a conspiratorial glance with his wife, and then with Richard. "I used to think that a pirate with a peg-leg could come through the wall and take me on adventures. Sometimes, it was so real, I think that I could describe that ol' pirate, right down to his brace of pistols and his peg-leg."

"There <u>was</u> a lady, singing to us," Amy insisted, before devoting herself to her breakfast again. Richard exchanged an indulgent social smile with her parents and continued on his rounds through the Crystal Room.

On his way back to his office, he spoke to Bianca at the front desk.

"I wonder if we should add an additional charge to Room 310, for baby-sitting services? The guests say that a ghost came in and began singing to their children in the wee hours..."

"Oh, the Lacey Lady," Bianca replied, without turning a hair. "She shows up whenever there's a little one staying in that suite. I don't think she's visited in quite a while."

"Stone the crows," Richard stared at Bianca, utterly dumbfounded. "A ... a ... ghost, who sings to children?"

"Usually only babies," Bianca replied. "It's been a while since we booked a family with a baby into that suite. Usually, they don't handle it very well, when she makes an appearance in the middle of the night. I'm going to have to speak to whoever took their reservation and booked them into that suite without telling them about the Lacey Lady..." Bianca scowled, in a manner which meant no good for whoever had lucklessly assigned the Sebold family to that particular set of rooms.

"A ghost?" Richard was still dumbfounded. "'Strewth, back in England, we would charge extra for the visitation!"

Bianca regarded him with astounding tolerance. "Well, the Cattleman does host three regular spectral visitors. We've been a regular stop for ghosthunters since forever, but the Lacey Lady is eccentric, as hauntings go. Only <u>that</u> room, and <u>only</u> if there is a baby or a small child in it. That's probably why she made an appearance."

"Eccentric, indeed," Richard was still dumbfounded. "Hang on ... exactly how many ghosts do call this place their favorite haunt? I hope that none of them are fond of the kitchen. All that we need there is a violent poltergeist, what with all the knives and hot pans at hand..."

"Mainly three," Bianca allowed, with an indulgent smile. "They've been around for years. Didn't you read Katie's article in the *Talk of the Town* Blog? OK, so it was posted years ago. None of the ghosts haunt the kitchen, although Cowboy Bob hangs around the bar, rattling the glasses. The Lady in Black manifests on the second floor as a dark shadow at midnight, and Mavis the Maid only on the fourth, mostly as a directionless breeze blowing dust bunnies across the hall floor." Bianca assumed a most professorial air, as if briefing a guest regarding the otherworldly features of the Cattleman. "Cowboy Bob was murdered in the Cattleman stables after a not-so-friendly game of poker sometime around 1890."

"Sore looser?" Richard ventured, and Bianca nodded.

"Very sore. The story goes that Cowboy Bob cleaned out a pair of professional gamblers. They were not accustomed to losing to a hick from the sticks and took it very personally. When they were hung at Huntsville the next year, the crowd of spectators was standing room only. Mavis the Maid was murdered too – by a jealous boyfriend. I think he was caught and convicted as well, but I don't know if the hanging drew a good crowd. The Lady in Black supposedly killed herself with poison after being jilted by her lover. No one really knew for certain what her name was, or why her lover ditched the hot date. She appeared heavily veiled, and no one ever saw her without it ... or so the story goes."

"But the Lacey Lady..." Richard thought that he might steer the conversation back to the fourth resident spirit, the one with an affection for babies and small children. "What is the story with her? Murder or suicide?"

Bianca shook her beautifully coiffured head. "No one is entirely certain, Chef. She arrived, stayed for months sometime in the 1890s, hardly ever leaving her room, meals brought on a tray. The legend is that she was friends with the wife of the original owner. You remember – that rich Italian dude, who thought he could make Luna City into a fine spa resort in the European style? They say that the Lacy Lady came for her health, being pregnant and all. The baby was born, according to the story. Then the next morning, they found her in her bed, dead. They thought at the time she had some awful kind of seizure after the baby was delivered. Preeclampsia is what they call it these days. I'd guess that the Lacey Lady suffered from the same condition as what Jess Vaughn had with the twins before they were born. Ask Kate; she researched all the ghosts of the Cattleman for that article."

"That would explain the ghost being attracted by the presence of children," Richard observed, and then noted the time on the monumental and ornate lobby clock.

His days were metered out in fifteen-minute intervals. It was time to go oversee preparations for luncheon and for the mid-afternoon tea service. The matter of the ghost in Room 310 slipped his mind entirely, until the following Monday. Richard and his intended bride, Kate of the Karnesville Heisel clan, met every Monday evening for a quiet supper together at the caravan in the lumpy field at the Age of Aquarius Campground and Goat Farm which – at a squint – passed as a trailer campsite. Richard had lived there for five years and more.

It was too chilly after the sun set to sit under the little pavilion and watch the stars come out. He and Kate had withdrawn to the tiny Airstream, where it was cozy and warm. Kate savored another glass of the peerless mustang grape elixir produced by Richard's landlord, Sefton Grant, while Richard fussed over the tiny cooker. He loved cooking, loved cooking for Kate, as they shared accounts of their week.

"Meant to ask you," Richard turned the sole filets browning in butter, and lifted the lid over the velvety sauce meant to envelope the finished dish. "One of the guests told me that their kids were visited by the Lacey Lady ghost. Bianca told me that the Lacey Lady is the shyest ghostly emanation of all the Cattleman haunts. I meant to ask more, but I had to get back to the kitchen. She said that you knew all about the ghosts, having written them up for your newspaper blog."

"Oh, yes – the Lacey Lady," Kate held out her wineglass for a top-up with one hand, while administering a good skritch to Ozzie, lounging in her lap. "Gosh, it's been forever since she manifested. Sad story, actually. My sources always thought she was looking for her baby."

"A baby?" Richard exclaimed. "What does a baby have to do with a haunting? Other than apparently the presence of an infant brings out the ghostly mother instinct. Did she kill the sprog herself, and now is sentenced to look for it, throughout eternity?"

Kate shuddered. "I know. An awful thought. But there <u>was</u> a baby and then the baby was nowhere to be found. She was pregnant, the story goes and gave birth in her room at the Cattleman. That much is confirmed by hotel records. The local doctor paid a visit and put in a bill for having attended on a live birth to a woman guest at the Cattleman. Second of November, 1896. One of the expert ghost hunters I talked to was certain that Lacey Lady killed her baby and hid the body somewhere in the hotel. I can't buy that, knowing how much of the fabric was torn down to the studs in the renovations. Cousin Roman's crew would have found the bones, for sure."

"She might have hidden the baby's body elsewhere," Richard suggested. The sole filets were nearly done. He lowered the heat of the burner and gave the sauce another stir. Kate shook her head.

"After hearing what 'Celi and Jess have had to say after giving birth. I can't see any normal woman going any farther than the next room, let alone leaving the hotel and dumping the baby somewhere else. It's that draining. Even back then, the Cattleman was a busy place. A woman staggering out of a third-floor room with a baby in her arms on a winter night would have excited interest and comment." Kate's left hand gave Ozzie one last loving head-skritch. "Oh, now you have got me wondering, lover. What did happen with the baby? Now I'm not going to stop wondering until I find out!"

"Save it for Friday at the VFW guest night?" Richard suggested. He knew very well that the light of his life was single-minded in pursuit of answers, once her curiosity was aroused. Kate's mother always insisted that her first intelligible word was not "Mama", but "Why?" Richard could well believe it. Inspector Javert was a lazy slug, compared to his dearest Kate, when she was hot on the trail of a story. "Miss Letty will be there, and if anyone knows where a body is buried in Luna City, she would be the one."

"A bit before her time," Kate admitted judiciously. "But Miss Letty's father and mother both lived here for all of their lives, and they would have been around at the time. They might have passed on a story like that to her. And her brother Douglas wrote the definitive history of Luna City. I'll ask her, then."

"Good," Richard turned off the gas burner, and began plating the sole. "In other important news, Kate of my Heart, supper is ready."

That Friday, at the VFW's regular Guest Night, Kate broached the matter to Miss Letty, after Richard explained about the ghost of the Lacey Lady manifesting herself to a pair of small children. Miss Letty, whose personal memories of Luna City went back to the 1920s, regarded the pair with a degree of mild surprise.

"What I really need to know, Miss Letty," Kate explained, "Is that happened to the baby? The Lacey Lady's baby, who totally vanishes from all records."

"No, not all records," Miss Letty replied, with perfect equanimity. "The baby was named Emily Violet. She grew up on a little ranch near Nixon and married an oilman from Houston … oh, in about 1922. Mother was one of her bridesmaids, as they were the best of friends,"

Richard was boggled. "You mean to tell us that the mysteriously vanishing baby who was born to a mysterious hotel guest in … what was it, Kate – 1896 – who subsequently shuffled off this mortal coil and joined the choir invisible, becoming the famous Ghost of Room 310 … that baby grew up, lived a normal life and married? Just like that?"

"Well, of course," Miss Letty sipped her own drink – a soft drink and set the bottle down with a click on the tabletop. "But it was a slightly more complicated story than was let on at the time. It was a different era, and mores were very … complicated than they are now. Or perhaps less complicated. But the circumstances of Emily Violet's birth were difficult. Scandalous, even; her adoptive parents wished to spare her any taint. Children can be very cruel, as I have good reason to know. To become the object of gossip in a small town can be incredibly hurtful. Emily Violet's mother and father of record engaged in some mild subterfuge. They did not consciously tell any lies; they merely encouraged anyone who took an interest into the matter to assume a certain predestined conclusion."

"I fail to follow," Richard felt as if his head would ache.

"I'm not certain that I follow, either," Kate added. "And I'd like to know how you know the whole story, since no one else seemed to have a clue."

"Mother told me," Miss Letty replied. "Years later, when I was about to head off to college. I was just barely eighteen, myself, and going to the women's college in Denton. Mother meant it as a cautionary tale, I think. There would be temptations, and Mother feared for me. Men, you know."

Richard tried to imagine Miss Letty as an 18-year-old, tempted by any earthly sin other than an illicit sarsaparilla at the soda fountain in company with a callow youth of unsuitable background, and failed utterly.

"Denton," Kate remarked with a sigh. "Hardly the Sodom and Gomorrah of Texas. Even then, hardly a den of vice."

"Mother thought I should be fully aware of the temptations that I might face, and the tragedies that might result from yielding to them," Miss Letty replied, austere as a Mother Superior. "After she made me promise never to breathe a word to anyone who might know Emily Violet's family."

"So, what was the story?" Kate persisted, and Miss Letty looked pensive. Richard thought again that the senior Mrs. McAllister sounded like one of the most censorious old prudes that the 19th century had ever produced.

"It was all so long ago; I suppose that it is safe to tell it now. Times have changed so much. The woman who gave birth to Emily Violet was not married to the father. Her name was Violette De – De something or other. French, I think. Married to a much older man – but having an affair ... from which she became pregnant. Apparently, the scandal was horrific. You would have thought that being French, they would have been more willing to turn a blind eye, even then. But Violette was sent away for the duration of the pregnancy, under strict orders to consign the child to an orphanage, once born."

"As far as Texas?" Richard wondered if he should have another drink. This sounded as if it would be a long story and Kate would want to hear every single detail and word. "Surely that was a little unusual. Weren't there discreet sanatoriums in Switzerland or someplace where she could go hide her shame for nine months?"

"Probably," Miss Letty agreed. "But Violette de-something-or-other was a dear friend of the wife of the man who founded the Cattleman. Upon hearing of her difficulty, they offered her sanctuary. Only then it was called the Grand Palazzo Vittoria. Signore di Barreca had dreams of Luna City being a spa destination to rival anything in the old world. But that is neither here, nor there. Violette de-something-or-other arrived with her personal maid and was settled into one of the better rooms on the third floor. I should imagine it was terribly boring and lonely for the poor woman. The maid was an older woman, a most dreadful gorgon, who really served more as a jailer – no friendship here, I fear! Being under a dark cloud of disgrace, Violette had but one friend in all of town. She couldn't even come downstairs and patronize the restaurant; all her meals were brought to her on a tray. As it happened on most days, the same waitress brought her meal tray. They struck up a conversation which very soon turned into friendship. The waitress was a local girl. Eva Eilerson. Her father was a small rancher with a place near Beeville. Eva's older sister Trudy had married a young doctor with a local practice in Karnesville for a time. Dr. March. I don't recall much about him. He wasn't our family doctor, you see. But he and Trudy March lived closer to Luna City than Beeville, and Eva came to live with them. Being bored with country life, she was allowed to live with her sister and work at the hotel. Girls did want to see a little bit of life, even in those days."

Richard considered several comments on that observation, considered them all, and then responded with the mildest. Sarcasm was not appreciated by Miss Letty, especially when she was waxing historical. As a matter of professional interest in the history of the place where he worked, Richard did want to hear the full story.

"I'm sure they did, Miss Letty. My Gran has had some wild tales about what she and her chums got up to as Land Girls during the Big War. What did Miss Eilerson have to say regarding Violetta de-whatever, the Ghost of the Grand Palazzo?"

"She was very lonely in isolation," Miss Letty was austere, but sympathetic. "Heartbroken over how her husband had rejected the baby, how her family refused to aid her in any meaningful manner. Abandoned, really – and in a time of great emotional need. But she wanted to see her baby placed in a good situation. It soon came about that Eva Eilerson provided the poor woman with the promise of a loving home with her sister Trudy and Dr. Marsh. The Marshes wished deeply for a child, and it seemed at first that they were not able to have one of their own, naturally. Once the notion of adopting Violette di-whatever's child of shame was suggested to them, they embraced the notion heartily. To the point where they embarked on a program of subterfuge. They did not wish that a stigma should later be attached to the child. Being resident in a small town, they were certain that ... well, gossip would fly on wings, regarding an adoption. Gossip which would be hurtful to a child, you see. Their neighbors and their children would never let the matter die, which would render schooldays very difficult for a child."

"So, what did they do, then?" Richard broadly hinted, as Miss Letty seemed lost in thought.

"They did not engage in outright falsehood. The Eilerson girls were had been very strictly brought up in a Methodist household. And Doctor Marsh was a doctor. His personal probity must remain without a shadow or blemish. Because his patients must trust him, you see. Trudy Marsh merely began to pad her abdomen with increasing quantities of stuffing underneath her clothing, allowing everyone to assume a certain happy conclusion. It was ... quite astonishing," Miss Letty added, "...How merely smiling and appearing to agree with happy congratulations on at last being in the family way served the purpose, without the necessity of ever voicing an untruth. It all went perfectly, according to plan. The infant was safely delivered one evening by Dr. Marsh and given into the care of Eve Eilerson; bundled into a basket, apparently full of soiled towels and carried away to the Marsh home. Her natural mother only asked that she be given the name of Violet, and when she was old enough, be given a silver locket in the shape of a heart, with a tiny picture of her mother inside. Dr. Marsh and Trudy agreed. As planned, they announced the safe delivery of their child to their friends and relations the very next morning."

"But what about Violette de-whatever?" Richard asked. "Didn't Dr. Marsh stick around, if he thought there might be complications, after the birth?"

"I'm certain he did," Miss Letty replied warmly. "I had never heard that he was anything but conscientious in the care of his patients. I suppose that Violette was most exhausted, following delivery. She would have wished to sleep and rest, after bidding a loving farewell to her little daughter. She did have her dreadful maid to attend on her, after all. But several hours later, she experienced a dreadful kind of fit – and died of it before her awful dragon of a maid could even send for Dr. Marsh ... so very sad.

Within a few years, there were stories of an apparition of a woman in a lace-trimmed dress, appearing in that very room. No one ever connected that apparition to Emily Violet Marsh, the doctor's little daughter. Besides the Marshes and Eve Eilerson, only the gorgon of a maid knew of the connection at all – and she soon returned to France. However, when Emily Violet was eighteen or so, she became curious, wondering why she didn't look anything like her parents, or their kin. Being painfully honest folk, they confessed the whole story, and gave her the locket and picture. Since Emily Violet was quite dreadfully shaken by hearing the truth, she told her best friend, my mother, after swearing her to confidence."

"And she told you – years later," Kate noted. "Well, that answers my question – about the baby. At least, that has something of a happy ending."

Miss Letty nodded, in sober agreement. "The Marshes were ecstatic upon have their prayers for a child answered, even in such a curious manner. And they went on to have two more children. Two little boys, after Emily Violet. It was so very curious, how that worked out. I'm told that it is often the case. But Emily was deeply loved by Dr. Marsh and his wife. My mother said that she was always beautifully-dressed and had everything she ever wanted. Mother and Emily Violet wrote to each other for years, after Emily Violet moved to Houston with her husband. It was almost as if a higher power was trying to make it up for the tragic fate of her birth mother. Our Lord does work his miracles in the most mysterious ways, you see."

Invitation to the Wedding

Mr. And Mrs. Frederick Heisel
request the honor of your presence
at the marriage of their daughter
Katherine Carolina Heisel
to
Mr. Richard Astor-Hall
son of
Mr. and Mrs. Alfred Astor-Hall
Sunday, the sixteenth of February

two thousand twenty
at six o'clock
At Shepherd of Galilee Lutheran Church

Karnesville, Texas

Reception to be held following the Ceremony

at The Cattleman Hotel

On Town Square, luna City

RSVP

Famous

"I thought you should know, *cher*," remarked Richard's boss, Lew Dubois, the C-suite level manager who had become at least a much of a friend over the years of their acquaintance, "That Anne's good friend – you will recollect Madame Creighton Doyle, who writes the novels most romantic and amusing? Her newest novel is to be launched upon her millions of breathlessly waiting fans tonight. Alas, the formal party sponsored by her publisher will be in New York, and not here."

"Oh, the best-seller. Yes, I recall – and I honestly I can't say that I mind in the least," Richard replied. When he cast his mind back to the previous year, he remembered briefly encountering Trish Creighton

Doyle on several occasions. She was a woman of certain years, given to wearing flowing, chiffon-laden garments. The customary dreamy expression on her countenance suggested that her mind was most usually occupied somewhere other than the here and now – unimaginably far, far from the mundane here and now. "We are simply full up with guests at the moment! Even with forewarning…"

"This is in the nature of a forewarning," Lew replied. "But not as it concerns the Cattleman or the Crystal Room, but rather some of our dear friends. First, I am nearly certain that many of Madame Doyle's readers will fall upon her latest like famished wolves on a tasty piece of filet mignon … and decide that they simply must see for themselves the enchanted circle of stones … that real circle which was made so many years ago. Madame Doyle has put the pictures which she took of the pagan monument on her website as part of the advance publicity…"

It was mid-morning at the Cattleman Hotel, the hour when Richard and Lew could both be found in Lew's office, confabulating over what to expect in the near future, about any foreseen and unforeseen events affecting management of the ornate boutique hotel which had dominated the western side of Town Square for more than a century.

"The stone circle at the Age of Aquarius? 'Strewth – I had better warn the Grants," Richard considered the prospect with a shudder of horror. "It was bad enough the last time that they were mobbed by visitors; treasure-seekers, ghost-hunters and UFOlogists all converged on the place a couple of years ago. It was a mob scene, culminating in a riot, and then in their old place burning to the ground, although the all-hands brawl had nothing to do with the fire. I couldn't get a decent nights' sleep for weeks. At least this time, they have a pleasanter place to live in… and Judy will be thrilled no end, having oodles of imaginative visitors to listen to her tales of New Age this and that…"

"Oh, most definitely, my friend," Lew agreed. "Tell M'sieu and Madame Grant to expect any number of visitors to their magnificent stone circle…"

"Which, alas, looks much more impressive with the aid of artful photography and the cooperation of nature," Richard replied. "The marker stones aren't anything like Stonehenge or Avebury, being about a quarter the size. I'm afraid the baying fans will be quite disappointed…"

"But not in another aspect," Lew was fiddling with his computer, and the printer across the room whirred and clanked into life. "My wife has sent me a copy of the news release regarding Madame Doyle's book … the cover was embargoed until the very last minute…"

"So, the Grants will get a boost in visitors to the Age," Richard mused, as Lew collected a sheet of paper from the printer tray. "And likely the good Colonel Walcott's reenactor group … I do recollect that the Doyle woman was taking pictures of their encampment and costumed reenactors at the 4th of July celebration in the square … what is the plot of the book? I know someone told me once, but I can't recall. Something about a woman going through the stone circle and traveling into the past…"

Lew nodded in grim agreement. "A woman of the most modern American times … and discovering fulfillment and love in the arms of a fearless Comanche warrior chieftain of almost two hundred years in the past…"

Richard snorted with rude laughter as Lew handed him the paper. "According to some of the stories I've heard from the reenactors, that would have been about the last … oh, f**k me running! Has Joe Vaughn laid eyes on this… this … Oh, my god. He will absolutely lose his mind when he sees this, let alone what Jess will think…"

"I suspect that Madame Vaughn will be amused," Lew observed. "To discover that her husband has been made into the bare-chested hero on the cover of a best-selling romance…"

"Joe will die of embarrassment," Richard replied. "And he will most definitely do gross bodily harm to the first person who ventures a jesting remark…My god, I suppose I shall have to tell him. I can only hope that he will not reach out and slaughter me, once I show him this abomination!"

"You will be most tactful, revealing this information, of course," Lew appeared to have been relieved of a dangerous burden. Someone else would take on the fraught chore of telling Joe Vaughn that a casual picture of him, snapped as he came from a turn in the civic dunk tank the last 4th of July and briefly embraced and kissed Jess, had been utterly transformed by a cover artist … transformed every possible detail save Joe's clearly recognizable dark, hawklike countenance. He was recognizably on the cover as a bare-chested, dark haired Comanche warrior embracing a slender woman with flowing hair and a diaphanous drape of some kind. Now Richard recalled Araceli's description of Trish Creighton-Doyle's output – always the studly romantic hero, embracing a woman clad in something flowy … only the period details and setting distinguished one of the Creighton-Doyle oeuvre from another. Lew appeared to have handed off that dangerous assignment to Richard – a case of discretion being the better part of valor.

"Lew, I will be the very soul of diplomacy," Richard assured his boss, while taking a good long look at the full-sheet picture of the book cover.

A Time-shattering Romance, from the best-selling author of *Those Bolyn Girls.*

Richard's heart sank, right down to the level of his kitchen clogs. For a long moment, he wished that he could hand this off to his redoubtable Aunt Moira, a woman who was unaccountably adept with blades, small arms, and the physical martial arts, ostensibly a traveling international journalist but most likely an operative for a secretive governmental agency designated M-something-or-other. But there was no hope for it; it was a Friday. This was the day when the VFW was open to non-member guests. The little reconverted classroom under the trees in back of the Tip-Top Gas & Grocery was the acknowledged male hangout in Luna City, where military service over the generations had left a solid geographic layer underlaying all. That and the volunteer Fire Department – Richard had done his bit loyally for the VFD, and made it a practice to appear at least briefly at VFW guest night, as part of cementing his credentials as a stalwart citizen of Luna City. And Lew was no slave-driver; Lew, in fact, insisted that his employees should live a balanced life – leave room and space for things like … a few moments frivolously spent at the local pub. Which in Luna City meant a Friday early evening at the VFW. That hour approached … gradually, but inexorably, like a long, slow, heavy-laden freight train, rumbling over the tracks near the Heisel's family home in Karnesville.

(Tracks which avoided Luna City, due to a monumental fit of pique on the part of Doc Wyler's grandfather. Toweringly angry over how his cherished yet flirtatious daughter Bessie had eloped with a handsome train engineer employed by the San Antonio & Aransas Pass railroad, Captain (late CSA) Herbert Kling Wyler had personally and vengefully seen to scuttling plans for the SA&AP to route their line through Luna City. H.K Wyler was a man of considerable riches and even more considerable capacity for holding grudges. The planned railway avoided Luna City as if the location originally planned to be the county seat and health resort had suddenly developed an incurable and embarrassing social disease.)

Guest night at the VFW would be the best time to encounter Joe Vaughn and break the news to him gently ... unless Richard could acquaint some other mutual friend with the intelligence about Joe's potential fame as an object of sexual worship by the masses of romance-reading fans.

Richard's spirits rose, almost immediately upon reception of this flash of inspiration. Of course – inveigle someone else into handing the radioactive intelligence! Telling Joe Vaughn that he was now spread across the front cover of a best-selling novel! Just the ticket! Practically everyone in Luna City had known Joe Vaughn longer than he had, and almost every one of those came to a place where he could encounter them ... Town Square! The Café! Sometime during this remainder of the day, he could find and hand off this task to one of them!

Richard's spirits revived, almost at once – yes, that was the ready solution. His position as senior chef-manager of the Crystal Room was such that he might absent himself from kitchen for brief periods of time without exciting comment, or allowing the high level of service expected of Venue Properties to collapse a single degree. It was now time for lunch service, and his expected round of the Crystal Room, assessing various patrons as to their degree of satisfaction with their meal, and that conditions generally were up to standard. No one would remark on it, if he drifted out of the lobby, through the main doors and into the Square ... and perhaps in the direction of the Café.

He still felt a few pangs of mild desolation that the Café was no longer his turf – that he was not the absolute master and commander. The working minions there no longer felt obliged to quail and quiver at his every slight frown, or run for cover behind performing some absolutely essential bit of kitchen prep. Café operations had been turned over to the firm management hands of Araceli, and the crew of kitchen staff that he had trained. Or, in the case of Luc Massie, one whose recruitment to the force he had approved.

Still, it would feel very odd, to approach the Café as ... an outsider. A guest.

As he stepped out of the monumental double front doors of the Cattleman, he spotted a single Luna City Police Department SUV drawn into a nearby nose-in parking slot, and his spirits rose! There! His escape route! That was Sgt. Milo Grigoryev, just getting out to speak to a couple of guests at the Cattleman – apparently, they had mistaken a no-parking zone underneath the cedar tree at the edge of Town Square park as a legitimate place to situate their enormous RV. Milo Grigoryev apparently was enlightening them on that score, in a mild and helpful manner. Richard waited patiently for that enlightenment to be completed. Things were done politely in Texas, or at least in Luna City. There was no need to escalate.

It looked as if this encounter between out-of-state visitors and local law enforcement was being concluded on a mutually cordial basis. The driver of the RV got back into his gargantuan vehicle, and it lumbered slowly away. Richard hurried across the street to buttonhole Milo Grigoryev before he could make a similar exit.

"Milo!" he gasped, as Joe's right-hand man pocketed his citation book and opened the door of his PD vehicle. "I'm so happy to see you! Look, there's this situation … a dire situation! Regarding Chief Vaughn and this wretched woman's book! She's making it out that Joe is this … this romantic god, and …"

"Sounds like a nice problem to have!" Milo chuckled. "And I'm sure Jess would agree … good old Jessie Four-Eyes, we used to call her back then. Don't forget, Chef – we all go back a long way! Course, it was the 4th grade. By the time we got to high school, all the girls were mad for Joe the football god…"

Before Richard could protest, the dashboard radio spat out one of those cryptic radio short-hand near-to-impossible-for-a-layperson to understand. Richard didn't – although he had become fairly fluent in official radioese, through participating in regular training sessions at the Luna City Volunteer Fire Department.

Milo, an abstracted expression on his face and his attention very obviously elsewhere waved him off, saying, "Sorry, Richard – save it for later, OK? Gotta run, crime is waving…"

And he closed the patrol vehicle door with a definite-sounding slam, and made what Richard termed an utterly cowardly escape, obviously fleeing personal responsibility.

Well never mind, Richard told himself. *There were others.* He would search them out, remorselessly – and hand off the responsibility of giving Joe the bad news…

He set his footsteps on the path towards the Café, knowing that the hour was propitious; after the breakfast rush, and in the slack time before preparing for lunch. And it might be that some of the regulars who liked an early lunch might be also approachable … like yes! Jess Abernathy-Vaughn, appearing regularly to consult with Araceli on the Café's financial doings, on behalf of the titular owners. Even now, he could see Jess with Araceli and one of the outdoor tables – with a massive stroller parked next to that table. The stroller was a three-seater, all the better to accommodate the Abernathy-Vaughn offspring: toddler-aged Joe Junior, and the twin infant girls, Alice and Lizzie. Richard hoped that the girls were sleeping, and that Small Joe was in one of his more tractable moods. The time was perfect to approach Jess –*Who better than Joe's wife and mother of his children to tell him that he was about to make an even bigger media splash than Romeo Gonzales, the handsome convict, made so flamboyantly famous through the internet that he found a whole new career as a male model from it.*

Richard crossed the street, picking up his pace – obscurely pleased that he was not puffing and out of breath. Routinely pedaling a bicycle to and from work over the last five years had definitely paid off; he was in the best physical shape of his life, all without having to pay a mint to a gym and a personal trainer.

411

"Jess! I was hoping to catch up to you!" He exclaimed. "Look, there's something that I have to tell you…"

"Richard!" Jess's expression warred between pleasure and mild dismay. "Look – glad to see you, happy that you're landed in a good place with running the Cattleman restaurant! If I wasn't an independent contractor, I'd love working for a guy like Lew Dubois … which every corporate boss was a boss like him!"

"It's about Joe…" Richard was deflated, observing that Jess was packing up her briefcase, stowing the spread of papers and files into her enormous work briefcase. Obviously her work here was done for the moment – and he had better take the bull by the horns, in a manner of speaking.

"Can it wait, Rich?" Jess's attention was obviously elsewhere. "Sorry – the girls have an appointment with their pediatrician; the practice is in Karnesville and I'm already running late. Shoot me a text or something, if it's urgent. Promise I'll get back to you, but I really have to run, now."

"Of course I understand," Richard replied, not entirely disheartened. He still had the rest of the afternoon – and he still had a chance of handing this off to Araceli, who also had known Joe since primary school.

But softy, softly … faint heart, fair lady. Araceli was a Gonzales/Gonzalez and as shrewd as any woman of her clan, plus knowing him very well after five years of close association, working at the Café. Richard cleared his throat, upon deciding that a frontal approach was best.

"Look, Araceli – there's been this … this thing which Lew just brought to my attention. About Joe … and that silly woman writer – you remember that gal-pal of Lew and Anne's who stayed here doing research on her novel …"

"Trish Creighton-Doyle," Aracely nodded, "Yes, I remember. Our book club read one of hers, a couple months back. She has a new release out, hasn't she?"

"She does," Richard breathed an interior sigh of relief. "Matter of fact – Lew tipped me the intelligence that the cover was to be released tonight … and there might be a wee small problem. You remember how she was hanging around taking pictures of features and people in Luna City … Katie did an interview with her, and she told Katie that she likes to use those pictures … well, anyway, she took a picture of Joe. And it turns out … well, this should explain it. The cover of her new release. Anyone on it look familiar to you?"

Richard took the folded printout out of the pocket of his chef's coat and passed it to Araceli. A whole series of expressions passed over her face; puzzlement, doubt, disbelief and finally hilarity.

"Oh, my," she finally replied. "This will … Joe will be … oh my god, I hope that he never meets up with Trish Creighton-Doyle again. She had better not ever come back to Luna City, once that he gets a load of this. Or Clovis Walcott and his gang of reenactors. Even Georg Stein might go all Teutonic on her ass, since he is one of the local authorities on Comanche tribal life."

"So … do you want to be the one to break this to Joe?" Richard breathed – yes, the trap was set. All he need do now was spring it, hand the fatal printout to Araceli, once she agreed. "He'll be at the VFW

413

tonight, when he's done with work. I think he will be in a mellower mood, once he has had a beer or two. And it might go better from an old friend like yourself. Better than me, anyway…" It didn't seem quite cricket to hand it off to her, knowing that Joe would likely erupt in a volcanic rage … but better a woman who had known Joe since primary school days. Practically anyone else than himself would better be able to calculate the rage-splatter range.

And to his absolute horror, Araceli shook her head.

"I can't do it, Ricardo – I'm stuck here until six, and then I absolutely have to make a showing at a parent-teacher school conference tonight. Matty is floundering at fifth-grade math, and Pat and I arranged this appointment days ago. Either you'll have to give the bad news to Joe …"

"Or palm it off on some other berk," Richard sighed. "One with mad self-defense skills, because I'm afraid Joe will go absolutely bonkers, once he sees this wretched cover."

"Another vet?" Araceli's expression brightened. "Cousin Sylvester! Just the one – and he's here in the Café now! He stopped by to grab some lunch and take some pictures of the new product line for the website he's building for us…"

"Strewth!" Richard marveled, momentarily diverted. "You've set up a website?"

"We had to," Araceli replied. "For the Café-made line of gourmet foods. They've gotten to be very popular – customers want them through mail-order, and don't mind paying the postage. So we commissioned Sylvester to build us a nice little commercial website. We might also branch out," Araceli added, "And offer meal delivery –

local only, of course. People around here adore Café-cooked meals, so why not?"

"Sounds like..." Richard gulped and dredged up a sincere compliment from the very bottom of his professional soul. "You're really making a go of this, Araceli ... I knew that you would, honestly I did. I thought you were the best bit of front house managerial talent I had encountered in years of working in this mad business, but you've been outpacing those expectations."

"I do what I can," Araceli seemed honestly touched. "And I'm sorry that I can't possibly help you with the Joe thing. Maybe Sylvester can. At least," she added fairly, "If Joe tries to hit him, I'm certain that Sylvester can hold his own. Go on in," she encouraged him. "He should be done with the photo shoot. Catch five minutes with him before he goes."

7 Minutes later

"I can't do it, Ricardo – I would, but I can't tonight. Got an important client in Floresville, installing a system for his office, after his employees go home for the day. It's probably gonna be an all-nighter and training over the weekend, so his office staff can pick up work on Monday. I can't re-schedule, not even to do you a favor."

"Damn," Richard said with feeling. He had rather counted on Sylvester's fine-honed survival skills. But a job was a job, a paying client was a paying client, especially for Sylvester's small information technology business. "Well ... I suppose there'll be others at the V tonight, being guest night and all."

"Strength in numbers, Ricardo," Sylvester offered that crumb of comfort. "I don't think he'd lash out at the bearer of bad tidings in front of witnesses. Well, I hope that he wouldn't! Good luck, anyway."

"Thanks," Richard took little comfort from that reassurance. His last and final hope was that someone at the V tonight would take on the chore. He had been away from the hotel and his duties there for long enough. Unless a suitable candidate for passing the bad news on to Joe presented him or herself at the Cattleman sometime during the afternoon, Richard was doomed.

With a heavy heart and even heavier footsteps, Richard headed out the back of the Cattleman, late that afternoon. He tossed the day's worn and crumpled chef's coat into the wheeled bin for hotel laundry that was parked just inside the staff entrance at the back of the Cattleman and let the heavy door fall closed behind him. His bicycle leaned against the brick wall. No hope for it. The folded print-out crinkled softly in the pocket of his jacket. He wheeled his bicycle out into the service drive and made his way slowly towards the old, pink-painted repurposed classroom which currently housed the VFW. This was a building which had for thirty years served as a temporary facility at the high school, until a permanent addition to the main structure was completed. Now it sat in a grove of tall sycamore trees on the bank of the San Antonio River, out in back of the Tip-Top Icehouse, Gas and Grocery.

Recalling that circumstance raised Richard's spirits somewhat. Chris Mayall, the manager of the Tip-Top was another military veteran, and guaranteed to be present at guest night, since he usually tended bar. And even if the presence of Chris and the rest didn't entirely dissuade

Joe from unleashing violence – Chris was also a trained and experienced emergency medic. If it came to violence, Chris was one well-equipped to handle the aftermath.

Still – Richard hoped devoutly that if it couldn't be avoided, would a merciful deity ensure that it didn't hurt too much, or leave any visible half-healed wounds or scars on his person – scars which wouldn't look good in his and Kate Heisel's wedding pictures…

He came by the well-trodden footpath to the VFW – a short-cut through the empty tracts at the edge of Luna City, avoiding what little traffic there was on the two side roads off Route 123 which led into town. It was entirely possible for travelers on that route to drive past and see nothing more than the Tip-Top, and the old McAllister house opposite. Curious motorists might pause to read the historical marker by the edge of the road in front of the McAllister house, and then drive on, never guessing that Luna City lay beyond the fringe of trees, fields and the distant sprawling roofs of those sheds which housed Gonzales Auto Repair.

It looked as if there was a good crowd gathered already, to judge from the various automobiles and pick-up trucks scattered haphazardly in the cleared and sparsely-graveled space around in back of the Tip-Top. Richard took a deep breath, skidded his bicycle to a halt at the nearest door, and left it leaning against one of the battered picnic tables which adorned the riverside aspect of the VFW.

His doom awaited. He opened the door and strode in, radiating superficial confidence, that stagy actor confidence that had served him so well in his days of being a celebrity chef – a confidence only dented invisibly when he saw that Joe Vaugn was already there, seated at a table, with a scattering of other guests and veterans, including Sylvester Gonzalez, Chris Mayall and Benny Cordova, the manager of Mills Farm.

"Joe!" Richard exclaimed, inwardly feeling that he had to lay on the enthusiasm as thickly as stage makeup on Marcel Marceau. "I've got something that I need to tell you about…"

"Later, dude," Joe replied. "Lemme finish my story …it was the damndest thing, guys – I shit you not! Here I was, by the side of the road about half a mile from the dirt road to the age, writing out a speeding ticket for a car full of forty-something gals – and they weren't bad-looking at all, they had obviously been taking good care of themselves…"

"Or their husbands had," Remarked Benny Cordova, who was long divorced from a serial bride with half a dozen scalps and alimony payments to her credit. Joe waved that comment aside.

"Look, they were OK-looking gals, and the thing was – they all giggled a lot and every one of them asked for my autograph! The driver – she blew me a kiss, and I swear to God, fellows – she folded up that ticket and stuck it inside of her bra!" Joe shook his head, and repeated. "The damndest thing. If I weren't a happily married man, and this wasn't a line-of-duty thing, I might have had the most incredible Friday night that you can imagine…"

"There's a reason for that…" Richard ventured, carefully taking out the folded printout from his jacket pocket. "It seems that you have become famous…"

"Oh, that book cover?" Joe seemed to be refreshingly unsurprised. "For Creighton-Doyle's flight of improbable fancy? I knew about that months ago – the cover artist got in touch, asked for a signed release. I had a good laugh. I thought I'd surprise Jess with it, once the thing was released. You haven't spoiled it for me, have you?"

"No," Richard answered, as he crossed his fingers behind his back.

The Enchanted Circle

Visit the Enchanted Stone Circle!

Now Open Daily
From 8 AM to Sundown

At The Age of Aquarius Campground & Goat Farm

Texas Route 123, 2.5 miles south of Luna City

The enchanted stone circle is a faithful copy of the prehistoric Drombeg stone circle! This replica, constructed in the 19th century is the very location made famous in Trish Creighton Doyle's best-selling new historical romance novel;

Sweet Savage Love!
Travel back in time!
Share the mystic adventure!

Those Wedding Gown Blues

"I don't know about you," Kate confessed one Monday evening, "But my mother is driving me mad over this wedding. I'm thinking more and more that we ought to do what Joe and Jess did – run away to San Antonio and get married at the Bexar County Courthouse and avoid all the trouble and fuss."

"Fie upon you, my darling, for even considering such a heretical notion," Richard replied. "This matter has gone too far. Our families have invested too much – in time and airline tickets, if nothing else. We simply cannot back out now. All we can do is gird up our loins and power through. The date has already been set, my sweet."

On Mondays, the *Karnesville Weekly Beacon* went to print, and Kate had long been in the habit of driving back from the commercial printing facility in San Antonio, once the weekly issue had been put to bed; taking a break from the newsgathering machinery by partaking in a custom-created classic French meal prepared by Richard. Although Richard was now the head chef at the Cattleman Hotel's glorious Crystal Room, he had exercised his managerial prerogative by declaring that Monday evening was his day off. He continued the pleasant custom of a regular date night at the Airstream with his beloved – his female beloved, of course, although Ozymandius, King of Kings was usually present and loopy in a catnip haze, but ever-ready for affectionate skritches and a cuddle with Kate.

"It has," Kate sighed. "Mom and Dad's church; Shepherd of Galilee Lutheran in Karnesville. Mom's been in the altar guild forever. She is already drawing up the lists of guests to be invited. She wants the names of your family and friends to be added, by the way. And we need to set a time for a talk with Pastor Lunberg – you know, for premarital counseling."

"Strewth," Richard replied, after a moment of thought. "Aside from my parents and Aunt Moira, all of the guests are our mutual friends. Most of them are probably on your mother's list of your friends already. Premarital counseling ... do you think you are marrying a total barbarian and hope to dissuade you from the prospect?"

"No," Kate replied, and held out her wine glass for a revivifying refill. "Just that you aren't a Lutheran and aren't someone who went to catechism classes with me and were properly confirmed in a proper church. Pastor L is a real sweetie. He just wants to assure himself that I am marrying someone worthy. Or at least, not a purple-haired freak with facial piercings and outrageous sexual tastes ..."

"No, that would be Luc, at the Café." Richard topped up her glass. Kate sipped from it and leaned her head back against the banquette cushions.

"It's all so dreadfully complicated," she lamented. "When did getting married have to be such a production number? We aren't rich! We aren't royalty – was it written into the laws someplace that we have to spend a bomb on a single day! I swear, every vendor Mom has spoken with hears the word "wedding" and immediately writes out an invoice for ten times the estimated cost of services! I mean – I would like a special day to celebrate with our friends – I don't want to be charged something like the national budget!"

"It's all to be expected, oh my best-beloved," Richard set the gallon jug of Sefton Grant's best white mustang grape elixir on the tiny countertop, where it would be handy. Kate's nerves were inexplicably worn to shreds over the prospective wedding, although he previously would have been prepared to swear an oath that she was fairly bomb-proof in the nerve department. "You and your dear mother need only concern yourself with the ceremony itself. I am handling the reception. My friends who have been married – and some of them remain married to this day – all assured me that it was planning the reception which precipitated so much agony! Sit-down or cocktail party with generous nibbles? Chicken or beef, or vegan abominations? Country club or hotel? Live orchestra or disc jockey? And would the best man fatally embarrass the wedding party, or at least, humiliate the bride ... and the groom. I have it all in hand – and Lew Dubois promises me that it will be every bit as splendid as was the Wyler wedding bash ... My sweet Kate, if I top up your glass again, you will be in no condition to appreciate fish quenelles with mantua sauce. What is really troubling you about this wedding ... not the prospect of marital bliss with Ozzie and I?" he added, suddenly apprehensive. "Or do you just prefer commiseration, rather than my suggested solution. I'm told that is what women commonly want, and it annoys them excessively when the man in their life gives them a solution and hopes that they belt up about the situation..."

"No," Kate hiccupped. "Never. I adore you, just as much as I adore Ozzie-cat. You would look so handsome in a black tux, with that darling little bow-tie! And you are right – it is the wedding. It's the prospect of me being expected to spend thousands of dollars – dollars that I don't at the moment have ... on a stupid white dress that I can only really wear once! And a white veil!" Kate took up her refilled glass. "I promise – not another drop until after we eat. Furthermore – I can't and don't want to ask Mom and Dad to spend out that much either. It's just a stupid, stupid custom. I'm thirty-four years old and not a virgin either, so the white dress and veil feel like a bit of a fraud anyway. When I thought about getting married – you know, most girls do – I wanted something simple and frivolous, even fun ... and..."

"Inexpensive?" Richard offered, and Kate nodded.

"I just didn't want a big fuss over it all ... but with Mom and Dad involved, it seems like it's all getting out of hand!"

"Well, you are their only daughter," Richard tried to sound as soothing and reasonable as possible. He gave the mantua sauce a careful stir. It was the sauce which made the dish, since fish quenelles were otherwise rather bland. "And if I am not mistaken, only granddaughter, too. You may not have wanted to make a big thing out of a wedding, but I'll bet that your dear old mum has been quietly planning your big day for decades. As a matter of pure fact, I've been waiting simply years for an occasion to wear black tie at an evening event. So elegant, so proper, so ... formal. I'm certain that we can find something for you that will be equal. Something simple, elegant ..."

"And cheap," Kate capped. "I'm starving, lover-man! Is supper nearly ready?"

"It is," Richard replied. "But it's fish, so let me put Ozzie in the bedroom and close the door, else you will have to fight him to the death for a bite."

"He's pretty zonked on catnip," Kate replied, with only a slight slurring. "Just park him on the bed. We can kick him off later."

"Promises, promises..." Richard replied.

***

Much later in the evening, curled up together in the cozy double-bed at the back of the Airstream, with Ozzie at their feet, purring rapturously, Richard murmured sweet nothings into the ear of his almost-asleep spouse-to-be.

"Kate, my sweet ... love of my life... can I beg of you a ride to Karnesville, tomorrow morning? I need to collect a set of classic gold and black enamel shirt studs that Marisol Gonzales messaged me about. You know she has this precious little second-hand shop, and she found them for me at an estate sale ..."

"I know her place," Kate yawned, and nestled even closer to Richard. "Mom collects Fiestaware place settings, and Marisol keeps an eye out for her. First thing. Then we can go to Mom and Dad's for lunch, or something."

"Perfect," Richard replied.

And it was. Monday evenings with Kate were always perfect.

Marisol Gonzales resale and thrift store, *Second Time Around* was tucked away just off Karnesville's old downtown Main Street. The buildings along a three-block stretch of Main Street were an assortment of late Victorian brick and stone storefronts; about the same vintage as the buildings lining Luna City's Town Square. In Richard's admittedly biased opinion, they were not anywhere near as scenic and attractive as Town Square. A few came perilously near to being run-down, with fading paint and dusty windows offering evidence of small-town decay. At either end of that three-block stretch the quant old store buildings raveled out into uninspired modernity. The main retail establishments in Karnesville, consisting of a massive HEB grocery store, a Costco wholesale outlet, and a Walmart had set up half a mile to the east; ultra-modern stucco and plate glass boxes surrounded by acres of parking lots and fast food franchises.

Second Time Around had premises down one of the side streets in old downtown; a store front from the 1930s with a curving entablature adorned with a couple of rows of colored neon tubes. Marisol Gonzales was one of the Luna City Gonzales clan – to what degree Richard had never fathomed. Likely, no one else could, either. When he had first fetched up in Luna City with nothing much in the way of luggage but an overnight bag containing two bottles of Cristal, a cellphone and a bandanna, Marisol was one of the Gonzaleses who had seen that he had every comfort of a home – including two bags of second-hand clothing in approximately his size. Since that time, he had made the most of his pay from managing the Café by continuing to patronize Marisol's shop.

"It's not like I ever wanted to be the form of fashion, anyway," he justified his tastes in denim trousers and plain polo shirts to Kate.

"No, not like Cousin Sylvester," she agreed; referring to the Gonzalez cousin who affected a sort of retro-nerd look. Sylvester also favored thrift shops, but was much more discriminating in his selections, which ran to chinos worn with vintage Hawaiian shirts and alternately, tailored mid-century suits.

There was parking available on the street in front of *Second Time Around* for Kate's late model VW Bug – there nearly always was. In all the times that Richard had been patronizing the shop, he had never seen anyone else in the place, although it was always immaculately clean, and as tastefully organized as any upscale and expensive boutique. When he commented on the mystery of how Marisol managed to stay in business, Cousin Roman Gonzalez – yet another bright star in Clan Gonzalez/Gonzales – replied,

"Oh, she gets most of her business on Ebay. She inherited the store premises, so she doesn't have rent to cover, and her oldest son is a plumber, so he and his pals take care of maintenance. It's just a good place to show off what she has at any one time. And she does get the occasional walk-in customers, especially on weekends."

Now, as the bell over the door – the same silver chime on a spring as adorned many of Luna City's mercantile establishments – Marisol appeared from the back room.

"Oh, hi, Rich – you got my message about the studs? Oh, good. I'll get them out of the safe. Look around, see if anything else takes your fancy."

"Thanks, Marisol," Rich had his attention already drawn by a rack of mens' trousers, including several hangers of lightly-worn and practically new blue jeans, especially as they were not displaying the current fashion for ragged hems, worn-out patches and rips in all the essential places. There was also a pair of barely-worn black Justin boots with grey embroidery on the shafts on display above the assortment of shoes and work boots. The boots looked like they were in his size, and Richard regarded them with acquisitive lust.

It didn't matter that he could afford new clothing and footwear these days; new from the finest stores in the big city, or even internet order straight from the big names in men's haberdashery. The new position as managing chef/catering director for the Crystal Room paid generously. But four years of relative poverty had set a mark on him; a mark like a stern Calvinist conscience, whispering in his year about waste, and reminding him that there were better things to spend his relatively paltry pay on.

One of those things would be a home for himself and Kate. They both couldn't possibly squeeze into the tiny Airstream for long. Even in Texas, even in Luna City – a permanent home for them which didn't come with wheels attached – would cost a bundle. As much as Kate loved working at the Weekly Beacon, her pay packet was not overflowing; responsibility for their home after marriage would fall to him. Richard considered the boots, was tempted mightily. He was not aware, at first, that Maisol was talking to Kate – and that Kate was leafing through a rack of evening dresses, with increasing excitement.

"... this one," Marisol was saying, as Kate looked at something in a very pale, rich ivory shade with a brief bodice and a bell skirt suspended from the hanger by narrow fabric ribbons.

"Not for a wedding dress in a church," Kate replied with a shudder. "Not sleeveless with bare shoulders. But the color is pretty – I'd like it, otherwise."

"It's practically new," Marisol was saying. "Didn't you see – the original tags are on it. Heavy satin. No stains, no bad smell. I'll bet it's never even been worn. Or maybe worn once for a big event and then some clever bitch with no morals about exploiting retail returned it the next day to the shop for a refund. It's your size, too," she added, wooingly.

Kate wavered, but her resolve strengthened. She shook her head. "Not sleeveless, Mom would have a fit. It's supposed to be a church wedding, and Pastor Lundberg is old-fashioned about things. Something styled like this is more in the approved style." She pulled out another dress on a hanger; a saggy and forlorn thing with a high neckline and long sleeves of heavy pale cream lace, overlaying an underpinning of mauve taffeta. The lace overlay went down to about hip-length, where a full-gathered skirt of many layers of darker mauve gauze fabric sagged depressingly, like dreams sadly abandoned. Marisol crossed herself.

"*Hermana*, sweetie – that's something you would make your mother-in-law wear ... especially if you hated her guts."

"But the lace is pretty," Kate said, with a considering expression. She fingered the lace on sleeves and bodice and looked again at the cream sleeveless number. "They're practically the same shade. How much for both dresses? I know you have a business to run... but I have an idea."

"For you, Katie *cariño* – a discount, because this is for your wedding and because you are family!" Marisol named a figure, which Richard – and more importantly, Katie did not boggle at. "What are you planning?"

Katie grinned. *"Pretty in Pink."*

Marisol's slightly baffled expression cleared at once. "Ah. I see – very clever. Look – would you like that I take them both to Patricia? You know how well she does alterations and dressmaking. She will fit you and alter these entirely to make the perfect outfit – and she won't charge you much."

"Of course," Now Kate looked so relieved, as if a weight the size of the Pyramids of Giza had been lifted off her shoulders. Richard, slightly baffled as to what exactly had been agreed to, asked if he could try on the Justin boots.

He did wonder why both Marisol and Kate were singing "Isn't she ... pretty in pink!" as they walked out of the store.

The dresses weren't pink...

From Mrs. Abernathy's Recipe Box

Pecan - Lemon Bar Cookies

Cream together until well-blended: ½ cup butter and ¼ cup sugar

Beat in well: 1 egg and ½ teasp vanilla

Combine and & to the above: 1 ¼ cup sifted flour   & 1/8 teasp salt

Pat dough evenly into a greased 9x12 inch pan and bake at 350° for fifteen minutes. Remove from oven.

Combine: 2 beaten eggs, 1 ½ cup brown sugar, ½ cup flaked cocoanut, 1 cup chopped pecans, 2 Tbsp. flour, ½ teasp double acting baking powder, ½ teasp salt and 1 teasp vanilla.

Pour over cookie layer and return to oven for 25 minutes

Combine 1 ½ cup sifted confectioner's sugar with sufficient lemon juice to make a smooth, runny glaze. Pour over warm cookie/pecan/coconut layer and allow to set.

When cool, cut into bars or squares.

The Secret Life of Brownies

Letty McAllister was just twelve years old and her older brother Douglas fourteen in summer of 1933, the year that the brownies appeared in Luna City. That was also the fourth year of the Great Depression, although Letty and Douglas and their friend, Stephen Wyler were barely aware of that. Something to do with a stock market crashing Letty gathered from overhearing adults talk it over, with somber faces and worried voices.

"I think it means the Fat Stock Show in Fort Worth," Stephen Wyler assured them, late in 1929 when Letty and Douglas consulted with their friend on this matter. He was the son of a rancher, familiar with matters to do with cattle and other beasts of the Wyler Ranch.

"Are you certain?" Douglas asked, not entirely convinced. The adults seemed to have been most particularly worried. "I don't believe there are cattle in New York City."

"Perhaps it was some other kind of stock," Stephen conceded.

As it turned out, the depression had nothing at all to do with the Fort Worth Fat Stock Show. What it meant to Luna City was that lean times marched in through the front door, hung up it's coat and hat, and settled down for a long lazy spell of lounging in the most comfortable chair in the parlor. Local small ranchers and farmers went bust, losing home and properties to foreclosure by the bank. Then a cascade of failing banks and small businesses closing up doors for good. All that and an increase in the number of bums and hobos drifting through, looking for work or just a free meal. Since no one had any money to spare to hire farm hands, the hobos mostly drifted on, although there were some who were agreeable to doing chores by the day in exchange for a few meals and a place to sleep under a roof.

The McAllister siblings and Stephen Wyler, together with a handful of friends from school, had built themselves a clubhouse with odd planks and tree branches brought down by winter floods. They settled on a sheltered declivity in the riverbank not very far from the burnt-out ruins of the Sheffield house, an old mansion on a low hill which had commanded a view of the river, and the washhouse and bathrooms for a tourist camp which had never really gotten off the ground. The owners of the derelict tourist camp had long given up on the property, even before the stock market crash, and left the cabins, the washhouse bloc, and the paved spaces to molder away, baked in the harsh Texas summer sunshine and blasted by winter winds. Perhaps this proved that even in good times, the tourist camp wouldn't have made a go of it. Nothing had lived anywhere near the owl-haunted ruins of the mansion for decades. There was a shed, leaning perilously to one side, Not far from the pile of burnt timbers and brick of the mansion was an icehouse, with thick and insulated walls built into a sloping hillside. The icehouse itself was a dank, dark cave, hidden by brush and tangled mats of wild morning glory vines. Stephen, Douglas, their tag-along acolyte Artie Vaughn, and Letty's friend, Retta Livingston sometimes dared aspirants to membership in their private club to brave spiders and other creepy-crawlies who inhabited the ruins of the roofless bathhouse and the icehouse as a condition of membership. So far, no one had accepted the dare.

It was Retta, who lived with her family on a small farm on the outskirts of Luna City, who first mentioned the brownies. Retta and Letty were in the same Girl Scout troop, a troop led by Mrs. Rowbottom, who was the wife of the Reverent Calvin Rowbottom, head minister of the Methodist church in Luna City.

"Mrs. Allison told Mama last week that she is being visited at night by helpful brownies," Retta commented one afternoon, when they had gathered at the clubhouse to share out a little bag of penny candy that Stephen Wyler had brought with his allowance money. "Like the story that Mrs. Rowbottom told us about brownies coming in at night to do chores for people who leave them a bowl of milk or something."

"Who's Mrs. Allison, when she's at home?" Stephen asked, flippantly. "And how can she tell?"

Retta regarded Stephen with an impatient expression. "Mrs. Allison lives across the small pasture from us – on the edge of town. Her husband finally got a job helping to build that big ol' Hoover dam in Arizona and such. They have a little boy – Samuel, but he caught polio this summer and it took him really bad. The doctors said to keep him in in the hospital in Karnesville, he was that sick. He even got put in that iron lung machine for a week! They were afraid that he might die of the polio or be paralyzed for life. Mrs. Allison, she tries to keep cheerful about his condition, but she told Mama that he might never be able to walk again. Mrs. Allison goes to Karnesville purt' near every day on the bus, so that she can see to Samuel in the hospital. He's only six years old – the same age as my little brother."

"What about the brownie visiting?" Letty was fascinated. The bus to Karnesville came by the McAllister house, and the Tip-Top Icehouse & Gas around nine o'clock on weekday mornings, ten on Saturdays. *(The bus didn't run on Sundays.)*

"It was right curious," Retta answered. "Mrs. Allison went into town to wait for the bus … as she didn't want to miss it. It stops by Dunsmore's grocery …"

"Only it isn't Dunsmore's grocery anymore," Artie Vaughn added, rather unnecessarily.

"We know that!" Letty pointed out, "It's just that the man who owns the grocery store ever since Mr. Dunsmore went to prison and had to sell up never has anyone working there who stays long enough for anyone to remember their names. They don't stay in Luna City long enough to matter."

"Well, anyway, there was a lot of people standing around! Mrs. Allison was saying that she came away in such a rush that she forgot to let the chickens out, and stack up the cord of firewood that was delivered. She talked about that and so much else. When she came home after dark that evening, she saw that all the wood had been stacked ever so neatly, the chickens let out – and put away again. There was a little note left where the milkman had delivered two quarts of milk to her ice-box first thing. One of the bottles was gone, but the note said; *'We took the milk, we needed it for the baby'* and just a little scrawled 'B' for a signature."

"No one ever locks their doors around here," Stephen remarked. "It could have been anyone, walking in." He looked around at the ring of faces. They were gathered in the Club; a ramshackle tipi of branches and odd planks brought down by previous winter's floods leaned up against a mostly-dead cottonwood tree. Stephen, the McAllister siblings and their other friends had built it for a secret clubhouse, in an out-of-the-way bend in the river, below Luna City. "Maybe Mrs. Allison ought to start locking her doors when she goes to spend all day, every day at the hospital. There are a lot of scurvy rogues on the tramp, you know. Just to be on the safe side." *Stephen had picked up the phrase "scurvy rogues" from an adventure book about pirates on the Spanish Main and used it at every opportunity.*

"She does at night," Retta allowed. "Being that she is all alone in the house, and her husband is away…"

"She ought to have a dog," Artie Vaughn said. "Dogs are the best guardian. Like Rin-Tin-Tin…"

"A dog would chase her chickens, less'n she kept an eye on it," Retta replied. "Anyway … maybe a dog would chase away the brownies. And then they wouldn't ever come back."

"Did they?" Letty was fascinated. It all seemed as if a fairy story was coming to life – and in Luna City! "Come back again to Mrs. Allison?"

"They did!" Retta replied, triumphantly. "She thought at first that one of her neighbors was playing a little game with her, so she left a note on the stoop under the empty milk bottles. She thanked the Brownies for stacking the wood and looking after the chickens and asked if they would dust the parlor and hanging out the wet washing for her, as she wouldn't have time to do it in the morning before she went to Karnesville. When she came home, the laundry was all dry and folded up neatly, and the parlor was as clean as a whistle!"

"Was it a neighbor, funning with her?" Artie was deeply impressed.

"She doesn't think so," Retta answered. "She says now that she wouldn't do anything to frighten them or chase them away. The Brownies have been such a help when she is so worried about little Sammy, it doesn't matter to her who they are or where they came from. She leaves a bottle of milk and a note for them about the chores that need doing every morning while she is away. She also leaves them bread, cookies, and other things to eat. And every evening when she comes home, the chores are done, and the milk and food she left for the Brownies is gone."

"That sounds like a miracle," Letty ventured, and Retta nodded.

"It's someone doing a good deed, without wanting any credit for it," Douglas agreed. He was older than the other children by two years, thoughtful and intelligent. He was their natural leader, because he could see and understand aspects and matters of the larger world, matters that others frequently found baffling. "But look, guys... *(and Douglas used that generic denominator to the Club, although two of them were girls.)* ... do your brownies in the stories have babies among them? They said in that first note – they needed milk for a baby."

Letty shook her head. "Mrs. Rowbottom never said anything about baby brownies."

"I don't think they do have babies," Letty replied, after a long pause. "They are just sort of helpful spirits."

"Look, guys," Douglas continued. "I can believe in being helpful. Neigborly. I can believe that someone is helping Mrs. Allison, but I don't believe in helpful spirits – brownies, elves, Santa Claus, Easter bunnies or any other fancy. That's not logical in the real world."

Artie Vaughn's face fell, in disappointment. So did Retta's. Letty thought how comforting it must be, to still believe in stories. But she was twelve, and like Douglas, of a logical nature. There was something strange about Mrs. Allison's brownies. Not dangerous, just ... strange.

"Who – or what do you think is doing Mrs. Allison's housekeeping, while she's away in Karnesville?" Stephen ventured. He wasn't one for believing in fairy stories either. Douglas considered the matter gravely, before he replied.

"I think that someone, or more than one someone – since the note said "we" it must be more than one – who are doing Mrs. Allison a good deed are human beings. For some reason, they can't show themselves." Douglas looked earnestly at the young faces, gathered in the dim shade inside the tipi-hut, and ventured. "I wonder if they aren't kids. Kids like us, and afraid to show themselves. They're on the road, like all those hobos, looking for work and a meal. They don't want anyone to see them. But they have a baby with them. And I find that real worrisome. Kids with babies ought to be able to ask for help. From Chief McGill. Mr. Drury, or our father. The Reverend Rowbottom."

"Strangers," Retta commented softly. "If they were from anywhere around here, they'd know to be able to trust Reverend Rowbottom, or Chief McGill … certainly the mayor of Luna City."

The mayor of Luna City was Letty and Douglas' father, and there was no man in Karnes County who was a softer touch for the troubled, ailing or indigent, as long as they were truly in the condition and not freeloaders looking for a handout.

"We ought to do something about that," Stephen said then – very decisively. He was the only son of the richest rancher in the county; a family well-accustomed to doing something positive regarding any matter which attracted concern.

"What ought we do?" Artie looked around the circle of faces. He was not entirely gormless, but one of those children made to be a follower, which is why he latched on to the McAllister siblings and Stephen Wyler.

"I think we out to set a watch." Douglas sounded as if he had thought a plan out very carefully. Just as Stephen loved movies and books about bold pirates and scurvy dogs on the Spanish Main, Douglas was devoted to the exploits and logical deductions of Sherlock Holmes, the famous detective. "Letty and Retta ought to watch Mrs. Allison's house and see who comes there during the day while she is away in Karnesville. It's summer; school is out until fall, so no one would think anything of kids just hanging around. Meanwhile, Stephen and Artie and I will go around every business in town and see if there are kids that we don't know hanging around, cadging work."

"Everyone around here notes strangers," Artie Vaughn nodded an assent to the plan. "You should make us up a list, so we can split up and save time."

"Let's do it," Douglas, being an intelligent boy, did not disdain sensible suggestions from other members of the club. He nodded, in slightly surprised agreement, pleased that Artie had been absorbing Sherlock Holmes' logical methods. "And meet tomorrow afternoon at four, to compare notes."

Letty told her mother that she was going over to spend the day at Retta's, once she had finished her daily chores. Retta told her mother that they were going to spend the day outside, and Retta's mother kindly supplied them with a thermos of lemonade and some sandwiches wrapped in waxed paper. The mothers of members of the Club were well-accustomed to their offspring spending the summertime daylight hours on kid-business of their own. All the various mothers asked, not with any real conviction that such requests would be scrupulously observed, was that such activities not be physically risky, unlawful or likely to involve blood being shed.

Retta and Letty both were working towards Scouting badges in First Aid and had – so far – been able to staunch any flows of blood resulting from various misadventures, without drawing parental attention to them. Douglas and Stephen were quite grateful for this ability.

The girls took some books with them, and a pair of bird-watching binoculars which had belonged to Letty's grandfather; the architect who had laid out the plans for Luna City and designs for all the public buildings, back in the waning decades of the previous century. Letty borrowed the binoculars from her father's study. The Mayor was not a birdwatcher. In any case, he would be in town all day long at his office, so the binoculars would not be missed. Retta borrowed her family's wind-up alarm clock, also hoping that it would not be missed during the day. Douglas had suggested that the girls keep a log, noting the times. For that, a clock was essential.

Retta's father had built a treehouse in the far-distant quadrant of their yard, for the benefit of Retta's three much-older brothers. Those brothers were now all well-grown and distaining such childish amusements, so Retta had the treehouse to herself and her friends. It was a simple platform of weathered planks with a crude waist-high rail around it, nestled in the center of a many-branched oak tree. This perch offered a good view of the back of the Allison house across a meadow of unmown grass, as well as the long dirt driveway between it and a rack of mailboxes on the main paved road. Veiled by leaves all around, the platform could not be seen by a casual viewer, but from it, anyone coming to or from the Allison house would be spotted. It was the ideal position, as Douglas had pointed out, to surveil the Allison's place. Retta and Letty climbed up the rough ladder formed by planks nailed into the oak tree trunk, emerging through a small trapdoor in the middle of the platform.

They had also taken the precaution of bringing some books and a pair of cushions to soften what they expected to be a day-long vigil. Letty loved spending time in the treehouse, for when the wind strengthened, the platform swayed gently, like a ship in a rolling sea.

"There goes Mrs. Allison," Retta made a tidy note. "Eight-forty. Just in time to catch the 9 o'clock bus to Karnesville. The milkman already has been. She took in the milk and let the chickens out. I saw Sgt. Drury's car first thing, coming back from Karnesville. I wonder if he is investigating someone?"

John Drury was an older man, once a Texas Ranger, who served as a detective for the Luna City Police Department, at such times as required extra-special detecting skills. Crime did not often wave in Luna City. Such offenses as occurred were most usually quite transparent.

"Probably coming back from visiting kinfolk," Letty replied. "His son lives in Karnesville. It's eight-forty now," Letty double-checked the time. "I hope this isn't a day when the brownies don't show up. I want to be the ones who solve the mystery."

"Stephen was going to go to all the shops on Town Square," Retta ticked them off on her fingers. "All the ones who might have hired boys to run errands, or something. Artie was going to Bodie's, and to the Cattleman Hotel."

"Douglas was going to the Tip-Top first thing," Letty continued, "Then to speak to the folks at Gonzalez' garage. He thinks that because the Gonzalez place is so close to the main road, someone looking for work might go there after first asking at the Tip-Top. They're going to meet up at noon and go around to everyone that they might have missed in the morning."

"Makes sense," Retta agreed, as she opened her book. "I think we got the easy part, though."

"The boring part," Letty propped the binoculars on the railing, and focused them on the Allison's back porch. They had agreed to alternate every half an hour.

It hardly had been forty minutes before Letty looked up from her book and spotted the girl, out on the paved county road that ran past the Allison and Livingston home places.

"Look now – over there, just by the mailboxes," Letty said, softly. "See that girl? She's pulling a little wagon … an old Liberty Coaster, looks like …"

"I see her," Retta swung the binoculars around, and trained the lenses on the girl, walking along the roadside verge, pulling the little wagon after her. She was very obviously a girl, as her light brown hair hung down in two braids, although she was wearing faded denim overalls like a boy's and a baggy shirt several sizes too large for a skinny frame. All this was plain to Letty, even without binoculars. "There's another in the wagon. Could that be the baby they meant – that they needed milk for?"

The girl, the wagon, and the smaller child in it were lost to their sight, momentarily screened by a thicket of hackberry bushes. Retta continued, almost whispering, "She's … yes, coming down the drive to the Allison place."

"If they go inside, they're for certain Mrs. Allison's brownies," Letty whispered in reply. The girl with the wagon and smaller sibling was so far away that they might have conversed in normal tones but the necessity for discretion compelled whispers.

Almost holding their breaths, Retta and Letty watched the girl go to the back door of the Allison place. The strange girl moved confidently, as if she knew what she was about, and had no apprehension about being there. She bent down and picked up the smaller child. Letty thought the smaller child was another girl, for the mop of yellow ringlets, and a baby smock which once might have been pink. Then the two girls vanished into the house – casually, as if they had every right to be there, leaving the wagon by the back porch steps.

"Nine-thirty-five," Letty looked at the alarm clock, and made a lot in their watch-log. "The brownies are in the house. I wonder how long they will stay?"

"Depends on what Mrs. Allison has asked them to do," Retta replied. "Say. What do we do when they go?"

Letty thought it over, very carefully. "I think that we should follow them. At least a little way. That way, we can tell the boys where they are staying."

"They must be living somewhere," Retta agreed.

For some time, silence fell in the tree house, broken only by the faint rustle of turning pages, metallic ticking of the alarm clock, and a slight scuffle as Retta and Letty handed off custody of the binoculars. The girl they were watching appeared in the Allison's yard three times; once to open the henhouse and scatter feed for them, an hour later to sweep the back porch with a broom, and finally at around 1:30 to chase

445

the hens back into the henhouse. Then, she emerged one last time from the house with the smaller girl in her arms. Retta and Letty noted the time and duration, in between bites of their own sandwiches. When the older girl set the blond child in the wagon and set off down the long drive towards the county road, Retta and Letty were ready.

They crouched behind a stand of overgrown sunflowers by the rack of mailboxes until the girls and their wagon had gone past. Letty wondered if they were sisters, although they did not look much alike, or as nearly as she could judge from a close inspection through the binoculars.

"Not too close," she warned Retta in a breathless whisper. "We don't want them to see us following them – but we ought to see where they go."

It helped that neither of the girls looked behind; the older seemed to have all her attention focused on pulling the wagon, and the blonde toddler with the curls was too little to be taking notice of much. Letty and Retta still lingered behind cover as they found it; overgrown roadside bushes and bends in the road, as it straggled southwards from Luna City itself, in the direction of the derelict abandoned tourist cabins, the burnt-out ruins of the Sheffield mansion, and the derelict Mills home place.

"I wonder if they're staying on Old Man Mills' land," Retta whispered, "I'd be scared to death of his pet alligators!"

Letty shook her head. "I don't think they would dare … even if Ol' Man Mills is practically a hermit, these days. Mrs. Mills is plenty sharp. I don't see that she would abide strangers, much. Even if they are kids. Those Millses are the biggest bootleggers in Karnes County. Everyone says so."

The girl and her wagon, with the smaller child in it had drawn somewhat farther ahead, lost to the sight of Letty and Retta around a bend in the road. They were nearest to where there remained a lightly-beaten track towards the Sheffield mansion ruins; now a pile of weathered stones and timbers burnt to ashes and blackened slate shingles thirty years previously. Locals insisted that the low hill above a bend in the river was haunted. When the two girls ventured stealthily around that bed, the road which stretched out before them was entirely empty.

"We've lost them!" Retta despaired, but Letty shook her head.

"Maybe not. They weren't all that far ahead of us. Look, Retta – there's gaps in the fence, and all those paths leading away from the road. I'll bet they went through one of them. We ought to look for the tracks that wagon would make in the dust. There's plenty of spaces between the weeds where wheels and shoes could leave marks." Letty smiled at her friend and nudged her shoulder. "We're Scouts! Remember – we should be able to spot tracks!"

It took the two girls merely fifteen minutes, exploring the first three gaps in the sagging wire and the wandering trails beyond, beaten into the hard summer earth.

"They went this way," Letty announced with confidence. Yes, there they were – the straight tracks of narrow wheels, and the footprints of someone whose' shoes were about the same size as Letty's were marked in the pale dust between patches of low-growing weeds.

"Towards the old Sheffield place. I wonder if …" She left that thought unfinished, and Retta finished it for her.

"They're camped out in the icehouse? It's got a roof on it, for sure. If I wanted to stay hidden, and had a place to hide out from everyone, I'd sure as certain consider the icehouse … I wonder how they found it?"

"How did they find out that Mrs. Allison goes on the bus to Karnesville every day and spends all day at the hospital?" Letty replied. The two girls walked on silent cat-feet along the narrow-beaten path through the thicket of oak trees and scrub brush, brush which covered a low rise above a bend in the San Antonio River – a rise hardly sufficient to be termed a hill. They had nearly reached where the old icehouse had been dug into that hill, when they heard a small child giggling, somewhere hidden by the thick undergrowth. A girl's voice – startlingly close to them, but unseen, called –

"Coral! Time for your nap! Don't be a naughty girl, now!"

Retta looked over her shoulder at Letty, who nodded and gestured that they should walk away. The mystery brownies clearly had set up housekeeping in the thickets around the Sheffield ruins, likely taking shelter at night in the ice house. Retta and Letty hurried away, not daring a sound until they had reached the road.

"Well, we shall have something definite to report, now," Retta commented, wholly satisfied with what they had been able to discover. It was a real person, and not a familiar household spirit, doing chores at the Allison home. She consulted the alarm clock – which she had carried with her in her little bag of First Aid supplies. Retta wanted to be a nurse when she grew up, and the aid kit accompanied her everywhere. As a Scout, she was always prepared.

They were only a short distance from the clubhouse; the girls had a shorter distance to cover than the boys, who needed to travel the farther distance from Luna City. It was a few minutes after four, when Douglas, Artie and Stephen finally appeared, sweaty, breathless and only moderately triumphant.

"They're living in the icehouse?" Douglas sounded skeptical, and Letty reassured him.

"We followed them almost there – the girl and the baby. They can't be anywhere else. What did you find out in town?'

"We went everywhere!" Artie was in full, enthusiastic flow. "Looking for strangers who might be kids like us! Even to Abernathy Hardware – every shop along the Square. I think we talked to everyone. Sgt. Drury even asked what we were doing. I told him we were doing a scavenger hunt and had to get a copy of a newspaper from someplace else. Pretty clever, huh?"

"Yes, but what did you find out?" Letty could hardly contain her impatience. "How did the girl find out about the Allisons ... and the old icehouse..."

"There are two boys," Douglas explained. "They weren't from around here; everyone is certain about that. Also – the talk different. Like country folk, but not quite like from around here. One is about my age, maybe a bit older. The other looks to be seven or eight. Everyone we talked to, who noticed the boys says that they've seen the older boy running errands and making deliveries for the grocery store. For tips, mostly. And Mr. Mason – that's the guy who runs it now – he says he don't bother with asking for a name, since he's not paying wages. But he lets that boy and his brother pick through the trash and spoiled things that he's throwing away at the end of the day, 'cause it's unfit to sell."

"Yuck," Retta made a face. "That's disgusting."

"You get hungry enough, you'll eat what you can that won't bite back," Artie pointed out, with feeling. The Vaughns were hard up, everyone in Luna City knew that. Mr. Vaughn, whose little ranch property near Beeville had been foreclosed on at the very start of the crash, made only a pittance as a policeman for the Luna City Police Department – hardly enough to support a wife, Artie and his younger brother Harry. If it weren't for them keeping hens and a garden in back of the Vaughn place, and their father regularly going hunting … they'd also be scavenging what they could from the grocery store, like those unnamed boys.

"Where did they come from?" Letty asked. "Did anyone know that?"

"I went and talked to Manny Gonzalez, at the garage," Stephen answered. "I thought that he might have seen something, since so many travelers go past his father's place."

Manny – or Manolo, was an older teenage boy, who was interested in nothing but engines and mechanical things, to the exclusion of practically everything else. Manny quit school as soon as it was allowed, to work in the Gonzalez family enterprise. This was an auto repair shop on the very edge of town, situated – like the Tip-Top Icehouse Gas & Grocery – to take best advantage of travel on the main road between San Antonio, Beeville and Rockport.

"Did he?" Retta demanded, impatiently. "Stop keeping us all in suspense, Douglas – it's not fair. What did Manny tell you? Did he see the boys? Did he know anything about them."

"He did, indeed," Douglas replied, with something of the air of Sherlock Holmes explaining something to Dr. Watson. "He told me that a trucker with a busted brake line and a load he simply had to get to Brownsville stopped at the shop about six weeks ago. There were four kids with him. Four kids with an toy wagon and a couple of bags and an 'ol suitcase strapped onto it. The two boys, a girl about eleven or twelve, and another little girl – just about able to walk, Manny says. The littlest had curly blond hair and looked sort of like that cute little girl with the ringlets in the movie shorts. That's how come Manny took notice. He also noticed that the four kids didn't stick around, until the trucker got his brakes fixed. When he moved on, the kids weren't with him. Manny thinks the oldest boy is the one doing errands for the grocery store."

"If he was hanging around there, looking for work," Stephen had already made the logical deduction, "Then he might have overheard Mrs. Allison talking to the others, waiting for the Karnesville bus. What are we going to do now, Captain?"

Douglas sounded as if he were thinking out loud. "I really think that we should talk to them. These kids. Find out what's going on. Why they're on the road, without any family to look after them. I've never heard of kids going on the bum all alone, 'cept in the movies. Maybe a boy by himself, looking for work and hitting the road. But with his little sisters? There is something odd and curious about this situation. I think we ought to get to the bottom of it, before we tell anyone else.

Tomorrow is Sunday. The bus doesn't run on Sunday, and the grocery store is closed. I think we ought to go out to the icehouse tomorrow afternoon … after church and talk to these kids. Find out what the story is. Agreed?"

"Agreed," Stephen nodded. "Meet here first, then go all together. Not a word about this to the grownups until we find out what the story is."

They all agreed, although Letty saw that Retta hesitated.

Finally, Retta mumbled, "With a baby, who still needs milk? We really ought to tell someone. Someone who really cares. And can do something.

"We will tell someone, as soon as we know that their story is," Douglas assured her. It was nearly suppertime. Their mothers would all be highly irate, if they were late to the table. There was no more time to talk about the matter of the family of children living surreptitiously in the icehouse. They headed for home, as speedily as their various means could take them; Douglas and Letty on their bicycles, Stephen on a spry ranch cowpony, Retta and Artie on foot.

The following afternoon, they met again at the ramshackle tipi clubhouse. Douglas, Letty and Stephen had changed out of their Sunday best, church-going clothes into their worn play clothes. So had Retta – but Artie had no Sunday best to speak of, although his shirt and too-large-for-him overalls were at clean. *(Mrs. Vaughn did laundry on Saturday, just so her family would have clean clothing on Sunday.)* It was only a short walk from the clubhouse to the scrub covered hill above a bend in the river where the old Sheffield mansion once had been, with an extensive array of outbuildings – stable, icehouse, well-house, summer kitchen and servant's cottages, all now gone – save for the icehouse.

They heard the voices of children, as they approached the shaded glade where the icehouse was – voices and carefree laughter; a girl's voice, chiding someone called 'Billy' for getting his shirt all dirty, and a boy – presumably Billy – replying, "Aww, Edie-May, don't you fuss none, over nothing at all! It's only a little dirt, won't do any harm!"

"But you have to look respectable, when you …"

At that moment, Douglas and Letty, with the rest of the Club following after, appeared in the little clearing among the thicket which covered the hill. This appeared to surprise Billy, Edie-May, and the two smaller children out of any comment at all for a long, long moment – a moment which seemed to stretch out to at least five minutes.

The girls were the ones that Retta and Letty had seen the previous day at the Allison house. Edie-May. That must be the older girls' name. She might be Letty and Retta's age, but thinner and smaller, clad in boys' overalls and a shirt sized for a much larger person, which hung on her skinny frame like laundry flapping on a line. The curly-haired baby would be Coral. The two boys … Letty squinted at the older with a start of recognition. He must be Billy. Yes, he did look familiar. She had seen him hanging around the grocery store on Town Square over the last two or three weeks, when she and her mother came to the weekly grocery shopping.

The children had created a rough camp and home out of the little space at the entrance of the old icehouse: a crude bench of tree stumps and weathered timber, battered footstool obviously salvaged from the dump, and the wagon that Letty and Retta had spotted earlier. A clothesline had been strung across one end of the space – bearing a couple of threadbare garments.

"What do you want?" demanded Billy, the first to recover his voice. He sounded belligerent, and his hands were already balled into defensive fists. The younger boy stood at his back – also belligerent, looking at the Club as if he were also ready to defend his sisters.

"We wanted to talk to you," Douglas replied, his own voice and manner calm and conciliatory. "Please … we don't mean to tell on you to the grownups."

"We saw your sisters yesterday at the Allison place," Retta sounded pleading. "And we thought that maybe you were in some kind of trouble … and maybe we could help you."

"We don't need no help," Billy scowled. "We're doing jus' fine!"

"Hiding away in an ol' hole in the ground and getting your meals from a garbage can?" Stephen snorted, "Yeah, that sure spells 'jus' fine' to me."

Letty hissed, "Shut up, Stephen! That's not helping any!" She saw that Edie-May looked about to burst into tears, or failing that, to grab her little sister and run off through the scrub woodlands. "Look, we know about how you've been helping Mrs. Allison – and that's right kind and neighborly, and we can see that you're good people … so we really want to help. Mrs. Allison's a good person, and you must be also good, to help her so in her time of need."

"Besides," Douglas' voice sounded as calm and soothing as if he were talking to a fractious traveler at the Tip-Top. "When winter comes, do you still want to be living here? Look; this is a small town, an' folk around here notice things. Pretty soon, someone is gonna take notice and wonder who you are, and what you are doing here. Where are your parents, and why aren't you in school. An' maybe they won't be as polite as we are. So … truce for a parley?"

"All right," Billy still didn't look happy. "Parley …"

At that moment, the little curly-haired toddler ran up to Letty and wrapped her arms about Letty's legs, smiling up at her – joyous and affectionate.

"I'm Coral Browne," she lisped. "Who are you? Can you take us to our Pa?"

"I'm Letty," Letty replied, utterly and unexpected touched by the open trust and instant affection. "Leticia Mary McAllister. But Letty will do for now. I don't rightly know if I can take you to your pa, if I don't even know where he is. Where are you from, Coral Browne – and what are you doing here in Luna City?"

Coral Browne only giggled and embraced Letty again. It seemed as if that open gesture of affection had opened a floodgate of honesty with her older siblings, although at first it was only a moderate trickle. Billy Browne replied for his little sister, Coral.

"All right … we're from Tennessee… Memphis, Tennessee. I'm William Lee Browne. Y'all may as well have a seat." The boy suddenly appeared humble, vulnerable as a desperate boy must be, scrounging a living for his three younger sibs out of grocery store garbage, and the charity of a woman desperately worried about her own child. Douglas, Stephen and Retta likewise introduced themselves. All found seats in the little clearing. Coral leaned confidingly against Letty, as her brother continued.

"Pop took a job out west someplace. He drives a truck. It's what he does, and it pays good, better than most, even if it keeps him away from us for weeks at a time. We thought he was working out of St. Louis, leastways that was what we heard. Ma ..." Billy gulped a little. "Ma got sick last year and took a real bad turn this spring. Finally, the doctor ordered her took to the big hospital in Memphis. She ... she couldn't even get out of bed; she was that sick of the consumption. TB, they call it, I guess. Before they took her away, she made us promise that we should stick together; me, Edie-May, Bobby, an' Coral, no matter what happened to her. Miz Janine, that's our next-door neighbor, an' Mr. Ted Harkness – that's her husband that also drives a truck like our Pop – they were looking after us. We would have made out jus' fine," Billy lifted his chin defiantly. "But for that ol' witch Miz Tann, from the Children's Home! She had to stick her interfering nose in, where it didn't rightly belong!"

From the way that Billy said that name, and the sheer venom contained in the words of that last sentence, Letty reckoned that Miss Tann was the main reason that the Browne children had taken to the road and run away from Memphis. She wondered how much of a witch this Miss Tann really was, and if she were as bad as Billy and his siblings seemed to think.

"What did Miss Tann do?" Douglas asked, quiet and level-voiced. Billy scowled, but it was Edie-May who answered first.

"Ma had to go to the sanitarium. Maybe she'll get better, Miz Janine said that she didn't think so. Miz Tann and her assistant showed up one day in a big fancy Packard car with a driver, saying that Ma had signed over custody of all of us to the Children's Home, since Pop was

456

away on the road, no one knew ezactly where. Miz Tann had a look on her face as if we smelled bad, or something, when she looked at us, looked around at our house. But it wasn't!" Edie-May almost cried out in frustration. "It was perfectly clean! Ma brung us up right, even Miz Janine said so, and she used to be housekeeper for a rich family in Memphis! Miz Janine was there at the house, an' she told that Miz Tann a thing or two. Didn't do no good. Miz Tann, she done tol' us then that she would be back the next morning with the sheriff's orders, like it or not. The judge had made it legal and all! We'd have to go to that Children's Home, because our parents were sick an' no-account, an' we'd all be better off. What <u>we</u> wanted didn't matter none."

Billy added, resentfully, "What we had promised Ma about staying together didn't matter none, either. We found that out soon enough, because of what Bobby overheard! Miz Tann and her assistant were talking when they didn't think we could hear. Bobby likes cars, and he went out to the road, where Miz Tann's driver had parked hers."

"A big fancy car," Bobby chimed in. "With all the extras, and so much chrome trim! The King o' England doesn't have a car that fancy. Anyway, I sneaked down to look at it … an' I heard that Miz Tann talking to her assistant about us! Gloating about how much money she would get from some rich folk in Hollywood for adopting Coral, 'cause she was so pretty an' friendly. An' other things she said. How much she might get for adopting out Edie-May and me to people who wanted hard workers and didn't want the bother of paying wages. She didn't think Billy would be worth the trouble to bother with. He was too old to be really biddable, she said. No one would want him.'"

"How horrible!" Letty was utterly appalled. There were orphans, and orphanages in Texas – she knew that for sure, but selling little girls like Coral to people who wanted a child to adopt? That was purely outrageous. "But you aren't orphans! How can she do that! Isn't that against the law, anyway – selling children!"

"Not in Memphis, I don't think," Billy answered, with a bleak laugh. "Anyways, Bobby came running back to tell us all what he heard, especially about selling Coral to some rich folk. Miz Janine about hit the ceiling when she heard that! She was that angry. She said that slavery days and being sold down the river were over and done with, years since. She went and woke up Mr. Ted, and tol' him what was going to happen when Miz Tann came back with the judge's order the next day. They decided that we ought to pack up that very night and go to Pop in St. Louis. Since that Miz Tann was a high-society woman an' friends with all them best people, she would have all the laws on her side. Miz Janine got even madder when Mr. Ted said that. Our Pop was in St. Louis, and Mr. Ted would drive us there, and we would stay together, no matter what Miz Tann and her high-ass society friends would say."

"We packed up our things and the little wagon that Pop bought for us, when he was flush. We were on the road in the back of Mr. Ted's truck before midnight. He took us all the way north to St. Louis, because that's where Pop was supposed to be working out of, living in a boarding house by the railway station when he wasn't on the road. Mr. Ted figured that if Pop wasn't there, someone at the boarding house, or the dispatcher where he worked would know where he was and let him know. Mr. Ted was in a hurry to deliver his shipment and get back to Memphis. He said that we'd be OK. Here was where Pop was supposed to be … and he drove away. I can't fault him none," Edie-May added, honestly. "Mr. Ted done us a great favor, getting us out of Memphis, away from Miz Tann an' her friends. He was breaking the law to do it, you see. But it turned out – Pop wasn't there. Folk at the boarding house said that he was gone to work in Texas, or maybe all the way to California. So, we set out on the road to where Pop might be working, looking for Pop. Anything was better than staying in Memphis and letting Miz Tann sell our baby sister to some rich folks and break us up. Leastways, this way we're all together."

The members of the Club sat in appalled silence, upon hearing this horrible story. Douglas was the first to speak.

"That's more awful than I can say, Billy. But I can guarantee you one thing. We don't allow anything like that around here …"

"We run scurvy dogs like that Miss Tann clean out of Texas!" Stephen declared, his face afire with indignation, "They run faster than ol' Santy Anna after the San Jacinto fight, when we're done with them!" while Douglas continued,

"Look, Billy – we decided that we wanted to help you, once we knew what the story was … and now that we know it, we want to help you even more. If we were to tell some grownups that we really trust … will you trust us to be straight about helping you?"

"Depends on the grownups," Billy looked as wary as a cornered cat, but Edie-May's woeful countenance brightened, as if she saw the gates to the Big Rock Candy Mountain opening before her.

"I would!" she exclaimed. "So I would! Miz Allison's right nice. You can tell things, from the way she keeps her house and leaves food and milk for us. Are folk in Luna City all as nice as Miz Allison?"

"Nearly all, save maybe Old Charley Everett," Retta answered. "He keeps pet alligators to eat up the bodies of his rival gangsters!"

"He does not!" Letty added instantly, upon noting the horrified expression on Edie-May's face. "That's only a story! He is an awful man but he hardly comes to town anymore, since he got nearly lynched in Town Square."

"The trusty adults we would ask for help for you," Douglas cleared his throat and adroitly took command again, "The first would be our father; mine and Letty's. He's the mayor of Luna City. And I think after that; Sgt. Drury. He was a Texas Ranger, back in the day. One of the youngest rangers ever to ride in a Ranger company. If anyone can find your father, in this whole US of A – that would be Sgt. Drury!"

"Sgt. Drury?" Billy's expression brightened at once. "That old man? He's been pointed out to Bobby an' me! They say he was a tough customer when he was in his young days an' he's only gotten tougher since!"

"He might already suspect something about y'all," Artie confessed. "Last night, my pa asked me why we was going around town asking questions. My pop's a policeman. He works with Sgt. Drury."

"I reckon you have no choice but to trust us," Douglas concluded. "Can we tell our father and Sgt. Drury about you, and you promise you won't high-tail it out of town before tomorrow?"

"Yeah … sure," Billy's narrow shoulders straightened as if he was a soldier, ordered to brace at attention. "I promise. Tell them. Or … let me tell them myself." At Bobby's barely stifled protest, Billy continued, "Bobby, we're plum-out of luck, looking for Pa. Winter'll be here in no time flat, and we hardly got enough to move on. I don't b'lieve we have much of a choice, since there ain't a better one on offer. Ma always told us that we should reply in good faith when we saw good intentions offered to us. We been here long enough to get a sense of what folk are about here."

"It took us near onto a minute to get a sense of what that witch Miz Tann was about," Edie-May solidly backed up her brother; no doubt as solidly as Letty as accustomed to back up Douglas. "An' it didn't take much longer to figure out who is dealing straight with us … and who isn't. You go ahead with these folk, Billy.   I'll wait here with Bobby an' Coral."

"If I ain't back by nightfall," Billy said, over his shoulder. "You'll skedaddle … go where we talked about next."

"You'll be back before then," Edie-May answered, serenely.

461

A Home for the Brownies

The first thing that Mayor McAllister did, after listening grave-faced and non-judgmental, to the story told to him by Billy Browne, accompanied by a chorus of comments from Letty, Stephen, Artie and Retta, was to put aside his evening pipe and go to the McAllister's telephone. This instrument – almost the first in Luna City, was in a small niche in the kitchen, where Letty's mother was fixing supper.

"I guess that I should set four more places," Mrs. McAllister ventured, after overhearing the conversation of Mayor McAllister, with serially, Sgt. Drury, and then with the Reverend Rowbottom."

"Not to worry, Matilda," Mayor McAllister replied, wholly serene. "The most urgent matter is being appropriately dealt with."

He returned to the shaded verandah where the interview had been taking place and carefully refilled his pipe, before addressing the juvenile assembly. "Now, young Billy … a friend of ours, Mr. John Drury will arrive presently, in his car. He will take you out to the old Sheffield place, where he will collect your brother and sisters, and whatever you have with you of your trash and traps and take you to a foster home … a safe place, where you all will live, until we can sort out this almighty mess and locate your father. I would like you to promise, on all that you hold sacred, to remain there and not go haring off on another dangerous wild goose chase. Will you so promise?"

"I will, sir," Billy replied, after a sideways glance in the direction of Douglas and Letty. Douglas nodded very slightly, which seemed to provide all the reassurance required.

"Good," Mayor McAllister nodded – and consulted the old-fashioned pocket watch, extracted from his waistcoat picket. "Ah … half-past four. You youngsters may run along now – I am certain that your parents will all be wondering where you are, as it is nearly suppertime. Consider this matter taken care of … for now," he added, as Stephen, Artie and Retta made their departure, going down the steps, with many a backward and reluctant glance over their shoulders. "Douglas … Letty – go and wash up, for supper. You've done a good day of work in this matter. Leave it now for those who are best positioned to deal with the situation."

"Yes, Papa," Letty and Douglas obediently scampered into the house and upstairs. By most standards, their parents were indulgent but there was a limit. An order, even a gentle one like that was not to be defied.

When they came downstairs again, Sgt. Drury's Ford sedan was just pulling away from the McAllister house, with Billy Browne in the passenger seat. But supper was on the table, and both Letty and Douglas were ravenously hungry. Douglas did venture to say, as their father carved up the Sunday roast,

"What is going to happen with the Brownes, now, Pops? Where is Sgt. Drury taking them?"

"Curiosity killed the cat, Douglas," their father reproved them. "They will be safe enough for now; that's all you need know."

"Yes, sir," Douglas subsided, and turned to paying attention to his plate. Their curiosity regarding the Browne siblings was not satisfied until supper was finished, and Mrs. McAlister was serving up scoops of peach cobbler. Sgt. Drury returned alone to the house and knocked on the door. On being invited in and offered a helping of cobbler and a cup of coffee, he sat down at an empty chair at the dining room table and thanked Mrs. McAllister for the hospitality.

Mayor McAllister looked across the table and waited until Sgt. Drury had eaten several bites of Mrs. McAllister's most excellent peach cobbler, warm from the oven and redolent with the scent of spices – cloves, ginger, and a dusting of nutmeg shavings. "Well?"

Not only was Sgt. Drury a man of few words, he also required little in the way of a request for information. He answered, "All settled at the Allisons' for as long as necessary. Mrs. Allison very kindly offered on the instant, upon hearing of the need from Mrs. Reverend Rowbottom. Her boy Sammy is coming home from the hospital tomorrow. She told me she would relish the company for him, and the help too, seeing that the girl was already taking care of her house! We'll need to send a telegram to Memphis, though. Find out where their parents have gone."

"I'll authorize the expense," Mayor McAllister replied. "Might even go as far as a trunk call. Don't suppose the neighbors they spoke of who helped them leave town would have a telephone, though."

Sgt. Drury shook his head. "No. Poor folk. Doubt they'll talk frankly to any lawman, either. Seems like that Tann woman put an almighty scare into them. Reckon I'd have better luck getting a line on the father's latest employer."

"I'm sure you'll get results," Mayor McAllister assured him. "Don't the Rangers always get their man?"

"The Mounties do," Sgt. Drury grinned. "And so do the Rangers, without fail and usually without tracking them through the snow."

With that, the Browne children were safely deposited in the Allison household, under the benevolent supervision of Mrs. Allison, assisted by Mrs. Reverend Rowbottom and the ladies of the Methodist ladies' association. Sgt. Drury and Chief Magill wrote letters of inquiry to police departments in all the cities where it was thought that the senior Mr. Browne had gone, seeking work. Sammy Allison returned from the hospital – not entirely recovered from polio or confined to a wheelchair, which is what everyone had feared, including the Allison family doctor, but with his pale matchstick legs encased in cumbersome metal and leather braces.

He was exactly the age of Billy Browne; the two boys immediately became inseparable.

"They have been such a help to me!" Mrs. Allison exclaimed to Mrs. Reverend Rowbottom at the weekly sewing circle, held at the McAllister's house. "Edie-May is such a love! She is minding her sister, and Sammy just now. Such a relief, to have such trustworthy children living with one! Billy and Bobby are mowing the yard and moving the chicken's enclosure. I will miss them so much, when their father is located and takes them to wherever he will settle down."

"Surely, he will not return them to Memphis," Mrs. McAllister ventured, and Mrs. Allison snipped off the end of a thread and replied.

"No, most certainly not. What a ghastly woman, this Tann creature! I can hardly bear to think of how cruelly these poor children would have fared, once under her guardianship!"

"I think you have done a very noble Christian deed, giving them a safe refuge," Mrs. McAllister noted. Letty agreed, overhearing this while bringing in a fresh pitcher of lemonade to the verandah where the sewing circle met. She and her mother had encountered Mrs. Allison that very morning, shopping for groceries. Edie-May had her hair neatly combed into curls tied with pretty ribbons. She was also wearing a dress – an outgrown one of Letty's. Letty, already wise in the ways of poverty and how it shamed the proud to be seen accepting charity, did not say a word about the origin of the dress, but only said how pretty

466

and grown-up Edie-May looked in it, and saw Edie-May glow like a lantern with happiness.

And that was how the situation remained, as the summer of 1933 dwindled to a close, and the school year began. The older Browne children and Sammy Allison, stumping gamely along with his legs encased in those heavy braces, assembled in the playground of the magisterial brick building that housed the public school on that momentous first day of school. Billy was assigned to the same grade as Douglas, Edie-May with Stephen and Letty to the sixth, Bobby and Sammy in the fifth, along with Artie Vaughn.

Mrs. Allison dispatched Sammy and the Browne sibs but for baby Coral, every day to the halls of academe, armed with neatly starched clean clothing, and a simple luncheon of a sandwich and an apple packed in a tin pail.   Meanwhile, Chief Magill, Sgt. Drury and Mayor McAllister dispatched letters to every city they could think of where one Robert Lee Browne, of Memphis, might have found employment, driving a truck or as anything else – to employers and to police departments, begging such employers and departments to tell Mr. Browne to communicate with them, on a matter of great importance. Mayor McAllister now and again mentioned what progress, if any, had been made, to Douglas and Letty. Not much, it appeared.

"There is a lot of possible territory to cover," he explained, one evening. "And most of the parties we are communicating with have much more important matters on their plate. Patience, Letty – patience."

"Finish your supper," Mrs. McAllister admonished Letty and Douglas. "Your friends are safe and in the care of Mrs. Allison. I am certain that their father will be located soon. Sgt. Drury and Chief Magill are unsparing in their efforts to find him."

"Yes, Mama," Letty replied. Obedient, because she was always obedient. Mama and Poppa always knew what was best. If Poppa said something was so … well, of course it was.

The following week, some news about the Browne parents did appear. It was the week before Thanksgiving, when the class was preparing for a final school assembly on Wednesday before the holiday. Letty's class would reenact the feast of the Pilgrams and Indians, with other selected students performed readings, choral singing and recitations. Letty had been picked to be one of the Pilgrims, along with Edie-May Browne. They would dress in old-fashioned grey gowns down to their toes, with prim white bonnets and white aprons. Halfway through the rehearsal in the assembly hall, where the stage was already decorated with autumn leaves, whole pumpkins and sheaves of dried corn, the school principal, Miss Donninger appeared in the doorway. She beckoned to Mrs. Kronberg, the 5th grade teacher, and whispered a few words to her.

"Edie-May, sweetheart," Mrs. Kronberg said. "Miss Donninger wants you to go to her office … no, you aren't in trouble," Mrs. Kronberg added hastily, upon noting Edie-May's apprehensive expression. "There has just been some news about your family…"

At that, Edie-May, her face nearly as pale as her apron, hurried down from the stage and vanished with Miss Donninger. She didn't come back to the rehearsal. When class was dismissed for the lunch break, Letty found her, sitting on one of the benches by the playground, all alone, and still dressed in the Pilgrim-pageant cap and grey gown.

Edie-May was just watching the smaller children play. The older students, who lived close enough to go home for lunch, were scattering out of the school gate. Letty went and sat on the bench next to Edie-May, feeling somewhat responsible for the girl. She and Douglas and the others in the Club had all had been a part of calling the attention of the authorities to the existence of Edie-May and her siblings in the first place.

"What did Miss Donninger tell you?" Letty ventured, after some moments. Edie-May gave a small sigh and replied.

"Our Mama is dead of the consumption. Chief Magill heard from the hospital where she was at."

"TB," Letty nodded. "That's what they call it, now. I'm so sorry, Edie-May."

Edie-May looked at the ground at their feet, her expression composed and her eyes quite dry. "We kind of expected it. She was so sick that day when they took her away. Miz Janine … our neighbor back in Memphis. She has the Sight. She told us that Mama had the look of death on her, when they took her to that place. I really can't say we hoped for better news, Letty. It's just that Mama wanted us to be safe, and together and I dunno if she died knowing that we were. We had months of believing that Mama was in heaven, so we got used to the notion. It's just that we know it for certain now."

Letty, at a loss for anything comforting to say, could only think of one thing. "I'm certain they'll find your father, soon. My father says that Chief Magill and Sgt. Drury between them will turn the whole west upside down, looking for him.

"I know," Edie-May answered, with a watery smile.

Encouraged by this, Letty added, "In the meantime, you are playing Priscilla Alden in the school Thanksgiving pageant and that will be something fine to tell your father, when you see him again."

"I guess," Edie-May's smile was still a bit watery, but she didn't seem apt to start crying, which was something, at least.

Mayor McAllister was noncommittal when appealed to over the supper table by Letty and Douglas that evening for further information as regards the Browne children.

"I really couldn't say," he replied. "The investigation is wholly in the hands of Chief Magill and his department. The children are doing well, according to what Mrs. Allison says. She has become quite fond of them all. And you say they are all well-regarded by the others in their classes? They have made friends?"

"Everyone likes Edie-May," Letty admitted, truthfully. Everyone did, even the kids from farms outside of Luna City, who normally viewed newcomers with deep suspicion, especially those who hailed from far away. "Mrs. Kronberg says that she was behind at first but caught up fast enough."

"Billy doesn't much like school," Douglas replied. "I guess it is different for him, being on the road and working. He says that he wishes it were still possible for him to run away and sign on to be a Texas Ranger, like Sgt. Drury did, back in the day."

"We'll see how it goes, when their father is finally located," Mayor McAllister sounded as if the matter of the Browne children were concluded; or if it wasn't, he had no intention of discussing it over the supper table. "I have every confidence that Chief Magill will meet with success, in the search. Now, your supper is getting cold."

Douglas exchanged a glance with Letty as they picked up forks. No, their father had nothing more to say. When they went upstairs that night, to prepare for bed, Letty whispered,

"What do you think will happen to Billy and Edie-May if they can't find their father? What if they turn out to really be orphans?"

"The State Orphanage in Corsicana, I think," Douglas answered, thoughtfully. "Or one of the orphan asylums in Galveston. I expect any of those that have a place where they can stay together. Don't worry, Letty," Douglas added with a comforting smile. "I just bet that Mr. Browne will be found soon."

On the day of the assembly, Letty and the other girls donned their costumes in the girls' lavatory; Letty, Edie-May and four or five others in Pilgrim grey dresses and white bonnets, and the remainder in fringed buckskin smocks, with brilliant headbands and their hair braided into long plaits adorned with feathers and beads.

"I wish that I were an Indian," Letty confessed to Retta. "Your outfit is so much prettier than this!"

"We get to dance, too!" Retta replied with a smug expression and tied another beaded band around her braid. She had long dark brown hair. Letty and the Pilgrim girls were tow-headed or with otherwise light hair. Retta and the other girls who portrayed Indians for the pageant were those who had brown or black hair. At that moment, Miss Kronberg put her head around the bathroom door, pointing to the watch on her wrist, saying,

"All ready, girls? The curtain goes up in ten minutes."

There really wasn't a stage curtain in the assembly hall – just a proscenium arch over the raised stage at one end. Today, the stage boasted a painted canvas backdrop of Plymouth village, produced by the Sixth-grade art class, behind an array of tables, barrels, stands of dried cornstalks and a campfire of artfully arranged logs, and flames cut from red and yellow tissue paper. A concealed tabletop fan made the paper flames waver most convincingly. The stage settings were produced by the senior grades boys shop classes. The Thanksgiving pageant was a beloved and well-practiced tradition in Luna City's public school, much looked forward to by schoolchildren and parents alike. School let out for the holiday at the conclusion of the pageant.

The pageant opened with some poetry recitals, a reading of a contemporary account written down at the time, and the school chorus singing *"Come Ye Thankful People, Come; Raise the Song of Harvest Home"*. On the decorated stage, Letty and the other Pilgrims mimed bringing the corn, the pumpkins, while the Indians brought in the deer and turkeys – all created by the art class of painted papier-mâché. The Indians performed a solemn dance, the Pilgrims bowed and offered them food and drinks in tin tankards which were actually measuring cups given away by the flour milling companies.

With the stage lights shining on them all and dazzling their vision, the players in the pageant really couldn't see much of the audience. All they could see was just a dark expanse, on the other side of the lights. But Letty and the others were fully aware of a large crowd in the auditorium. She and the other players could hear them; the murmurs of awe and approval, proud mothers pointing out their children to approving fathers, older and younger children, a rustle of pleasure at the sight of a clever artistic effect, and a roar of applause at the high points. She was also aware that about three-quarters of the way through the pageant and during a quiet moment on stage, there was the sound of a door opening, indistinct male voices while several tardy people entering the auditorium, and a low buzz of comment and a scraping of chair legs as the latecomers looked for empty chairs.

It wasn't until the pageant concluded, and the row of her classmates, all hand in hand, advanced to the edge of the stage, and bowed in unison. For the first time before the performance began, they could look out and clearly see the ranked faces in the audience. There were several men standing at the back; Letty saw that Chief Magill and Sgt. Drury were standing at the back of the auditorium, along with a tall, strange man in drab working clothes and a cloth cap. Letty didn't recognize him.

At that moment, Edie-May tore her hand out of Letty's, and Retta on the other side, and cried,

"Pa!" She ran down the three steps at the side of the stage, and the aisle in the center, flinging herself – grey Pilgrim dress and bonnet and all into the embrace of that tall man. In the next instant, both Billy and Bobby sprang from where they had been seated with their classes and elbowed their way between the rows and followed suit. As the assembly dissolved into its' constituent parts – participants struggling through the crowded room to rejoin their parents, Letty saw that Coral had joined her brothers and sister, while Mrs. Allison hovered nearby and Chief Magill and Sgt. Drury watched with expressions of quiet satisfaction.

"So, how did Mr. Browne find out that his kids were here in Luna City?" Douglas asked that evening over supper. He and the others of the club hadn't any time after the assembly to speak to each other, or the Browne children. It was all a matter of perplexity for Letty and her brother.

"Chief Magill briefed me regarding the matter," their father replied calmly. "Apparently, Mr. Browne had been informed that Mrs. Browne had passed to her heavenly rest and his family taken into the care of the Children's Home. He came rushing home to Memphis as soon as his duties permitted, but weeks – nay, months had already passed – and none of the authorities could tell him anything, I do not believe," Mayor McAllister added with an air of mild disapproval, "That Miss Tann or any of her associates would have been honest about the disposition of the children, even if they had managed to keep ahold of them. It is Chief Magill's professional judgement that her operation skates along the thin edge of ethical conduct, and likely verges over it on many occasions. But because of her social connections and position, likely nothing will ever be done. However, that is a problem for the city of Memphis and none of ours."

"How did Mr. Browne find out, though?" Letty murmured.

"I was getting to that, Letty – of course that Tann woman and her associates were not in the least helpful to a grieving father. When Mr. Browne went to the house where he and the family had lived, the new tenants couldn't tell him anything useful. But the neighbor woman who had looked after them told him how her husband had taken them to St. Louis. She and her husband assumed they were safe there with him in that city. The poor fellow was searching for a needle in a haystack. It never occurred to him that the children were on the roads, also searching for him. No, it seems that when he finally went to the nearest police station weeks later, on a return to that city, one of the desk officers finally recollected speaking with Sgt. Drury. for a wonder, he remembered that Sgt. Drury was calling long-distance from Luna City, Texas. It was only a matter then, of Mr. Browne's employer locating a cargo needing to be transported to South Texas. And so he traveled here as swiftly as could be managed."

"What are they going to do, now?" Douglas asked, over an additional helping of mashed potatoes.

"Mr. Browne has a cousin in California, who has offered assistance in helping them all to settle there. I assume they all will be traveling there as soon as can be arranged."

"California…" Letty mused. "Perhaps Coral will be in the movies after all. Like that little girl she looks like – the one who sings and dances."

"A silly place, and not a suitable occupation for a child," Mrs. McAllister added, with the tone of a judge laying down a verdict. "Still – I am so glad that we were able to help such nice, conscientious children."

Found and Lost and Found Again

"Richard, my old – can you be spared from your kitchen for the afternoon?" Lew inquired on one Monday afternoon late in winter. "There is something that we wish to show you, now that you and your estimable Katherine have set a date."

"Of course, Lew," Richard answered, sneaking a quick glance at the clock. He could, in fact, spare the time. The kitchen brigade behind the grand Crystal Room restaurant was well-trained in the old-school manner, honed to a highly polished professional sheen. This freed him from the necessity of keeping constantly after them in the manner of an obsessive-compulsive sheep dog. He could, in fact, spend the remaining afternoon with Lew on whatever thing Lew had in mind. Lew was essentially his boss, and operated on the principle of training your staff so thoroughly in your way of doing things that one could safely take a few hours from the duty day.

"Come with me, then," Lew commanded. "You do know that VPI established a new development at Mills Farm?"

"I know that the stables had been enlarged," Richard took off his chef's jacket, and assumed his outdoor coat. Texas did become surprisingly chilly in winter. "You spoke about expanding to support more outdoor sports ... a new cabin, fitted out especially for the hunting and shooting fraternity, with trophy heads and hunting memorabilia."

"All that, as well," Lew was shrugging into his own coat, as he and Richard walked out the private side entrance, where there was a little parking lot for staff. "But I want to show you something which I mentioned to you some months ago – Mills Farm's private retreat lodges; houses for upper staff such as yourself, and to accommodate visiting senior management from Houston. I thought you might like to look at the residence which will be offered to you when it is finished. Some of the structures are complete," Lew added, "But for the final touches, essential cabinetry and such. I hope that you will approve," Lew added, in a somewhat austere manner, "More importantly – that your lovely bride will also approve..."

"I am certain that whatever you and the design team come up with will be satisfactory," Richard assured him. Lew grinned like a mischievous boy.

"My dear Anne has the project firmly in hand. I will drop a hint to her that perhaps she should invite your Katherine for coffee some delightful morning soon, to determine what she might prefer for your little nest. In the meantime, I thought to show you the place."

"I'll be glad to see the new development," Richard replied. In the rush of recent events and wedding plans which demanded whatever interest he could spare from the Crystal Room, he had quite forgotten – or at least, set aside the matter aside as a secondary concern, or even tertiary. The matter of where they would live together would be resolved for as long as he worked for Venue Properties. His employer would provide quarters. Richard had assumed that it would be one of the tiny flats on the upper floor of the Cattleman. It had been obvious that Kate couldn't possibly move into the tiny Airstream caravan, and he certainly couldn't move himself into her tiny flat in Karnesville. Moving in with her parents in Karnesville wasn't on, either. For one thing, although their house might have been large enough, but since Richard couldn't drive, he absolutely had to be within bicycle-distance of Luna City.

"Excellent!" Lew beamed, as he led Richard to the beautifully maintained vintage Mercedes sedan which was his main ride. Lew drove expertly, and with a Gallic flair which Richard could only envy helplessly. His own early attempts at operating a motor vehicle were so disastrous that he had been forever put off the prospect of getting and keeping a driver's license. (*Also at the request of his insuring agency, his parents, past employers, and the police traffic authorities of several nations. Something to do with bad or nonexistent depth perception. Richard was totally incapable of calculating distances when traveling at speeds of over twenty miles an hour. The considerable damages incurred when he was on anything but a bicycle were too much for Richard and others to risk.*)

The Mercedes swept along Route 123, south in the direction of the next eventual almost-metropolitan area; that of Beeville. Just short of the turn-off to Mills Farm, which was clearly marked with some tasteful signage, a planter full of seasonal decorations and a clearly-marked turning lane, Lew directed the Mercedes off the main road and onto a modest unpaved driveway, which might have been mistaken for the entrance to a small ranch holding, or perhaps an oilfield facility. There was, however, a very businesslike tall fence with a barred gate in it – a gate with a combination to open it through some legerdemain with Lew's fancy cellphone. The gate swung ponderously open, they passed through, and the gate   shut after them.

Richard realized that this was the private back way into the far reaches of Mills Farm; the extension built on the river-front acreage purchased from the Grants which contained the stables and the 1912 Boathouse. Months ago, Lew had said something about the uber-private luxury compound. In the rush of events since, that had all slipped to the back of his mind. Now that mention was retrieved from the back of the messy filing cabinet that resembled Richard's memory.

A little way past the gate, the road branched. A small period-style signpost directed left towards the stables and 1912 Boathouse. The turning to the right was as yet unmarked with anything other than a lettered temporary sign directing construction deliveries and vehicles in that direction.

"The landscaping will be done as soon as the work is finished," Lew explained. "But I think that there will not be much required ... there was a small natural pond. Very scenic, which has been deepened and enlarged, to serve as a central feature. The gardens of all the villas will focus on it. My dear Anne recalled Queen Marie Antoinette's little home farm at Versailles, when she suggested the overall layout for this complex ... only adapted in accordance with local custom. Some of the cottages are based on the charming little houses built by Alsatian immigrants more than a hundred years ago in Castroville. European in sensibility, but refined by Texas ... and of course, with every modern convenience ... but tastefully done, of course," Lew added, in response to Richard's raised eyebrow.

"Where I came from," Richard commented, "Modern convenience meant that the loo was indoors, instead of in a little hut at the bottom of the garden. But I get the intention ... I'm certain that this ... a kind of grace and favor residence? ... will be perfectly adequate for Kate and I ... oh, my!" he added, as the well-traveled road passed through a stand of small trees and emerged with the view of the new Mills Farm enclave spread out before them like a particularly choice *hors de oeuvres* platter. "Very nice! Your lady wife is an absolutely splendid designer."

"She does very well," Lew replied, all modesty. "The company is quite pleased with her designs! I should add that she is well-compensated as a consulting designer, although M'sieu Norberg once complimented us by saying that VPI had gotten two superior talents for the wages of one. I put him right on that score, of course."

"Of course," Richard could barely contain himself. It was a lovely vision of half a dozen small houses of varied design star-scattered in the sloping meadow that ran down to the small lake. Although three of the nearest constructions were still frame skeletons, rising up amid a litter of empty pallets, piles of brick and concrete block, churned earth gouged by truck wheels, and a cement truck sending down a rivulet of grey slush into timber forms while the light still held. The three farthest along the margin of the pond appeared nearly complete, with tile or shake roofs com and windows so new that they still had manufacturer's stickers adhering to the glass. One was being painted, a rich cream over rough stucco textured to appear ancient, contrasting with dark wood trim. The other two were already done. Lew parked the Mercedes by the last in the row; a tidy little cottage with a round window in the gable over the front door.

"I am told that this will be completed on the inside by the end of the month – would you like to see the inside?"

"I would, indeed, "Richard answered, and followed after Lew as Lew opened the front door and stepped inside. The room inside was empty; just bare, white-primered walls, with splatters of paint and assorted small construction litter on the concrete floor. A bank of windows in one wall framed a pleasing view of the tranquil pond, the meadows and a band of trees beyond. An arch in the wall opposite delineated another room; a smaller one, with more windows, and lengths of plumbing pipe rising from the floor, or out of the wall.

"The kitchen," Lew gestured towards it. "The cabinets are on order to be delivered next week. The appliances will be installed once that is accomplished. There are two bedrooms, with a comfortable bathroom and a small utility closet between ... through this little hallway... Observe."

"I think this will do very nicely for Kate and I," Richard allowed, after a short pause to examine the three smaller rooms, the windows of which all looked out to the grove of trees which masked the lower half of the stables, and the distant belvedere tower on the 1912 Boathouse. The bathroom was mostly finished, tiled in white penny tile, matching pedestal sinks and tub installed; plain and slightly old-fashioned facilities which merged perfectly with the mildly antique aesthetic of Mills Farm. "It's certainly larger than where either of us are living now! Kate will be so pleased to have where we will live sorted for the present. I can't thank you enough, Lew – for making a charming little cottage like this available ..."

"VPI values good employees," Lew replied, appearing slightly embarrassed by Richard's gratitude.

As if it had been arranged, the sun was already beginning to drop below the western tree line, sketching long and picturesque shadows across the greensward. At that moment, Lew's cellphone chimed a short, jingly tune.

"Pardon, my dear Richard – I must answer this call," Lew murmured, and Richard nodded acquiescence. For privacy's sake, Richard went into one of the rooms designated as a bedroom, and thought to himself,

Yes, this will do – do very nicely indeed. The other room can be a shared office for me and my darling Kate of Kate Hall ... or for Ozzy to claim as his own. Yes, we can live here very happily, until the day when we can afford something that isn't grace and favor...

"Richard, I must go and talk to Benny Cordova," Lew called from the main room. "I regret – it is a matter of extreme urgency; a crisis with the new irrigation system for the golf course. It is not functioning as was guaranteed, and the golf course is slated to reopen tomorrow. Do you mind waiting until I can drive you back to town? I regret that this may be an emergency of some duration."

"It's almost five," Richard replied. "Look, it's just a short walk to my place at the Age, and Kate will be there soon. I've left my bicycle at the Cattleman, but I can hitch a ride in the morning with her. Don't worry, I'll just walk home from here. It's just half a mile or so, along the riverbank. See you in the morning. Do you mind if I take some pics with my phone of this place, to show her tonight?"

"Not at all," Lew grinned, almost fatuously. "Show your lovebird her new nest, cher! I will see you in the morning, then."

"Perfect," Richard answered. In the moments that he wandered from room to room, he heard the Mercedes engine start up and then diminish into the distance.

It was strangely restful for him, walking from room to unfinished room, considering how he and Kate would make it into a comfortable refuge. He would leave it up to Kate and her mother to sort out things like furniture, drapes and pretty towels for the bathroom. He did know that between them, the wedding gift registry *(since their many friends had been generous in gift-giving)* and an attic crammed full of inherited furniture at the Heisel family residence – that would be sorted. Lucky man; he would not be obliged to lift a finger, unless it was to assist with something heavy. Yes, he would relish coming home at the end of a long day to this little cottage with a view of the pond.

"I'm a simple man, with simple tastes," he observed aloud, as he wandered into the smaller designated bedroom. "Wherever I hang my hat … and park my boots … that's my home. One thing sorted, after this wedding, thank God!"

There was no lock yet on the front door, so Richard simply closed it after himself, oriented the way down to the 1912 Boathouse, and walked away in that direction. Some of the workmen were also departing the site, as it was the end of the day. They waved casually to Richard and he waved in return, although he didn't exactly recognize any of them. Likely they were patrons at the Café, where his full English breakfast had become a standout favorite among those in the construction trade, and given to eaten early and substantially.

Richard rather relished the walk through the carefully groomed back reaches of Mills Farm, down towards the margins of the San Antonio River. It wasn't raw Texas countryside, which he was given to understand was full of plants to which sensitive people were allergic, cacti full of sharp spikes, poisonous snakes, and dangerous critters like feral hogs of massively unusual size. This was a nature not quite as willing to kill the unwary human as Australia, but a safer and tastefully edited version, planted thoroughly with colorful wildflowers and shrubs. Paths had been laid out here and there, graveled or filled with wood mulch. It was all a very pleasant walk, considering. He hoped that he might see fireflies, among the lush spring grass and rushes along the river, when twilight fell.

Perhaps he and Kate would see early-evening fireflies dancing among the tall sedge along the pond from the window of their grace and favor cottage, once spring came again.

There was a scattering of guests around the 1912 Boathouse – the aftermath, he surmised, from a private event; a celebration of some kind. It did not involve or interest him, so he skirted the boathouse, and strolled along the well-groomed path along the bank – a path which eventually led to the boundary of the Age of Aquarius Campground. There was a gate, with a notice on it, informing wanderers that the Age was a privately-owned property, although considerate guests were welcome as long as they treaded lightly upon Mother Earth and did not pester the goats, harm wildlife, and closed the gate after themselves. It was to this gate that Richard was heading; a shortcut to the campground, and to the Airstream caravan which had been his home for five years. A little distance from the Boathouse, he overtook another pedestrian. He saw to his mild astonishment that that other person was someone he recognized: Gunnison Penn, the semi-famous treasure hunter.

Gunnison Penn was a man of late middle age, originally from Canada, and lately married to a member of the sprawling Gonzalez-Gonzales clan, Professor Miranda Rodrieguez-Gonzales. Richard recalled the events of that wedding through a haze of panic, as he was on the temporary outs with Kate at the time, due to a colossal misunderstanding. That morning, Miranda Gonzales-Ramirez was on the temporary outs with her grandfather, Don Jaimie of the Rancho, over her sudden and inexplicable resignation from the staff of the private and quite up-market university where she had tenure.

The reason for that resignation and the purpose of the wedding was now in one of those marsupial-style baby-carriers, hitched to Gunnison Penn's chest; a sleeping infant, revealed around the margins of the carrier as a matched set of tiny, clenched fists, bootie-clad feet and a tuft of dark hair.

"Hey, Penn," Richard exclaimed, as he came close enough to speak without shouting. "Good to see you! I didn't know you and Dr. Mindy were back in town."

"Richard!" Xavier Gunnison Penn turned, beaming unalloyed pleasure on his bearded countenance. Richard noted, with mild surprise, that the beard was now neatly trimmed, and the dyspeptic expression which Gunnison Penn once had worn almost routinely had been banished. Marriage and fatherhood must agree with him. The man looked almost happy, content, even – although there were suspiciously blue shadows under his eyes, which suggested sleep-interruptions caused by the baby. "What a surprise, seeing you here! Yes, we returned for a visit to Mindy's family, and to introduce Little Carmen Miranda to Don Jaimie! A first great-granddaughter for the Rincon de los Robles family."

"Carmen ... Miranda?" Richard was slightly boggled, and Gunnison Penn beamed proudly.

"Carmen Miranda Rodrieguez-Gonzalez Gunnison Penn. Carmen for her great aunt, and Miranda for her mother."

"Quite a mouthful for such a little tyke," Richard commented, after turning over several possible comments in his mind, including a reference to towering fruit-baskets as a hat and rejecting them as untactful. The baby slept on, undisturbed.

"Yes, but she's going to grow into it, the wee darling," Gunnison Penn smiled fatuously, appearing to take every possible fatherly pride in the baby. Standing closer, Richard now could see the tiny sleeping face – yes, she was his, all right. The peevish expression was identical to that of the great treasure hunter in a bad mood. Richard could only hope that the wee darling would grow out of that, before commencing kindergarten.

"I hadn't heard that you and Mindy were back in Luna City," Richard sighed and accepted his social obligation. "Else I would have sent you an invite. Kate and I are getting married in February – do you and Dr. Mindy have any plans for the 16th? Six o'clock at the Lutheran church in Karnesville."

"Alas, our immediate plans take us to Central America," Gunnison Penn actually looked quite regretful. "The reservations are already made, and the airline tickets purchased. We leave on Monday next week and anticipate being away for months."

"Another honeymoon?" Richard asked. He couldn't imagine a less inviting place, and Gunnison Penn shook his head, lowering his voice to a conspiratorial whisper.

"No ... another treasure draws us! Mindy has been studying the existing documents in Mexico City, and we are certain we can pinpoint the exact location of the stolen treasure of Lima. Piracy was involved, you see ... but it is all documented – the apprehension of the miscreants ... Mindy being a scholar and an archivist, you see. She has researched deeply in the official colonial archives. For some documents, she was the first to examine them in fifty years. We have every hope."

Richard just barely stopped himself from observing, "So you always do – have every hope!" Instead, he said, "Then I'll have every hope for your success."

Gunnison Penn beamed. "Thank you! I've been lucky twice, so no reason I couldn't be lucky a third time. There is one thing, though … can I leave … a certain package with you? It's … well, something that I don't want to leave with anyone else, and I trust you implicitly."

"It's not something that will bring me a packet of trouble?" Richard was wary of much to do with Xavier Gunnison Penn. Penn was the most famous unsuccessful treasure hunter in the known world, and also the record holder for being banned from museums, auction houses and whole third-world countries. If there was trouble following Gunnison Penn, Richard didn't want to be a speed-bump in that particular road.

"No," Gunnison Penn replied. "It's just that Mindy and I are older parents, and following our passions might be somewhat hazardous … well, we want to leave a legacy for Carmen Miranda. Just take the sealed envelope that I'll bring to you … you are still living in that caravan on the goat farm?"

"Yes, I am," Richard replied. "For now. But during the day, I can generally be found at the Cattleman Hotel. I have an office there. And if security is required, there is a safe in the office, and I am one of those employees permitted access to it."

"Excellent!" Gunnison Penn beamed. "I'll bring the envelope to you tomorrow. Just put it away and keep it safe … and give it to Carmen Miranda on her 21st birthday. I'm certain you will be around, since you are also marrying into the clan."

"Right … yes, of course," Richard promised, now having second thoughts about such an obligation. *Hold onto a sealed envelope for twenty years?* But he had already committed. Yes, now he would be a member of extended Clan

Gonzalez/Gonzales, although to be absolutely truthful, merely perched on the farthest outlaying branch of that family tree. "My word on it, as an Englishman," he added. Gunnison Penn beamed.

"I'll see you tomorrow then," he said. "Farewell for now – Mindy is collecting me at the Boathouse in a few minutes. I just wanted to walk with Carmen Miranda in the peace and quiet, you see."

"Ta, then," Richard said. They had reached the gate into the Age of Aquarius – the point of parting for now. "See you on the morrow. I'll keep your documents safe. My promise on the matter."

"See you tomorrow," Gunnisen Penn replied, and in short order, he and the slumbering infant were out of sight. Richard closed the gate after himself, and only at that juncture began to wonder.

Lucky twice? To the best of his knowledge, Xavier Gunnison Penn's lifetime record for unsuccessful searches for lost treasure troves had been blemished only once; by finding the Gonzaga Reliquary welded into a set of tacky Christmas ornaments. A Renaissance work in gold, crystal and gemstones, reported to have been created by Cellini, painted by Da Vinco, brought to the New World, much battered by the centuries of being used as a mobile bank account by Gonzaga descendants, despoiled of half the inlaid gems in it and replaced by glass fakes. A sad treasure, but still undisputably a treasure ... so what was the second time lucky? Richard mused on that for a few moments, but then he looked ahead and saw that Kate's little Volkswagen Bug bumping down the rutted roadway that was the driveway into the campground at the Age, and put that puzzle aside, in favor of more interesting diversions.

The Mills Treasure

The Contents of the Envelope Entrusted to Richard Astor-Hall, January 2020, to be held in trust for Carmen Miranda Rodrieguez-Gonzalez Gunnison Penn until her 21st birthday.

1 – key to a safe deposit box, in the Karnesville Savings Bank security vault.

2 – 1 20$ Gold piece – American coinage, circa 1892

3 – a hand drawn map of a tract of land in the loop of the San Antonio River, directly south of Luna City, showing buildings and landmarks as existing in 1937, with an overlay showing the same in 1978: the historic and renewed Mills Farm complex.

4 – 10 pages of printed documentation, addressed to Carmen Miranda as 'our dearest child' and signed by Xavier Gunnison Penn.

To Carmen Miranda, our dearest child and heir; this written account is left for you as an explanation for the contents of the safe deposit box, which is your inheritance. Your mother knows nothing of this matter, since I conducted my search in deep secrecy, and under conditions which might give rise to legal disputation. However, a search for the Mills Treasure had long engaged my interest. I had studied all available records and performed preliminary and unsuccessful searches for it before your mother and I ever met and married. You may know of the legend of the Mills Treasure, from your familial connection to the locality – or may not. If you do, then you may safely skip over this brief account of Charles Everett Mills, of Mills Farm – as it was known before becoming the property of Venue Properties, International and the spa, resort and event venue that it is.

Charles E. Mills was the dissolute son of the original owners; a respectable and hardworking family whose prosperous farm property was the pride of Karnes County in their lifetime. Charles Mills, however, spent most of his adult life on the far side of the law, to the shame of his surviving family. He was recorded as having been an active member – if not the leader – of several notable criminal gangs in the late 19th century, gangs which specialized in robbery of trains, banks, and payrolls. Upon the deaths of his parents in the early years of the 20th century, Charles Mills returned to the family homestead. It was rumored locally at the time that he possessed a fortune in gold coinage and ingots; the takings from such robberies. It is a matter of historical record that even while the family farm went to rack and ruin over the subsequent thirty years, Charles Mills still maintained possession of the property and lived in a certain degree of comfort until his death from natural causes in 1937. In spite of his known activities as a bootlegger and producer of illicit alcohol during Prohibition – which may have accounted for the appearance of prosperity during that period, rumors persisted of a cache of gold somewhere on the property. Nothing was ever found to substantiate them until an archaeological excavation of the area adjacent to the modern show barn was conducted in 2016, after a small boy found an 1892 20$ gold coin in near to pristine condition, during a holiday Easter Egg hunt.

The final results of that dig were kept confidential by the VPI corporate powers, but I was able to access them through private means. The area excavated encompassed what had been the privy of the original farmstead; with the usual valueless discards in the form of bottles, broken crockery and other trash – but among them were some small silver coins and another 1895 20$ gold coin, confirming that Charles Mills had indeed possessed a quantity of gold and gold coinage, and that for a time such items were likely concealed them in the put underneath the farm outhouse.

From my long experience in the treasure-hunting profession, I was convinced that the gold cache removed from the privy was taken to some other hiding place on the Mills property by Charles Mills himself during his lifetime, but he took the secret of that new location to his grave. After his death in 1934, the property fell even further into disrepair. In 1972, the derelict farmstead and property surrounding were sold by the Everett heirs to Venue Properties, International. Any existing structures, or their remains were demolished, and the site extensively terraformed to accommodate construction of various new or relocated structures. It was obvious to myself and to other searchers that if the remaining gold had been hidden in what was left of the Mills's original house and outbuildings, that it would have been found – and if not by Venue Properties demolition crews, then by any number of searchers over the decades when the property lay vacant. Therefore, logic and experience suggested to me that the Mills gold must have been secreted underground, in a location which Charles Mills believed to be utterly secure against detection.

In pursuit of this theory, I embarked on an extensive search for information about the original Mills property. Maps, photographs and personal accounts contemporary to Charles Mills' occupation of the property turned out to be extraordinarily rare. He was not personally well-disposed towards his neighbors and had few visitors to the place during his lifetime. Indeed, in his final years, he lived as a recluse, rarely leaving the property. One of the last visitors to the property – and present there shortly before his death – was a writer for Federal Writers Project, Percival A. "Perry" Woodstone, who was collecting material for a guidebook to South Texas and collecting interviews with such aged citizens as he could convince to speak with him. Woodstone's materials were available in the project's archives, along with photographs taken at the time of that visit to the Mills farm. One landscape which was of particular significance to me was of Charles Mills standing next to a fenced stock pond containing three alligators. He was notorious locally for a number of peculiarities. One of them was for his collection of alligators. It was rumored for many years that the bodies of enemies murdered by Mills were disposed of by being fed to those beasts.

The thought came to me then – what if Charles Mills treasury of gold coins was hidden in or buried adjacent to the alligator enclosure? The longer that I considered that possibility, the likelier that it seemed. What better location wherein to conceal a fortune than in a place where the boldest trespasser would fear to venture? I began an intensive study of those maps which I could locate, comparing aerial views of the contemporary area with those extant in the 1930ies, and of historic photographs – those taken by Woodstone and others, of the Mills Property. Eventually I pinpointed the area most likely to correspond with the alligator pond: the vicinity of a large sand-trap adjacent to the 11th hole of the Mills Farm golf course.

At that juncture, I was stymied. Mills Farm is the property of a large corporation; it has been my bitter experience over the years, that such entities are reluctant in the extreme to permit any infringement on their prerogatives. However, I could not see that they had any moral right to the Mills gold, merely by owning the land upon which the previous owner had concealed it. They had no interest in searching for it, in any case – and not only had I such an overwhelming interest, I had been seeking it for many years. I was secure in my own conscience that the Mills treasure was rightfully mine – if I could find it.

Fate intervened at this juncture; I was made aware that extensive work on the irrigation system for the golf course would be taking place over the next month. Fate then played into my favor: with dozens of workmen coming and going onto the property, and conducting extensive excavations in the area of prime interest, it was a simple matter for me to assume the guise of one of them, and conduct a surreptitious series of excavations without exciting comment from anyone, even when I brought in a metal detector. When casually queried about what I was doing, I explained that I was merely searching for those pipes previously installed. You would be astonished at how openly I was able to conduct this search, and how little interest in my activities was excited among the legitimate workmen. A frank and open demeanor, a confident bearing – and a superficial and apparently legitimate reason for being present is a passport to many places which may be otherwise out of reach to a seeker of treasure.

I uncovered the Mills hoard after two weeks of careful reconnaissance and excavation, when my metal detector pinged repeatedly in the area marked with a circle on the attached map – approximately one meter from the south-east border of the existing sand trap. I assumed that the hoard was originally deposited within the alligator pond. I presume that Charles Mills marked the position in some manner, so as to be able to retrieve portions of the contents such as were needed. Among the quantity of coins and cast gold ingots were the metal fastenings and reinforcements from some kind of satchel or Gladstone bag.

I assume from these scraps of base metal that the gold was originally contained within such. In any case, I was able to transfer the gold into my pockets or the tool bag which I had with me as part of my pretense as a worker. I managed this without ever being detected by other laborers, or the management of Mills Farm. I procured a safety deposit box for a bank in Karnesville, for which the key is now in your hands.

This is your inheritance, my dearest child – yours to do with as you wish. Let discretion be your guide as to how you use what I have bequeathed to you.

Your adoring father,
Xavier Gunnison Penn

Endings

"Letty, can you come out to the house today? I'm feeling like cr*p, and I don't want to expose anyone else at the Café. I'll wear the stupid mask and avoid coughing on you," Doc Wyler growled over the phone – the ancient wall unit that Miss Letty McAllister maintained in the kitchen of the house that she had inherited from her parents. The only phone in the house was mounted on the wall in the same small niche built for it when the McAllister family took the plunge in 1928 and joined the early 20th century telecommunications network. Back in the day, Mayor McAllister's family had been on a party line. Miss Letty still recollected the pattern of long and short rings which meant a call was for their household. She had also never overcome a certain discretion when it came to discussing personal matters on the telephone. One might never know who else on the party line might also be listening in.

"Of course, Stephen," Miss Letty replied. This was their usual once-weekly meeting, to discuss matters affecting their mutual ownership of the Luna Café and Coffee, a project dear to both hearts in their love of Luna City. "Christopher can drive me, as usual … but may I ask for a ride home when we are done? I do not like to impose on very much of the dear boy's time."

"Of course," Doc Wyler growled. "I'll have Ken or one of the hands drive you back, when we're done. Or maybe Pat can give you a lift. She came this morning, bearing bone broth and lectures about minding my health… I'd much rather have some of those lemon pecan coconut cookies that your mother used to make for us. If you have made a batch of them, bring a few for me."

"If course I will. Patricia has always been very fond of you, Stephen," Miss Letty replied, and Stephen Wyler merely grunted, ungraciously. He was Miss Letty's oldest and best friend left to her in the world of the living.

Miss Letty gathered some late roses from her garden, wrapping the cut stems in a wet paper towel, and then in a plastic bag. She also took a pasteboard box with a few homemade pecan-cocoanut bar cookies with a lemon drizzle frosting, cookies which Stephen asked for, specifically. He had always been very fond of them when he and Letty and Letty's older brother Douglas and their friends had run in a group as children. They had organized a kind of secret club among those friends, a select association dedicated to small juvenile adventures and excursions. For a while, they had even built a small ramshackle hut built of river-wrack and scraps of lumber for their meetings. Those cookies were a favorite treat among the McAllister childrens' friends. Their mother made them often, as they used plumb pecans and lemons from their own garden; the only additional expense being for dried grated coconut from the grocery store. Mrs. McAllister had written down the recipe in her own spidery handwriting on an index card filed in a little wooden box which still sat on a shelf in the McAllister kitchen.

Of that long-ago group of friends, only Letty and Stephen Wyler survived and lived in Luna City. The last remaining among other regular members, Dym Marcus, was still alive, living in Colorado Springs, but his signature on the most recent Christmas card which Letty had received was pretty shaky. Harry Vaughn still lived in Luna City, but he had been so much younger than the others, he was more of an unwelcome tag-along when his older brother Artie was forced to baby-sit his younger sibling.

"If you can drive me out to the Wyler place this morning," Miss Letty told Chris Mayall, when she met him at the front of the house, when he came across road from the Tip Top at the accustomed hour and opened the passenger door of the little red coupe which was his ride. "Dr. Wyler is not feeling well – and asked me to come to the house, instead of the Café. He didn't want anyone else to risk catching what he has…"

"But what about yourself, Miss Letty?" Chris demanded. "Shouldn't you have a care, then?"

Chris tactfully left unsaid that Miss Letty was just as aged; vulnerable to the stray seasonal cold or flu virus developing into pneumonia and carrying her off to join the choir eternal. Miss Letty appreciated his sensibility on that score. Now she replied,

"Nothing to worry about on that score, Christopher. Curiously, I have rarely contracted the seasonal influenza, and when I did, I only felt out of sorts for a day or so."

"Cast-iron immune system," Chris agreed. "God's gift. All right, Miss Letty – fasten your seatbelt."

Miss Letty did not close her eyes during the brief drive to the front gate of the Wyler Ranch; along Oak Street to the edge of town, past the high school, and then into open tracts where Luna City proper unraveled out into open meadows. She had traveled that way for decades, beginning when she was seven or eight years old, on a bicycle and trailing after her older brother Douglas. It was all so very familiar, even though a lot had changed. During the prosperous 50ies, after the War, newer houses and a separate high school   filled in empty tracts to the east of town, right up to the tall perimeter fence which surrounded the vast acres of the Wyler ranch. Chris Mayall's little coupe rumbled over the cattle grid at the main gates, elaborate wrought-iron gates which almost always stood open. A long scenic drive, attended by white-painted pasture fences on either side, curved away into the ranch property. A few russet-red cattle browsed companionably among the scattering of tall oaks.

"They say that a really high-class house," Chris remarked, as the Wyler home ranch house appeared; a three-level columned wedding-cake of a house, perched on a low rise in the middle distance, "Is one that you can't even see from the road. All the same, I'd hate to be the one that mows that lawn. By the time you get to the back forty, you'd have to start all over again."

"I believe that Stephen's flock of goats takes care of the lawn," Miss Letty replied. "His father's notion, back in the day. I believe that old Mr. Wyler – Stephen's father, that is, used to keep a whole crew busy with the landscaping, when I was a girl. Mostly to provide jobs for them during the Depression. When the War began, of course, most of them went to work in defense plants, or in the military. So the Wylers brought in a herd of goats … oh, there is Patricia's car. Don't worry about returning for me in an hour – Patricia will give me a ride back to town."

"Okay-doke," Chris drew into the final approach to the house; a neat half-acre-wide apron of raked and edged gravel. "You'll be OK on the stairs, Miss Letty?"

"I'll be fine," Miss Letty took out her cane from the car and straightened her hat. "I know this house very well, and I'm accustomed to stairs."

"I'll wait until you get inside," Chris said firmly. Miss Letty knew there was no arguing with him. The dear boy was very fond of her, and of course he was good to be so concerned. She climbed the twelve stairs carefully, walked carefully across the wide veranda and rang the doorbell. When Conchita Gonzales, the Wyler housekeeper, opened the door for her, she turned and waved to Chris – who waved back, set the coupe into gear and drove away towards the gates.

"Doc is upstairs, on the balcony off his private office, Miss Letty," Conchita said, as she closed the door. "He's expecting you. Go right on up. Pat and I are having coffee in the kitchen. She says come on down when you're finished and ready to go home."

"Thank you," Miss Letty replied. "I won't be very long, I don't think. I brought some roses, and the cookies that Stephen has always liked. What mood is he in, this morning?"

"Feeling better, I think," Conchita was a stout, motherly woman a generation and a bit younger than Letty; another member of the extensive Gonzales/Gonzalez clan, and one who had passed through Miss Letty's Kindergarten class some forty years before. Conchita had been plump then, too; a round somber face framed in a pair of dark braided pigtails. "I'll bring them up with his lunch. Oh, don't they smell wonderful! No one in Luna City grows such lovely roses as you do, Miss Letty! But be sure you don't tire him out. He's one of those men who thinks because that he's feeling better, he can go back to doing what he normally does … and then he overdoes it and is sick in bed again."

"I'll be careful," Miss Letty promised. "I'm not getting any younger myself."

The grand sweeping staircase which ascended to the top floor in a series of gentle arcs under a domed glass skylight, was an easier climb. Letty knew the way very well. Not only had she been coming to the Wyler mansion for most of a century as a friend of Stephen Wyler's, she had also been the best friend of Miss Alice Everett; Mrs. Stephen Wyler for nearly half of that time. Dear Alice, who had adorned the Wyler household as wife and hostess! Miss Letty still grieved … grieved for Alice and for other long-gone friends.

Yes, she knew her way around the Wyler mansion, nearly as well as she knew her way through the little stone house that she had been born in, grew up in, lived in now. She went to the second door on the left, at the top of the stairs to the second floor, rapped softly twice and then opened the door and went in. The room was fitted out as a study and library, redolent of another century, fitted out with heavy Belle Epoque furniture and an antique partner's desk, the walls lined with bookshelves and genre western paintings in oil, some of them better suited to a museum. There was a more modern overlay, of a computer and monitor, with a printer; the only imposition of the lamentable newer century. The room was empty, although the French door giving onto the veranda which went all round the house stood open, the long curtains stirring in the fitful and blessedly still cool spring breeze.

"I'm on the balcony," Stepen called from outside. Miss Letty followed the sound of his voice.

This side of the grand Wyler mansion offered a view of the distant roofs of Luna City's taller buildings, set among the green tops of the oak trees. The balcony was set with a number of comfortable wicker chairs and a pair of chaise lounges, some flowering plants in pots. It had long been Stephen's most favored place, as it offered a view of Luna City and the rolling green countryside out towards the southwest of the mansion.

"How long have we known each other?" Stephen asked. He leaned against the cushioned back of the chaise, a light blanket covering his legs. It was chilly on the shaded balcony at this time of year. Miss Letty eyed him, surreptitiously. He did look terribly frail. The regularly appearing seasonal influenza seemed to have hit him terribly hard this year; he who was normally as tough and stringy, as impervious to wear and tear as boiled leather.

"All of our lives," Miss Letty replied – a literalist at heart. "We were born three months apart. Me first, then you. I think Dr. Haugen delivered us both. Not in the hospital, of course. At home, as Mama felt was only proper."

"But do you recall when we first officially met?" Stephen Wyler persisted, and Miss Letty cast her mind and memory back over the decades.

"I do, indeed," she replied. "Your third birthday. Your parents held a party for you here, and invited Douglas and I, and a few other children of about the same age. I recollect that they ordered up a small traveling carnival, with a little Ferris wheel and a merry-go-round. Only you were very rude to the other children at first, and your mother took you into the house for a lecture and a good spanking."

"Better memory than me," Stephen replied. "I don't recall the spanking; must have blown it off. I usually did. The merry-go-round is what I recall. Painted horses on it. I wanted one for myself to keep. I believe that is what I had the tantrum over. Ah, I guess I always was a spoiled brat. Single-minded – my way and my way only."

"It made for a very pleasant little party," Miss Letty reminisced. "Such fun, the merry-go-round! The cake that your parents' cook made for us had lemon-curd between the layers, and the most heavenly-tasting whipped white icing. I thought that was the most original and delicious thing I had ever tasted. We had such a good time; I believe that Douglas and I thought about that party for months afterwards."

"Must have been about 1925," Stephen mused. "One of those good times, before the Crash – when the money flowed like water, and Mother and Father spared no expense when it came to throwing a good party. I don't believe that we saw good times again until beef prices revived during the war. That didn't last for long, though. Too many folks got a taste for moving around – wanted the thrill of living in the big city. Never saw the sense in that. Our town damn near died, until VPI bought the old Mills-Everett place, and then the oil boom picked up a few years ago. Broke my heart, seeing all the small one-off small family businesses closing up around the Square, what with everyone preferring to go to shop in Karnesville."

"We did our part, Stephen," Letty reminded him. "We kept Luna City alive … well, us, the Abernathys and the Bodies between us. The hardware store, the feed mill … and the Café."

"Yes, the Café," Stephen sat up a little straighter. "That's what I wanted to talk to you about that. I've decided that I'd prefer to step back from regular involvement at this point. Richard put the place on a stable footing and put it on the culinary map – worked a damned miracle, as far as I can see. Now, with Araceli as the manager, riding herd on some good reliable local staff who won't quit on a moment's notice over some stupid tiff or other, I'd like to think that we can leave it in her hands. Young Walcott is shaping up very well, what with his notions about mail-order gourmet items. All that newfangled stuff about a website and an on-line store … beyond me, Letty. You can't teach an old dog new tricks and I'm not gonna even try. Besides … I'm tired."

"Quite understandable, Stephen," Miss Letty favored her old friend with a wintery smile. "We are not either of us getting any younger. I have already made a disposition of my estate. I have decided to leave the larger portion of my own share of the Café to Araceli in my will, with smaller shares willed to Robbie Walcott and Luc Massie. Although I do not intend to inform them of this. As Mr. Dickens so wisely counseled in *Bleak House*, such expectations of a fortune – even a small one –   can entirely ruin the character of an otherwise admirable young person."

Stephen snorted. "Very wise, Letty. I've made it simple for my lawyer; the ranch and my local holdings are all in a family trust, with Patricia controlling the majority of shares for the benefit of her sons, and my daughter Pamela for her kids. Collin has his own fish to fry, he gets nothing more than a few trinkets for sentiment's sale. I'll leave it for Patricia to sort out what to do with what I hold in the Café. She's a good, sensible woman … must have got it from her mother, lord knows it didn't come from Collin. Anyway, I thought I'd let you know that I want to step away from directly overseeing the Café and get your thoughts on it."

"Very sensible, I think," Letty agreed. "Let the children have their head – make their own decisions. Stephen … are you feeling unwell?" Letty added, with sudden concern, for it seemed to her now that Stephen did appear … very pale, and almost unnaturally exhausted. She was afraid that her visit had tired him out.

"I'm fine, Letty … you know, I think I would relish one of those cookies that you said you would bring."

"I left them with Conchita. She told me she would bring them up with your lunch." Letty answered. "Shall I go tell her to bring them up now?"

"Yes, do," Stephen replied. He closed his eyes and leaned back against the chaise.

Letty rose from the wicker chair. "I need to use the ladies, anyway … I'll go downstairs and tell her that you are ready for lunch."

Knowing the mansion as well as she did, Letty retired to a plush lavatory on the second floor – one bountifully set about with fluffy towels and a mat the size of a polar bear pelt next to the bathtub. Alice had overseen modernizing and redecorating the second-floor rooms, sometime in the early 1950s, when pink porcelain was all the rage for bathroom fixtures. Letty often wondered what Stephen had thought, of all the ultra-feminine touches that Alice had favored. Likely called it all kinds of useless feminine, frilly fru-fru, Letty thought – but not where Alice could have heard. She finished attending to matters and made her way carefully down the grand staircase, following the sound of feminine laughter to the kitchen and offices at the back of the house.

In the vast kitchen, Letty found Conchita and Patricia sharing coffee and gossip at the vast old oak kitchen table. The Wyler mansion kitchen was approximately twice the size of the severely practical and professional Café kitchen, and four times the size of the kitchen in Letty's house. When it was first built in the 1870s by Stephen's grandfather, Captain Wyler, (late) Confederate States Army, the mansion had often hosted events for a hundred or two hundred guests, and the kitchen was constructed along the lines of industrial-sized hospitality. In the bout of renovations in the 1950s, Alice Everett Wyler had retained those most attractive late Victorian features and upgraded kitchen facilities to a more comfortable and practical degree.

The subject of a wedding – of Richard *(formerly of the Café, now of the Cattleman Hotel restaurant)* and Kate Heisel, a second-or third-degree connection of the Karnesville branch of Clan Gonzales/Gonzalez was of intense interest to both. Especially since both Richard and Kate were mildly renown locally as media personalities. Afterwards, Letty wondered if the fifteen minutes she spent idly exchanging pleasantries and local gossip with Conchita and Patricia made any difference at all, after the time she had spent in the bathroom.

Conchita followed her upstairs, with Stephen's lunch – of course, set out on a silver tray, with two pecan-coconut-lemon bar cookies on a small plate, beside a bowl of chicken soup and a few soda crackers.

"He's got so that he isn't real hungry at lunch," Conchita remarked. "Is he still out on the balcony?" she added, as she and Letty returned to the office. The tall French window was still open, the long filmy curtain stirring in the light breeze like a cartoon ghost.

"He is," Letty replied, as she stepped out on the balcony. "Stephen – your lunch is here. Oh, dear – he has fallen asl—"

Stephen Wyler lay unmoving on the chaise where he had been when she left – lean, grey, irascible. His eyes were half-open still, seeming to gaze out at the distant vista of Luna City, the little town which he and Letty loved to the last little fiber of their being; the place which they had given their hearts to, long since – long before any other residents of the place had been born.

Letty, suddenly alerted and recognizing the signs through ancient experience in the War – picked up Stephen's slack wrist and felt for a pulse in it. No. Although his hand was still warm. He was gone. The oldest friend of her life.

No one left to remember. Only her.

"Conchita," she said, very calmly. "You had best call for the ambulance. But they need not hurry. I believe that it has already been at more than half an hour."

Conchita had the presence of mind not to drop the tray. Instead, she set it down very carefully on the desk and came to stand next to Letty on the balcony. She made the brief gesture of crossing herself and closed her eyes – a moment of silent prayer in the face of the final unknowable. When Conchita opened her eyes, they sought out Letty, almost as if she were the plump, solemn-faced kindergartner again, looking to her teacher for guidance. Letty answered that silent entreaty.

"It's all right, 'Chita. Go downstairs and break the news to Patricia before you call the dispatcher. I'll stay here with him."

Conchita nodded; her face was solemn, but her eyes were still dry. Perhaps she would cry later. Likely she and Patricia would have a good weep together, down in the kitchen.

As soon as Letty heard Conchita's footsteps descending the stairs, Letty drew the light covering up and settled his hand underneath it. Not pulling it over his head – it was too soon for that final covering,

Goodbye, my old and dear friend. Send my love to Alice, when you see her. Say hello to Douglas, Artie and Retta for me when you see them. Tell them that I will probably be along presently.

When Two Hearts Entwine

"I am wholly convinced that there will be some hideous, unavoidable, unpreventable disaster at the last minute," Richard confessed in a low voice to Chris, as they stood side by side in front of the lectern at the front of Shepherd of Galilee Lutheran Church. Chris was immaculate in a rented black-tie formal utfit with a white gardenia in his buttonhole. It was a real gardenia, and the perfume of it was heavy and almost too overwhelming for Rich's well-honed sense of smell. But the choice of flowers was up to Kate and her mother … and this was their wedding.

"Nothing to worry about, pal," Chris's barely moved his lips. He stood in a relaxed parade-rest position, feet slightly apart, hands clasped behind his back. "Your lady – she got this. It's all under control. Just go with the flow."

"I know," Richard answered. Likewise, his lips barely moved; set in a fixed half-smile. The church of which the Heisel family were long-time members was one of those 1920s mock-gothic edifices. The sanctuary boasted a set of outstanding stained-glass windows, and vintage hanging light fixtures dependent on bronze chains from a ceiling of pointed arches. The setting sun through the west-facing windows cast vivid scattered patches of colored light on the floor below. If Richard half-closed his eyes and pretended very hard, he might have thought himself standing in the English medieval church which this one copied. The church itself was better than half-filled already and rapidly becoming even fuller.

"Congratulations, Dude, you got a full-house," Chris remarked, as Lew Dubois, resplendent in faultless black tie of his own (not rented) escorted Judge Anita Blake-Silva to a length of pew on the groom's side on an end, towards the back. She had the dachshunds Felix and Oscar with her, on leashes, of course. They settled down obediently side by side, in the aisle, out from under careless stray feet, noses on paws. "And her little dogs, too. Hope they behave themselves around your furry friend."

"Oh, good lord," Richard sighed. "That would take the cake, wouldn't it? Felix and Oscar chasing Ozzie! My god, Chris! That would be a disaster!"

"Relax, Dude," Chris added. "Looks like they're behaving themselves...I don't recognize the elegant dame with Harry Vaughn ... is she one of your relatives?"

Sylvester Gonzalez, yet another immaculately black-tie clad usher was conducting Harry Vaughn and his lady to the second pew on the groom's side. The lady herself, in a long-sleeved pale lavender evening gown aflutter with silver gauze, caught Richard's eye and blew him a kiss. Richard sighed.

"My Aunt Moira the spy. Don't ever piss her off. She knows half a dozen ways to kill you without leaving an unnatural trace."

"You don't say!" Christ favored the lady with a wholly admiring look, and Richard hissed at him in warning.

"She likely has a stiletto-knife in her sleeve, and a garotte in her handbag. I'm warning you as a friend. Do not trifle with her ... there's been a trail of bodies in her wake, over the years. Most of them are still alive," Richard added fairly. "Stunned and twitching helplessly, but still alive."

"I'll keep it in mind, dude," Chris let the lascivious grin show for a moment and then resumed the regulation neutral expression. "Look, there's Joe and his mom. They don't have the babies with them. Guess they got a babysitter."

"Kate considered drafting Little Joe as a ringbearer," Richard nodded. "But she and her mother decided that he's too young to be reliable. An evening event is way out of his expected range of good behavior. Araceli volunteered her two for the wedding party instead. They are thrilled to have been included in such a solemn adult occasion."

Richard had become quite fond of Matty and Angelika, ever since the days when he first was hired for the Café and Araceli's son and daughter helped their mother after school, wrapping up silverware sets in cloth napkins and banding them with a paper wrap, ready on the morrow. He approved of children being trained up in a useful trade.

Chris sneaked a look at the watch on his wrist, before reassuming parade-rest. "Five minutes," he whispered. "If you're gonna run, Dude, do it now."

"Asshole," Richard whispered in return, hoping that no one in the almost-filled pews could read lips. The moment was nearly upon them. The church organist was noodling away at some inoffensive classical-sounding melody in a minor key. Just about every pew in Shepherd of Galilee was filled. Only the first row reserved for immediate family were empty.

Richard recognized a handful of Kate's family and friends on the brides' side, but the rest were relative strangers to him. He assumed they were her co-workers and old school friends, neighbors and distant connections of Clan Heisel. On his side, he did – refreshingly. The pews contained large contingent of Luna City Gonzales/Gonzalezes: Roman and his wife, Conchita *(who ran his construction firm office)*, Abuelita Adeliza, who ruled the clan with an iron fist, Araceli's husband Patrick and her younger brother, the guileless and gormless Berto, Bianca from the Cattleman and her cousins, the Battling 'B's, Beatrice and Blanca and some callow youths who must be their plus-ones for the evening. Patricia Wyler-Pryor and her husband and sons sat next to former Mayor Martin Abernathy and Martin's own plus-one, Joanna Garcia the tragic-romantic former prima ballerina, who was also a Gonzalez by birth. Richard wasn't entirely certain how. The connections in Luna City ran deep, complicated and defying the efforts of genealogists to untangle.

His landlords from the Age of Aquarius sat in the pew behind the Wyler-Pryor family: Sefton and Judy Grant. Mercifully, they had not brought any of their pets, goats, chickens, or Azucar the Ill-tempered Llama on this solemn and formal occasion. Their granddaughter Bree was with them. She was holding hands with Robbie Walcott. Colonel USA (Ret.) sat with his fire-cat spouse, Sook, sitting on the other side from her son. Richard sincerely hoped that Sook did not observe the signs of obvious affection between Bree and Robbie. She was a fiery-tempered creature and determined social-climber; with lofty ambitions baffled by her two older children in their choice of profession and possible spouses.

And there was Miss Letty, easily the most cherished and honored of all his guests saving only his parents. In the manner of a senior royal, she adorned and graced this gathering with her august and revered presence. Chris had seen her settled in the second pew *(on the other end of that now occupied by Harry Vaughn and Moira Astor-Hall.)* Richard's eyes roved a little farther back, where the other ushers lingered, waiting to settle the very last guests, before escorting his parents and Kates' to the

515

pews of honor. There was a flurry of movement beyond the sanctuary doors. It sounded as if the last handful of guests had just barely made it.

"Oh, f**k me running!" Richard murmured, frozen with horror. His heart sank down to the level of his black oxfords, as two women appeared in the doorway, framed by the light behind them like a pair of avenging angels. Beside him, Chris barely kept a grin from spreading from ear to ear.

"Hey, looks like it's the bunny-boiler herself! Miz Wyatt from Mills Farm! And is that your old girlfriend? Sunny, Sammy, whatever – that one that Collin Wyler put a ring on? Damn, from what I heard tell about Doc's boy and his dozen ex-wives, I reckon he buys wedding rings by weight."

"Sammi," Richard whispered through lips frozen into something that he hoped looked like a faint smile. "Swear to god, Chris … if anyone in this lot dares whisper a word when the Padre asks if anyone has any reason…a single, flipping word, I won't be held responsible for what I'll do then!"

"Relax, Ricardo," Chris slanted his eyes sideways towards Richard, suddenly concerned and contrite. "They're both happily married. Look, there's Romeo and Collin, coming through the door. Guess they were looking for parking places. It's OK, Dude. Take a deep breath. Wiggle your toes. It's going to be OK…"

Chris went on talking, in his best authoritative, soothing medic-to-accident-victim tones. Richard hardly heard a word of it, so close was he to the edge of panic over the unstoppable disaster that he was certain was roaring towards him with the inexorability of a freight train. Sylvester was showing Sammi and Collin Wyler to the groom's side. There was only room for them now in the pew next to Anita Blake-Silva and the dogs. As a Gonzalez, Lew Dubois squeezed Roman Gonzalez, the handsomest Gonzalez of his generation and his elegant wife, formerly Susannah Wyatt, once the operating director at Mills Farm *(and a fellow former senior executive in Venue Properties, International)* to the bride's side, in a pew among the constellation of Gonzalezes and Gonzaleses.

The distant tolling of a bell in the steeple above their heads striking the hour brought Richard back from the far edge of panic and sent him spiraling at light speed towards the opposite border of acute nausea. The outside church door was closed, cutting off the light and a thread of ambient street noise. The organ music was a little louder now, or perhaps it just sounded louder with the doors closed.

"Deep breath, Rich," Chris straightened to attention. "Action stations. Here come your parents, and Kate's mom."

"I think I am going to be sick," Richard murmured.

It was all coming to this pinnacle of a moment. All the planning of the last few months. The discussions with Kate, with her family, with Pastor Lundberg. The doubts and fears that he had in his own mind. The five years of his life in Luna City ... indeed, all of his life until that point. It all coalesced.

"Deep breath again," Chris replied, "Don't worry, Dude, I got a barf bag in my pocket with your name on it."

His parents, Alfred and Dorothy Astor-Hall advanced up the center aisle, to murmurs of curiosity and interest from the Gonzales/Gonzalez contingent, most of whom had never met Richard's parents. Dorothy was matronly and glorious in lavender-grey, with a matching fascinator. Her outfit reminded her son of something that Her Majesty, the Queen, might have worn to a regular Sunday evening service at Sandringham. Dorothy's corsage was a medley of rosebuds and gardenia, not nearly as large as the one which adored the covered wicker basket adorned with ruffles of white lace and trailing ribbons. Through the latticed door to the front of the basket, Ozzie's one-eyed brindle face could be seen. A single paw reached out to snag one of the trailing ribbons, to draw it within as an idle plaything.

Curiously enough, Richard's stomach settled. Just seeing Ozzie was ... reassuring. Even if Ozzie was stupefied with a bouquet of catnip, which affected and mellowed him in much the same way that a couple of gallons of neat brandy affected his human servant. Kate wouldn't hear of Ozzie being left out of the ceremony, which was against Richard's considered judgement ... but there he was.

And there was Mrs. Heisel, smiling as Lew deferentially conducted her into the pew with Kate's brothers, their wives, and older children. Her father-in-law, Grandpop Fritz, the aged veteran paratrooper with a ferocious dislike of all things English scowled like a walrus with indigestion from the pew immediately behind. His one-plus sat next to him, with a calming hand on his arm. She was the nice senior care nurse who kept him behaving more or less in a civilized manner towards Richard on public occasions such as this. Still, he was glad that Grandpop Fritz didn't have an electric carving knife within reach. He was certain that between Kate's father, mother. and her brothers, they all had taken care to confiscate any other deadly weapons that Grandpop Fritz might have concealed about his person.

But then there was always Aunt Moira as a second line of defense against an irate German-Texan with a decades-old and wholly-understandable wartime grudge.

Richard was jolted out of that contemplation by a single loud note from the church pipe organ. Pastor Lundburg joined Richard and Chris, standing on the first step into the chancel, resplendent in formal, old-fashioned church vestments. Pastor Lundberg boggled Richard on first acquaintance, for his resemblance to Father Christmas – beard and all. Richard almost expected him to be wearing a velvet mantle trimmed with white fur and carrying a bag full of toys on his shoulder.

"We will begin the ceremony now," Pastor Lundburg observed conversationally to Richard and Chris. The Reverend Lundburg had the most soothing voice; in another profession, he could have made a mint narrating natural-history documentary films. It was a wonder anyone stayed awake during his sermons, listening to those gentle soporific tones. Richard could only nod, suddenly dry-mouthed.

"Too late now, dude – you gotta go through with it!" Chris whispered under cover of the music as the organist roared into the processional. Which for a mercy wasn't the "Ta-dun-dun-

dun!" of the traditional wedding march, for which generations of school-boy wits had composed scurrilous lyrics but was instead was something spritely and Mozartian. Lew Dubois stood in the doorway with Araceli on his arm – elegant and smiling in something in rose-pink, still as slim as a teenager in spite of two children. *(Long days at the Café constantly on her feet must have had more to do with it than workouts at the gym.)* Just behind her, Jess Abernathy-Vaughn paired with Sylvester. The adults were so tall, they hid the next pair until they were halfway down the aisle: Angelika and her brother Matty. Angelika carried a basket of pale pink rose petals, Matty the small cushion with the wedding rings on it; rings carefully secured with a ribbon bow against any last-minute accidents. A solemn-faced Angelika scattered rose petals in precisely measured handfuls. Matty proudly strutted bearing up the ring-laden pillow as if he carried the crown jewels.

And then – it was Kate and her father, framed perfectly in the gothic arch of the center door, as the rustle of those gathered in the church stood and marveled. His lovely, beryl-eyed, dark-haired Kate, smiling and glorious in the cream satin and lace gown which Patricia Gonzalez had cobbled together from a pair of thrift-store dresses. No veil – a convention which she was adamantly against; only a crown of flowers and a frill of lace and trailing ribbons woven though her dark hair. Her eyes met Richards' – and he knew instantly that now, it would be all right.

And it was, although Richard remembered only bits and images from the service of marriage, as if he were wrapped in a happy fog, dazed with his own incredible good fortune. She was his, and he was hers, from now and forever, to the world's ending: the rustle as she handed her bouquet – a veritable fountain of flowers to Araceli – her own capable small hand warm in his, and the solid cool metallic feel of the simple gold circlet sliding onto his finger, the end of Pastor Lundberg's formal stole wrapped around their ringed hands binding them together, the slithery sound of lace and heavy satin from Kate's full skirts as they knelt before the altar. The daze didn't lift until it was all done.

The church emptied like water running out of a broken bowl. Faces floated past his and Kate's, the buzz of congratulations merging into a single continuing chorus like the summer cicadas singing in the trees, congratulating hands shaking his, thumping his shoulder ... Richard didn't think he was really back in his own mind and fully cognizant of reality until the photographer was done with taking pictures of himself and Kate, and the wedding party with Pastor Lundberg, in front of the altar, lined up with their respective parents, and a catnip-blissed out Ozzie in his basket at their feet.

The only guests waiting patiently through this was Miss Letty, who had begged off attending the reception, pleading that she was tired and still in mourning anyway. Miss Letty offered to cat-sitting Ozzie over Kate and Richard's honeymoon. She waited now for Chris to deliver Ozzie and herself back to the

McAllister house before Chris continued on to the reception at the Cattleman and his duties as best man. Berto also waited, as designated driver for the wedding party at the wheel of his uncle Tony in Elmendorf's luxurious white stretch limousine.

This automotive beast which was about half a block long and now sat outside nearest Shepherd of Galilee's main front door, adorned with ribbons, streamers, a garden of white paper flowers and a "Just Married!" poster across the back. Another smaller limousine had already departed, bearing Alfred and Dorothy, with Kate's parents and Aunt Moira, with Sylvester to assist the oldies – although Richard wondered why Aunt Moira and Sylvester had their heads together, and seemed to be mutually amused. The Gonzalez hire car service was doing a bang-up job on this day of all days. Richard was pretty certain that Uncle Tony in Elmendorf had offered a friends and family discount.

"Your one-eyed lawn panther doesn't do parties," Chris said by way of excusing his absence from a ride in the limo with the rest of the wedding party. "Neither does Miss Letty."

"How is she getting along?" Richard asked, quietly. "After ... you know."

"As good as can be expected," Chris replied. "They were friends for as long as she remembers. But Miss Letty is philosophical about all that. She told me the other day that eventually it does come down to the last one standing. She's bearing up. You and Kate getting hitched cheered her up no end, so that's all to the good." He lifted Ozzie's ornamented basket. "I'll see you at the reception. Don't start the honeymoon early."

"Not a hope," Richard sighed. "Especially not in front of the kids. Are they going to take any more pictures?" That was directed towards two of Kate's professional associates in the media business – a videographer and a still photog winding up the last of the formal photographs. It was a wedding, a wedding of the 21st century. It would naturally be extensively photographed or videoed. All that he could hope for was that the results would only appear in albums, or on private social media accounts belonging to their nearest and dearest.

He reminded himself to ask Kate if it was possible to obscure his face, or most of his face in anything released to the general public. But oddly enough – staying hidden away didn't seem so important now. Here was his place, his people, his wife. Perhaps Kate was correct when she told him months ago that no one in the larger world gave a waffle-fried damn about the Bad Boy Chef anymore. Richard had just barely managed to repress the urge to flinch whenever the lenses pointed in his direction.

Finally, it was all done. Now they could leave for the reception. It was a Sunday evening, the streets of Karnesville were all but deserted as evening fell – or rather, collapsed on the last whisper of a weekend in a place where most folks had jobs. Kate, Richard, Jess, Araceli, Lew and the two children gratefully climbed into the long limousine, relishing the opportunity to sit down for once, as Berto closed the doors after them. Chris' little red coupe proceeded the limousine out of the near-empty parking lot of Shepherd of Galilee and soon sped out of sight ahead, on the long country road that ran between fields, pastures, patches of woodland and the occasional oilfield installation, and ranch house.

"Well, that's one bit done and dusted," Kate commented cheerily, as she leaned back against the back of the luxuriously-padded seat which ran the considerable length of the limousine. "Oof, my feet are killing me."

"I told you to pick flats," Jess commented, "Especially for the reception. You have to dance, you know. At least twice – once with your Dad and again with Richard."

Kate groaned. "I wanted to look as tall as everyone thinks that I am. I wear flats every day."

"I had Joe and Myrna take my bag to the reception, with a pair of white flats in it for the dancing," Jess replied. "Look, as your bridesmaid, I had to think of this."

"Bless you, my friend!" Kate was also sagging against Richard's shoulder, their ringed hands still entwined. Richard judged that she was tired – but energized. As he was, himself, with half the tasks of this momentous, memorable public day completed. He was accustomed, though, to such long and eventful days,

Lew Dubois was, in the meantime, investigating the contents of the limousine mini-fridge. "Some champagne, *cheri*? There are two bottles here, nicely chilled and plenty of glasses..."

Kate shook her head. "I'm sorry. Lew – not for me! I haven't eaten all day through being so nervous about everything!

If I drink anything now, I'll fall flat on my face, getting out of the car."

"Then, champagne for all, and this for you," With an extravagant flourish, Lew brought out a bottle of fruit-flavored energy drink and handed it to Kate. "Thinking that all of us need fortification against the next few hours, Anne had the sous-chef prepare these for us." With the air of a stage magician producing a slightly stunned rabbit from a top hat, Lew brought out a series of cunningly-packed bento boxes, full of chilled and revivifying assortments of appetizing, blissfully drip-free finger foods, snacks which the adults fell upon like a famish horde, thanking Lew for his intelligent foresight with every bite as the limousine rolled ponderously along, trailing streamers and flapping strings of white silk flowers.

It appeared that none of them had taken the time to eat, certainly not after having dressed for the occasion. Araceli, hovering over Matty and Angelika, permitted them each a champagne flute in which a tablespoon or two of champagne was diluted with mineral water. Everyone congratulated the children on having performed flawlessly those ceremonial tasks assigned to them, in the full view of an enormous crowd. Matty and Angelika, in return, were thrilled to silence over being included in such an august and adult event – and the sheer fun of riding along in Uncle Tony in Elmendorf's extended-body limousine, a vehicle which had featured in weddings, proms, anniversaries, and other significant events in Karnes County over the last fifteen or twenty years.

"I was surprised as heck to see Collin Wyler and his current wife at the wedding," Jess remarked, around a mouthful. "I didn't think he had been invited."

"He wasn't," Kate explained. "Well, not invited specifically. We did send an invite to the Wyler ranch for Doc. Conchita said it was on his desk with the date marked on his personal calendar, and he sent an RSVP almost at once ... but when Collin and Sammi flew home for the funeral, Collin saw the invitation and called Mom to see if it was OK if he represented the Wyler family instead. It was a bit of a surprise, but Mom said it was all right. She knew Collin when they were in college together. Not friends in that way, but they knew each other from being from Luna City. Since the guest list was already finalized, the numbers would all add up. I really didn't think his wife would show up, though. That was a bit of a surprise..."

"Tell me about it," Richard confessed. "It was the most ghastly shock! I was about to run screaming, when I saw her and Susannah Wyatt coming into the church together!"

"Poor darling," Kate giggled fondly. "Both of your exes, appearing at our wedding!"

"I'm glad you find it amusing," Richard snapped, while Jess and Araceli joined her in mirth. "My nerves were in shreds ... absolute shreds. Susannah Wyatt was NEVER an ex of mine. She was a stalker, an unrelenting stalker, haunting my every footstep until Romeo took her off my doorstep, in a manner of speaking ... thank God!"

"At least the current Mrs. Wyler was pleasant to me," Kate patted Richard's cheek. "She may have been a heartless, manipulative tart to you, but she was civil, at least. Not like Susannah Wyatt! Didn't you hear what she said, as she and Romeo made as if to move along?"

"I did not," Richard replied. "Romeo was too busy briefly regaling me with tales of his adventures in the male modeling trade."

"She looked over my dress with that — expression on her face ... you know, that one that certain women have when they're about to be total cats to someone who can't slap them silly in public, and she ... she cooed at me with that sneering expression! She said *'Oh, such an original dress, darling — suits you so very well. Alexander McQueen, or Dolce and Gabbana?'*"

"Oh, lord — what did you say to her?" Richard asked. He hadn't heard a word of this exchange, possibly because it was carried on in a frequency above the ability of male hearing to detect it.

Kate smirked. "I said to her, *'Same as yours, Susie sweetie — Dolce and Goodwill. It's not everyone who can carry off that color.'* Susannah looked as if she had bit into her breakfast taco and found half a cockroach in it, before she and Romeo moved on."

"Sounds as if you had a grudge, there, girlfriend," Jess remarked. Kate giggled again.

"Oh, I do! From when she was still the main point of contact for Mills Farm, and I would be trying to get a statement from her for a story in the Beacon about one of their big public events. She was so snotty to local small-market media, you simply can't believe. So I was happy enough to say that ... not to mention how she tormented my darling hubby Richard with unwanted sexual attentions!" Kate drew their clasped hands to her lips and kissed Richard's fingers. "It was a positive pleasure to pay her back in her own bitchy coin."

"I always heard people who worked there calling her 'The Witch in Pink Boots'," Araceli chimed in. Lew appeared faintly horrified at the realization that his predecessor at Mills Farm was not held locally in anything like respect.

"She did wear pink boots," Jess confirmed. "Vintage Ariats ... limited edition... what is the matter with the limo...why are we stopping here?"

They all realized at that moment that the white limousine had been going slower and slower, accompanied by increasing hesitation in the engine, almost as if it were gasping, and running out of breath. Finally, it slushed to a stop, slightly and awkwardly tilted at an angle on the grassy shoulder.

"Strewth! I KNEW something would happen!" Richard exclaimed, as Berto set the parking brake and came around to open the passenger door. "What's wrong with the car, Berto? Why have we stopped."

"I don't know!" Berto replied, his countenance utterly disconsolate. If he had been the age of Matty, or even younger, Richard was sure that he would be holding back tears. "I gassed up before leaving Elmendorf ... it's a cranky old beast, though.

Uncle Tony keeps it running out of sentiment, 'cause it was the first big one he ever bought for the business."

Lew Dubois sighed, very deeply. "Cher, we should not panic. How far away are we from Luna City? Can you call for another car and let everyone know at the hotel that we will be unavoidably delayed, until another car can be sent for us? The one that the good parents of the bride and groom would do, although it will be a tight squeeze."

"Sure," Appearing immediately reassured and cheered, Berto dug a cellphone out of his pants pocked, but even as he opened a screen and began punching in numbers, his face fell. "Uhh ... my battery is run down – almost to nothing. Anyone else got their phone handy?"

That was when the disaster which Richard had fully expected to strike all through this day finally made a touch-down, pin-point landing. He had turned off his own cellphone and asked his mother to take custody, since she carried a good-sized handbag. There wasn't a pocket in his vintage black tie large enough to accommodate the phone without revealing an unsightly and obvious cellphone-shaped bulge.

Kate was the first to speak. "<u>My</u> cellphone! On my wedding day! For pete's sake, where was I supposed to carry it! In my bouquet, or stuffed in my cleavage!? I left it with Mom! What <u>was</u> I supposed to do with the darned thing?"

Both Araceli and Jess were shaking their heads, with similar expressions of dismay, regret and bafflement.

"Patrick has mine," Araceli explained. "I mean – really, where the heck should either of us have stashed our phones. There's no pockets in these dresses. And can you imagine the horror of your phone ringing as you're halfway down the aisle?!"

"Joe has mine," Jess nodded agreement. "If there ever was a time to unhook from the internet of things, a wedding is about the top of the list ... along with the honeymoon. What about yours, Lew – did you bring your phone?"

They could already tell from Lew's expression that he also had taken a similar precaution and given his cellphone into custody of his good lady wife.

"Who might have thought such an emergency would overtake us!" Lew sounded stoic and philosophical. "On a more cheery note, our failure to arrive in a timely manner will be noted at once. I am certain that a search will be initiated in a manner most prompt."

"It'll still take considerable time," Kate fretted. "And all the guests will be freaked out, because they can't eat until we're seated. What can we do, Richard?"

"Are we close to any houses," Richard suggested, feeling vaguely heroic, because his best-beloved had appealed to him for a solution. "Can we see any lights, anywhere at all?"

"If the ladies will remain in the car," Lew suggested, "Lest their gowns be disarrayed ... perhaps cher Richard and I, and Berto should explore the immediate vicinity..."

"We passed some lights, just back there," Berto pointed down the road where they had just come. "A house, and close enough to the road. Not an oil-drilling site," He added, for the locality was dotted with such, most of them uninhabited.

"Where are we, exactly?" Richard asked. As a member of the volunteer fire department, he had studied the maps extensively, but he was not a driver and lacked first-hand familiarity with the network of roads around Luna City. He couldn't relate where they were, precisely, not without connecting to a known location.

"County Road 342, almost to Horseshoe Lake," Berto explained. "I wanted to take a back road, avoid the weekend traffic coming from Beeville. See, there was a big road rally this weekend ..."

"Irrelevant, cher," Lew tactfully cut short what would likely be a lengthy and unnecessary explanation. "Let us then, you and I walk to that place and ask for the use of their telephone. You said there were lights, so someone must be at home. Richard will remain with the car, to protect the ladies ... not," he added hastily, "That there is any particular danger from wild beasts and certainly the ladies are capable in any emergency. Be assured – we shall return with good news."

"This is certainly something which we can hope for," Richard allowed. He was still somewhat torn between horror that disaster had fallen upon the wedding festivities, and relief that it had and was still not as awful as it could have been. His own fears had been along the lines of a meteor crashing onto the church, or Sammi Wyler stripping stark naked in the church and declaring her undying passion for yours truly. Or Grandpa Fritz Heisel going all murder-mad with a machete or his beloved electric carving knife.

The dark outside of the limousine's tinted windows was pretty impenetrable; all that remained of daylight was a pale smear on the west horizon, casting a distant tree line into a silhouette as sharp as if it had been cut by sharp scissors from black paper. In their dark suits, Lew and Berto were soon lost to sight along the deserted and unlit back country road.

"I don't think that the house was very far away," Araceli was putting a brave face on it, for Angelika and Matty's benefit. "Well, it's a memorable adventure you'll have to tell everyone at school tomorrow."

Kate leaned back against Richard's shoulder with a very deep sigh. "You know, I think I could handle some champagne now, if there is any left."

"Just a smidge," Jess was closest to the mini-fridge, and the rack of glasses above it. "It's still cold, but it's probably going flat already."

"I'm not picky," Kate replied. For a while, there was a silence in the limo, a silence only broken by the quiet ticking sound made by cooling metal, and the light rustle of tall grasses rustling against the side which was deepest in the unmown verge.

It seemed as if at least half an hour had passed, although by Richard's watch, it was only fifteen minutes, when Lew reappeared, a jovial smile on his pleasant middle-aged features.

"Rescue is at hand!" he explained. "Perhaps we will arrive at the reception somewhat tardier than expected – but with ceremony individual!"

"How so?" Richard was wary. This required further information, which Lew was happy to provide.

"A M'sieu Barton is the owner of the property to which young Berto and I made appeal! Alas, his good lady has taken their only car to San Antonio, leaving him with only his farm truck, which alas – is not running at the present time. But he has generously offered the use of an alternative ... and since we are only ten minutes by road from Luna City – the delay will not ruin your reception, Richard!"

"If Mr. Barton's truck is in the shop," Richard asked, "Then what transport is he going to provide us? A magic carpet, per chance?"

"An old-fashioned hay-ride!" Lew replied. "He has brought out his tractor and hitched it to the wagon which he has adorned with hay-bales, in the configuration he uses when offering hay-rides at the yearly fall festival! We will transfer the white ribbons, flower adornments and the just-married sign from this vehicle to Mr. Barton's wagon, and voila! A ceremonial arrival – one which will be talked about by your children's children!"

"You can't possibly be serious!" Richard was horrified, but Kate was laughing to tears. So were Jess and Araceli, while Matty and Angelika squirmws in their seats from excitement.

"I love it!" she exclaimed and hiccupped as a bit of flat champagne went down the wrong way. "What a wonderful idea! And surely we can ask Mr. Barton to the reception as a reward!"

Behind the stalled limousine, a pair of lights were bobbing their way slowly along the road – soon revealed as a small tractor pulling a low, flat trailer-wagon. The sides of the wagon were lined with bales of hay. Someone had thought of adorning it by hanging strings of white icicle lights along the sides. The tractor and wagon pulled around the stranded limousine and parked on the verge ahead. It looked festive, in a very rustic kind of way. Still, Richard was not reassured that this was a dignified alternative; certainly not as dignified and stately as the limousine.

"You can't be serious!" Richard exclaimed again, and Kate giggled.

"Well, it's better than walking all the way! Or delaying our grand arrival at the hotel any longer! Don't be such a stick in the mud, lover! This is the perfect vehicle for a country wedding!"

"My father will never live it down, if his French wine-making pals ever hear about this," Richard grumbled, but everyone else in the wedding party seemed to be so chuffed about the unorthodox transport, that he soon resolved to not be such a wet blanket. He joined Jess, and Aracely, who with the children were eagerly stripping off the flowers and ribbons adorning the limousine and transferring them to the wagon. The battery in the limousine still held enough power for Berto to shine the headlamps helpfully on the wagon, to assist in the work. With many willing hands, this was achieved in a bare five minutes.

Mr. Barton turned out to be a middle-aged cove tastefully dressed in jeans and cowboy boots which almost a requirement for working men in that locality, accessorized with a ZZ-Top sweatshirt with the sleeves cut off. Obviously, he had not had the time to assume more tasteful attire, or to shave that morning ... although Richard briefly entertained the unworthy assumption that perhaps that_was tasteful attire at *Chez* Barton. Mr. Barton, swung down from the tractor seat, to come around to help load up his new passengers. He pulled a small wooden bench from the trailer and set it with some ceremony to serve as a step up into the trailer.

"Hey, Miz Kate!" He exclaimed, upon observing for the first time, that he and his tractor were coming to the assistance of someone that he knew. Although Kate, as a hardworking reporter for the local newspaper, was on first-name terms with practically everyone in Karnes County. "I didn't know it was your wedding party, all stranded out here! Could knock me over with a feather!"

"Charlie!" Kate replied, giving her hand into the callused grasp of a friend. "I didn't see that we were near to your place! Yes, it is my wedding! Had you met Richard, my husband? We were just on our way to the reception, and my gosh, you are a friend, indeed!"

"Richard – him that usta run the Café?" Mr. Barton appeared to be tickled pink. "Cap'n Kitten in the Kitchen! Waal,

535

I am that pleased to be of assistance! My kids love that cooking series that you have! Step up lively now, and we'll have you where your guests are waiting in two shakes of a lamb's tail!"

Between Mr. Barton, Richard and Lew, Kate, Jess and Araceli were boosted up into the trailer, somewhat hampered by their long skirts. Matty and Angelika followed without difficulty, excited all over again at riding through the back country in an open trailer lined with bales of hay. Charlie Barton handed up the step-stool after Berto and Richard scrambled in, and they were off. The noise of the tractor engine made conversation difficult to carry on a conversation in a normal voice – but at least they were moving again.

The stars came out, bright and silver in a velvet dark sky that seemed to go on forever; even brighter since there was little in the way of city streetlights or illuminated advertising to dim them. Kate leaned against Richard's shoulder, and he had one arm around her waist. The narrow country road curved around a long bend, a bend which edged around a slough on the margin of a small lake, or maybe a stock pond.

"Look, Kate of my heart," Richard said, seeing that early spring fireflies sparked brief flickers of light as they danced among the dark spears of grass. "Fireflies. I've never seen quite so many. Is it an omen, do you think?"

"It is, lover," Kate replied, with a sigh of deep contentment. "Everything will be perfect from now on."

Postscript – Where Are They Now?
A Retrospective for Media Stars of the Noughties   *People Magazine* – May 2029
Rich Hall – the Bad Boy Chef

Now known as Richard Astor-Hall, the astonishingly young and versatile classically trained Cordon Bleu chef burst on the television audience as a contestant in a British IRT-1 classic French cookery contest show, *Doing it the French Way* in early 2000. He was a stand-out as a final-round contestant and emerged in the 2001 season as a viewer favorite. He did not win the final round, placing only second in the opinion of contest judges, but made such an engaging appearance over the course of the first two seasons that he was signed to do his own series *The Bad Boy Chef Cooks For You*, which became a hit, first in the UK, and then in the USA when the show was syndicated on   The Food Network. Guest appearances on various TV morning shows and *No Reservations* with Anthony Bourdain followed, including a second series for The Food Network, *On the Road With Rich Hall*. The Bad Boy Chef appeared to be riding high in the celebrity firmament, with guest appearances, profitable product endorsements, and a number of highly visible celebrity romances.

Towards the end of 2012, Rich Hall announced plans to open Carême, an uber-luxurious restaurant of his own on Hans Crescent in London's exclusive Knightsbridge neighborhood. No expense was spared, according to releases from Rich Hall's production company, Bad Boy Enterprises, Inc. The opening night was set for October 3rd, 2013; an event widely anticipated among the glitterati, the wealthy and well-known. Throngs of spectators gathered on the street outside the restaurant, as well as photographers from major media outlets, so when disaster struck, it was well-documented in subsequent news reports. A virulent case of apparent food poisoning, deliberately afflicted on guests at a single table initiated by a jealous waiter, set off a horrific round of mass hysteria and sympathetic vomiting on the part of other patrons. A veritable traffic jam of ambulances and emergency personnel responding to frantic cellphone calls joined crowds of paparazzi outside the Carême premises. In the midst of this hysteria, Rich Hall apparently experienced a complete metal breakdown. Before he could be restrained by staff members, he stripped naked, put a colander on his head and ran along several blocks of Brompton Road screaming nonsensical nursery rhymes before being apprehended and restrained by three Chinese tourists in the Hyde Park rose garden.

Heavily sedated, he was released into the care of family members and senior staff of Bad Boy Enterprises. He dropped from public life at that point and was widely assumed to have been confined to a private nursing home for most of the following decade. He was nowhere to be found on the food scene, either in the US or in the UK. Carême never reopened after the total disaster of opening night. The premises were sold, along with Bad Boy

Enterprises' other London real estate holdings, in order to pay legal judgements filed against Richard Astor-Hall and Bad Boy Enterprises. Both television series were dropped by the Food Network and never renewed, although it was rumored that Richard Astor-Hall was briefly considered as a co-host with football legend Allan Lee Mayne, on his travel and restaurant series *Ala Carte with Quartermayne*

Today, as best as can be determined by investigators for this series, Richard Astor-Hall lives quietly in rural Texas with his wife, the former Katherine Heisel, and their two children. He refused all requests to be interviewed, photographed or filmed for this series. He currently maintains a low, if not near to invisible public profile as catering director for the international hospitality corporation Venue Properties, Int'l. He is also reputed to be culinary developer and advisor for a small local company, Luna Café Gourmet Foods, a mail-order specialty firm offering small-batch sauces, preserves, spice mixes, and salad dressings. He is rumored to be a neighbor of former child star, Amy Butler, and her husband, Alberto Yasbeck-Gonzales, who also own a small ranch near Karnesville, Karnes County, Texas.

www.ingramcontent.com/pod-product-compliance
Lightning Source LLC
Chambersburg PA
CBHW070354030726
47504CB00001B/180